A.J. SCUDIERE

NIGHTSHADE

FORENSIC FBI FILES ◆ BOOK 3

THE
ATLAS
DEFECT

NightShade Forensic FBI Files: Atlas Defect

Copyright © 2017 by AJ Scudiere

FIRST EDITION

A big thank you goes out to all my beta readers . . .

You all are the ones who help grapple these stories into shape and remind me when to twist my readers up and when to let them breathe.

A huge thank you is reserved, always, for my family. My husband and kids are just all-around awesome. They make this possible more than they could ever get enough credit for.

This book is dedicated to Jack and Christina Pines.
An author could not wish for two better fans. They showed up at
conventions, told their friends about my books, and eventually
invited me to their home for a writing retreat. After making sure they
weren't huge Stephen King fans (Misery, anyone?) I booked a flight.
This book was partly written in their home. We started as writer and
fans but are now true friends. I cannot wait until I see you guys
again!
Thank you for everything. This one's for you.

"There are really just 2 types of readers—those who are fans of AJ Scudiere, and those who will be."
-Bill Salina, Reviewer, Amazon

For *The Shadow Constant*:

"The Shadow Constant by A.J. Scudiere was one of those novels I got wrapped up in quickly and had a hard time putting down."
-Thomas Duff, Reviewer, Amazon

For *Phoenix*:

"It's not a book you read and forget; this is a book you read and think about, again and again . . . everything that has happened in this book could be true. That's why it sticks in your mind and keeps coming back for rethought."
-Jo Ann Hakola, The Book Faerie

1

Eleri looked around, unable to deny the prickle at the back of her neck but not seeing anything.

She high-stepped through the snow, sinking up to her knees more times than she cared to count. Though she was carefully wrapped up, the snow came above the top edge of her boots each time she sank in. It was just a matter of time before it snuck inside.

Following Donovan's tracks, she tried to catch up, but her partner was nowhere to be seen.

Trees stuck out of the landscape, snow weighing branches and muffling sound in the stillness around her. Everything else was a blanket of thick white. All her senses told her she was alone. Only two things denied this clear fact. One—she knew Donovan was out there, ahead of her, sniffing out what needed to be found. And two—the prickle at the back of her neck.

She pulled her foot out from the hole she'd sunk it into and climbed once again onto the surface of the snow, hoping it held. She could see farther, hear just a little better from this spot about a foot and a half higher.

Donovan's tracks went out of sight, a straight line of holes and drags where he, too, kept breaking the icy surface and then bounded forward.

She had all his clothes in her pack, as well as a blanket and emergency gear for both of them. Which was all well and good if they didn't get separated. It was always a gamble: outfit him with what he needed and make his oddity more obvious or send him out unencumbered and bank on him returning safely. He hadn't always. Eleri thought about the last time he'd been taken out, how she'd had to rouse him, cover for him, make up for the fact that he'd gone missing in the middle of a crowd.

Lifting her hand, Eleri checked the GPS. Donovan was headed off in a different direction from the coordinates. She frowned.

He wouldn't go that way if he didn't smell something, right? She'd have to catch up before she could ask.

Surveying the area once again, she spotted tracks in the distance. Not Donovan's. She had flags in her pack, ground flags—which she now laughed about, she hadn't seen ground since she got here—and tall flags. She pulled one and marked where she stood. Then for good measure, she grabbed a pink ground flag and used the weight to toss it up ahead, near where Donovan's tracks shot off in front of her.

Just the thought of marking her trail sat uneasy. The national forest they were in was closed to the public now. The signs at all the entrances said it was due to weather, but Eleri knew that wasn't true.

Some college professor had reported the human bone found in the forest, in this area. The initial filing triggered an FBI alert for a missing man, which hadn't panned out. Whatever they had found, though, got through to her boss. Special Agent in Charge Derek Westerfield decided he needed his people on the case, and the next thing Eleri and Donovan knew they were headed to the Huron-Manistee National Forest.

Eleri veered off the trail, heading for the tree line and the other tracks she thought she saw. Had she been taller, she might have been able to look down enough to distinguish them, but she wasn't. She managed three steps before she hit a weak spot and crashed through the thin skin of ice on top of the snow.

It didn't hurt; it would just be embarrassing had she been trying to impress anyone. There was a sound, but she was pretty certain it had come from her own throat as her foot suddenly dropped out from under her. Still . . . something was off.

She should have climbed back out and headed on. Honestly, she couldn't stay on the surface for all that long any way. Every handful of feet, she would crash through, then climb up and continue on. But right now, she stayed low, peeled her arms out of the pack as quietly as she could and scanned her surroundings.

The bulky clothing hindered her; she was no Donovan, that was for sure. For a moment, she considered leaving the pack, searching the area. But if she was caught away from her things, then what? She wasn't fast even without them—the coat, the boots, the ski pants, nothing moved well enough for an easy escape. So she surveyed.

Nothing.

Eleri sighed. No evidence at all to back up what she was feeling.

In her old life, she'd occasionally followed her hunches and eventually found specific support. Since joining NightShade, those hunches had been admired rather than thought odd. She'd been pushed to develop them, use them, and believe that they weren't just the occasional blip on her radar that may or may not be true. In NightShade, sometimes she was the only evidence.

Three years ago, even just one, she would have brushed this

feeling off, told herself she was making it up. Now she knew better.

But there was nothing to support her odd feeling.

Slipping the straps of the pack back over her arms, she stood up. Waiting a beat for a shot that didn't come, Eleri gave a mental shrug and headed again toward the tree line. She fell through the ice a handful of times, making the journey slow and probably getting her even farther behind Donovan.

The ranger had offered them both snow shoes. Donovan had, of course, declined. He had no need for snowshoes when he was going to do that weird double-jointedness/werewolf thing he did—that he *still* hadn't let Eleri see him do—and go off bounding through the snow as his bad wolf self. Eleri, on the other hand, had read up. This time of year, the snow would have an ice layer on top of it, and at her weight, she wasn't that likely to go through.

Well, she did. A lot. But she really couldn't say if that was better or worse than sludging around in snowshoes—which she'd never used before. The rangers asked if she'd been in snow before. Of course, she had. Her family had homes in Kentucky and Virginia, both of which saw what she thought was decent snowfall. Especially Bell Point Farm, just outside Charlottesville. These past years, as the weather had gotten wonkier, they'd seen even more of it. So she'd said yes, she had seen snow. She'd ridden her pretty horsies through it. It sounded just as dumb in her head now as she crashed through one more time.

She was in great physical shape, dammit. Her heavy breathing was more the result of sighing than lack of stamina, but she felt like that kid in the Christmas movie, the one whose snowsuit was so bulky he couldn't put his arms down.

As Eleri approached the tracks, she became more worried.

"Son of a bitch," she muttered as she got close. Probably cougar. Looked like a big one, too.

She wasn't worried about herself; she was hardly bait-worthy in all her winter gear. But Donovan was a threat, and he was heading right through the territory. Surely he could smell the big cat?

She told herself he would, then set about examining the tracks a little more closely. Had she not known what she was seeing it would have looked like only two feet hit the snow, but many big cats were known for stepping their back paws directly into the tracks of their front ones when in deep snow. The method was more efficient and meant the cat probably hadn't just hopped down from a tree and gone for a stroll; it was definitely conserving energy for something.

"Son of a bitch." She muttered it again. The tracks headed in the same general direction Donovan had. There was nothing she could do about it. She had a gun, but the ability to pull the trigger on anything but the flare gun was questionable in this get-up.

She headed back to her own tracks, to the path Donovan had laid out as he bounded happily ahead. At least the pink flag she'd thrown saved her from backtracking.

Maybe the cat was what was watching her.

The thought didn't make her feel any better.

Picking up her pace, Eleri followed Donovan's tracks still not seeing him. She did find a spot he'd marked for her.

The snow had been dug up in a neat paw-marked pattern, tossed back into a pile, revealing a singular neat bone. Eleri came to a dead halt. Tracks forgotten, she stared down at what Donovan had revealed.

It was a humerus. Her first thought was bear, the bone was so thick, the two pieces revealing that the marrow was long gone and the bone itself made to support more weight than the human version. Pulling out her camera, she snapped off a series of pictures before she touched anything. Then she grabbed a forensic scale and brushed away parts of the snow before laying out the marked ruler and taking more pictures.

In her previous cases, evidence was usually brought to her. One time, she and Donovan had searched a yard for pieces of bone, but there would have been no court case, no need to catalog it.

Now she just might need some of her skills. Or not. It might be an animal bone. She was cataloging it anyway, because Donovan dug it up. There were surely tons of animal remains out here. So why would he have dug it up if it wasn't pertinent? She took another picture, then stared at the site, thinking.

Looking around, she saw nothing of use. Normally, she would find north with a compass, lay out a line or a grid if she wanted. Mark the site by GPS coordinates and triangulate the remains to several immovable objects. She sighed. Well, one out of three would have to do.

She looked down at the GPS and marked the spot. She would have liked a paper document but her gloved fingers were too fat to work a pen with anything better than kindergarten skill. This would have to do, the hair on the back of her neck was prickling again. She wouldn't take the time to map it full out. Donovan wasn't here and there wasn't the option to call in more people.

She dug out the spot more, still not sure yet what she was looking at. She'd be more careful if it turned out to be human. But she kept her eyes open. Donovan marked it as something important. It wasn't just that he'd dug it up. Small x's marked the snow, a signal they'd worked out before he ran off. So she kept digging.

The pieces were scattered, but she found a radius and ulna —the lower arm. She moved the scale, took more pictures. Now she was equally convinced it wasn't bear and it wasn't human.

Forty minutes and seven bones later she was more confused than ever. What had Donovan found?

Down near the ground, she was practically soundproofed by the snow piles she'd added to the one Donovan had started. She peeked her head up and looked around, still seeing nothing but white. The sky was a little overcast, keeping the snow from glaring, but that didn't make much difference. The snow huddled in lumps that could hide rocks, bodies, or a plant that created a stop, building up a drift. The trees formed the edges of the white expanse, but beyond the first line lay only a dark tangle of branches, trunks, and undergrowth. Unless something came out onto the snow, Eleri wasn't going to see it.

She rolled her shoulders, wondering why she still felt watched. They'd been out here for hours, separated, each with a task and she was following hers. Maybe it was because she'd learned some interesting facts on their last case. Donovan and his direct line weren't the only ones of his kind. They could smell each other and they could smell something on her they didn't seem to like. So maybe her paranoia was founded but not real, not here.

Eleri dug further, following where the bones pointed. There was every possibility the skeleton was scattered and she wouldn't find any more, but she had a little more time before she had to go after Donovan, before the light faded. At least the day hadn't been a wash. She got to dig up some animal.

With the break in the humerus, she'd made an educated guess about which way to look next, hoping for a shoulder, spine and skull. Instead she found the lower arm and some finger bones. That's what had convinced her it wasn't human. The fingers, too, were thicker than human hand bones should be. But she was pretty certain—had the body decomposed intact and not been scavenged by other animals, hacked by hunters and tossed, or worse—she was aiming toward the skull now.

She stopped, stood up, took a drink of water while turning a full three-sixty and seeing nothing but the same trees and snow staring back at her. This time she set her timer. Forty-five minutes then she was done here. She'd have to come back. Normally, she would flag the site, but honestly, she didn't trust this place. This spot was marked on her GPS and that would have to be good enough.

Eleri looked into the tree-line, uncertain if she saw a glint of light there. She didn't take the time to cap her water bottle, just tossed it to the side and reached for her binoculars. As she held them to her eyes she saw nothing but trees. Dark patches in the woods that could conceal anything. She felt nothing but paranoia. There were three creatures out here that she knew of: herself, Donovan, and that cougar. Two humans—well, in both their cases there were arguments against full status—and one animal. She was certain there were other animals out there, but none that she could specifically account for.

Tamping down the feeling she couldn't do anything about, she turned back to the work at hand.

Thirty minutes later she had several more arm bones and was blinking at the skull.

It was human. She should have put down the scale, taken photos, but she picked it up, her mind churning. It was heavy. Heavier than it should have been. Just like the other bones. The eye sockets didn't come to a delicate edge, but were rounded. Her first thought was Neanderthal—something before Homo sapiens—but the shape was sapiens. The size was sapiens. Still, it was all wrong.

Holding the skull in one hand she quickly dug around for the mandible, her gloved fingers brushing against something quickly, but it turned out to be spine. C_1, the top bone of the vertebral column, and it was wrong, too. She found C_2, with its telltale spike, fitting perfectly into C_1. Setting the skull down, she held the two together, then set them aside, too, still wanting the mandible.

Her fingers closed around it and she pulled it from the ground. Her professors would be so mad. The investigators would arrest her for mishandling evidence if they could. But she was protected by the umbrella of the NightShade division. It wasn't free rein, but the fact that she feared for the evidence itself, that she was afraid to leave it? That would save her the shoddy work. She didn't think of that much as she looked at the mandible. It, too, was thick.

That wasn't that uncommon. Not normal, but not abnormal either. Many humans, more men, had what was known as an "iron jaw." This thickened bone that took a punch easily, delivering more damage to the hitter than the 'victim.' The teeth were what interested Eleri, most were intact. And they were distinctly human.

Just then, her timer beeped. She was turning it off, punching awkwardly at the buttons with fat, gloved fingers when she heard it.

Three heavy barks. Angry, low, and definitely issuing a warning. They stopped as abruptly as they came, her head snapping in the direction of Donovan's path.

Then she heard a male sound, low and distinctly full of pain, followed immediately by Donovan's voice.

"Eleri!"

2

Donovan stood up, knowing full well he was completely naked in sub-freezing temperatures.

"*Eleri!*" He yelled it again. He could hear her out there, not that far behind him. She'd lingered just beyond where he could see, his ears always keeping tabs on her. She'd dug where he marked.

He'd smelled the cat in front of him a ways back and had been on alert. To say he'd been ready would be an understatement, but he'd known this was a possibility. He'd thought ahead. Hence the change.

As a man, he was taller. His fingernails still strong, his muscles still ready. He'd hoped the act of changing would frighten the cat off.

It hadn't.

The cougar stayed a handful of feet away, stalking back and forth in front of him. Her eyes stayed focused on him regardless of which way she turned.

"Eleri!" He hollered again, his heart pounding at the possibilities. He did not want to die here in the cold. Not at the hand of this hungry cat. Not naked in the middle of nowhere.

"Coming!" Her voice carried back to him.

He was sure if he could turn his head, he'd see El behind him. But he couldn't afford to look away from the hungry, two-hundred-pound female in front of him. He could hear his partner, her heaving breathing indicating her work to get to him. She was almost here.

Donovan lowered his voice and offered a deep growl. The sound was human, given the change in his vocal chords, but his growl was still better than most. He also knew which growl to do. He didn't offer a "stay away" sound, but an "I will fucking kill you" in return to her low threats.

"I'm here." Eleri had come up behind him now, her voice whispering to him. It didn't matter what she did. Simply outnumbering the cat should mean they were the automatic victors and the cat would stand down. She'd go find food for the cubs he'd smelled on her somewhere else.

But the cat didn't turn away. Still she stalked.

Donovan's heart pounded.

"Don't breathe." Eleri's voice carried on the still air, reaching his ears almost as if by psychic power.

Her hand appeared over his shoulder, glove missing, bare fingers wrapped around the can of bear mace.

Oh, go, Eleri, he thought just before the mist rushed forward.

He stepped back, his arms out, taking Eleri with him. Just a few steps. She backed up with him, her puffy coat brushing against his bare skin.

As he predicted, the cat stepped forward, making an aggressive move toward him. It stepped directly into the spray before issuing a pained yowl and retreating.

As Donovan watched, the cougar headed for the tree line. It shook its head as though it could shake off the oleoresin capsaicin that was stinging the ever-loving hell out of its eyes and mouth.

Donovan pushed Eleri back farther, hoping to keep both

her and himself out of the spray she'd unleashed. He didn't
know if she was sensitive to it—most people were—but he
knew he was. His eyes were already starting to water.

Eleri added to the sting. "That's a nice outfit you're wearing,
Donovan."

"Listen Stay-Puft, I don't need your comments. I just stared
down a cougar bare-ass naked." He didn't turn around. She
was, after all, his professional partner.

"You want your clothes?" She asked casually, as if it was a
perfectly normal conversation.

"Yes," he ground out, still not turning around. He watched
as the cat passed into the trees and disappeared out of sight.
Holding his hand up over his shoulder, he waited as he heard
Eleri rummage through the big pack she carried until she
slapped a stack of clothing into his hand.

Tucking pieces up under his arms, he hopped into pants,
then a shirt. The cold finally was starting to hurt his feet, the
adrenaline that kept the sensations at bay receding. He hopped
around thinking about how to get his socks on, then boots
while standing in snow.

"Here." Eleri was holding out one sock and his left boot.

Donovan didn't know if she was reading his mind or if she
was just smart enough to see what he needed. She even offered
a shoulder for him to brace one hand on while he pulled on his
sock, then boot, before setting his foot back down into the
snow. They did the other boot and he finally stood on his own
two feet.

"Hey, El, that's a human skull in your bag—actually, in *our*
bag."

"Yeah, kind of." She nodded while she searched the landscape as though looking for something.

"Is that legal?" he asked before re-thinking it. "No, wait. Just
how *il*legal is that?"

"Pretty illegal," she replied. "I'm counting on Westerfield and NightShade to cover my ass on this one."

"Why didn't you leave it?" He was frowning at her as his body heat warmed his clothing. He was grateful he had it. He needed to maintain it, as the rumble in his stomach reminded him. Pushing past the handful of bones she'd apparently also stolen from the site, he reached into the inside pocket where he'd stashed his energy bars.

Eleri was standing with her back to him; she spoke just a little louder to make up for it. "I took them because I don't feel confident they'd still be there when we returned."

"No one's supposed to be out here, Eleri." But now he was looking around, too. "I didn't pick anything up. So if someone was here, they wouldn't have come through the main area and would be staying downwind."

He turned his head to look at her, just enough to see her nod before she turned back to him. "You picked up on the cat, right?"

"Sure, but she was trying to alert everyone she was here. She has cubs."

"True." Eleri shrugged, "I mean I didn't know it was a female or that she had cubs, but I saw the tracks and recognized that it was a cougar."

He sniffed at the air, wishing he was still in wolf form with his nasal passages more open. Even so, his smell now was superior to a normal human and he took in the air around him. Mostly, it smelled like snow. He inhaled again, this time slower, letting the air slide past his nose in an easy, steady flow.

"El." He frowned and did it again.

She watched, not asking, waiting.

He got it again. "Something's here." He couldn't place it.

"What? Some*thing*?" She was looking around again, trying to see through the trees, beyond the snow covered rise that kept her from examining the site.

"Some*one*." Then he recanted it. "Maybe." It was only a hint. Could be someone who'd been here before and was long gone. "Someone could be here now. Look at you, you're all bundled up, you're masking most everything. Then again, it could be residue. I can't tell."

She was looking at him again, another—different—frown on her face now. "We have to make camp."

"Oh, hell no." Then he sighed. "Why do we need to camp?"

"You saw the bones."

"And they'll be there tomorrow," he countered. Changing clothes in the great white north was not his cup of tea and he'd already done it once. Donovan looked up. The sky had been a pale shade of overcast all day, making it harder to track time. Still, the day was waning; they would have to start the trek back to make it to the station before it got too dark.

"I'm not sure they will."

"El," He sighed. Donovan wanted a bed, but the case always came first. "Whatever happened, that body stayed there, covered by snow, decomposing with little interference. So why would that change today?"

She shook her head. "I don't know."

"But you know that it does?" He looked right at her this time. Eleri's hunches had become legendary at the profiling division she'd been a part of before she went into NightShade. SAC Westerfield told Donovan about it once—her hunches led to arrests and amazing finds and some accusations that she'd been involved in the crimes in the first place. Her stint in a mental health hospital afterward pretty much erased any desire for anyone to track her. Westerfield snatched her up, making her Donovan's senior agent partner and training her to push those hunches.

Eleri's ability netted them some serious finds. But right now? When it wanted them to stay overnight in the frozen wilderness? He wanted to believe she was a sham.

Eleri took a deep breath as though she, too, could smell the air. "I have a feeling. Someone's watching."

"Not the cat?"

"No. Human." She looked worried. "We need to get back to the site and set up camp. I didn't get the whole skeleton."

"Did you get enough?" He spoke as though he remained hopeful of a bed and hot shower. In reality, he'd given up on that already. His question was just a Hail Mary.

"No, I want the whole thing. It doesn't match the one on the report, so it's a second find."

"How so?"

She looked up into the sky for a moment as she thought. "The report said 'humerus, right.' Well, I found the right humerus and the left, so unless they have absolutely no knowledge of bones, this one isn't that one. Come on." She turned and started to lead back the way she came, her footprints showing a clear path from the site to where they now stood.

"Wait, Eleri." Had they been on solid ground, he could have run two steps and grabbed her arm. As it was, he was sinking into several feet of snow and any fast movement was nearly impossible.

Luckily, they'd developed a level of trust. She turned. "What?"

"There's another site over here." He pointed just to the right of where they stood. She'd veered off his path to rescue him, missing the other site he'd found.

Her head snapped around, immediately seeing what she'd missed. From here it was just a pile of snow and an obvious spot where he'd dug.

She was already doing the odd, high-step run required by more than a foot or two of snow. "What was it?"

"Another skeleton." He was right behind her, his long legs eating up the ground.

"Human?" She wasn't looking at him and the word was nearly eaten by the space around them.

"Pelvis. Looks like." He'd seen enough of them in his days as an M.E. But it had been almost a year now. Maybe he wasn't quite up to speed, and he'd only looked at it quickly, but . . . "Something's wrong with it."

She stopped, turned again. "Like what?"

"Don't know really." He picked up the pack and easily passed her, leading the short distance to the other site. "You check it."

Despite being a trained forensic pathologist, she was the one who was better equipped to say when something was wrong. She had degrees in forensic chemistry and toxicology as well as a strong forensic anthropology background. Had she not gone into the FBI and been tapped by the behavioral unit, she would have been someone the medical examiner would have called to help with skeletal cases like this.

He was standing over it when she pulled up behind him and stopped. Like the last time, he'd dug down to reveal what it was, then he marked the surrounding area with the small x's. Turning to let her lead, he asked, "How are we doing this?"

"We're noting the location, digging quickly, and hoarding what we can." Her mouth was set in a grim line.

"Hoarding?"

"I don't trust these bones will still be here when we come back. I want to see enough to determine which site is more forensically interesting. Then we cover the other and camp near the better one." She dropped to her knees and pulled the small spade from the pack.

After breaking the surface of the snow in short, sharp jabs, she tossed the spade carelessly to the side. Using her gloved hand, Eleri picked up chunks of the surface ice and tossed it, too. Then she began hand-digging.

Donovan dealt with bodies that were brought to him. On

very rare occasions—before his NightShade assignment—he'd visited scenes. Eleri was the one who taught him to dig without disturbing the body, to catalog the pieces, to do all the things they weren't doing now. He looked around again, still not seeing anything.

He inhaled deeply, searching for the scent of other humans but finding nothing. So he dropped to his knees next to her and began shoving snow aside, trying to achieve the opposing goals of being careful and quick at the same time. The sky was already just a little darker; he didn't like it.

"This." Eleri held up the coccyx, matching it to the two major pelvic bones he'd already exposed. "You're right. It's weird."

She tipped her head one way then the other, looking at the bones she held together. "Looks juvenile, well, not fully adult."

"That's not *wrong*, though, is it?"

She shook her head, but didn't say anything about what she was seeing that was so off. Eleri dug further, following a pattern that she saw but he didn't.

In a few minutes, she said, "The bodies appear intact. The bones seem to be resting where the body lay. So nothing scattered them. Not that I can tell with what I can see."

"How long have they been here?" Donovan asked as he uncovered the torso and Eleri headed toward the skull.

"Total skeletal decomp—in this weather—it wouldn't happen. The temperature hasn't gotten above freezing since the beginning of December." She sat back for a moment, grabbed a bottle of water from the pack and took a deep swig. "So it must have happened last summer. If not before."

Donovan nodded at her and continued to push back the snow and dirt. The first skeleton looked like it had decomposed on the surface of the dirt, but this one was partially buried. The pelvis had stuck up out of the ground a little, giving Donovan something he could see, something he could leave for Eleri to find. He hadn't expected the cat to come after him. He should have smelled too odd for her to approach him; she must have been starving. He pushed more snow and dirt, ruining his gloves. He hoped he wasn't staying out here overnight, but he was pretty certain he was.

He dug his fingers down until he hit something hard. A few more swipes and he saw the thing he'd hit. Dark with both smooth and lumpy patches, it was rounded, long. "I think I have the humerus."

Eleri didn't answer. Donovan knew what she wanted, she wanted him to be certain. He pulled a plastic art tool from the bag Eleri kept. It shouldn't be hard enough or sharp enough to damage the bone, but fingers and brushes were preferred. Still, daylight was fading and a bed was preferred. Neither of them was going to get what they wanted. "We don't have much longer."

"Humerus?" was her only reply.

Five minutes later, he told her, "Yup. Right."

"Shit." She drew the word out on a Southern drawl and some astonishment. "This makes skeleton number three. Unless someone had three arms."

"I haven't seen any gross anomalies in anything I've dug up." He treated her ridiculous statement as though it deserved scientific merit. "Nothing that would indicate the kind of malformation necessary for three arms. It's getting late, Eleri."

She nodded but didn't quit. She only dug faster.

Giving up on a good night's sleep, he asked her, "Which site are we covering?"

"This one. I think."

"You gotta decide quickly, El."

"Skull!" She yelled it the same way a kid might yell, "Birthday cake!" and dug a little harder. "I want to get this out. To be sure the other site is the more interesting one."

Donovan still didn't know what she meant, but he came and dug his fingers into the dirt.

THE WOMAN WATCHED from the woods as the two in puffy jackets covered the spot where they'd been digging. The smaller one—presumably a woman—stuffed some of what they found into her bag. Stealing finds from a national forest was illegal. Maybe she could get charges brought up.

Then the taller one sat up and looked right at her.

3

Eleri sat in the tent, knowing she was warm enough, even if she didn't feel like it. She stayed on the inflatable mattress, the only place to sit that wasn't hard earth.

"Donovan, look." She had two skulls, though only one lower jaw. "See this one—" She hefted the one in her left hand toward her partner. "—it has a more regular weight, but the top of the head is flatter than normal. The shape of the eyes is off. Whereas this one—" she turned the other skull toward him, "—is more normal shaped, but the weight's all wrong."

Eleri handed him the skull, watching as he tested the heft for himself. He seemed to agree, but she got the feeling he might not have noticed it on his own. His previous work had been mostly wet stuff—bodies with tissues still attached.

"Look." She pointed at the eye socket. "See how thick this is?" She didn't wait for him to nod. "Look at the zygomatic." She referenced what was usually a slim arch of bone. "See how thick it is?"

This time his head snapped back. "Oh, wow. The nasal area

too, the sinuses are all . . . *wrong*. What I can see of them." He was tipping it and looking up through the spaces into what should have been there. "What is it? Is there a disease that you know of?"

"No. That's your jurisdiction." She was looking at him oddly now.

"Paget's. Arthritis, but—"

"That would cause deposits. This looks like the bone just grew that way." She was discounting the diseases outright.

Donovan was, too. "This density isn't clustered at the joints in odd growth patterns. It's a uniform thickening of the bone. I don't know a disease that does that."

She inspected the skull she still held, turning it one way then another. She'd photographed them, labeled them, done what she could, given the circumstances. Donovan had dug out this spot, set up the tent, and inflated the mattresses, while she used the last of the light to get decent photographs of the specimens she'd basically stolen.

Eleri prayed her decision wasn't in vain. She'd destroyed a good bit of evidence—some of which they might never recover —based on the idea that there was someone out there. Someone she still hadn't seen.

"So is this a birth defect?" Donovan broke into her depressing thoughts. "Or something that happened after?"

"Hold on." She had the broken humerus. It was from the thicker skeleton. Setting down the skull she'd been holding, Eleri picked up one piece of the long arm bone and looked at it end on. "Hmmm. Hard to say."

She flipped it around and examined the end, checking the epiphyseal plate. "It looks like it maybe wasn't from birth. But if it wasn't it was only a little while after that the changes started. The laydown of bone is so normal, except for being thicker."

Donovan traded her the skull for the long bone and examined it himself. "It's definitely thicker. Is the break ante-mortem?"

Eleri shook her head. "It looks like it was not only *after* death, but relatively recent. Maybe even someone stepping on it."

"That makes more sense than someone with bones this thick breaking them in a fight or fall or something."

"Fight or fall?" she asked, wondering how he'd gotten to that. Her stomach growled and she reached into the bag for yet another energy bar.

"Well, do you think he died out here? Or was he brought here?" Donovan flipped the bone over again as though it might speak to him. He sniffed it, sniffed again. "Do you think he was shot? Maybe hit by a car and dumped here?"

Eleri didn't think a car hit could have left no marks on this bone—although with the thicker shaft it was possible. "Gunshot could have happened, we'll examine the whole skeleton for that. Tomorrow."

She was looking at the zipped-up tent door wishing she could see out of the tent. She'd seen clear ones advertised in the past, but it would also mean someone could see in. "If we're lucky, there will be some anthropological information on the bones indicating manner of death."

"Part of the skull is missing," Donovan pointed out. "Head trauma?"

"Looks post-mortem, too," Eleri told him. He should know that.

"No, I mean, the missing piece might hold the evidence of a trauma."

"Gotcha," she was conceding just as his head snapped to the side wall of the tent as though he could see through it.

"What—" she started to ask, but his hand was already up, indicating she should be quiet.

"Stay here." He spoke in a low voice, knowing whispers carried better than true voice.

Before she could protest, he'd lifted the zipper and stuck his head outside the tent. Then he was back in. "Kill the lights, El."

He was stripping even before she got the light turned off. She heard a sound like knuckles cracking and something akin to Donovan suppressing his own voice. She felt the shift in the air around her, but he was out the opening before she could do more than reach out and touch fur as he went by.

She was left sitting in the dark tent, now alone under the starry sky and in the middle of almost one million acres of wilderness. Donovan had wondered if the body was dumped here, but that didn't make sense. Who would dump a body in the middle of an open field in the middle of massive amounts of forest? Under the trees, the undergrowth would have covered the body. It would have been harder for someone to stumble upon it. It made more sense that he died there. Well, she thought it was a "he." Given the anomalies in the bone formation, she wasn't sure of the gender.

Tomorrow, she told herself ignoring the fact that she and her partner had been split up again. Tomorrow she would examine the bones and see if the skeleton was male or female and if there were any identifying marks indicating manner of death.

Her head jerked up at a sudden series of sharp barks.

Donovan.

She knew his bark now and his growl, which she didn't hear. She knew the panting noises he made when he'd run hard. But this was just the bark. Then another. Another.

She considered climbing out of the tent. But if he'd heard or smelled something he thought he could take care of it.

He'd changed and she'd been dumb. Now, quickly, she reached for her weapon, slid a magazine into place and chambered a round. No longer distracting herself, she focused.

Listening into the sounds of the night, she thought she heard more than just Donovan's paws. Did she hear feet? She did hear another low growl, of that she was almost entirely certain.

Eleri waited, both her hands on the gun now, bones set aside. Donovan had gone after whatever was out there, so it was her job to protect the find. She was ready, but she wasn't comfortable.

She didn't check her watch, but it was a while before a nose pushed through the half unzipped tent opening.

"Donovan!" She kept her voice low, setting the gun down with one hand, using the other to feel his fur in the dark, examining him briefly as he went by.

He shook her off and she waited while he changed back.

She was fascinated. He'd never changed so close to her before. He never let her watch, despite her need as a biologist to see what exactly he was doing. Donovan didn't care. He equated it to watching her shower, so she didn't press. But he was changing in the tent! Right next to her in the dark! "Donovan?"

"One sec, El." He was breathing heavily.

"Are you hurt?" It was the most important question. She knew from history that he wouldn't tell her about changing.

"No. Just tired. That was fast." His breathing was calming down.

She reached in the bag for the small container of fruit she'd brought. She had oranges, apple slices, and grapes. A small indulgence should she get caught out in the open overnight.

"Here." She held the now open container toward the sound of him shuffling into his clothing.

He answered as he snaked out a hand to grab several pieces of the fruit. "Someone was out there."

"What?" She paused, the orange slice only halfway to her mouth. She'd been right?

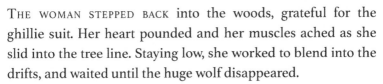

THE WOMAN STEPPED BACK into the woods, grateful for the ghillie suit. Her heart pounded and her muscles ached as she slid into the tree line. Staying low, she worked to blend into the drifts, and waited until the huge wolf disappeared.

Her breathing heavy, she waited. She'd thought he was going to eat her right there. Though he'd barked at her harshly, advanced on her until she nearly ran screaming, and growled low like he was going to attack, he didn't.

Once she calmed down and the wolf didn't come back, the woman retreated farther into the woods back toward her camp. It was a mile away, not easy going in the snow in the woods in the dark. But she knew her way around out here.

She'd been out here a while now and she'd seen some strange shit, that was certain. But none weirder than that crazy-ass wolf. She'd seen him during the day, too, running in front of the woman in the red puffy jacket, almost as though as they were together. The two hadn't interacted, not anything she could put her finger on, but that was exactly the problem: they hadn't interacted. That close? The wolf should have run away from a human so close behind him. Or else the human should have. Neither had.

Then the wolf dug up the bones but left them behind. It made sense that the wolf didn't want the bones, they were just bones, but the woman came along behind the animal and worked at the site he'd dug. Was she tracking him? It was hard to tell. If she was, she was doing a piss-poor job, stopping for a while and ignoring him. It was confusing.

Later, the woman heard the snarls of the big cat. The cat had been around for a while. She was doing her best to stay clear of mama cat, though she'd seen the cubs out one day and they were freaking adorable. She'd watched from a distance as mama found a snow hare and let the babies play with it like the cute little murderers they were. The hare didn't last long with three cubs and one mother cougar. They were magnificent, but deadly.

The big cat had come up against the wolf later in the day. She'd heard the barks and yowls, then the woman's voice. Then a man's voice.

She hadn't watched the interaction. She couldn't afford to be seen. So she'd stayed hidden, listening but not seeing and becoming more confused than ever.

There was a man and a woman. Even if she hadn't seen the man, she'd heard him speak. They covered the second site, pushing the snow, backfilling the hole the wolf had dug earlier. With the freshly fallen snow from two days ago blanketing everything in a smooth sheet of new, white powder, the spot was easy to find. So as far as hiding anything it was a crap job. All it did was cover the bones. So why would they do that?

But nothing about this had been anything but confusing since day one.

She kept up her pace on the trek back to her camp, wearing herself out in the process. She'd gone out under moonlight, wanting to check out the bones the wolf found. She dug up the site the man and woman had backfilled. She wanted to check the other site, too, but she could see a tent there. They were guarding that one.

She'd thought she could just come out and see what they'd done, until the wolf came out. He'd snuck up behind her and barked, scaring the shit out of her.

Back in her tent she did all the necessary work, shaking off the snow, checking the small heater and the battery she was running it off. She checked that nothing flammable was near the heater and peeled the outer layer of her clothing. She climbed into her sleeping bag and passed out for a while, trusting in the camouflage netting and snow she'd covered her space in.

When she woke, she reached into the bag and pulled out the three bones she'd pilfered from the site.

4

"Shit." Donovan stood over the second site, the one farther from the tent.

Eleri stood next to him, her ski pants and jacket turning her into a puffy, touristy-looking red lump. She shook her head and muttered Southern-drawl-laced swears.

Finally, she looked up at him. "Man or woman?"

"Woman." He answered. "I.D. by smell, couldn't tell by look. Only height."

"So she was all dressed for the weather like me." It was a comment rather than a question.

Donovan answered anyway. "Actually—shape unidentifiable like you, yes, but she was in a ghillie suit."

A ghillie suit was white, fluffy warmth and camouflage, usually used by military. Eleri's head pulled back. "She was ready for this."

Donovan agreed, though he didn't have to say so. "She was ready for snow, ready for night, and she stole some of our find." He turned to Eleri then, an action that required his whole upper body to turn in the outfit designed for the subfreezing temperatures. "You were right that we needed to camp out and you were right to grab what bones you could."

"It's a good thing you stopped her." She replied.

Now that the acknowledgments were done, he had to ask, "What did she want?"

"Same as us. The bones. Knowledge of what they'll reveal." She shrugged.

"You know," Donovan said, looking at his partner now, rather than at the bones of the dead kid in the ground. "I thought this case was kinda cool when we started. Now it's pissing me off."

Her head tipped. "Only proves that something is going on here and Westerfield was probably right to send us." She looked around and seemed to be taking stock. Donovan did the same.

"So we take the bones out?"

"Yeah, we get them all up today, photograph them and head out tonight." She checked the area again as though she would see the intruder. "Make a sled? Or carry them?"

"Carry," Donovan voted. They'd brought a second pack, rolled into the first, in case they needed to bring things back. "We don't have time, resources, or even an empty park like we're supposed to." Then he smiled. "We can at least arrest her for trespassing on closed federal land."

"And for stealing archeological finds. That's a little bigger." Eleri dropped to her knees almost as though she'd been shot, and started pushing the snow back again.

Donovan took a deep breath, not getting anything human, and joined her. The other woman had cleared out the snow they'd used to backfill the site, which made the job a little easier. The morning helped.

This was the harder skeleton to excavate, the one half buried in the soil—packed soil. Donovan used the small tools on the painstaking work. If they nicked anything, they would ruin any finds. They might not be able to figure out what killed the kid.

Working side by side, they periodically stopped to take pictures with the scale. Occasionally, Eleri would look up at him, questioning. Donovan shook his head. No, he didn't smell the woman.

"Do you still feel it?" he asked.

She nodded, her eyes flitting one way then another, looking for the source of her concern.

They turned back to the work, finally exposing the whole skeleton. Eleri stood up then, looking down. Standing next to her, taller than her by almost a foot, Donovan tried to see what she saw. He made his best guess. "Juvenile. My guess is male, given the height."

Eleri nodded at him, agreeing but disagreeing at the same time. "You can't do more than guess at sex though. It's not a given."

"Yeah, I'm used to things with more obvious signs of gender," he conceded, then looked up at the sky. A light snow was starting to fall. "I don't like the look of this, Eleri."

"Me either." She didn't look up. "The bones are basically full size, but they don't show full gender development. Not even early secondary sex characteristic development. This would be a nearly six-foot tall eight-year-old. Not impossible, but pretty implausible." She was picking up the bones now, examining them since they'd mapped the layout and taken their pictures. She rotated them in her hand, looking at the ends. "Also, the epiphyseal growth plates are fused, not indicative of an eight-year-old."

Donovan picked up another of the long bones and examined it for himself. "Are all the growth plates fused? This one is."

"All the ones I'm looking at." But she didn't look at him, didn't look up.

"So female growth plates are usually fused around twelve to fourteen years. Males later, by around sixteen." He thought the bone looked odd too, but nothing he could put his finger on. "That would make this skeleton more likely female than male."

"Right. Not adding up." She pulled out a bag and labeled it "left hand," then began scooping the small carpal pieces into the bag. Then she made a second bag for the right hand. She scooped the other set of nearly identical pieces, then sealed the bags before looking at him. "Donovan, it's snowing."

No shit, Sherlock, he thought. He'd been trying to tell her that for five minutes while she worked her way through her thoughts about the skeleton. But he didn't say that. "There's a front coming in. It looks like it's moving our way pretty quickly." He didn't like the way the sky had darkened. "We need to gather this up and get the hell out."

Now she was looking up, worried. "I'll get this, you get the tent."

"Only what's necessary." He scanned the sky. *Shit.* It was rolling up fast. He hopped up and headed for the tent, the wind kicking up at his back.

Donovan picked up his feet and headed toward the other site, the tent. At first, he was trying to beat the storm. He worried about Eleri behind him, still packing up bones. He worried about them getting out of the damn area before the weather hit, but as he crested the rise, he had another worry.

The camp site had been picked over. *Fuck.*

At the top of the little ridge, he turned back to Eleri and yelled into the wind. "Get it all. Fast! We need to get this site, too."

She was standing, looking at him, her heavy head tipping in question. She could tell he was yelling but not what about. The wind had stolen his words. Donovan tried yelling at her again, but found quickly that it didn't work any better the second time. Using his hands, he gestured toward the site, then made a big X.

Eleri took off running for him, but he held a hand out to stop her. "Get that!" He yelled even knowing the words were useless. Then he gestured to her until she turned around.

Point made, he took off toward the first site. Toward the ghillie suited figure he could now see running into the tree line. Taking off after the person, Donovan gave chase for just long enough to use up his resources and to know it was futile. The storm was coming down now, enough to distort his vision of the fleeing figure. Then again, that was the idea of the damn ghillie suit—the white streamers blending with and distorting the never-ending whiteness of the snow.

When Donovan hit the site he saw that the bones had been picked up. Moved. *Shit.*

Then he looked up. The tent flapped open.

ELERI SHOVED the baggies with hand and feet bones down into the big pack with the larger ones. Despite the missing pieces, she had a good portion of the skeleton.

The snow was coming down harder now as she stood and looked over the ridge toward Donovan and the other site. He was down in the dug out portion, probably putting bones into bags like she had.

The site wasn't as obvious with the daylight getting sucked away, with the tent down. Hopefully he'd gotten it rolled up and bagged. The mattress inflators reversed and packed up, too. She wasn't sure now if she liked the red jacket she wore and the bright blue he did. It made them easier to spot, which might no longer be a good thing.

Donovan was kneeling over the other specimen, pushing things around that she couldn't see through the flurries. When she got close, she saw that the site was empty—but was that because he'd gathered it up or because something had happened?

"Donovan?"

He didn't look up, couldn't hear her even though she was just a few feet away. She could now feel the wind through the heavy clothing she wore. It pushed at her, tried to knock her over, push her around.

"Donovan!" She yelled it this time and he finally looked up. Though she still wasn't sure if that was because he was done or because she'd yelled. He did seem a little surprised to see her there.

"We have to go," he urged.

Duh. She almost said it out loud but figured she'd need to conserve her energy. The weather report had only listed a low chance of light flurries today. The rangers said the same thing, telling them they'd be pretty safe. Then again, maybe the rangers were mad because the offered escort was turned down.

Not Eleri's decision. Westerfield's. He hadn't wanted anyone in the loop on this. Which Eleri now counted in the "dumb as shit" column. If she and Donovan died out here, then the only person in the loop would be whoever that woman was running around in the ghillie suit and stealing the damn bones.

Turning, now sideways to the wind, she pulled out her compass and GPS as Donovan lifted the smaller of the two packs and helped her into it. It wasn't made for hiking, just a spare, big, lightweight pack they'd brought along just in case. It didn't slide easily over the bulky parka. Once it was on, she reached back and tried her best to brush the snow out of the hood she'd let flop back during the earlier, sunnier part of the day. She pulled it up, snapping it in place and essentially deafening herself. But the storm had already done that.

Beside her, Donovan was shouldering the bigger pack himself. It had an internal frame and was made for this. Well, it was made for humans to carry it, so Donovan wasn't changing and running off. They would stick this out together.

"Come on!" He grabbed her hand as the words carried to her on the blowing snow and started off on a path between the distant lines of trees.

They each had their talents, and while she had a fine sense of direction, she was no wolf in the woods. She let him lead. He also had longer legs and it didn't take much before she realized he was stepping a little short to allow her to use his tracks. It was kind, but it still made her roll her eyes at the thought of all the short jokes she would wind up enduring after this.

An hour later, she was hoping for short jokes.

They'd barely covered half the ground they'd made in the same time on the way out. The landscape had grown more and more unrecognizable. While before she'd had wry thoughts about dying with the evidence out here, she hadn't really believed it. Now...

As Eleri looked around and saw virtually nothing she could identify, her heart kicked up. Her thoughts took off even as she tried to slow her heart rate. She was already exerting herself in the high snow.

Who was out here pilfering their sites? Who even knew about them besides Westerfield?

She put one foot in front of the other despite the fact that she was wearing thin, despite the fact that there wasn't time to stop and get water or food out of the packs. The storm was coming up behind them faster than they were getting ahead. She pushed the worry back with logic.

The professor had reported something about the find to the FBI. He'd thought it was a missing person, and so did they. The case had fizzled and died—it didn't match anyone on the missing list.

That right there, that was a bunch of people. But none of them should have any reason to come back here. She didn't know how much of the other skeleton had been gathered. Westerfield said it was incomplete; she knew they had a right humerus. So neither site that Donovan had found was the skeleton from the original find. So how did that woman in the ghillie suit know about them?

Eleri stepped higher, the snow drifting up around her knees now. Each step was requiring more work than the one before. She wanted to ask Donovan if they were close to where they'd left the ATV, but didn't have the extra energy to yell. Besides, she had no idea if they'd been walking for three hours or fifteen minutes and her heavy breathing was already concerning her. She turned back to her thoughts to keep the worries at bay.

None of the people on the initial report made sense as the culprit here. So had someone followed them out? Maybe one of the rangers, pissed that they hadn't been invited to join the party? That theory had some serious flaws, too. None of the rangers they'd seen on the way in had been female. They had only spoken to a few officers, been offered escort, and politely declined. Well, Eleri had politely declined. Donovan had remained silent. Sometimes a little too blunt, his version of etiquette was often silence. Southern girl Eleri knew how to lay it on, and she thought she'd slathered those national forest rangers in charm. So she found no connection between rangers who thought the two Feebs were making a mistake and the woman in the ghillie suit following them around.

Donovan stopped for a moment and Eleri nearly plowed into his back. She would have, had she been going any real speed. Her thoughts stayed on a disturbing track, one she hadn't wanted to admit before.

The missing bones, they didn't seem random. There was no way to tell, but if she had to steal just a few bones to take back with her for the most evidence possible, she would have sampled the skeleton exactly the same way.

As she finished the thought, Donovan turned and looked at her.

Then his arms flew up, startled, and he dropped completely out of sight.

5

The top of her tent curved with the weight of the snow and it was still coming down. The heater was off, too dangerous to run it in this weather. The woman knew that.

The sleeping bag she was wrapped in was made specifically to withstand this kind of cold for a long time. She was tucked down into it, only occasionally sticking her face out, looking at the inside of the tent. The poles were designed to hold up under the weight of the added snow. She didn't worry; she was set up for this.

She did hate being stuck. She couldn't check the bones like she wanted. If she wanted to survive the storm, she had to stay in the bag. In the morning, she hoped she could dig out.

The glow stick she'd popped was starting to fade. She had five more, then she'd be in the dark. Daylight or not, the tent would be pitch black inside. She listened and still just barely heard the storm beyond the growing blanket of snow that insulated her. She was going to wait until the glow stick completely faded. Then she might wait more, not knowing how long the snowstorm would last.

The storm hadn't been on the radar. She knew; she'd checked. But her grandfather taught her to be prepared—he'd probably saved her life today. She sent up a prayer, thanking him, and huddled down further into the bag.

She thought about the bones she'd stolen, the sites these two had uncovered. None of it made sense.

The first bones, almost a month ago, had been *her* find. *She* was the one the police called to help them. *She* was the one who found the anomaly; she had her own network, knew the right people to call. Her professor didn't know the people she knew. Maybe it came down to professional jealousy? Whatever it was, he'd insisted they turn the find in to the FBI. She hadn't been against it, just asked if she could check a few things first.

Before she knew it, the feds had shown up and confiscated her research. Two whole human long bones. Five hand and foot bones and various pieces, fragments she'd been sorting.

They took it all.

Those bones were a little odd, too. That had been worth investigating. Honestly, she wasn't surprised the feds reported back that the bones didn't match any missing persons reports.

She—as a student—worked for the school, under their umbrella. She was set up to help identify the body. And why wouldn't she? That was what she was getting her PhD in. So why wouldn't they give the bones back? They didn't even return them to the medical examiner's office, where she would have had access to them.

Now, the entire national forest had been shut down with a weather advisory for a storm that didn't exist. Then these two had shown up.

She wasn't sure if these two were feds or not, but they had some kind of science behind them. That wolf had gone straight for the bones. Two more sites they'd found. She wouldn't have discovered those until the snow cleared, which would be at least March if not May. So these two had at least helped that way, even if the new finds opened up some serious scientific puzzles.

Then she'd committed a federal crime by stealing the bones.

Next the storm had come. Making the closure legit and stranding her and probably the two scientists/feds, too. If she was lucky, she could catalog what she had in the tent with her. Write up her own notes, take pictures, see if she could figure out what it was about this skeleton that was off.

Then maybe she could put them back before the two returned. They didn't have her tent. She'd seen them trekking off into the woods, not in the same direction they'd come from.

They would notice the bones were back. It looked like they'd packed up everything they could when they left. So it would be clear that she'd replaced them.

But how would they find her?

She hadn't even touched the bones bare-handed. She was in the ghillie suit, so they probably had her general height and that was it. They couldn't even tell her race or her gender from the distance they'd seen her from. So as long as she got the bones back before they returned—and why wouldn't she be able to?—she would be fine.

ELERI ASSESSED her partner and Donovan was in rough shape. Bruises lined his ribs—at least across the front of him where she'd opened first his jacket, then pulled up his shirt, then the undershirt.

"Donovan, you aren't fine." She sighed. "I'd ask if you have broken ribs, but you'd probably say no even if you did."

"Doctors are the worst patients." He said as though that excused everything.

"You work with dead people. That probably makes you

even worse than the rest." Eleri just stared at him. Then she poked him in the ribs. She was no MD like him, but she knew enough to diagnose the look on his face as "bad." Then she waited while he took a deep breath, and couldn't quite hide the grimace at what clearly hurt. Probably hairline fractures if not worse. "At least you didn't fall in water. Let's bind you up."

"Too cold."

Though they were inside a building, the open spaces were sucking the heat out of them. They'd need to find power, heat, or something better and quick. "You stay."

She had some exploring to do.

The building wasn't on any map of the national forest that she remembered, and she had a pretty good memory for that. Which would mean that they'd wandered in a different direction from which they'd come. Not surprising after the GPS crapped out on them. Too much snow and too many clouds between them and the satellite. But if her memory of the area map was accurate, that would mean they'd wandered beyond the forest boundaries. Something she didn't want to contemplate.

They'd never made it to their ATV, and without the GPS, with the storm coming in, she was just glad to be inside a structure. They'd been trained in survival techniques, but Eleri hadn't thought she'd ever have to use them. Stupid Westerfield sending them up here in the snow. Not her forte. She hoped he was worried that they hadn't called in. It would serve him right.

Then again, her new boyfriend Avery was probably worried, too, especially if he was watching the weather here. That didn't serve him right. He worried about her. Clearly, with good cause. She worried about him, too—though his ice involved blades and sticks and big guys who liked to hit each other. Hers was coming from the sky.

She left Donovan to put his multiple layers of shirts back together as she headed down the hallway. The room they entered looked like a cafeteria, maybe. Open space, windows in the cinderblock walls, kitchen space behind the windows. The only furniture was industrial chairs and tables and the low, built-in counter she'd set Donovan on.

The hallway opened onto another hallway, then to another hallway—at least as best she could see through the wired glass with the flashlight she was using. Some of the doors were jammed shut or bolted, leaving her to look but not check them out. Later, maybe, she and Donovan could force them open.

Heading back toward the room where they started, she peeked through little windows in the doors. Looked like offices, mostly still containing long unused furniture. Those would be better, smaller, not so much space to suck the small amount of heat they had.

"Donovan," she called out when she came back in, "I think I have a better place. I'll carry stuff. Just get yourself down that hallway."

He was already on his feet, having put himself back together, and he grabbed the smaller of the two bags, seemingly unwilling to not carry something. She let him do it if only because arguing would take too long. "In here."

Eleri opened the door to the smallest office that would fit.

"It's still cold." He told her.

"Yup, but it has windows." She pointed to the nearly floor-to-ceiling windows fully whitened by the flurries beyond. "We can see out if the snow stops."

"But if it stops snowing anyone can see in, too." Donovan set the bag onto the floor almost too casually.

"Who?" she asked, thinking ahead to the long trek back tomorrow. Or the day after. "There are restrooms across the way."

"That's good." He curled his lip, revealing how his scale of "good" had degraded.

"There's still running water." She shrugged. Though it felt frozen, it wasn't. "This place must be insulated as hell."

"Up here it would have to be." He looked around, his hand absently wandering to his ribs. "You really want to sleep in front of a window? And it's still too cold. We need a much smaller space."

He was right, they would never get even the smaller office heated up. "Ready for the solution?"

She opened the pack and pulled out the bag that held the compacted tent. Pulling out the lump of it, she flicked her wrist and watched as the wires popped it open. It settled onto the floor with a feather glide, almost four feet tall and a good seven by seven feet across. The pale color wouldn't be seen by any one unless they were specifically looking for a tent inside the building. "The drifts outside are high enough to cover us. Let's get in, get some heat, and get you fixed up."

"I'm fine." He was already leaning over to unzip the entrance though it clearly hurt him to do so.

"You lie well about some things, but this one you suck at," she told him, then followed him inside the tent. Eleri reached down into the bag, the organization making it easy to grab at what she wanted. The first aid kit came right out. She pulled out the rolled-up mattresses and set them to inflating, wondering how much juice the batteries had in them. "Sit."

This time he at least listened. The "sitting" wasn't pretty.

They had a tiny heater and she fired it up. It wouldn't be warm enough for a while, but soon. "Peel."

He rolled his eyes at her, but obliged. *Shit.* He must be really hurt.

Hopefully the satellite radio would work tomorrow. Hopefully.

With some direction from Donovan, Eleri got his ribs wrapped.

"Tighter." He brushed his hands over the wrapping. "It needs to be tighter."

She did it again, then again, until he was wincing as she pulled it into place.

"That's it." He nodded even through his gritted teeth. Donovan used his arms and apparently his clenched jaw to push himself up onto the inflated mattress. Then he waited while she rolled out his sleeping bag behind him. The bag slowly puffed up, and Donovan sat, silent, while she unzipped her pack and checked it.

Shit. And shit again.

Eleri took stock. They had enough heat for three more days if they didn't use it continuously. They had enough food for four days if they were careful—not crazy low rations, but *careful*. They had all their provisions, top-of-the-line tent, sleeping bags, tools, the skeletons. Most of it could be left behind, but they'd already gotten lost once. It didn't bode well; they were at the mercy of the storm.

It hadn't been on the radar; maybe it would pass quickly.

She could only hope.

But instead, she let herself out of the tent and stood at the window, her red parka a beacon to anyone who was looking. Not that anyone was. The snow was blowing wildly, but whether it was coming down or going up was anyone's guess. She couldn't see more than five feet beyond the glass.

Back inside the tent, she turned off the heater to conserve it and set her alarm for three hours. When she lay down, Eleri felt her eyelids start to close. Donovan was out cold and she stood no chance of serving as the night watch.

But they were in an abandoned building, in the middle of a snowstorm, maybe still on national property. They were as abandoned as they could be, but she wasn't going to worry yet. She was going to take advantage of being alone. She felt her head tip back for just a moment before her alarm went off.

Eleri hit the button, the cold telling her that she'd been asleep for longer than it felt. Looking over at Donovan, she saw that he was still fast asleep. It should be someone's turn to take watch, but it wouldn't be his. He'd fallen down a ravine hidden in the drifts of the snow. If the snow hadn't cushioned the fall, she didn't know what kind of shape he'd be in. She pushed the thought away and didn't wake him.

Flipping a small light on, she yawned into the space, then she froze.

There was a noise beyond the hallway.

She turned the light back off and waited, hearing nothing. Animals were probably all through this place, even though it had appeared to be locked down pretty tight. Just because she hadn't come face to face with any creatures didn't mean they weren't here. Her shoulders were just relaxing when the noise came again.

6

Donovan jolted awake to pain, his ribs notifying him that he was being repeatedly stabbed. This lasted half a second before he remembered that his ribs were most likely broken and no one was stabbing him.

He sat up, thinking it would make things better, but they weren't.

His breath caught as he saw Eleri, poised on the edge of her mattress, as still as she could be. Donovan couldn't even see her breathing.

He mouthed her name, or at least part of it. "El?"

Silently, she held up one finger asking him to stop. He, too, froze, unsure what he was waiting for but knowing that Eleri didn't give warnings lightly.

For long moments they stayed that way. He watched the zipper to the tent as though it would yield secrets if he just stared at it long enough or hard enough. Eleri looked into the middle space, and as Donovan watched her he realized she didn't see anything—she was listening. Right about the same time that she caught on and pointed to her ear then to him.

He could hear far better than she.

Now he, too, quit focusing on the ultralight poly-fabric of the tent and shifted his attention to waking all the way up and listening.

Donovan heard the building settle. He heard the snow outside, hitting the window in tiny, icy particles driven by small puffs of wind. The storm had died down, but that wasn't what Eleri was waiting for.

Then he heard it.

His head jerked toward Eleri and she saw.

"What?" she mouthed the word.

Not wanting to alert whatever was out there and not wanting to make any noise that might cover what he was listening for, he only shook his head. This time he was the one who held up a finger for her to wait.

A small nod showed she was still listening, but understood that he had better odds than she did.

They sat that way for three more minutes. He was about to give up when he heard it again.

Shit.

Turning to Eleri, he motioned to her to follow. Pushing to his feet, he ignored the burn in his ribs and rolled softly up. Behind him, he heard Eleri rise to her feet, too. She wasn't as quiet as he was, but she didn't hear the noise she made—he figured to herself, she was silent.

Her hand landed on his shoulder as he reached for the bottom of the zipper. He hadn't heard the noise again. Looking back at her, he mouthed another word. "Person."

"Animal?" He could read the shape on her lips.

He shook his head.

"Shit." She mouthed it back and he couldn't fight a grin.

Someone was in the building with them. Only Eleri could make that into a moment to smile.

It wasn't an animal. An animal wouldn't lay in wait, not that long before it made another sound. It would most likely run away from them. This person was coming toward them. He was tracking the marks they'd carelessly left behind, thinking no one was here. Someone was.

Donovan lifted the zipper slowly, the sound making a massive racket to his sensitive ears. Whoever was coming might hear it, but that was better than the person getting in the door before he and Eleri could move.

Behind him another sound zipped and made a metallic crack in the stillness. Eleri had pulled her gun. Her hand touched his arm again and he reached back, understanding. Donovan didn't think of reaching for his weapon. Despite his training, it still wasn't a natural reaction for him.

With the gun in his hand, the motion came back to him. The butt of the gun hit his palm and he was triggered to run the whole cycle. He dropped and checked the magazine, popping it back into place, then he racked his own slide, the sound breaking the silence with a clear call.

The way the person was waiting, sneaking in, Donovan had no doubt they knew what they'd heard. He lifted the zipper now, no longer caring about the noise. The guns had been a warning.

As he stepped softly forward into the cold, his breath clouded in front of him and he heard it. Eleri was right behind him, and he nodded at her soundlessly. From the look on her face, she got it. She was ready, probably more ready than he was, but Donovan was the ears, so he was in front. His gun was in his hand, down by his side, not aimed. Eleri was leading with the barrel as he slowly turned the knob and opened the door.

The hallway was as empty as he'd suspected. Whoever it was hadn't made it further than the first set of doors, and though they were quiet, he heard them retreating. With his hand, Donovan motioned that to Eleri. With that, she became more bold, stepping forward, bringing his attention to her face.

"Who?" she mouthed with a frown.

Donovan shrugged. It was too cold. People were wrapped up; they weren't touching things, not leaving the same kinds of traces they usually did. He heard the person, but hadn't scented them yet.

The two of them moved forward, the low crouch suiting Eleri's smaller shape. It had never been natural to him, and now it contracted his ribs, making his already painful breaths excruciating. Still, dying out here would suck worse than the pain in his ribs, so he stayed low and moved forward.

"Shit!" He whispered it, then turned to Eleri. "Running," and he took off, Eleri close on his heels.

Whoever it was had given up on stealth, footfalls smacking through the big room he and Eleri had opened up first. Then Donovan heard other noises. Loud and overlaying the sound of the running footsteps away from him, over his and Eleri's noises, too.

Something was wrong with the sounds though Donovan couldn't and didn't have time to place it. Another noise entered his brain now that he'd located the source and could give chase. Heavy plastic and metal sounds clicked and knocked before he heard the telltale zip of a spring pulling back.

A gun.

Then a door, heavy, the hinges un-oiled. He scented the cold the same as the snow, catching only the glimpse of a heavy boot as the door allowed the escape of whoever was here.

Full out running now, bruised ribs be damned, Donovan bolted across the open space. The door was closing, letting the perp get away. He scented something that grabbed him for a moment, but it wasn't as important as catching—or at least seeing—who'd invaded the building. Their closed national forest. Their find.

Eleri shoved past him, knocking his wounds as she went. He was irritated for a moment until he realized she was trying to get in front so she could take the brunt of opening the door.

A quick thought flashed that she was Southern to the core: even giving chase, she was thoughtful enough to get a door. But it didn't matter.

Out in the snow, tracking was easy enough.

The steps went just far enough to clear the door and then ducked behind it.

Eleri jumped out, giving up her cover in favor of sight. Donovan let her. One—because he couldn't stop her, never could. And two—because she'd need a damn doctor if she got herself shot up making herself a target like that. It took another heartbeat to remind himself that her instincts outranked his smell and hearing. She was already shaking her head, dropping her hands from where she'd popped out with her gun aimed and ready.

"Gone." She pointed.

As Donovan made it around the corner, moving much more slowly now that the threat was gone, he saw the tracks. They headed straight for the corner of the building and disappeared. Eleri was already following, though he didn't put any money on finding anything. Still, he trailed her out into the cold, trading precious body heat for information.

The tracks bolted from the side of the building directly into the woods. Whoever it was probably wasn't far, but they weren't willing to shoot. The day was eerily silent as they ducked back beyond the corner of the building, seeking safety in the belief that things were as they appeared.

Standing in the sun, holding up a hand now to shield the glare that came from above and glanced off the tinted windows as well as the snow, she told him, "One person. Not too tall, not too heavy."

She pointed at the tracks that weren't much different from her own. These broke the surface at every step, the new powder not having formed an icy layer that could be carefully traversed. Also, there was no "careful" in these steps. Just flight.

"The boots were black," he offered, not sure what it meant.

"Came from this way." She pointed back in the other direction.

Whoever it was had come in the same way they originally had, but had run off in the opposite direction—where the woods, and therefore cover, were closer. That meant the person either knew their way around relatively well, or they'd come into the building with an escape route planned. Donovan didn't like either option.

He tapped Eleri on the arm. "Let's get back inside."

"Then what?" she asked.

"Plan. Get out of here?"

She nodded, apparently not thinking much more than he did of someone tracking them this way. "Are you up to it?"

"I'll have to be." Despite his love of what dead bodies could tell him, he didn't have plans to become one. Certainly not out here, where who-knew-who or what was digging them up and letting them rot. He'd be happier being left out somewhere green and being pulled apart by coyotes. With that thought, he knew the pain had gotten to him and he'd turned morbid. "We'll wrap me tighter, dose me with Advil, and I'll be peachy."

She raised an eyebrow at him. A good response as even he wasn't sure when exactly he'd ever been "peachy." Then she ushered him back into the main room.

Their breath still clouded in front of their faces as Eleri scrounged around, looking for something to brace the door with. Admitting to his own limitations, Donovan let her. It still felt new to him, unfamiliar, letting someone help. He wasn't sure yet if it felt good, but it felt better than doing it himself. Better than alone.

He leaned against the counter, gun aimed at the door, ready to take all comers—well, all of them he could take without moving. He sniffed the air again, catching something familiar. He kept his gun trained until Eleri returned with a broken piece of re-bar, which she jammed against the door until she was satisfied it would hold. "Come on."

She held out a hand to him and his brain *clicked*.

He didn't know why that made his brain absorb enough of the smell, or maybe just place what he already had. He turned to her but didn't take her hand. "I know who was here."

WITH A HEAVY AND IRRITATED SIGH, the woman picked up her pack and slung it over her shoulder. Her injured shoulder.

"Ugh," she protested, not sure why she was speaking into the void. If only the little birds would come and sing her home, a la Snow White.

She was no Snow White. She was a rich kid, camping illegally with all the best equipment while she stole things she'd been specifically prohibited from being near. No, no little birdies were going to sing her home.

She'd slept hard, obviously needing the rest, but missing the sunrise and her planned early start to the day. Given the storm, she'd barely been able to track the two feds. Her major goal had been to return the bones she'd taken. That meant backtracking, and given her snow skills, she wandered around for quite a while before she found the spot. Which meant she'd left prints everywhere. First chance she got, these boots were going in the trash.

The ghillie suit was great at covering her visibly and did a decent job keeping her warm. But it was heavy as hell. Eventually, she'd dug up the site where the bones had been found and replaced them. She'd thrown a little snow over them, though she wasn't sure what that was worth. It was clearly a hack job. If she got lucky, another storm would come along and cover her tracks, literally.

She headed back to the tent. Her campsite was now as

obvious as if she'd set up klieg lights and red arrows. She was getting out of here.

It had taken far longer than she planned to pack it all up. She couldn't leave anything behind. Her illegal activities meant any screw-up would become evidence. It meant whoever it was out there could prosecute her. Prison was not a place where she would fare well. She thought about it as she hauled the huge pack through the woods.

She could kill someone with a half-inch deep cut on seven different places on the body. Most of them weren't obvious, so no one would probably stop her slicing at them with her prison shiv. Plus she knew how to hide evidence of her crimes. Okay, maybe she wouldn't die in the clink, but it still wouldn't be good.

She made it three miles according to her GPS and backup map before she heard the growl.

She was too close before she saw the cougar.

"R eally?" Eleri asked again, thinking there was no way Donovan had said what he said.

"Really."

"But why would she be here?" Eleri couldn't wrap her head around it. "No one would be here unless they were involved in this."

"Or tracking us." Donovan added between steps, the wince in his voice betraying what the trek was costing him. Eleri would have taken an alternative route had she known it. But without any communications—which still hadn't linked back up—she hadn't found any. And they couldn't stay where they were.

"That makes more sense." Eleri conceded. "There's no reason for her to be involved in this. I told you I thought someone was watching us."

"Well, it was obvious early on that you were right."

"Sure, but I never would have guessed it was Walter." What the hell was Walter Reed doing here? They'd left her back in Los Angeles several months ago.

The ex-MARSOC marine was beyond helpful in their last

case. She'd started homeless, helped them track people, and by the time Eleri and Donovan wrapped the case, she had an apartment, a PI license and relatively steady work from the FBI branch in L.A. So why was Walter Reed—actually Lucy Fisher —here?

Eleri was usually really good at reading a situation, using logic and her own intuition to put together the basis of the idea. This time she had nothing. She could think of no reason Walter would be here ... "Donovan, have you been talking to her?"

"Sure. Emails. The occasional phone call." His shrug was all but hidden by the bulky clothing he wore.

"How much?" That was a thread Eleri intended to pull. Was Walter following Donovan?

"Maybe one email a week?" He took in a deep breath, thinking. "Probably two calls."

"Long ones?" Now she was curious about any romantic connections. Because if that was the issue, this was a whole different ball of wax.

Still Eleri couldn't fathom Walter as a romantic stalker. Though she could certainly pull off tracking them up into Michigan and into the heart of the wilderness.

"No. Not long conversations," Donovan countered before her brain could wander other places. "I'm not involved with her and I don't think she's the kind to have misread anything from that. Our calls were pretty business oriented."

"Yeah, I don't see her as the stalker type either." Still something along those tracks bothered her.

Eleri didn't get very far at tugging on that thought either. "Look!"

She pointed first, then took off running. Donovan would catch up when he could. "Don't run," she hollered back, not sure if he could hear her. She ran forward anyway, toward the break in the smooth surface of the snow.

Too well-trained to ever run right into a scene, she stopped at the edge of the marks. Footprints. Boots. She'd seen these before. Yesterday.

The tracks wandered the area as though the site wasn't obvious—and probably it wasn't under the new blanket of snow. The prints indicated that the spot was found and digging began. A single line of footsteps pointed away from the site and headed into the woods with purpose.

Pulling out her camera, Eleri photographed as best she could. She knew there would be snow, and she had filters, but she was only minimally equipped for this. They had expected to find a set of bones that matched the pieces originally brought to Westerfield's attention. Not a stalker, a thief, and who knew what else. She'd expected any crime scene she was photographing would be a very old one.

Once she had it recorded as best she could, she moved into the scene. She was brushing back the snow as Donovan arrived.

"Fucking Westerfield," he muttered under his breath, but Eleri caught it. She wasn't Westerfield's biggest fan either, not after he'd sent them out in the snow for this.

"Look." She didn't move the bone, but cleared it. *"Son of a bitch!"*

Unlike Donovan she didn't mutter her swear, she yelled it.

"Those weren't there yesterday. This is our site."

"Yeah, she returned them!" Eleri was pissed.

"That should be a good thing."

"Unless they were altered, exchanged, who knows!" She felt the heat in her body, her anger spreading as she realized what had been done here.

She was pretty good at understanding why people did what they did, but the impotence that came when she didn't know why drove her nuts.

Clearly, Westerfield had a bead on this case. He had more information than he'd given them, letting them come in and put the pieces together for themselves. Even that, Eleri understood. Setting them to find it out for themselves would reveal anything Westerfield was missing. It was obnoxious, leaving them working without all the data, but Eleri understood it.

This, though?

Why would anyone take the bones? Then return them? Why was anyone even out here?

She posed that to Donovan out loud.

"I don't know. But it's a crime to remove evidence from an active investigative scene," he answered back. "So maybe she was trying to minimize the crime?"

"While that makes some semblance of sense, what would Walter want with the bones?" Eleri picked them up and bagged them. They'd be kept separate from the others, in case something was wrong with them. "It's still a crime, even if the bones are returned. Walter would know that."

"Does this make the skeleton intact?"

"Close. Aside from some small hand and foot bones, I think this would be everything." Not that she was all that happy about it.

Eleri stood up then. Stuffing the new bag down into the pack, she pulled out the phone again.

It was a good excuse to let Donovan rest for a while. He knew what she was doing and gave her the stink eye. She would have protested had it been her, but some days it was good to be the senior agent.

So she stood in snow up to her knees while she turned on the radio and waited for a signal to get through. After five tries through frequencies that should have connected to the rangers' stations, Eleri gave up on the radio and switched to the satellite phone.

It, at least, made a connection. The day was sunny, she was in the middle of fucking nowhere with a MARSOC-trained soldier on her ass and a wounded partner. Oh, and it was cold as crap. She said none of this. Just asked for an airlift out of this godforsaken land.

Turning back to Donovan, she gave him the news. "There's another storm coming in. Tonight."

"Oh, shit monkeys."

Her face showed her surprise at his on-the-spot swear but it was appropriate.

"So, no airlift out?" he asked.

"Sure. But not today, and maybe not tomorrow." It was not the conversation she'd hoped to be having. "They're afraid the chopper will wind up grounded or worse."

"Then it's just more people stranded out here. It's not a requirement that they rescue us. Nor for a classified FBI case." He put his hand on his hip, not a normal movement for him. It was definitely a tell of how much pain he was in. Stupid doctor.

"Do you have an idea about how this should go down?" she asked him, hoping he would plan for his injury, since he wasn't telling her about it.

"Let's get as far in the right direction as we can. We'll find some shelter and set up the tent. Hunker down through the snow." He looked at her then, as though to test her.

Eleri wasn't sure if she passed or failed, but it sounded like the best plan anyway. "Alright—we continue the direction we were headed. Two problems, though. The cougar—we should be able to avoid that—and Walter."

"Walter." It was all that needed to be said.

"I have no idea how to avoid Walter," Eleri admitted. "I have no shame admitting that she's superior to both of us on the stealth front. It was good when she was working *for* us, but now? I'm pretty sure she'll find us if she wants."

"Yup." Another non-Donovan-like response. He was definitely in pain. "Honestly, I think we should do exactly what you said. We'll avoid the cougar and we'll deal with Walter if and when she shows up. Trying to avoid her would be stupid since we'll fail epically." He pulled out his GPS and checked coordinates. "Do we have a location for the helicopter pickup?"

This time she pulled out a paper map. Without a pickup in the next few hours, she was all about conserving batteries and rationing supplies. She pointed. "This is the best spot for a chopper evac."

"That's completely the opposite direction from where we want to end up."

That fact had not escaped Eleri's notice either. "We have to commit to one plan or the other. If we head farther north, we'll catch a lift when the snow clears, but we'll definitely wait until they come get us. If we head back southwest, there's probably no lift. Just us, getting ourselves out."

She looked up at him. Donovan didn't answer. She waited.

"Look, I'm in favor of getting ourselves out. We have the snowmobiles. They have gas. If we can just get to them, we can ride out of our own free will. Don't have to wait for chopper weather either, just clear enough."

"I agree." She folded the map back up. "The snowmobiles are our best chance of avoiding Walter, should it come to that. I think the chances are that getting ourselves out is the slower method, but we'll be in control and the repercussions of it going wrong leave us closer and easier to find. I don't like any of this."

"Are your feet cold?" He startled her with the change of topic.

"No. I'm okay." Despite what she'd expected, they really had been outfitted with the best gear and snow hadn't leaked into her boots. "Why?"

"When your feet start to get cold we have to change tactics. Hands, too."

"I'm good. Pretty warm-blooded." She flexed her fingers, glad for what she'd always thought of as an oddity. She hopped back on the sat phone, wanting to call while the line was clear, and told the rangers she and Donovan would get themselves out.

The rangers agreed to have someone at the main station where they'd originally entered the federal land. Though the officers disagreed with the plan, Eleri stood firm. These people were national forest rangers, not army rangers. They didn't know that Walter was on their tail and stealing bones, and they didn't know what training Eleri and Donovan had. She assured them they were fine.

That was the truth. She just hoped it remained the truth. Her gun was at the ready though.

She and Donovan folded up and headed out, aiming southwest. Eleri knew where the snowmobiles were. Looking up at the sky, she guessed at the amount of daylight they had left to burn. When did they have to stop in order to get set up and ready before the next wave of the storm hit?

According to the sky, they should have some time. Last time the warning hadn't come early enough. She wasn't getting whatever weather report the rangers were working from. In fact, she wasn't getting much of anything at all. "Let's head out."

At least she didn't have that tickle at her neck.

They marched for an hour before they stopped for water. Eleri both desperately wanted to keep moving forward and wanted to set up camp and let her partner sleep.

The going was disturbingly slow. Donovan's injuries were a concern, but avoiding more problems was more important. The snow blanketed everything, dragging at their feet or making them high step. Either way, simply walking required about five times the usual energy. This time, she was in the lead, letting Donovan step in her tracks to save him some effort. Being the lead also meant keeping a solid eye on the landscape in front of her, so they didn't miss another drop-off, or head straight into a rock or river. Out here, everything looked the same except the trees—and the trees apparently had cougars.

"How are your feet and hands?" Donovan asked her as though she were the one who needed checking.

"I'm good." She was. It was his ribs she was worried about, but she didn't bother to ask. She would get a better assessment just watching him. He winced slightly as he screwed the cap back on the water bottle.

They didn't talk much, just drank and ate and tried to conserve energy. Eleri pushed them forward, pretty sure the sky was a little darker than it had been an hour before. The snowmobiles were just beyond the tree line, under cover in a small effort to make them less obvious.

Walter had probably found and dismantled them by now.

That thought bothered Eleri. Now that she thought it through, the odds that the vehicles wouldn't work was higher than she'd estimated. For a moment, she believed she should have gone the other way. *Shit.*

Well, what was done was done. She wasn't going to say anything to Donovan.

"What?" he asked just then.

"What what?" She was confused. "Clarify."

"You just thought of something. I can see the change in your posture. You don't like it."

Fuck.

Well, she wasn't going to lie. Turning to face him and realizing then that the snow was swirling up behind them in a bad sign, she told him her thoughts. "I just realized we've been stupid—"

"—distracted—" he filled in as she nodded.

"—there's a good possibility Walter got to our snowmobiles and dismantled them."

"Oh, shit."

"Exactly." She pointed now, the day getting worse by the second. "Snow blowing in the distance behind us. Sky's getting darker, too."

"Shit."

"You keep saying that." It was droll.

So was his response. "You keep giving me reason to."

The fact that Donovan hadn't considered the possibility of Walter tampering with their ride again told her he was in more pain than she'd initially thought. He was focused on it. He was supposed to be their lookout. She wondered what he missed.

It only took fifteen minutes to figure it out.

"Let's get beyond the trees." They'd been staying close in case they had to get under the canopy quickly. Sure there were cougars here, but their tent was pop-up and would possibly collapse under too much snow. They would add the supports tonight.

They were setting up the tent when a familiar voice chimed in.

"I didn't disable your snowmobiles. They were fine when I checked them last."

8

Donovan jerked at the sound of the voice and immediately regretted it. His ribs protested with sharp jabs of pain, reminding him what he already knew: he was a dumbass who didn't watch where he was going well enough. It was embarrassing to have the injury; the constant reminder was just insult.

He didn't speak—nor did Eleri, he noticed—as he turned to face Walter.

To his surprise, she wasn't in a white, fluffy ghillie suit and she wasn't aiming a gun at them. She was, however, carrying one. The bitch was dressed in pale camo pants and a jacket that blended into the landscape almost as well as the snow camo suit did. Her hat was knit but run through with the same pale colors changing position just often enough to break up the light, to keep you from spotting her. Her boots were darker, but again, not enough to get someone as good as Walter in trouble.

"Hi, Lucy." He said it just to be facetious. If he was going to get killed out here in the great beyond discovering what Westerfield probably already knew, he was at least going to call his killer by the first name she hated.

"Donovan." Lucy Fisher/Walter Reed stepped back. Not much, but enough to be noticeable.

He thought he detected a change in smell—to fear? He couldn't be certain, she was as bundled up as always. Walter had nothing to fear from him. She should fear Eleri, maybe, but him? He was practically dead on his feet, trekking through this god-forsaken land when breathing was a damn chore.

As he glanced forward, he saw Eleri's eyes flick back and forth, from him to Walter and back. He hoped to hell his senior partner had a damn plan.

For maybe a minute, no one spoke. Donovan took stock. If Walter wanted to kill them, she could just steal their pack and run away. They wouldn't last another few hours without it. Then again, she had a gun in her hand. It was better suited to a long-range shot than she would need right now, but at her hip was a pistol. Both were painted in the same muted shades as Walter herself.

At his first glance, she looked completely underdressed for the weather. But as he examined her now, he noticed she was thicker than he remembered and he figured she was wearing standard camo—snow camo probably being of warmer fabric in the first place—over thermal gear. Whereas he and Eleri looked like overgrown kids out on a snow day. He was going to die out here in a puffy jacket.

"I didn't disable your snowmobiles," Walter repeated, but didn't offer anything more.

"Why not?" Eleri was more willing to question the woman in front of them than Donovan was.

"I'm not here to sabotage." Walter looked at him again, something odd in her expression.

"Then why are you here?" Eleri pushed. "This isn't your usual stomping grounds?"

Donovan heard the question in it, when it should have been

a statement. It just showed that—despite the vetting they'd done on her—they didn't really know Walter Reed at all.

"No, not my usual," the other woman answered, her hand still on her gun. "I'm not here to take you out or anything." She sounded wonderfully offended.

"Then why?" Donovan pressed. He'd emailed her, talked to her on the phone some—more than he did to just about anyone but Eleri. He found he was hurt by her following them even if she wasn't coming to kill them.

"I'm just following. Recon." She clipped the words as though the very idea bothered her.

"Who sent you?" Donovan found the questions now rolling off his own tongue, no longer willing to wait for Eleri's measured interrogation. He was pissed.

"Just me." Again the flat expression. Walter gave away nothing more. "Storm's coming. We should stake out for the night."

Eleri's eyebrows rose again. "So we just hang out with you and your guns?"

Walter tucked hers away, though there was still an element of wariness that bothered Donovan. "You have guns, too."

"I just don't think we're up to your skills," he countered.

She stared at him, again giving him the odd look Donovan couldn't interpret. "You're not. I'm counting on it."

Well, holy shit. "Color me thrilled," he intoned dryly, but it hurt his ribs.

Even as he said it, Walter was dropping her own pack and pulling her clearly smaller tent from it. In fact it looked almost like an enclosed recliner. Though it popped up like theirs, it had a built-in inflator and she bolstered it with struts she pulled from the bag. "Be sure to add your supports. We're in for a few more feet of snow possibly. Don't want to collapse."

No, he didn't want to collapse. He didn't want the tent to collapse either. But Eleri was already setting theirs up and waving him off. He was to stand guard and watch over Walter. Donovan didn't mind.

It did piss him off that Walter looked good doing this. She was calm, collected, holding back information. There was something to her being here other than just stalking. Something niggled at the back of his brain, but he couldn't place it.

"I'm up," Eleri announced, waving him toward the tent as she looked back and forth between their set-up and Walter's.

"Don't worry. I won't shoot you through the tents. I won't come after you," Walter paused, "unless you start it."

Why did she turn and look at Donovan at the end of that? He couldn't start jack shit like this. It hurt to bend down to get in the tent. It hurt to lift the damn water bottle to his damn mouth, and Walter thought he was going to rush her in some way that would make her pull the trigger. "I won't start anything."

Eleri put her hands up. "I won't either. Just don't touch the bones."

Walter shook her head at them as though they were nuts, but a quick turn to look over Donovan's shoulder had him turning, too.

Shit. The storm was closer. Snow was kicking up around the three of them and the air had grown colder, the temperature dropping a handful of degrees in the last few minutes.

He didn't like it. "We need to get inside, Eleri."

"Yup." But she cast another dirty look at Walter before waiting while Donovan ducked inside, poorly. His ribs hurt and his brain hurt, too.

He was bothered by the very idea of being on the opposite side of whatever side Walter Reed was on. She'd never struck him as the kind to go off half-cocked. She'd go off, sure; Walter followed her own leads, but she was nothing if not reasonable. So why was she here? If she did have a good reason, then what had he and Eleri done wrong to deserve it?

Alternately, was it possible that Walter was truly out of it here? Neither option sat well with him. Neither made any sense. Walter knew they worked special ops. So the two of them going off into the wilderness to track a case shouldn't have set Walter off. He couldn't make heads or tails of it. He told Eleri just that.

"I got nothing," she answered softly, trying not to let her voice carry to the other tent.

That might be worse—that Eleri didn't have any idea either. He leaned back onto the mattress thinking he would stare at the roof of the tent, watching the snow build up. But he was opening his eyes from sleep before he could count the time.

Eleri was gone and he heard nothing he could parse out from beyond the blanket of snow that now covered the tent completely. Rolling off the mattress, he hit his feet to the ground, trying to be gentle and starting to feel like he really needed a shower. Gentle wasn't gentle enough and the shock went up his body to his damn ribs. Why he was angry at them for not healing in less than forty-eight hours was beyond irrational, he knew that. But he was still angry.

He climbed out of the tent, snow falling as he did, sounds becoming clear as the zipper slid up. Eleri and Walter were talking, but they stopped suddenly as Donovan appeared. The look on Eleri's face was not comforting and he hadn't even had breakfast. At least the snow had stopped falling.

The day had dawned bright and sunny, glare bouncing off the blanket of white. Donovan slowly inhaled, trying not to be obvious about what he was doing. He scented the cougar and her cubs nearby, that could only mean trouble. He scented something else, something human? But Eleri's voice cut that thought.

"It turns out Walter had a good reason to follow us," his partner told him, stern expression in place.

Donovan turned his attention to Walter now, looking for any semblance of an explanation.

"I don't have a lot of friends," she started. Not what he'd been expecting. "I was really grateful to you, and I hadn't left L.A. in so long that I flew out to South Carolina to bring you this military-grade support for your ankle. So you could walk and train on it before it was up to full strength."

That was nice, he thought. He'd broken his ankle during their last op. The damage had taken the team out of commission for his recuperation, leaving them both on desk duty for more than a month. But how had a kind gesture like that gone awry?

Walter was staring at him and he started to make a guess.

"It was stupid of me," she said, looking apologetic, "to come to your house unannounced. You weren't even home. So I waited."

He hardly ever left his house, except when he . . . Yeah, he knew now what had tripped Walter. "You saw me come back?"

"It wasn't you." She looked away. "I thought I was crazy. So I did what I usually do when things don't make sense."

He wished they weren't standing around in the cold. His sigh hurt his ribs, but not as bad as his brain hurt. "You investigated."

"I do have a license to do that." She again shrugged as though she was sorry. "It took a week. I turned down a paying job. But I figured it out."

He hadn't changed once during his initial few weeks at home, even though he'd itched to do it. Donovan hadn't been sure his ankle would hold up to the movement the change required. So he'd waited until he was mostly healed. Then he did little bits at first. Change and then change back. Change and pad around his own home as a wolf for a while. Change back. He hadn't gone for a run until just a few weeks ago. It was freeing, but it had been scary, too. What if he re-injured the ankle while he was changed? What if he couldn't change back?

Walter must have been there. But that had been only a few weeks ago at best. SAC Westerfield had sent them out as soon as Donovan was healed. It was part of his sheer pissiness about his ribs. He'd just gotten healed up, dammit! "So you tracked us up here?"

Nodding, her head aimed at him if not her eyes, Walter continued. "I flat out saw it. I don't doubt any more. You're the wolf-hybrid that came into the square with the vets. You listened and got intel."

Shit. Shit. Shit. Donovan was shaking off those thoughts, but Eleri—who'd stayed quiet until this moment—took another tack. "You got to see him do the change!"

It should have been a question, but it was awe.

Pulling back at his senior partner's vehemence, Walter nodded.

"*I* haven't seen it!" Eleri stalked a tight circle in the snow. "Goddammit, you got to *see* it?"

Another nod as Walter realized what she'd done. As Donovan realized what that meant.

"I blew the whole op," he said.

Eleri shook her head. But that didn't stop him.

"Yeah, I did. I made a stupid assumption that we were out here alone." His ribs were stabbing his internal organs again, but this time he realized he deserved it. "But we weren't! I was watched, and not just by the cougar. She saw it, she made me."

"Look Donovan—" Both the women seemed to be trying to soothe him, but he wasn't having it.

"Oh no." He held his hands out to ward them off. "She made me *twice*! Twice. Once back at my own home and again here, where she actually watched me change without either of us knowing it!"

Walter talked at the same time Eleri did.

"Look, I'm MARSOC trained. I'm really good at this. So you don't have to worry about other people finding out about you."

"She got past me, too, Donovan. I'm the senior agent. If it's anyone's fault, it's mine."

He wasn't going to let El go down for his mistake, and it had been his. He knew it. Turning to Walter he said, "Oh, so you're the only soldier who's ever been successfully trained to recon like this? Because I don't think that's the case. Which means any one of you who catches a whiff that I'm weird—" probably the softest way of putting it, "—can come find out the whole story before I even know you're there."

"Donovan." Eleri's voice was harsher. She grabbed his attention with that, even if he didn't want to give it. "She's good. Really good. We know this. And you're right—Cooper Rollins got past us, too. Clearly, there are people out there who are better at finding us than we are at concealing ourselves."

"*You, too?*" Walter asked, stunned as she now focused on Eleri.

"No." Eleri shook both her head and an open palm at Walter. "I'm not like him. I'm weird differently."

Now Walter Reed/Lucy Fisher, special forces trained Marine and part-terminator, was looking at both of them as though *they* scared *her*.

Eleri was ignoring it. Donovan didn't. If Walter thought they needed to be put down, she'd have them both dead in a matter of seconds and no one would ever find their bodies. Except maybe Westerfield—who knew what skills that creepy-ass man had up his sleeves? Donovan didn't want to know, really. Then there was Wade. Wade wouldn't stop until they'd been found. That was Donovan's only comfort.

Eleri kept talking, trying to soothe him, but it didn't work. "Look, Donovan, she's really good. You know this. I know this. And she didn't just get past you. She wore that damn ghillie suit and came in and stole our bones out from under both of us, then put them back, too." She sighed and looked at the sky, missing Walter's odd expression. "We got made. That's all. We'll report it to Westerfield and we'll get reprimanded. All we ever saw of her was that damned suit in the distance. We had almost nothing on her. If we hadn't seen that much, she would have completely been a ghost."

Walter interrupted. "I don't own a ghillie suit."

Eleri looked at her sharply.

"I don't. And I didn't steal your bones."

9

T
he rush of the engine of the snowmobile gave Eleri's
heart a happy jolt. She hadn't had a positive jolt to
her heart in the almost four full days they'd been out
here.

She'd watched her partner fall off the face of the earth in
front of her, tracked a stalker, and found out that they'd pretty
much screwed away their secret. But the revving of the engine
was something she found she cherished now.

Beside her another engine revved, indicating both had
started up exactly as they should. Eleri had half expected problems just because of the way the rest of this little expedition
had gone.

Rogue storms be damned. She was going back where there
was heat and a bed and a hot shower. To where she wasn't
running low on food.

And to where there wasn't some unknown woman running
around stealing bones. Eleri sighed. They had to get going to
make it to the ranger station before dark. At least she'd
managed a call—the forest service was not only expecting

them, but now knew their exact location and where to start looking if they didn't make it.

Walter was the wild card. She wasn't supposed to be out here.

Despite the extra time needed to stick together, Eleri didn't want to split up. She turned to Donovan. "How do you want to ride?"

Walter raised her dark eyebrows at Eleri. "Is he that injured?"

"Fractured ribs. Did you see him go down?" At Walter's head shake, Eleri explained. "A drift covered what was actually a ravine. He was walking and just dropped into the snow and onto a rock."

"Probably just bruised," Donovan added. "And I don't know if it's best to ride solo or sit behind someone."

"Solo." Walter offered. It figured she would know these things. "That way you're in control. If there's a speed or a method of taking the bumps that works better, you can adjust. I'll ride behind Eleri."

"Doesn't that scare you? Wouldn't you rather drive? I'm sure you're better at it than me," Eleri offered.

A grin lit Walter's face and she almost laughed. Eleri likened the other woman to a saber-toothed cat—beautiful, graceful, stronger than expected, and deadly as hell. "Well, actually that's why I want you to drive it. I tend to go fast and I think you'll be easier for Donovan to follow."

Yup. Walter politely didn't say "yes, I'm better at it than you" but it was pretty clear that's what she meant.

With their packs strapped down, Eleri slid into place and began the ride that wouldn't take them to the nearest ranger station but to where Walter had parked her own snowmobile. Apparently, she'd also made part of the trek in snowshoes, proving once again that she was the superior being out here.

In an attempt to not be found by Eleri and the werewolf she

was traveling with, Walter hadn't parked her own ride near theirs. She was afraid they might over- or under-shoot their marked spot and stumble upon her ride and know she was out here.

As they took the bumps and crossed the landscape at what was finally a satisfying speed, Eleri thought about what Walter had revealed that morning. She too had seen the woman in the ghillie suit, but by staying out of the way had missed her stealing bones from the dig sites. She'd come across the other woman's tent, too. High end. But Walter hadn't done anything about it because she hadn't known what was going on.

The soldier had said it was better to ride with Eleri rather than holding onto Donovan and his bruised ribs, but Eleri wasn't so sure about that. Walter still seemed pretty reticent about going near her partner. No wonder—the man could change into a damned wolf. On top of that, Eleri was having to tamp down her jealousy. Walter got to see Donovan change. Eleri had been asking the entire time she'd known about him, but he wouldn't change in front of her.

She insisted that her interest was as a scientist, but it was also as a damned curious human. The scientist understood that he hadn't *let* Walter see that. He was just as upset about it happening as Walter was about seeing it. Eleri was jealous as hell.

She wanted to tell Avery, but she couldn't.

She'd hardly thought about him since coming out here, but —points in her favor—she'd been worried about her survival. Eleri vowed to text him as soon as they got in. Besides, he knew she was on a case and might lose contact for several days at a time. Hell, she could have frozen to death in the snow and Avery never would have known where to find her. The Bureau wouldn't hand out information on a deceased agent to a non-family member.

The two snowmobiles were now headed a different direction from how they should come in to the ranger station, cutting two sides of a triangle instead of a straight line. Eleri lied and told the rangers they had a pickup to make. It was actually a drop-off. After that, Walter would follow them until close to the ranger station and pass by.

The ride was long and bumpy, her thoughts as rough as the terrain. When she finally let Walter hop off and waited while the other woman started her own snowmobile, it was the first time she'd felt cold.

FINALLY READY, Eleri stood in the lab. She would have felt bad about the time frame, but she couldn't muster it up. There were no kids in a cult to rescue before they died. There were no bombs threatening any cities—at least not that she knew of. All her problems were dead now. For today, she was grateful.

She'd showered, slept in a real bed, and ate—both dinner and breakfast—before coming here. For the first time in five days she felt rested and warm. But she couldn't take the day off; the night was all she had. And she'd called Avery. He hadn't thought anything of her not checking in, hadn't even known he should. That hurt her heart, and it wasn't his fault. Not to mention he wasn't all that happy that she'd been that close to mortal danger and he hadn't known. The job was hell on relationships. Eleri knew that concern deserved a greater amount of attention, but the irony was she had a job to get to.

"What's first?" Donovan asked her, standing before her in latex gloves and a lab coat.

"You go to the doctor and get your ribs checked out."

"Can't. Besides *I'm* a doctor." He shrugged, then regretted it and tried to cover it up.

"Well, hell's bells." She set down the bone she'd picked up. "Let's do this shit ourselves then." They'd been given a lab in the Grand Rapids FBI complex. Surely they could cook up an X-ray for an agent.

It was three hours later that they'd determined Donovan had merely cracked his ribs. He was bound tightly back into his bandages before he told Eleri in no uncertain terms that he was not off the damn case.

"I'm not costing us more time," he said over the burger he'd ordered medium rare.

"You won't cost us time." She looked at him, not wanting to argue but needing him healthy. "You just don't want to get put on desk duty again."

He tipped his head. "If it was you?"

"Fuck." She said it softly. He had her there. The only reason it wasn't her was because he was being nice and walking first so she didn't have to do so much work on her stumpy little legs. Okay, her legs weren't stumpy, and that's what partners did. But in that same vein. "All right, then. We're mostly in the lab. We'll keep you bound tight. But no tackles; leave that to me."

"Oh, hell yes." He responded with flare, making her laugh. Until he followed it up with, "After Los Angeles, you don't even have to tackle anyone. You never got a handle on the black-eyes thing did you?"

"Never saw it again." Well, no one had reported it to her. Not Haley Jean, her friend she'd stayed with for a few weeks. Not Avery, and they'd spent plenty of time together when he wasn't playing away games with his team the North Dakota Executioners. So, no. Nothing to report there. At least that's what she told herself. She picked up her tray. "Speaking of weird things from Los Angeles, do you still have the gris-gris my grandmère gave you?"

He tossed his trash and set the tray aside. "Nope. Weirdest thing. I had it, then I didn't wear it for a few days, and then . . ."

"Couldn't find it, huh?"

"Same for you?" He asked it like a question, but he could

see that the gris-gris had disappeared the exact same way for her. "So it only shows up when you need it?"

"I don't know. I remember people coming to my grandmère for advice and help when I was a kid, but I didn't think it was anything unusual." She shrugged. "Now, I'm starting to wonder."

"Ever see her eyes go black when she got mad?" Donovan teased, but Eleri wasn't so sure it was all harmless. And she wasn't so sure it wasn't the job doing it to her.

"Sometimes, I think you made it all up."

He shook his head but didn't say more. Why would he? They were both weird enough as it was. "Let's hit the lab."

He seemed happier, then again, he'd just taken a small handful of painkillers. Nothing prescription, but it was clearly helping. She didn't think a burger and fries had hurt his mood either. After four days of energy bars and melted snow water, hot food was heaven.

It was almost two o'clock before she stood in the lab, in the same place she'd started—late—at ten that morning and she was exactly zero steps further along. "Okay, let's see if we can get any evidence off the stolen bones."

"On it. Filters?" He started to lay out the pieces on a tray.

She rattled off a few she'd like to try, but she didn't hold out hope. They searched for an hour, using every shade of light in the visible and unseen spectrum but hadn't found a single fingerprint on any of the bones.

"Well, it makes sense," Donovan conceded. "From what we saw, she wore gloves, and I can't imagine taking them off, knowing she would leave prints *and* opening her fingers to the risk of frostbite."

"You're saying she knew she'd leave prints and that we'd check it?"

"Everyone knows that. Especially people who sneak around

and steal human bones in the middle of a closed national forest in a snowstorm."

"It *was* pretty damn weird." Eleri's turn to concede. But she put the bones into a chamber and added a superglue fume to check. Forty-five minutes later they'd developed exactly zero fingerprints. They'd checked the other skeleton, the one sitting on the surface, for prints, too.

"So no one touched these bones after they were bones." Donovan spoke it out loud. "Except for us and our girl."

"It makes sense. I mean, both bodies appeared to have fallen there and rotted away." She put her gloved fists on her hips. "Except for the part where that's all wrong."

"Walk it." He prodded her. He knew bodies better than crime scenes. He knew human function; she knew bacteria, animals, and things left behind.

"Okay, let's talk about the second site, the one she stole from. It was partially buried, as though the ground came up around it. Which happens if something stays in one place for a while. That would indicate it was an earlier death than the other one—the first skeleton on the surface. But both were laid out as though they just rotted there."

"Why couldn't they?" he asked, as though it was a legit question. Maybe it was; she just hadn't found that angle yet.

"Why didn't some animal come along and take a bite? Take a leg back to feed their baby cougars? Left a mark, something!" Eleri picked up the femur from the first site. "I mean, the bones themselves are wrong here. It's possible that something was wrong with the body and the animals knew it. These are pristine, not a mark. I would have expected something like that to be buried deep. But it was on the surface."

"Is it possible that someone brought the skeleton and laid it out like that?"

"Sure, but it was anatomically sound. Like he died, rotted, got down to bones with no one bothering him, and then the snow came and preserved him." Her brain was churning options. "So the bacteria ate him—he didn't desiccate—but the bigger animals didn't."

Donovan held up the femur of the second skeleton beside the first. "This one's pretty pristine, too. I mean, there's dirt from the partial burial, but no gnaw marks and no missing pieces."

"Right. I mean a few of the small bones are missing, but nothing like we'd expect to see in a case like this." She looked back and forth between the bones. "Nothing else matches between the two. Not the age estimation, not the time since death. Only that nothing wanted to eat them."

"How could the longer one have laid in that field and no one tripped over him?" her partner mused. "We'll need to call the rangers and see what that likelihood is."

"I think it could happen. Tall grasses, field off the main trails, unless someone stepped right on him, they wouldn't see him. You could pass within a few feet and easily miss it if it didn't smell or anything."

"Always a disconcerting thought," Donovan added as he absently placed a hand to his ribs and set the bone back down. Then Donovan put the two skulls next to each other. "Maybe we're looking at it wrong. Maybe it's not about how they ended, but how they started."

10

I t had taken three days. Three glorious warm, healing days, by Donovan's count. But they had something.

Westerfield still wasn't telling them what he knew, if that was anything beyond what they were discovering. Donovan found himself amending his own thoughts. Westerfield *did* have something.

The initial report on the found bones—the ones that started the case—didn't trip anything on the outset. The FBI investigated, said the bones didn't match any missing persons cases, and then there was some equation he was missing. At some point after the FBI should have returned the bones to the medical examiner's office in the county where they were found, Westerfield picked up the case and handed it to them.

Some days Donovan wondered what kind of cases the other NightShade agents were assigned. He didn't even know how many other NightShade agents there were or anything about them. He only knew that Eleri's friend Wade had been an agent and left the FBI to pursue his chosen field. The other thing Donovan knew was that he had two fully skeletonized bodies and a third that he should have but didn't.

Eleri had already requisitioned the original skeleton, the one that started this, but they didn't have it yet. Donovan tried to think about other things while he ate breakfast alone. For a man who previously had a pretty solitary existence, even the day-to-day stuff with a partner was a bit much. He still wasn't able to shake thoughts of the case.

Heading back to the lab, he walked into a full set-up. Eleri was already at it. "What do we have today?"

She pointed to papers she'd spread out on the table. "We have results."

He looked, but the first thing he saw was the requisition. "They lost them?"

"Yeah. They went to pull the bones to send to us and what do you know? They're gone. All we have is the report." She shrugged, but it wasn't a kind one. She was pissed.

"There are pictures," he offered half-assed, knowing how much she hated pictures. She was right, they could show evidence you'd already found, but you couldn't find evidence on them. She wanted the bones. So did he. "Well, shit."

"Yup. Especially since these are so different. If there's a thread, a third set would really show it nicely." She paused, looked at him. He didn't like it. "You know those bones were found in the national forest."

"Of course they were. That's why we were out there in the first place. We were hoping to find the remainder of that skeleton." He put it together then. "Oh, Eleri, no."

"We didn't find it, Donovan." She pointed out.

She was right. He'd been avoiding it, pushing the thought away each time it weaseled its way in. They'd gone out to find a particular skeleton. They hadn't found it. "So the fact that we found two others doesn't count for anything?"

"It counts for a lot. It counts for this case being even weirder than we thought." She gestured to him with the ulna of one of the skeletons, a move she apparently didn't find odd. "I want a thread, Donovan. Two is a coincidence, three is meaningful. You know this."

He started to run his hand through his hair until his ribs protested. It was a useless gesture anyway. One thing he hadn't counted on was getting injured. He'd been injured more times since joining the Bureau than in all his years at the medical examiner's office. There he'd played with saws and hedge clippers and chisels sometimes. Then again, here, he played with guns. "I agree. I *want* the third set. I'm just not sure I want it badly enough to go back out and get it."

"So you don't go. You're injured."

"You can't go by yourself," he argued first, then he reminded her, "I have the nose."

"That you do." She nodded toward him, still gesturing with the bone she held. "But you also have the fractured ribs. I don't think you can change—or maybe it's just that you *shouldn't*—while you're injured."

"I'm getting injured a lot. So are you. If I can't do my job while injured, I don't think I can do my job, period." That was a sobering thought. As much as he liked to mentally complain to himself about being kept in the dark, about the beating he was taking, about the crazy cases they were dealt, he realized he kind of loved it. The puzzles, the intrigue, the fact that he was suddenly very useful even if no one knew it. He was a mental man, and the things he was soaking up were fascinating, if weird and even often scary.

"You shouldn't have to do your job while injured, though sometimes we just have to. Today isn't one of those days." This time she offered a full grin. "I have Walter. She's better out there than either of us anyway."

That pulled him back. They did have Walter. For all the wrong reasons, she was here. The thought flitted through his head of what she'd seen, but he tamped it down. Walter would happily head out with Eleri; she seemed somewhat scared of

Donovan these days. Why wouldn't she be? But it bugged the shit out of him that big, bad Walter Reed was scared of him. "If I couldn't find the bones before, how will you and Walter find them with your puny little olfactory bulbs? Huh?"

Eleri laughed outright as she set the bone back into place where she'd laid out the whole skeleton before he even arrived. The big bones were relatively easy, but sorting hand and foot bones could be painstaking. "If you can't find it, then Walter and I don't have a worse chance."

Then she looked up at him, a more serious expression on her face. "Look, I think we're dealing with something here."

He didn't interrupt to say, *When are we not?* but let her continue.

"Right now I have two theories. First, it's possible the bones weren't ever in the original spot. Not at the coordinates we were given. We would have found them. We were there. You have the nose. Which brings up more possibilities."

"They were moved," he supplied as he leaned forward onto the lab table, thinking the change in position might help his ribs. He needed super healing powers. He didn't have them.

Eleri ignored his inner monologue and answered his words. "Or they don't smell like human decomp for some reason."

Donovan thought on that one for a minute. "I can't think of any reason for that to happen. I'm trying to think if I smelled animal decomp and passed it by. Probably."

"These bones already got passed over by animal predators. We know *something* is off." She peeled her gloves and crossed her arms. "Option number two: they were never there in the first place."

"Why would someone—" He stopped himself. "So the person who reported them falsified the initial documents a little."

"Which would indicate they knew something was up and didn't want to share."

"It worked."

"Not for long. We have you and me and now we have Walter." Eleri shook her head. "With that person out there after the bones, I'm going to be glad to have a special forces Marine at my back."

"So the grad student falsified the docs?" He thought that through.

"I'm guessing it was the professor. More likely to notice any anomalies. More likely to have a ghillie suit? Or at least access or money to get one. And to get supplies to be out in the snow for four days. That's no easy or cheap feat out here."

Donovan agreed. "Yeah, I didn't know any grad students who could swing either the money or the time for such a thing. But the originating report is from a male professor."

"So how certain were you that the person in the ghillie suit was female?"

"Pretty damn certain." He looked her square in the eye. Things weren't adding up. They never did, but that was growing on him.

"Then we have a conspiracy." She shrugged as though conspiracies were everyday things. Or even plausible. Not in the long term, they weren't.

Donovan didn't like conspiracy theories. He didn't believe that aliens had been roaming the earth for decades and everyone involved managed to either keep quiet or be stupid about how they told the world. Enron was about as big a scandal as could contain itself and it didn't last all that long. So he could buy into the idea of a small handful of people covering up a weird set of bones, but . . .

"El, just what kind of people would have to be involved in this? I mean, they'd have to know what they had." He almost sighed then stopped himself, grateful at the thought of not having to go back out there. "The average person often doesn't recognize a human bone when they see it. These people not only did, they also recognized that it was scientifically interesting, and then managed to report the find while obscuring part of it."

Eleri did sigh in response. Not uncommon when there was no way to narrow down such diverse theories, or to even know if any were on the right track. "Option three—they don't know the bones are odd. They report them with the correct location and then animals come and scavenge the remains."

Something he could work with! Donovan was grateful. "No."

She waited.

"I would have found the spot. If animals scavenged it, that would mean the decomposition didn't put them off—meaning it was normal. I would have at least smelled that a body had been in that location. I didn't."

"So, Walter and I go back and scour the area. I search and she protects." Eleri shrugged at him.

"But you don't know where to search. You have no better shot at it than a random chance. Especially if the initial report is off."

"Donovan, we went to that location and didn't find the original bones, but found *two* other sets. Something is really crazy out there. What are the chances that we found the only other two skeletons in that area? Not high. My guess is that original location is close to the right one. They didn't know how many there were. Didn't know they were faking us into another find." She was getting excited and he had to admit that her math added up. "So we may not find the originals, but we might find more."

"The snow is a bitch." He didn't *want* to play devil's advocate.

"But time is, too," she countered, and she was right. Donovan found himself glad that Walter would have her back. Someone was out there, and maybe not just one person. That person had already messed with their finds, who knew what they were doing today while he and Eleri stayed in the lab?

Donovan looked out the window where snow swirled beyond his vision. Eleri tracked his gaze.

"If I'd thought it through earlier, I'd have gone back out today. I'm just grateful the bad weather means whoever's out there can't get much done either. Walter and I will head out tomorrow morning."

"Walter has agreed to this?"

"Not yet, but I have eight hours to convince her." Eleri shrugged. "So today, we comb the results, and tomorrow you take over the lab? Hopefully we'll be back by tomorrow night. The weather is supposed to be clear."

Donovan didn't say he'd heard that one before. He didn't get a chance. She was pulling out the papers she was looking at when he'd come in. "Here's what we have so far."

He picked up a plot of results from mass spec and read the sample name she'd fed into it. "Left Femur—Subject 2" Then he picked up a second mass spec sheet labeled "Left Femur —Subject 3"

"So 'One' is our missing guy?" he asked.

"Yes. I went with chronological order of find." She looked over his shoulder. "Do you see it?"

"They look to be from the same place." Bone was a living tissue and constantly remodeled. Checking the composition for tiny mineral deposits laid down as the person lived could give information about where the person had resided most recently. "How common are these ratios?"

She would have looked them up, he knew. Compared them to known samples. "Not positive. This element—" She pointed at a smaller peak on the graph. "—is relatively rare and the graph as a whole points to them living here for a while before they died."

"Or living somewhere with a similar isotope ratio and then

dying here. It's a national forest, Eleri. People come here from all over."

"True," she conceded, "But that one peak really drops that possibility. In fact, the place is so large, that peak is pretty isolated to this area."

"You mean they lived *in* the national forest? Like squatters?" He almost shook his head.

"It's a possibility we have to consider." She then turned back to the skeletons. "I measured the long bones to estimate stature. Neither was very tall, though I'm not surprised. Number two has such thick bones it's as though they grew round instead of long and number three didn't sex differentiate. Even in the skull measurements."

"Really?" He picked up her papers and scrolled through the computer screen. She'd logged a variety of cranio-facial measurements. He could see the calipers still sitting on the lab table.

"I did it twice for both of them." She took a deep breath. "I'm heading out for a snack. I want you to re-run the numbers with no input from me. I don't want to influence you in case I did something wrong."

He doubted she had, but he had to ask. "That bad? What is it?"

He picked up the skull of number two and looked at it. Often you could glean info just from appearance. But the program ran specific measurements against major ancestor groups and genders and could produce results that couldn't be found by sight alone.

Her answer stunned him. "According to what I got, neither skull has enough evidence to determine gender or ancestry."

Donovan almost dropped the skull.

11

Eleri looked back over her shoulder. She was feeling it again, only this time she knew it wasn't Walter following her. Walter was right beside her.

"We're being followed," Walter calmly announced through the mic and earpiece from behind Eleri.

No shit, Sherlock. Eleri thought it but didn't say it out loud. "Yeah."

As long as Walter didn't think they were in the crosshairs, Eleri didn't care. Mostly she was upset. It was harder being out this time. The snow felt colder, the glare seemed harsher, and she was irritated at the amount of time it had taken to get out here. She only had one advantage this time.

She high-stepped through the snow, each step more of a trudge than the last time.

"Why are we headed to this field?" Walter asked softly. "Ma'am. If it's okay that I know."

Eleri almost laughed at being called "Ma'am" but Walter was a soldier, Eleri the team leader of this op. She shouldn't balk. In a low voice, she spoke into the mic. "It's okay. I know we're being followed. I'm okay if she hears us. We have two snowmobiles. If we get her can we take her back?"

"Yes, ma'am. So speak freely?"

At Eleri's nod, Walter turned and went forward into the woods. This time she asked her question into the air, not into the tech, as if she didn't care who overheard. "Why are we headed to this new field?"

"I have intel."

"Anything in particular?"

"I believe the original skeleton is there." She didn't offer up the part where she'd seen it. She didn't even know when. Maybe she'd seen it while asleep, maybe not. Previously, she'd remembered when she dreamed of something. But this morning she'd just thought it. Was it a memory? Had she been seeing the location of the other skeleton?

She wasn't sure. She only had one of those hunches that the place she could clearly see in her mind now was simply a separate open field in the same portion of the grid.

Eleri had no way of knowing for sure. But she'd had hunches so many times that turned out to be exactly right. At this point she was going off the statistical model of "Eleri is right," and that was it.

So she was headed to yet another field she'd found on the map. When they got there, she sure as hell hoped she recognized it, or she was out of luck.

After maybe another mile, she started getting that tickle at the back of her neck. Whoever their stalker was, she was close.

They went another quarter mile in silence before Walter's voice came into her ear again. "Target is off to the left of us. Don't look."

Eleri didn't need to be told that, but since Walter was the tactical portion of this mission, she didn't balk at the reminder. Better to be told than to give away their tactic.

"Ma'am, wait." The voice came through the air again, not the tech.

When Eleri turned—not a graceful, easy maneuver in the deep snow—Walter was pulling something out of her pack. It became clear it was a map as Walter opened it.

"Ma'am, I wasn't sure if we were going to this field, or this one." She was pointing almost clumsily as she spoke, pointing out several possible places that would fit the criteria Eleri had.

It took a moment for Eleri to realize what was happening. She pointed to several of the spots on the map, holding up her end of the charade. In a low voice she asked into the mic, "Why are we checking the map?"

"I wanted to give the target a chance to get ahead of us. Without solid intel where we're going, she's our best chance of getting there."

"Because?"

"If she's part of some conspiracy to hide the original skeleton, then I'm assuming she knows where it is." Walter pointed at the map again. "Let's have her lead us to it."

"Good idea." Eleri shook her head and pointed to another part of the map. "Should we head in a different direction for a little bit?"

At Walter's nod, Eleri immediately regretted the question. It meant more walking in this god-forsaken snow. But if the other woman would lead them to the find, rather than leaving them digging up random snow for hours on end, it would be worth it.

They headed off toward their right for a while, talking about nothing. Just two girls, walking through three feet of snow on a random day. Yeah, she always did this.

After a short distance, Walter turned them sharply to the left and began tracking the other woman.

Eleri couldn't see her, but Walter sure seemed to. Eleri took it on blind faith that Walter was actually tracking someone. Her job was to stay low and not get them spotted. That, at least, she could do. It was an hour and an energy bar later that they approached the border between the woods and the open field they'd been aiming for.

Walter held her hand out, palm back, holding Eleri from running ahead willy-nilly—which she wasn't about to do.

"Yes?" She kept the word low, knowing the mic would pick it up.

"Bingo." Walter stayed low and pointed out into the field.

Damn, she was good. It took Eleri a moment to find the ghillie suited woman among the drifts. But there she was, in one spot, playing in the snow.

Likely, she was digging up another set of bones. Why else would she be on her knees in the snow in a still-closed national forest? Eleri watched.

The woman was bagging something.

"Walter." She spoke the word to the side, not wanting to take her eyes off the scene in front of her. "I don't want her to leave with the bones."

"Take her down? Or steal the bones?" Walter asked.

"Bones. Top priority. They'll be safe in the lab." She reminded herself that there were probably several more skeletons out here. At the rate they were going, the number was likely at least one and possibly almost infinite. Bones. That was what she should want. She also wanted to arrest this woman who was fucking with the case before it even got started. But, *bones.* She repeated it to Walter. "Bones."

Walter nodded, ignoring the repeat. Ignoring Eleri's real wishes and going in favor of the command. It was the right thing.

So they stayed put.

Eleri watched the woman, wishing she could have seen the bones as they were laid out in the field. But she gave up on that. This woman was already at the scene, thus, nothing Eleri saw now could be trusted, and nothing she got would be worth the fight. Still, Eleri wanted to see it with her own eyes. She sat on her hands, held her voice, and otherwise tamped down her anger.

When at last the woman stood up and threw the pack over her shoulder, Eleri almost stood up, too. It was Walter who slowly moved and started stalking their prey. "Stay here."

"*Really?*" She was a trained FBI agent. Then she reminded herself that on their last op, Walter evaded them and snuck up on them more than once. Walter was gone before Eleri could really protest.

Eleri stayed in the woods, back from the edge of the field so she could see but not be seen. She was virtually invisible this time, having been decked out a la Walter. The camo gear was a size too big and she was layered with thermal wear under it, but it was stealthier than the red jacket she'd worn the first time when she thought she was just gathering specimens. A mistake she wouldn't make again.

She wanted to go check the site. *Shit.*

Time was passing. There wouldn't be daylight left to check it if she didn't get there soon.

Executive decision time. Did she piss off Walter? Take advantage of the light? Or wait? Sometimes the op just had to be run as planned. Eleri thought through all the possibilities. If she was seen, if she was shot at, if she ruined the entire op.

Eleri stood up from her spot and pulled her weapon.

DONOVAN HOVERED over the bones of two nearly complete skeletons as he tried to figure out what he was looking at.

Today he'd been up early, seeing Eleri and Walter off. This time both were dressed in the snow camo, both practically disappearing in the parking lot. It was a good thing, too. This time they were hunting. Whoever that woman was, she was out there. She wanted what he and Eleri wanted. And Donovan had no idea how dangerous she was.

He was grateful for one thing: when it came to betting on who was the most dangerous, he would bet on Walter. That, at least, allowed him to focus in the lab.

Dead bodies told a story. Flesh wounds, burns, coloring, all gave up secrets about what had happened before the person died. Toxicology screens told about what they'd taken or had been given. The contents of their stomachs told what they'd eaten and when.

None of that existed here.

Bones were only the synopsis of the story. Just the bare basics of it. Sometimes they kept some of the evidence—knife marks, breaks and fractures, burrows from passing bullets.

These bones had none of that.

If a body came into his office fully skeletonized, he turned it over to the anthropologist. Instead, his anthropologist had just left. So he did his best.

He quickly checked over Eleri's layout of the skeleton, then completed his own write-up without looking at hers. The one skull was missing a piece, so it was conceivable that a fatal trauma had occurred in that one spot, leaving no other marks on the bones. Then, at some later date, that portion of the skull, the one spot bearing all the evidence was knocked out. Possible, but not probable.

The thickness of the bone made him wonder about how that break had happened, even post-mortem. The humerus was broken, too. Odd for bones that thick.

He hit the microscope then. When the skeleton didn't reveal anything visible to the naked eye, that was the next round. Forty minutes and seven bones later, he was looking at some kind of disease similar to osteoporosis. Maybe the bones had formed wider at the expense of density? But they were still heavier.

Rubbing his eyes, he realized he couldn't solve it now, but he wrote it up.

He next compared it to Eleri's lab notes. She hadn't gotten to a microscopic analysis, but the mass spec reading and the metals there might help solve it. Donovan wasn't up for that. His brain was abandoning him to pay attention to his stomach.

He'd changed several times while they were out, then marched for miles, been injured, and done it all on rations. He was still eating to make up for it. He checked his watch. No word from Eleri and Walter.

A full meal later, he hit the second skeleton.

It, too, had no clear marks indicating death or abuse or bone breakage. He worked up that skeleton, too.

Four more hours gazing at minutia under a variety of lights, through a microscope and a magnifying glass, and he was about to pass out. His eyes hurt and, worse, his brain hurt.

The second skeleton was almost the opposite of the first. They shared microscopic markers indicating they both lived in the area for at least a while. They likely died there. Number Three was undeveloped, whereas Number Two was over-developed. The hips and shoulder breadth indicated male, despite the skull not showing the same thing. Eleri's write-up concluded the same thing. But the sex wasn't a given.

Number Three had denser than normal bones. Nothing he could tell upon picking it up—not like he could with, say, a bear femur—but microscopically, it was denser. Which might explain why Number Two had broken pieces, even post-mortem, but Number Three had no breaks, nicks or even evidence of previous fractures and healing while alive. It appeared Number Three had never had a broken bone. But the bones themselves were longer, thinner, overall lighter weight.

He was so confused.

Stepping away from the microscope was the right thing to do. So he turned both the skulls over and checked what he could there. The teeth could reveal a lot. Or at least aim him in a direction.

One tooth was missing from each skull. Eleri had pulled it almost as soon as they arrived and sent it for analysis. DNA wouldn't be on the table until they had a direction to aim, but she was hoping for strontium isotope ratios to tell where these two had started life. Bones gave the most recent data, teeth the oldest. They formed in early life and were living fossils of that time. Additionally, the shapes could tell him a lot.

Number Two lacked a cusp of Carabelli, the absence of which meant almost nothing. Donovan had been hopeful. The front teeth had no shoveling at all. So likely no Asian or Amerindian history. The shape of the nasal opening was heavily Caucasian. The process of the mandible was average, another piece of evidence that might have said the skull probably belonged to a white person. Given the thicker nature of the bones all around, some of those thicknesses weren't indicators he could trust. The abnormal development would mean the normal signs weren't trustworthy, even as simple indicators.

He set Number Two down and picked up Number Three. This one had more useful signs. Maybe too many of them.

As he looked at the molars, he spotted the cusp here. This guy had some European heritage—not uncommon in the US. The teeth also exhibited some shoveling, a scooping out of the backs of the front teeth, which indicated some Native American, or Pacific Islander, or Indian, or Asian . . . He blew a frustrated sigh into the empty air. Then he made notes.

The nasal opening looked like a cross between the two Asian/Caucasian indicators. At least this one looked like he could classify it in some way.

His phone rang just then, nearly causing him to jump and definitely causing his ribs to protest. He ached from the constant sitting/standing/bending. Barely managing to not drop the thing and get it to his ear, he answered.

"El!"

"We're on our way back." There was a smile in her voice. "And we have bones."

"Do you think they're the missing ones?"

"Probably. I'll tell you more when we get in. We'll be back in the lab tomorrow."

He could not be less excited, but he wished her well and tried to estimate what time she and Walter would get back. He could hold off on dinner and eat with company, if Walter and Eleri could be considered that.

It took a while to put everything back and lock up the bones and double-check them. One sample had already disappeared in this case. Donovan wasn't taking chances.

His stomach growled as he finally headed out of the lab. He was locking the door behind him when a courier showed up with an envelope.

Frustrated, Donovan debated leaving the letter for morning or biting the bullet and reading it now. In the end, he decided to stand there at the door and read it. He would take it with him rather than go through the ritual of unlocking and re-locking the lab.

Peeling the strip from the pack, he found a big envelope containing two stapled printouts, one for each tooth sent in. He held them side by side and read as he walked.

Number Two showed isotopes that matched a biome—or area on the globe—in South America. A small spot in Africa was also a possibility as was a section of Egypt. Nothing matched Michigan or even anywhere else in the US. Donovan flipped a page, revealing a map colored by likelihood of origin. When he looked at the results for Number Three, he stopped dead in the hallway, his rumbling stomach forgotten.

They were both the same.

He quickly scanned the remaining pages. Other data was different, revealing that Eleri had ordered a few other tests. But the last page for both was an added letter—the same for both. It suggested that the bearer of the sample submit for further DNA testing at the expense of some group called "Las Abuelas."

Something about these particular results had triggered the sending of the generic letter. He would have to contact the group, they didn't know about him or his samples yet. The testing places included it as an outreach when certain results were triggered.

So where the hell had Number Two and Number Three come from? Because it wasn't from here. And who were Las Abuelas?

12

Eleri stretched as she got out of bed. Everything hurt. A long day in the snow, the tension of following the woman with the bag, the hike back, and even the snowmobile ride all left bruises and faint pulls, cramps and stiffness.

But she had the bones! The skeleton the woman had been digging up was missing the same bones that had been turned in on the original report. By Eleri's memory, the parts she now held looked like matches to the pictures she'd been sent. She hated pictures, but it would serve to match as best she could now. First step in the lab today was to test for rule-outs— anything she could find that would definitely prove that this skeleton was not the original.

So step one, name it. "X" until they determined if it was Number One or Four?

She'd checked out the site where the woman had dug up the skeleton. From what she could figure, this one had been partially buried, like Number Three. Maybe indicating that it had been there longer. Nothing in the dig site was deep, so the grave had been relatively shallow.

The shape of the dirt left behind was conceivably from a body laid out where it fell, but Eleri couldn't tell for certain. That was possibly the hardest part; giving up on what you couldn't know. It was even harder when she often somehow *knew*.

There was also the issue that the other woman had handled the specimen. Though from the way it was packed, clearly she knew what she was doing. That helped narrow down the suspects.

Because it wasn't like Walter or Eleri had seen the woman's face. At least Walter had managed to get the woman to leave the bag to save herself.

Eleri told herself she couldn't be happier. That Walter had followed the directive she'd been given, that bones were the priority. But Eleri wanted that bitch, too.

At least the second outing had gone more the way the first one was supposed to go. Out in the morning, work, and back in the evening. She slept in a real bed, even if it wasn't her own.

After showering and getting dressed, she grabbed breakfast and met Donovan at the lab. Today, he was in first. She grabbed a lab coat that didn't fit as well as she wanted. "Morning." She tried on a grin.

He didn't smile back. "We have results from the strontium isotope testing."

It took her about five minutes to read through the papers. "It's Argentina."

"Not Africa or Egypt? Those are possibilities."

"No, it's Argentina—at least I think it is. We need to age and date the skeletons. Las Abuelas wants us to run the full DNA for them."

Donovan frowned at her. "What is Las Abuelas?"

"You don't know?" Eleri was astounded that anyone could come out of a medical school in this day and age and not know about Las Abuelas. At his head shake, she told him.

"*Las Abuelas* translates as *The Grandmas*. You know about Los Desaparecidos?"

"No."

"Jesus, Donovan, you need to know your medical history better." She scolded him.

"I can't know my own medical history for clear reasons. I have a smartphone. I can look it up."

"In the eighties, the Argentinian government imprisoned and killed those who protested the tyrannical actions of the state—"

"Like killing them?"

"Well, that," Eleri conceded. "Any kind of speaking out against the government could get you killed. People weren't ever found. So no one really knows if the missing are missing or dead. *Los Desaparecidos* translates as *The Disappeared*. In a literary sense, it was the first time the word 'disappear' is recorded in use as a verb, as in 'to disappear someone.' But that's not relevant."

"So these protesters would have been at least twenty or thirty, in the eighties? That would mean they came here and died . . . somewhere between the eighties and last year." Donovan looked at the ceiling doing the math, mentally carrying the one. "I don't think these guys were out there too long. Do you?"

She shook her head. She didn't.

"Option two—someone preserved the skeletons and then dropped or placed them out here within the last year." The look on his face said he wasn't buying that one either.

She interrupted his off-track thoughts. "It's not them, because they aren't who we're looking at. When the women disappeared, they were often snatched off the streets, their infants and toddlers going missing with them. Some of the women were pregnant."

"Shit." Donovan uttered the word as though he couldn't have held it in.

"Las Abuelas believed their children were dead, but they suspected the babies had been adopted out to wealthy families with government connections or elsewhere. They hooked up with a geneticist in the US who was roughly the same age as their missing daughters. They didn't have their daughters for DNA samples, so they pioneered mitochondrial DNA matching, to show maternal lineage. Last I'd heard they'd found over a hundred of their missing grandbabies. But there are *hundreds* more that weren't accounted for." Eleri always got sad at this part. "Most of Las Abuelas have died. Many never found their grandchildren."

Donovan was staring at her. "You think these are some of the disappeared babies?"

"Yes . . . possibly." She shrugged. "More importantly, why did our samples trigger the invite from Las Abuelas? What is in that strontium isotope test that got us that letter? On *both* skeletons."

Donovan was nodding along now. "So we send in a tooth sample from the new skeleton and see if it triggers, too."

She agreed. "Let's get it sent out, ASAP. See if we can get it back by late tomorrow or the next day."

They turned around, heading to the back of the lab, and together they recorded all the data and photos they needed before they pulled the tooth.

The mandible was missing from this specimen. It was one of the bones cataloged in the first report. Donovan spent some time looking at what they had and the pictures.

Almost as if he was reading her mind, Donovan muttered, "I haven't found any of the missing bones associated with the first skeleton. So no rule-outs, yet."

"What if she stole the bones from the M.E.'s office and intended to put this whole thing back together?" Eleri shrugged. The thought that this thief and the other thief were one and the same had crossed her mind before.

"It's possible. All the same pieces that were logged in that report are missing from this one. And almost nothing else." Donovan sounded pretty convinced.

Eleri was growing convinced, too. More so from the match in the bones to the pictures on the report than the missing pieces. "The coloring fits. The aging of the skeleton."

"Was it good?" Donovan asked, and she automatically knew what he meant.

"Yes. I think so. They had the pelvis, the mandible and a long bone. So they had the pubic symphysis." Probably the number one spot on the skeleton to use for aging it. "They had epiphyseal fusion." Another way to determine adulthood from the ends of a long bone. "And evidence that all the adult teeth had emerged."

Donovan stopped and stared at her, fistful of wrist bones still clutched in his hand. "I didn't think of it until now."

Eleri followed his line of thought. "It's too odd."

"Yeah." He frowned. "I mean, a humerus, an os coxa and the mandible. What an odd combination to go missing from one skeletal find."

She could feel her own frown on her face, too, probably a perfect mirror of his. "They aren't on the same part of the body, so almost the whole skeleton would have to be there to get those three particular bones."

He was nodding.

"So either our grad student or the professor left the site relatively intact, thinking no one would come out here and mess with it, and took a sampling of the bones so they could age the find." She was nodding as it came together.

"That's pretty illegal." He commented.

"True, but nothing about this has been on the up-and-up." She was staring into the middle distance now, her mind churning. "So it wasn't that they just wanted their specimen back. It was weird from the moment they found it and whoever it was knew it."

"Forensics grad student—so yeah, they should." Donovan was tracking her thoughts.

"Do you think that's the woman who was out there? The one who's stolen from two sites now?"

He was nodding again. "Can we sic Walter on her?"

"Oh." She hadn't thought of that. "That's a fantastic idea. Let her lead us to any future sites. I'll call her."

She was turning to peel her gloves and grab her phone, when Donovan stopped her.

"I want to call this as Number One. Do you agree?"

"Yes, I think we have enough to declare this."

"So be it." He marked the records they were keeping. "So we have One, Two, and Three. Do you really think there are more?"

"Most definitely." She was looking at the bones now; why would there only be three? And why would they have found them all? She called Walter, who agreed—maybe too quickly?—to go back out.

"You have two goals, Walter. Number one, bring her in. But secondly, if you can, mark on the GPS any sites where she digs. I want to know what she knows and I don't want to have to torture her for it." Eleri grinned on her end of the line but was met with a cold silence.

"Walter?" She pushed, but nothing came back. "Walter? It was a joke. Really."

"Okay." The word was not delivered with Walter's usual military precision. "I'm on it. But if I find out . . ."

"Jesus, Lucy Fisher!" Eleri wondered if using Walter's given name would make a difference. "You won't."

Another pause, another moment for Eleri to wonder. Then, "I already found out more than I wanted to."

They'd had a talk about the necessity of Walter staying quiet about Donovan. Now Eleri was wondering if it would stick. What the hell was she going to do when Westerfield found out? She wanted to prove that Walter could stay quiet for a while before she told her boss just how badly they'd fucked up. "I know. But . . . Well, I won't joke about it anymore, okay?"

Weird. She was settling Walter's feelings. Walter had never struck her as anything other than an uber-competent soldier. She was an excellent P.I.—evidenced by the fact that she'd tracked Eleri and Donovan up here in the Great White North. She'd even tracked them through snow, where she would leave prints everywhere and Walter also managed to see Donovan change—a feat Eleri had not yet accomplished. But apparently that very feat had unsettled something in Walter. Maybe Eleri had just gotten too used to the fact that her partner could roll his shoulders and push his rib cage into a different shape. That he could pop his maxilla out, pushing the front of his face forward, opening his nasal cavities and pulling his skin so his ears appeared to be higher on his head. It had simply become no big deal.

Now they might pay the price for it.

"Can you get her, Walter?"

"If she's still out there, yes." This was the sound of the soldier. "If not, I may be able to track her and at least mark some sites for you."

"Thank you, Walter. Do you need a partner? Is it safe out there?"

"I'm better by myself, ma'am."

"Thank you." She said it with a smile, though the "ma'am" got to her every time. She turned back to Donovan. "She's on it. Thinks she can bring the woman in."

"That's good." But he had an odd look on his face.

"What?"

"So, they tested these bones already, assuming this is in fact Number One. Why didn't it get the letter from the Abuelas?"

"Who says it didn't?" They saw only the results, not all the accompanying paperwork. It was possible the letter had arrived with the test and been thrown out; no one had to answer it. She had another thought. "I think they just went for a DNA hit, checked against CODIS and missing persons. No hit."

"So if they didn't do the strontium isotope testing, they wouldn't find it?" He asked.

Eleri thought for a minute and shook her head. "Las Abuelas pioneered mitochondrial DNA testing, so, no, a standard genomic DNA test wouldn't necessarily pull one of their triggers. We may still get one from Number One. If we do, I'll be really curious to see if these guys are some of Los Desaparecidos."

"So, the bone density here is solid, but it has a lot more holes in it than it's supposed to." Donovan was frowning as she stood over the microscope. "I want to make a slide. I'm just looking from the outside, but this isn't normal."

"Lord. None of these are. We have the upper arch of teeth—all the wisdom teeth are in. So late teens at least. But the bones haven't fused, not in the skull, not in the long bones, almost not at all. I don't get it."

Donovan snapped up, his eyes coming right to her. "It's been bugging me, but I just thought of it. Don't know why I didn't."

"What?" she asked, confused now.

"We would have seen it when we went for an ID, but none of them have had any dental work."

Eleri felt her own head jerk. She'd registered it vaguely when looking at each skull, but hadn't put together that out of three specimens there wasn't a single indication of any visit to a dentist.

She pondered that for a moment, then went down the line

looking at the teeth. They had two intact faces and one without a mandible. "Shit, shit, shit. Why didn't we see this?"

"What?"

"Look at the incisors. Donovan, look." She held the skull up to his face, a move that didn't even register as being totally inappropriate in most social circles. "Trauma lines."

There were horizontal grooves on both front teeth. The line ran across both teeth, and was at a slightly different level on each set, one stronger, one fainter, but it was there.

Donovan took the skull. "The other thing I noticed, but hadn't had a chance to say since yesterday, is that all the teeth look well formed. Normal. Meaning whatever happened to the bones possibly happened a bit later in life, if the teeth formed normally."

A good portion of the teeth formed or started forming well before birth. Many were partially built by age three. So he made a good point there.

"There's so much information here, Donovan. And I really do think there are more skeletons out there. Hopefully, Walter will find us some."

He put the skull back down. "There's another thing, El. What was that building we were in? I looked yesterday, and I can't find anything—anywhere—about it. It seems that, according to records, it doesn't exist."

13

G J ducked into the old building seeking only shelter from the wind and a place to stop for a moment. She'd been out for three days and it wasn't any better than the first time.

For all she'd figured out and all she'd done, she had nothing to show for it still. Nothing.

Okay, she had a pelvic bone, a humerus, and a mandible— all completely illegal. There was no way she could brush it off as an honest mistake. Not only did she know what she was doing, everyone knew that she knew the difference. The only thing saving her ass right now was that people thought she was in the family cabin on vacation. At least she hadn't lied about being somewhere sunny, so she didn't have to fake a tan when she returned.

That was the only good thing.

She'd had the rest of the bones from the first site with her when she'd heard the click behind her head. She'd been certain it was a gun. In the end, she'd never seen it. She could have been played. If there was one thing GJ hated, it was feeling stupid. She should have turned around and checked. But, damn, she'd never been held up at gunpoint before.

Without checking, she'd dropped the bag. When she was told to walk away, she had. It was a woman who'd held her up. That was all she knew. She'd walked. GJ hadn't looked back. Not until she was certain it was safe, until she believed that turning wouldn't mean catching a bullet. She was not bulletproof.

She wasn't windproof or disappointment-proof either, it was turning out.

Once inside, she sat down on the cold, cold floor and put her head in her hands. Everything had gone to hell.

Okay, not everything. In the positives column, she hadn't been shot and she wasn't in jail. But that was about it. Her grandfather was likely going to kill her if he found out, and she wasn't sure how she was going to keep him from finding out. Her thesis was going down the drain faster than she could blink and she had no evidence of what she'd seen.

GJ had been so convinced she had the thesis of the century. Again. And once again it was pulled out from under her. These bones had something, something that would give her a chance to prove she was more than just Murray Marks' granddaughter.

Her grandfather had given her a love of old bones, solving the riddles of the past, and adventures beyond what any normal kid got to experience. He'd also given her all the baggage that came with his name. All the people who doubted her because they thought she was trying to ride his coattails.

Partly her own fault. She knew that. She had tried to do it for a while.

Shit.

Regroup, GJ, she told herself.

What did she have?

The cougar hadn't eaten her—always a plus. No one had seen her face. She had a tent, food, and more. She could stay

out here for four more days if she had to. Screw this bad idea of
a plan. She was collecting one more thing, then she was going
home.

DONOVAN TOOK a deep breath and rolled upright, putting his
feet on the floor. For the first time, it didn't hurt to move his
ankles or his knees. A good deep breath still reminded him that
he was an idiot who fell through the snow sometimes, but this
was at least better.

He and Eleri had talked about Westerfield. It wasn't a
matter of whether to tell Westerfield that Donovan had been
seen, but of when to tell their boss that they'd royally
fucked up.

Donovan's father hadn't been good for much, but he'd
taught Donovan two things. One—don't let anyone see what
you really are. Two—if they do see it, kill them.

Never able to get on board with the second directive,
Donovan had closely guarded his secrets all his life. Honestly,
NightShade and Eleri and all this, well, it just meant his secrets
were still guarded, just by more people. That was all.

There had been no discussion about what would happen
officially if anyone learned about him or Eleri or what either of
them could do. Donovan assumed it was understood that
neither of them would let that happen. El guarded him because
he guarded her. Well, that and they were actually friends now.

He felt his head jerk, his ribs pinch, and his thoughts
stutter.

He had a damn friend. Who knew? So now he had someone
to ride the hand basket to hell with him.

Not what he wished. Donovan would have sighed, but even
that was still ranking as "unpleasant" with his ribs. In the end,
he and Eleri had decided not to decide yet. They wanted to see

how Walter handled it, to have something to report to Wester-field before they called it in. Besides, they were handing in nothing on the case—or at least nothing of value.

Donovan was becoming aware that all their cases seemed to start this way, with a mass of confusing information. It was their job to find the threads and pull them until the thing unraveled. Unfortunately, Donovan had another thread, and it was out in the snow.

Sitting there on the side of the bed, he was unable to describe, even in his own thoughts, how much he did not want to go back out there. He didn't hate or even dislike the snow, it was just another season, and often a fun one. But getting stuck sucked, and it was always a possibility. Also, he couldn't change until his ribs were better, so he was only ordinary Donovan for the next outing.

Which meant he had to convince Walter to go with them, and she was still looking at him like he was a freak. Since that was an absolutely correct assessment, he had a hard time arguing with it. It would be easier to have Eleri do the asking, but he needed to be the one. He needed to talk big bad Walter into coming along.

Not his strong suit.

But Donovan pushed up off the bed, he had to get going. He had to go do a job that he was horribly bad at.

ELERI STOOD in the lab by herself. Not her lab, not even her lab coat. She didn't move well in here; she didn't fit. Donovan had gone to get dinner, needing his usual abundance of calories plus extras to keep him healing. She didn't.

Making slides out of the bone samples was tedious work, but something she couldn't hand over to a tech, even though lab assistants were here and on hand for exactly that reason.

Not knowing the techs personally, Eleri couldn't vouch for the work, so she couldn't trust it. She had to cut the bones herself. And cutting the bones hurt her heart.

The bones were the evidence, and she had to destroy the evidence to get more evidence. She was torn, looking forward to what the slides would reveal, yet gritting her teeth as she put each humerus under the saw.

She mixed epoxy and set the pieces, then waited while they set, puttering around the lab, looking at every bone they had once again. Searching for any additional clues that might pop out at her.

They didn't. Walter did.

Eleri jolted at the presence of the other woman. Walter looked normal today in jeans and a T-shirt and flats. Her hair was up in a ponytail, her face fresh. The only reveal of the super-soldier beneath the get-up was the metal hand replacing her original left. Her left leg was also prosthetic, but not obvious either by look or by gait.

Even her voice sounded normal, cautious, un-Walter-like. "Am I bothering you?"

"Nope." Eleri smiled, hoping to set the other woman at ease. "Just waiting while things set up. What can I do for you?"

Walter rubbed her right palm against her jeans, the nervous gesture so unlike her. "I have questions before we go out tomorrow. Can I sit, ma'am?"

Eleri almost rolled her eyes. They'd gotten past the military ranking last time they'd worked together. "Only if you call me Eleri." She crossed her arms and stood firm.

"Okay." She perched on one of the lab stools and faced Eleri, more confident now for some reason. "Tell me about Donovan Heath."

Eleri shrugged. There was so much and so little. What did Walter want?

Walter filled her in. "So . . . he's a werewolf?"

Eleri sucked in a breath. The answer wasn't no. "He hates that word."

"So he's not one, or he just doesn't like being called one?" Now it was Walter crossing her arms and standing firm.

"He definitely doesn't like being called one. Whether he is or not depends on your definition of the word." She paused. "And there is no true definition of it, so I'm not sure he can be one."

"You're not helping." Walter's expression was serious and Eleri knew the woman was capable of pulling a weapon and shooting her dead should she not like an answer. The reason Eleri didn't worry about it was because she knew it wasn't in Walter's code to do anything like that.

"Well, it's wrong if you're thinking of the fictional version, where moonlight forces the change and they hunt people down. If you think he's bloodthirsty or evil. Or if you think you need a silver bullet, again you'd be all wrong." Eleri tipped her head, trying to both read Walter and set her at ease. Not an easy task with this subject.

"Then what is he?"

"What did you see?" Eleri countered.

"Are you evading my questions?" Walter tensed in her seat, not a comfortable place for Eleri.

"No. I'm trying to explain from what you already know." Eleri leaned forward, trying to play the same game. "Tell me where to start."

There was a pause as Walter either decided to trust in what she was hearing or else decided that she wouldn't get what she needed if she didn't start somewhere. "I saw a dog, the same one from the square in Los Angeles—the one that kept showing up around the same time you two did—here in Michigan."

Eleri nodded. "Go on."

"Then I saw the dog start *bending*? Or something, and then

he changed into a man. Or specifically, he changed into Donovan Heath." She shrugged. "And I've never seen Agent Heath and the dog at the same time."

A bark of laughter burst out of Eleri's mouth. "Like Batman."

Walter didn't laugh.

On a sigh, Eleri stuffed her giggles down. "You know, I've never seen him change. But now you have."

That at least stopped Walter's brood from setting in further. "So you don't know how it works?"

"Not the same thing," Eleri pointed out. "Biomechanically, it's like a complex series of double-jointedness and dislocations. His bones aren't shaped quite like a normal man's and his tendons go in slightly different ways. This allows him to switch back and forth."

Eleri paused, allowing for Walter to ask questions. Apparently, Walter didn't have any more questions.

She sat down, taking a deep breath before she continued. "He's still himself when he's like that, but he can't talk to tell you; his vocal chords aren't lined up the same. So he can make more variegated sounds than a normal wolf could, but he can't speak. He can hear better than the rest of us, and smell better, too."

Walter sat still, as though her lack of movement would absorb the new information better. Looking at her, Eleri considered holding back. These were Donovan's details, not her own. Had she shared too much?

"He was naked when he stood up." Walter commented without any inflection.

"Yes." What did Walter want? "He was naked when he was the wolf, too."

"So his clothes didn't come back?" Walter asked, seriously.

It took a moment for Eleri to come to terms with that. Walter was too smart to really think that way. Too logical, tactical, precise. On the other hand, her brain was dealing with far too much, trying to fit what she was seeing into boxes that didn't have room for it.

"It's not like TV." Eleri added. "His clothes don't disappear and reappear. There are no werewolf fairies who fold his clothes and wait for when he comes back."

"No werewolf fairies?" Walter finally cracked a smile. "I also didn't see any sparkles when he changed."

"Oh good God, no. No sparkles." Then Eleri turned more sober. "I think it hurts. Like physical pain somewhat. I can hear bones popping when he does it. And when he twisted his ankle, he had trouble getting back."

Her mouth had run away again. Not her shit to tell, but she was spilling it all over the floor. She needed to talk to someone about it and Donovan himself had always been reticent. Wade had offered a little insight about what he and Donovan both were, but he was far away these days. Eleri didn't get to see him as much as she would have liked and didn't want to use what time she did have with Wade talking about Donovan.

In an attempt to rescue the conversation and not be a complete ass telling all her partner's details, she added in the last piece. "Most of what you may have heard—"

"I haven't heard anything about him." Walter shrugged. She seemed like a woman who dealt in hard facts.

"I meant about . . . legends, I guess, of his kind. Anyway, most of it is untrue." Eleri tried to lead things the way she could. "It's just legend. No silver bullets, no full moons, no biting and turning other people."

With that Walter nodded. "So I can trust him?"

That, right there, was the heart of the issue. Walter hadn't been concerned about heading out into the snow with only Eleri. She was concerned with being out with Donovan at her back.

"You can trust him like you trust me," Eleri told her.

Walter stood then, the movement smooth, not giving any hint of the prosthetics she sported. "Then I'll have your back tomorrow."

"And Donovan's?" Eleri asked the woman as she retreated from the room, but she wasn't sure Walter heard her.

14

Donovan was the middle of the train this time. Previously, He'd been the lead, making footprints for Eleri to step into, to save her energy. He'd been the caboose, slowly trudging along, trying to keep up with his partner, ignoring his hurting ribs.

Now he walked step-by-step behind Walter Reed. She was a machine—her pacing precise, her head turning as she constantly scanned the area for predators, clues, surprises.

He felt safer with her watching out for them. Despite Eleri's training—and even his own—Walter had them both beat when it came to lethality. In fact, Donovan didn't even know just how lethal Walter was, only knew he felt safer with her around. Better able to do his job, which was figure out what the hell was going down with these skeletons.

They were in a different field this time. The area was riddled with them. Between that and the trees, it was a nearly perfect scenario for hiding a body. Only these hadn't been hidden. That might be part of what was bugging him. There was no evidence of foul play on the skeletons; even the positioning of the bodies indicated that they'd decomposed where they'd fallen.

This was the field Walter had tracked the woman to, where she'd made her drop the bag with the third skeleton—the one that had turned out to be the first. Well, they were ninety-nine percent certain it was the first one. That last one percent would bug him until he could confirm it. Some M.E.s would sign off on identifications with just a tattoo, or some other piece of evidence that wasn't sound enough. Donovan knew his ass was on the line with his signature, and the last thing he wanted to do was have to appear in court any more than he already did. He did not want to get called to the mat. Ever. He didn't like people looking at him at all.

There was nothing to ID on these bones. There was no one to match them to, other than the DNA that had been pulled from the first sample. The FBI already declared it not-a-match to anything in the database, leaving them at square one.

The landscape pulled his attention back. He'd already stepped into one ravine, and the downside of a new field, a new direction, was that he didn't know where the pitfalls were. And he couldn't smell them. The one thing he really still had, he couldn't make use of on the land.

They walked in a silent line for a while until Walter suddenly spoke up, jerking his attention forward.

"Here." Her voice carried easily over the flat expanse.

Donovan knew what "here" meant. They'd reached the spot. Walter had seen some spots while out scouting the day before.

The three of them stopped, having already agreed that Walter would do a check first. So he and Eleri automatically stayed put as Walter raised her weapon and went on the offensive.

Donovan looked up at a sky he hadn't yet learned how to

decipher. "I don't want to get snowed in out here. I want to get done and head back."

"You and me both. But we don't know anything about this woman." Eleri countered as though he was considering walking out into the expanse.

"I actually do know a good bit about her. Like she hasn't been here in over twenty-four hours, but that damn cougar has."

Eleri looked at him sideways.

He shrugged. "It's not that big a territory and she has cubs."

"No, I meant that the woman hasn't been here in a day. You smell it?"

"Or I don't, really."

"Could she have masked her smell?" Eleri asked, growing curious.

"Against a nose like mine? Highly unlikely." He looked out at Walter, still stalking the perimeter. "She didn't do it before, why start now? She probably didn't even have anything to accomplish that task with her. So how? And I don't think she even knows she needs to protect against that. Why would she think the wolf that growled at her would have any communication with a person, let alone be me?"

"All valid points." Eleri sighed, then called out to Walter. "She's not here!"

"Great. Let's rub it in what I am." He grabbed her arm and tugged it back. Not an easy feat with the thick gloves and her padded arm. At least it was better than that big red puffy jacket. The one that clearly said they believed they were the only ones in the national territory.

"Sorry. Wasn't trying to do that." She turned back to him, her expression matching her apology. "I really am sorry. I have no idea what we're going to do about her."

"Me neither." Though he knew one thing: he didn't want to tell Westerfield. Donovan truly had no idea how his Agent in

Charge would react to them blowing his cover, and he didn't want to find out.

Walter came back to them, rifle lowered. "There's evidence of a camp over in the woods, but it's vacated. And there are two areas in the field where it looks like a human excavated something. One is the site Agent Eames and I saw the other day."

Donovan was grateful that she didn't seem to acknowledge Eleri calling out something they couldn't have known without some extra source of input. He also found the whole thing odd. Walter not acknowledging the obvious, speaking about him and Eleri as if she didn't know them at all. Calling them "Agent Eames" and "Agent Heath."

"Well, shit." Eleri intoned, deadpan.

Another skeleton would be good. But gathering the bones was a bitch and he wanted to get back to the Bureau Branch Office. It almost felt comfortable after all this. "Let's get to work. Which one do we start with?"

"Which one was she on when we tracked her down?" Eleri asked Walter and Walter pointed. "Then that's where we start. Assumedly, she gathered that skeleton and we confiscated it."

It took a disturbingly long time to trudge to the site. Though the snow was definitely disturbed, there was a fresh layer of powder over it.

Donovan looked at Eleri. "Nothing." He shook his head.

She touched her nose, silently asking if he smelled anything, but he shook his head. It smelled like damn snow. And he'd be happy not to inhale the sharp, too-clean scent any time in the near future.

When they decided they'd done everything they could, Eleri called them off and they headed to the second site. Somehow, Walter had stood guard the whole time, silent and wary, knee-deep in snow, without a complaint or a moment when Donovan felt he was in danger.

Walter tracked with them to the second spot, putting herself into a better position to watch around them. This spot was in the middle of the field and looked both more recent and more chaotic. When they arrived, they wasted time tracking around it, Eleri taking pictures.

"El, there are no bones here." Donovan was getting exasperated.

"But maybe there were," she insisted, snapping off another burst of pictures.

"There weren't. I would know."

She looked up at him, sharply. "Even if they'd only been here for a short while? Old, skeletonized remains?"

"Yes, the scents are strong and unique." he insisted, wondering why she didn't quit with the site. What was so damned interesting? Turned out, it was him. She was staring. "What?"

Eleri sighed. "You have to pick a side. You function like a cadaver dog, too, I get it. But you don't want me to make assumptions about what you can do based on dogs or wolves. One or the other, Donovan."

He didn't answer. It pissed him off when she had a point. He didn't know how to do this. He didn't usually make—let alone keep—friends for exactly this reason. But he had no excuse here; this was Eleri.

He was getting ready to open his mouth when he caught something. His head jerked at the smell, his little, stupid human ears trying to perk.

Human.

He could sense the change in Eleri, the alertness that was almost a smell, maybe an electric current. "Donovan?"

He held up a hand, noticing that Walter had seen his change, too. They were all three looking to the tree line.

Shaking his head, Donovan got frustrated as the scent went away. "Wind change. I can't track it now."

But Eleri pulled out her small binoculars and began searching. Eventually, she gave up too and they turned back to the churned snow in front of them.

"It looks like a fight," Eleri commented. "Of course, that's a damn wild hair of a guess. There's a small layer of powder on top of it, and it doesn't look like a dig site."

It also didn't have the distinct odor of human remains. Another new skill he hadn't known he possessed: cadaver hunting in deep snow.

Eleri was still examining the mess in front of her when she began to meander away, her eyes and her thoughts clearly wandering.

"El?" He looked at her, letting her do her thing, but wondering how far was too far to let her go on her own. She was his partner, after all.

"One set of tracks leading into this . . . *skirmish* looks like it came from that way." She looked up at him and Donovan knew it before she said it. "Back toward the building."

She was moving before she even finished the sentence. Donovan followed. Silently, Walter brought up the rear, her rifle at the ready. No one spoke as they abandoned the damaged snow and headed for the tree line, following the buried set of footprints. He couldn't track them. Not just boots, on a well-covered person. Not in this snow, not in this form, not in this mood. So he let Eleri lead the way as he looked up at the gunmetal sky, wondering how long they could chase the tracks before they were stuck out here.

His damn ribs still hurt. He shouldn't be doing this, he thought. None of them should. They were halfway to the trees when his hand shot out before he even knew he was doing it. He grabbed Eleri, momentarily stopping her forward motion. "El. Cougar."

It was close. The cat radiated a predatory scent as well as one of growing desperation. She was lean and hungry, and rapidly growing crazy with it. His hand still on Eleri's arm, he took a slow deep breath, letting the scents all around filter through him as he mentally sorted them out. The woods themselves offered an overlay of thick pine. Smaller deciduous trees softly cut through the sharp prick of ice and snow, their scent just detectable in their winter state.

Deer roamed freely, avoiding the cougar and leaving lingering trails. He smelled raccoons, mice, and—he froze.

"Human." He said it out loud, looking with his nose, his eyes all but glazed over. He inhaled again. "Male. Hot."

Eleri turned and raised one eyebrow at him. "Didn't know you swung that way."

He glared. "He's high temp, Eleri." Donovan said it before he realized Walter was listening in on them. *Shit.* It was hard enough with Eleri knowing what she did. Needing to see what effect his words had, he turned to look at Walter.

No response. She simply stood with her gun at the ready, as though she hadn't even heard him. Donovan knew better. But if she wasn't going to acknowledge it, neither would he. He looked back to Eleri and pointed. "In the trees."

"Well, let's go find him." Before she turned, he caught a gleam in her eye that reminded him of girls he'd known in high school and college. Crazy girls, adrenaline junkies who didn't have a good outlet like sports or vacations. Not in the progressively worse places his father moved them to. Girls like that wanted Donovan. He was a loner, a nerd, but they must have smelled the wolf on him and not known it. A few had even gone after his father. Eleri had that look now; she was on the hunt.

Her pace quickened, forcing Donovan to keep up. Pride stopped him from bitching about his ribs as his feet moved methodically into the holes she punched in the snow. Even going faster, they weren't fast. He didn't check to see if Walter was keeping up. He had no doubt about her abilities, only his own. And besides, he could smell her back there.

They hit the tree line, stepping from the edge of open field and the thick layer of white, to the dull gray of winter in woods. The clouds blocked any direct sun and the canopy took care of most of the rest. The snow here drifted more, lightened by the load caught by the treetops above. Occasionally, it would come crashing down, sometimes with warning, sometimes without.

He wasn't prepared when Eleri stepped off to the side, putting him at the front of their little line. She whispered, "Find him, Donovan."

He stopped, inhaled, and turned to the right. Side by side wouldn't work in here, so he couldn't put Eleri on sight tracking while he scent tracked. He would have to do both. As he looked down, he saw the broken and blown snow in front of him reveal more. Though the light was bad, the snow was easier to read. "Her tracks, coming from the direction of that weird building."

"I want to see that building again," she muttered.

I don't. But he only thought it. It would do no good to say so; they were headed that way anyway. The male was in the vicinity; from the smell of him, he was tracking too. But was he hunting the cougar, or them?

It was all of ten minutes later that Donovan found out. The scent had grown stronger, but there was no other warning as the figure dropped from the trees onto him.

15

E leri would have screamed, but her training took over. Donovan crumpled under the weight that suddenly appeared from overhead. For a fraction of a moment, she thought about her partner's already bruised and battered ribs, but it was quickly superseded by the realization that she was already fighting.

Her pack was on the ground and her gun drawn, but she was slower than Walter who had her rifle trained on whatever it was and was yelling, "FBI, hands up. Hands up where I can see them. FBI."

It was an ingrained litany they all had, almost like a dog-going-to-bed motor pattern. They would repeat varying phrases of "hands up" until the hands either became clear, or the suspect was shot.

Donovan was on his back, elbows and legs coming up as both defense and offense. He was in motion before Eleri could get a foot into the fight to roll his attacker off. He landed an elbow upside the man's head. It seemed to have no effect other than making Donovan wince.

Still, she turned away. It would do no good to defend

Donovan yet have five more people come down on them and catch her off guard. She scanned the scene, checking all directions, gun out. She even looked up this time, searching the trees. There was no time to berate herself for the miss. Donovan was still fighting.

She understood that time was passing slowly because of her adrenaline. She even understood the neurological underpinnings of the feeling, but it was time to fight, not analyze. Before she was even fully turned back, she had a boot planted along the torso of the man, shoving rather than fully kicking him off.

He rolled in the snow two full times, coming up on the balls of his feet, aimed toward them. That he hadn't hit a tree or rock on what had looked like a haphazard choice of direction scared her. Initial assessment put him on par with Walter, but probably more familiar with the area. She counted the numbers in her own favor at least.

As he stood, hardly even breathing heavy, he took their measure and they took his. Donovan rose gracefully to his own feet, the movement smooth and protected. Like the first man, he was putting distance between them, but Eleri knew he was fighting to not appear injured in the slightest. If he looked wounded, weak, not as well-trained, Donovan would make himself the target of the next attack, too.

The man stood, just beyond reach of an arm and a stick, his hands were raised, palms out toward them, but it wasn't surrender, not at all. He was ready for another fight.

It was these moments in between strikes, everyone on high alert, no one willing to break the undeclared truce that she noticed his hands were large, scarred, thick-fingered . . . and bare. His arms were covered in dark hair, his right forearm sporting a simple tattoo that she couldn't quite read from here. Again, she could see the tattoo because his sleeves were pushed up to his elbows. The sleeves were thin cotton, not even thermal weave. He was going to freeze to death out here, soon.

Or he was hot. Just as Donovan said. She wished for a thermal imager, but let the desire go just as fast as it had flashed in. She looked the man up and down, cataloging everything. Sunglasses, dark and dull—probably on purpose not to reflect light and give his position away.

His pants were sturdy but lightweight and Eleri was starting to develop an opinion. No thermals under there either. His boots were heavy with thick treads, though the way he moved and had climbed the tree, he wasn't hindered by the snow. It looked like he wouldn't be hindered by much else either, judging by the tools—knives, a small claw hammer, old police baton—that hung from his belt.

"You can't take me in," he said, startling her with the crisp clarity of his words.

"I had no intention of it," she replied, but recognized the change in his eyes before he moved.

He called her *Liar* with just a look and lunged for her in a single leonine movement, graceful and deadly all the same.

Her hands flew up, protecting her throat as though he truly was a big cat. Both hands together and fisted, she kept her palms aimed toward her. Though he wasn't wielding a knife, she didn't trust him to not produce one on a moment's notice— he had a fistful available, hanging at his sides.

With the backs of her forearms, she deflected his hit, sending his arm off to the right, but his other punch was coming faster and she blocked it only by force of habit and training, elbow by ear, duck and cover. Her foot shot out for his and she saw Walter raise the rifle again. But, like before, the two fighters were too entangled for Walter to risk the shot.

The man was fighting close, all bare arms and warm heat. Eleri was hindered by her layers of clothing, her gloves.

Shit.

She saw the punch coming at her face and rolled backward, hoping he would come with her. Donovan had reached just then for the back of the man, expecting the two of them to react in the other direction. Eleri had thwarted her partner's chances of containing the other fighter, or getting hit again and letting him go. They wouldn't know which decision had been right until the fight was over.

The man stayed with her, hovering over her head as she came up, a dangerous, disadvantageous position for her. She used the roll, buffering with her luckily padded shoulder as she pulled her gloves off and left them where they fell. She used her shoulder to pop up into him, throwing him off balance.

Then she opened her mouth, a wail coming out that was part scream, part battle cry, and she went for him in the weirdest ways she could think of. He was a trained fighter. He'd already recognized that she was, too, and that she wasn't as good as him. So she switched goals and tactics mid-fight. Hopefully confusing him.

It worked.

Though he defended against her landing any hard blows, he was unable to stop her from slapping, scratching, smacking —everything shy of biting him—like a madwoman.

The sounds of their battle changed. There was a smack of bare palm landing on the side of his head. She'd been going for his exposed ears, but he twisted away, leaving her hand to make contact with his cheek. She absorbed a punch, taking it in the shoulder instead of the face, rolling with it and letting her extra clothing suffer some of the force, but as she spun with it, she came back at him, claws out, swiping his neck then the back of his arm as she carefully recorded mentally what she was doing.

A boot hit the side of his ribs and a rifle took him upside the head as Donovan and Walter were finally in position to tag-team him down. The glint of metal revealed that he'd drawn his knife when she hadn't seen and they'd saved her from real damage.

She was still processing all of this as the man came to his

feet, unfazed by the heavy rifle barrel he'd taken to his skull. His eyes flashed, deep brown—his sunglasses probably lost in the fight—his face bleeding from Eleri's crazy-lady attacks. Then he was gone.

One moment, he was standing there staring at them. The next, he was running away. A half-heartbeat later he'd entirely disappeared into the trees, leading Eleri to again think that this man knew these woods far better than they did.

"Eleri." Donovan's voice cut her thoughts in two. "Are you okay?"

"Yup," she answered though she stood breathing heavily, her hands still clawed at her side.

With a quick survey for anything he might have missed, Donovan stepped into her line of sight, blocking her from watching the stationary trees the man had disappeared into. "What were you doing? You abandoned all your fighting skills."

"Yup." Her heart was beginning to slow. Her breathing only coming down from a chest-heaving need for more oxygen to replace what she'd burned in the fight. "He was a better fighter than me. I realized quickly that I couldn't win that way." Then she turned to look at her partner. "And I sure wouldn't get what I wanted."

She held up her still-clawed hands. "His DNA."

"Holy shit, El." Donovan reached out for her hands but stopped as he saw what she was presenting.

She didn't have to tell him there was a kit in the pack, she simply held her hands out, protecting them from loss of evidence while he rummaged for it. Walter naturally fell into place, too, now circling the two of them, rifle aimed for the ground a few paces in front of her, but ready nonetheless. Eleri scanned the area, too, now including more upward glances than before.

"I don't smell him anymore." Donovan said low enough for

only her to hear as he returned with the small tackle box and opened it.

Walter knew. Then again, maybe Donovan didn't realize all that Walter knew. It was Eleri who'd done the telling. So she kept her mouth shut. They'd gone head to head on their first case about protecting each other's secrets and understanding what the other needed. The distinct feeling that she'd fucked up again washed over her as she felt the cotton swab pulling blood from her hands.

She watched as Donovan expertly slid the plastic guard up the stick and into place where it kept the fresh DNA sample from bumping anything or becoming contaminated. He kept his thick gloves on, probably wanting to avoid the cold that she could now feel biting into her fingers. But even with the gloves, he expertly popped open the small box and inserted the swab for later testing. Another plastic envelope ripped open, another swab came out, then another. After he'd taken what he could from her hands, he pulled another and motioned for her to open her mouth. Her own genetic code would have to be removed from the samples to find the man's.

They didn't speak, just two scientists now, running a common pattern despite the woods, the cold, the snow, and the retired Special Forces Marine guarding them. He handed her a water bottle and she walked a few steps away to wash her hands. She dried them carefully on the small towel he held out, knowing she was already risking her fingers by having them so exposed for so long. Then she pulled her now-freezing gloves from the snow and breathed into each one a few times before pulling it on. It wasn't warm per se, but it was better than frozen. When she finally looked up at the other two she said, "Let's hit the building."

Donovan shook his head at her. "It's too late. We won't make it back."

"Yes, we will," she countered wanting to argue her way into

this rather than pulling rank. "If only because none of us wants to be out here late."

He stared at her and she kept going.

"It's very close. I think I can see a corner through the trees that way." She pointed, not confident at all of what she was seeing. "And we'll take a direct path back to the station. I'll lead."

She knew that someone else leading would help ease Donovan's ribs, the ones they couldn't seem to stop hurting. The thought made her pause. "Are you okay? Do you need to go back for medical care?"

He'd been attacked, too, taken some unexpected hits. *Crap.* She hadn't even thought to ask before.

"No. I'm okay." He stared at her, clearly thinking she was putting him in a position to either declare himself in need of medical care or acquiesce and go to the building. It hadn't been her plan.

"Are you lying?" she asked him. Doctors made the damn worst patients. They seemed to think everyone else's pain was their body talking to them, but their own was just a pest to be ignored. Donovan was sadly relatively normal in that aspect.

"No." He sighed, a good sign given his ribs and the fact that he didn't wince outwardly when he did it. "Let's go to the damn building. But you're buying me a hot meal when we get in."

It was an old back-and-forth between them. Whenever they were together, food was just a matter of handing in receipts for reimbursement. But that was a bit of a bitch, so she smiled even as he turned his back, grumbling.

Eleri took point and Walter stayed silent the whole time as they made their way to the building, which turned out to be much farther away than Eleri guessed.

This time, they were here to look, no longer on a mad flight for shelter, no longer hindered by swirling clouds of sub-freezing snow and wind. So she stopped and took stock.

The building was low—one story only—with a rough, boxy look as though the architect had hated the place. Dark brick covered everything except the windows and the roof. Trees grew tall overhead and she pulled out her GPS marking the spot, wondering if she'd be able to find it in satellite images when they got back.

"No markings." Donovan noted. "Not even an awning over the door."

That was odd. Most buildings had some kind of marking. Businesses put their names on their doors, offered a sign, a painted window proclaiming themselves. After circling the entire area, they couldn't even find a discoloration where a sign had once hung.

They also didn't find any recent prints in or out, but pulled their guns anyway and headed back toward the doors they'd entered the first time. Again, they swung open easily, the inside likely protected by the doors' strong hydraulic pull to close themselves—a necessary feature in this climate.

"The file cabinets were empty," Donovan offered as he paced through with his gun out, not caring if they were heard. He'd clearly rather scare someone off than confront them. She'd had enough of that for one day, too.

"I remember," she said it even as she opened the drawers and found nothing. They stalked a hallway, this time with Walter in the lead, sweeping offices before Eleri and Donovan went in.

Some offices opened toward the middle of the building, their windows showing off a courtyard in the center. Eleri stared.

A metal jungle gym filled the corner. Whoever played there would run right past these windows. A small platform stood at attention at one end, allowing someone to stay central and yet watch the whole course from above.

They left that office, checked another and another, constantly coming up empty.

"We have to quit, Eleri. Or we won't make it back." Donovan's voice was both weary and wary.

"We'll make it back."

"We can't do the whole building." He warned.

"Just a few more." She went out the doorway and across the hall before he could start bartering.

Three offices later she shouted out, "Got something!"

When Donovan came in and saw her holding up a stack of empty, used manila folders, he just stared. "You do know those have no information in them, right?"

"They are the information. Look." She showed him the front. "Axis."

"Probably the company that makes the folders," he deadpanned.

"We're investigators. So investigate." She held them out, showing him the tabs.

"Alpha, Bravo, Charlie, Delta." He let out a breath. "It's just the alphabet, El."

"I know, but look at these." Other folders had seemingly random three digit combinations on them.

"I don't get it," he said, his shoulders slumping.

"Neither do I." She smiled as she pulled an empty folder from the stack. "But this—" she held up the one labeled 820 "—is the number that was tattooed on that man's arm."

16

Eleri wandered through the snow, sinking to her knees with each step. When she looked behind her, she saw nothing but the field stretching out to a fuzzy horizon. At the edges of her vision, flurries muddled the lines and kept her from seeing farther. But she wasn't worried.

The trees were in front of her and what she wanted was in the trees. Slowly she kept walking, her legs and hands cold from the weather, her nose stinging with the frigid air. Eleri breathed deeply, knowing she had come with Donovan and Walter, but unconcerned with where they had gone to now.

As she passed under the canopy of the trees the cold stopped reaching out for her and the warmth began to seep in. Flurries had blown drifts into the spaces between the trees, but after a little while even those were gone, leaving only wet leaves and a humid, heavy air around her.

Eleri shed her coat, leaving it where it fell. She walked farther into the woods, breathing in the smells of fall even though she knew that wasn't right. That something was *off* here. She was headed to the house. She knew that much.

Leaves coated the ground at her feet. Mostly brown, a few

winked up at her in shades of yellow or red. She pushed up her sleeves as the thick air warmed her. The ground below her feet opened into an obvious trail. She walked it, pushing ever forward, toward the house.

When at last it came into view, she trailed around, looking for the front corner. The small house was almost perfectly square, not more than just a few rooms, white siding covering all the walls; Eleri ran her hand along the rough painted wood.

The front corner was as she'd known it would be—a small porch, just big enough for one person to stand on. Cut into the floor space of the house, the porch sat under the roof line. White wood railings ran along the two sides, not coming together at the corner of the house, leaving just enough space for Eleri to climb the one step up onto the tiny porch and knock on the door.

Her knocks made a noise just short of the requisite rap as the door swung inward in invitation. Eleri stepped over the threshold. The main room was empty. The nearly-white walls blank, the hardwood floors were dusty, but supported no furniture.

Again, putting her hand to the wall, Eleri traced her way through the house, passing the closed window, then into the small, equally empty kitchen. She wandered through a back room, then another, and only when she completed the loop did she see the old woman sitting in the rocking chair in the main room.

"Grandmère?" She spoke the first word.

But the woman kept rocking and gave no sign that she'd heard anything. Eleri wondered if it wasn't her Grandmère, if maybe the woman was deaf, and she circled around to the front of her.

It wasn't her Grandmère, and the woman did not look up.

Eleri knew if she could find the right name, the woman would acknowledge her. But Eleri didn't know her name.

The woman worked on something in her hands. She stitched an even rhythm, but Eleri could see it wasn't a blanket or even fabric. Maybe a doll?

"Hello?"

The woman didn't look up from her work.

"Can you hear me?" Eleri tried again but got no response.

At last she sat on the floor in front of the woman and looked for clues to her name. While she searched, she watched the woman fashion a standing doll from a collection of natural fibers and findings. Corn husks bent to the will of the old hands. Rough-dyed cotton wrapped the shape, held in place with needle and unidentifiable brown twine. A shard of bone and small pot of a thick black substance made pen and ink, but not a face.

The woman murmured to herself, not to Eleri, as she stitched and plucked and drew. Still, Eleri couldn't think of the woman's name. She sat for a long time, picking up scraps that fell to the floor, running the husks and twine through her fingers until it burned or cut at her. But nothing came to mind. At last she grew tired of trying to understand, occasionally attempting to get the woman's attention, or figure out what she was making.

Eventually, Eleri laid back on the smooth floor, grateful that it wasn't cold, but warm and far softer than she'd expected. Drifting into a drugged slumber she wondered if the old woman was doing more than making a doll. As the last bit of darkness overtook her, Eleri was certain. The doll would hold the spell as surely as it had been cast on Eleri.

∽

DONOVAN LOOKED up from the lab table when Eleri walked in. For the first time he was feeling better. His ribs were sore, but no longer pulling with each breath. No longer stabbing him if he overdid it. He was healing quickly, indicating the damage wasn't as bad as they'd initially assessed.

Walter disagreed. She was sitting on a stool nearby, watching him work and trying to convince him he had super healing powers.

"I'm not an X-man," he ground out between clenched teeth.

"Why not?" she asked back, no tone at all in her voice, the challenge purely from her words.

As tempted as he was to growl in response, Donovan knew that would only fuel her fantastical ideas. Instead, he ignored her. It wasn't as if he would just sit down and tell her that his father had been this way. It was a purely genetic condition, much like sickle cell anemia or cystic fibrosis. The scientist in him wanted to throw facts at her, but he started out doing that and Walter simply soldiered back at him.

She was ultimately as superstitious as a baseball player. She knew what she'd seen and she was trying to work it out. He wasn't in the mood to tell her a pretty story to help her.

A stilted silence settled between them as he played anthropologist and studied the bones of the three skeletons they had. He'd submitted the DNA samples from Eleri's attack the night before, even though they'd arrived very late.

Luckily, they made it in with no more incidents. Eleri getting bruised and scratched in a fight was no easy matter either. And just when he was healing up himself—at a perfectly human rate, his brain inserted. Did it matter that a small part at the back of him nagged that he wasn't perfectly human? He was a man. He knew that much. He belonged with this species, but he wasn't truly like them. He knew that, too.

Pushing his own thoughts aside, he sat at one of the tables and fired up his laptop. Which was when Eleri sauntered in, looking a little bitter for the rest he would have thought she'd gotten.

"Good morning, Donovan, Walter." She addressed them as

though she was at a formal breakfast and not hovering over a trio of dead people. The tone in her voice didn't match the one in her eyes or what the line of her jaw betrayed. She turned to Walter. "Can I ask you to give me some time with Donovan?"

Walter nodded, peeled herself from the stool and sauntered out of the room, the heavy door clicking locked behind her.

"Jesus," Donovan muttered under his breath. "That easy, huh?" He felt stupider than a pile of turds, the old saying of his father's bubbling to the surface.

"What?" she asked, moving her head to get a good look at his face.

"I just had to ask her to leave?" He almost scrubbed his hand down his face, forgetting he was wearing latex gloves and the gloves were wearing who-knows-what. It was a motor pattern he'd long since broken as a med student. Why was it back now? Was he too far out of the lab? Out of the morgue? At the puzzled look on Eleri's face, he explained. "I spent the last hour trying to explain that I didn't have super healing powers and that I don't belong in the Justice League."

"She said that?" Eleri blinked, knowing Walter well enough to hear the odd phrasing.

"My words, but pretty much, yeah."

She laughed until he countered, "Just be glad she doesn't know about you."

Then she sobered. Maybe a little too sober, but he didn't trust his judgment. He was used to shutting people out, not reading them. His skills of interpretation seemed to only extend to Eleri so far—clearly not Walter or he would have shuttled her out of the lab at the mere mention of "werewolf"— and he didn't trust the new senses yet anyway. He only asked, "What?"

"Weird dream last night."

"Anything important?" He knew what her dreams could do. Donovan was certain she was capable of a lot more than even she knew. It was easier seeing that from the outside. He ignored the implications about himself.

"No. Weird house in the woods. Front door cut into the corner of it." She frowned. "So it had an almost triangular porch."

"But what?" He prodded.

"I'm pretty sure this isn't the first time I've dreamed of it. I'm convinced that I've been there before, but whether it was awake or asleep or even if it's just my brain playing tricks on me, I don't know." With a breath in, then out, she signaled to him that she was going to say more, so Donovan waited.

"There was an old woman there, sewing a doll. It didn't make sense at the time, but I looked it up and it was almost a specific spell. Still, it was wrong." She shook her head, as though shaking off the thought. "But the woman dropped bits of twine and corn husk as she worked. I played with them until they cut me and I woke up with these."

She held out her left hand which sported two cuts and what looked like a burn in a straight line.

"It's from yesterday's fight." Donovan grasped at the most logical explanation.

"Nope. You cleaned me up. All my wounds were defensive —forearms. All the blood on my hands washed off. I did not have these before bed." She shrugged it off. As well she should; stranger things had happened to them. Manifesting skin lesions from a dream was small potatoes in his new world. Donovan changed the topic.

"Is that why you slept in?"

"I didn't. Though I did first send out an email to Avery." She didn't apologize for spending some of her time writing to her boyfriend and Donovan didn't fault her either. If her budding relationship with the hockey player was going to stand a chance, an early morning email keeping the man as up to date as possible was necessary.

"How's he doing?"

"Benched. Minor injury. Hopes to be back in tomorrow's game." She smiled. "Might be better that we're apart. He sounds like he's an actual bear when he's injured."

Donovan smiled at her. Maybe she'd get to see her hockey player before too long. Then again, the way things went down for them, maybe not. There was no "standard" anything in NightShade.

"Second email was to Westerfield," she said, breaking into his thoughts. "He's up to speed on Walter. He must have picked up the phone even before he read the email. I swear my cell was ringing before I finished clicking send."

It might be an exaggeration to tell the story, or it might be gospel truth. Westerfield picking up the phone to call Eleri about the topic she was emailing him before he even received it was well within the realm of possibility. What they knew Westerfield could do only opened the doors to speculating what they didn't know about. "What does he think?"

"He didn't make a judgment. Didn't say anything other than to keep her close and he'd check her file again." Eleri shrugged. "I mean she already worked with us once."

"So he knows she saw me change." Donovan let that sink in. It was bad enough to be caught, worse that it was no longer protected in the tiny circle of himself and Eleri and Walter.

"I didn't say that specifically."

So she wanted Donovan to tell their boss? Or not tell? He didn't know. He didn't ask. There'd be time for that later. He switched topics in a way he hoped was smooth but doubted he achieved it. "So we have electropherograms—" the portions of the genetic code that were used to legally identify someone "—but not full genome sequencing—on each." That was the part he loved. "I pulled the FBI program. No matches to any known missing persons."

"You ran them?" Eleri frowned. Now she was pulling a chair up beside him, peering at the screen over his shoulder.

He spoke before her thoughts fully gelled. "I ran every database I could find. There's NamUs and DoeNetwork, too."

"Those are run kinda by the same people," she pointed out.

"Sure, but they have public support. A lot of missing people on there that aren't in the official databases." He countered. As agents, specifically agents trying to help pair findings with missing persons, they had back door access to the sites.

"And?" she prompted.

"Nothing. Not any match on any of them." He shrugged.

"Not even on Eight-twenty?"

He shook his head.

Eleri didn't like that. "I get it if a body under a bridge doesn't match up. But bodies in a national forest? That doesn't fit the missing-but-no-one-missing-them profile. Certainly not three of them."

17

Eleri held too many things in her head. She had puzzle pieces, but not enough to put any of them together. She had an empty manila folder labeled "820"—the same as the tattoo on the arm of the man in the woods. She had a stack of other folders, labeled with three-digit numbers that she couldn't find any connection between. Not mathematically, not in code, not at all.

Donovan hadn't been able to get anything out of it either. And he was better at it than she was. She wanted to call it done. Declare it dead, but she held on, convinced something would shake out later. Though she didn't do it intentionally, she'd stared at the folders long enough to memorize a good portion of the numbers.

She set the folders aside for the FedEx envelope that had been delivered to her just moments ago. Donovan was on his way up, happy to be in the lab and not out in the snow.

Eleri tapped on the envelope, wondering if she should wait, then decided on a plan. Setting it aside, too, she pulled out her phone and found a text from Avery. Just the sight of it brought a smile to her face. A pulse of heat bloomed in her chest. She hated being away from him and was shocked at the feeling of resentment for the job—the first time she'd ever felt that way.

The job had once been all-consuming—her safety from her past, her refuge from a meaningless life of pretty colors and tight trappings. But lately, there'd been something else worth waking up for in the mornings. She tapped out a sweet message back to him, letting him know what she thought was important. She never waited to tell someone how she felt. Maybe it was more than he was ready for. For a while, she'd thought it was more than she was ready for. Now she knew that wasn't the case. She texted back again. And again.

When Avery's texts stalled out, she turned back to her work with a grin on her face. Donovan still hadn't shown. His ribs probably needed the extra sleep. She hadn't been kind to her partner's injury, and neither had he, really. Eleri understood. Having waited long enough, she ripped open the envelope.

The pages fell out into her hand, the same form as the previous two. She ignored the DNA samples for a moment, thumbing to the last page. This was where the letter from Las Abuelas was located on the other three samples.

It slid onto the black-topped lab table, slipping through her fingers to land perfectly in front of her.

The same form stared up at her, the same plea to contact them. Once again her sample held DNA suggesting it might be one of theirs.

The ages weren't right, though maybe for 820 it was. One of the skeletons appeared both juvenile and adult. Eleri paused. On second thought, the ambiguous aging of the skeletons *made* the Argentina connection possible.

Was 820 one of The Disappeared?

"Enjoying staring at a blank wall?" Donovan's voice startled her from her thoughts.

"Oh, absolutely." She didn't look at him. "I was thinking a

Degas would go nicely here." Eleri pointed at the place she was staring.

"Can your family afford those? Degas, I mean?"

"Yup. But not a lot of them." She grinned. "We aren't *that* rich."

"Oh, my bad." He scoffed with a laugh behind it. She liked it.

They came from massively disparate backgrounds, but something about their pasts pulled them closer than it pushed them apart. She'd seen his father and some of what Donovan had lived through with the man. But Donovan understood her feelings about her sister, her driving need to make something better, to make up for when she failed. Even if she'd only been twelve at the time. In that, they understood each other. The money didn't matter. She snorted her own little giggle. "Yes, our 'illions' start with 'm,' not 'b.'"

"Oh!" he mocked. "Only 'm's. You poor little thing."

She turned and saw his hand over his heart in a gesture that was both very Donovan-like and un-Donovan-like at the same time. She grinned. "I was thinking we need to do a full genomic comparison on all the DNA. They have the samples already, we just tell the lab to run it."

"You want to test them against The Disappeared?"

"We got a fourth letter. Eight-twenty triggered the request from Las Abuelas, too." She turned, holding it up as though it spoke for her. "We passed coincidence two letters ago."

Donovan nodded. "Do it. Then tell me what's behind door number eight-twenty."

She shrugged. "Don't know. Haven't looked yet." Eleri pushed the papers across the table to him where he picked them up and started thumbing through.

"Shit." He muttered, then muttered it again. "It's just as screwed up as the others. But differently."

"Well, shit." She echoed his earlier sentiment. Her brain

rattled in her head with the thoughts bouncing in there. "I'm going to call the lab."

It took no more than twenty minutes to order the full genome of the skeletons and Eight-twenty. She had account numbers for each profile. Despite the several layers of safety needed to obtain information on genomic samples, it didn't take too long.

"One last request," Eleri asked before she hung up. "We received a letter with each of the samples. It asked if we would submit to a full mitochondrial DNA sequencing."

"Oh!" the voice on the other end of the line sounded surprised. "You got one of the Abuelas' letters. Which account?"

Eleri didn't like showing her hand. Granted, all that was showing was that four sequences each tripped the trigger for the Abuelas, but she didn't like that information in civilian hands. The letters were computer generated, a request that could be accepted or denied without anyone being the wiser. So Eleri bluffed a little, a last-minute attempt to cover her tracks. "I don't remember which one. Just run it for all four. We'll cover the costs."

The feds would have covered it anyway. That way they owned the data. They could alert Las Abuelas on their own time frame. Eleri would make sure it would happen.

She'd read about Las Abuelas in school, about how they pushed science into the discovery of mitochondrial DNA—a direct gene link from mother to child, traceable through generations. The Abuelas were older now, dying. Eleri felt the urge to solve her case, quickly. Eleri hung up the phone and turned back to her partner.

Seeing that she was off the line, he started telling her about what he saw. "Eight-twenty has some relatively low occurring alleles."

"So he has rare genes? Does that mean something?" She

frowned, her brain still struggling to see a pattern in all the pieces. She didn't have enough pieces yet; she knew it.

"Don't know if that means anything. It's just weird."

Eleri sighed. "What I wouldn't give for a vial of his blood."

"One—you almost got it and two—you'd love a vial of mine, too. That's horrendously unethical." He shrugged at her.

"True, but I'd still love if he'd walk up and hold out his arm and volunteer. A girl can dream." So what if her dreams were dramatically different from other girls' dreams?

Her phone chimed.

—Your boyfriend's hot.

Wade. She grinned and typed back.

—You watching him on TV?

—Nope. Met his hot ass in person last night.

—What?

Eleri was shaking her head. Wade met Avery? She was typing back before he responded.

—You've been sniffing around my boyfriend?

She could almost hear Wade's laugh as his return message popped up.

—Literally. Got a VIP pass. Got close. He smells good.

—You hit on him?

Now she was laughing and having a brief moment of uncertainty clench her heart. What if Wade did hit on Avery? What if someone else did?

—Yeah, he turned me down.

Not enough, Wade. And he would know it.

The next message popped up right away.

—and he turned down all the buckle bunnies or whatever the hockey players call them. You serious about him?

—am I?

Wade was an excellent judge of character. Hell, he was like Donovan. If Avery even smelled like another woman, he would know.

—I would be if I had the chance.

A laugh burbled out of her, startling Donovan. He looked up at her, the question in his raised eyebrows.

"Wade." She held out her phone and let Donovan scroll through the exchange. It put a smile on his face, too.

"You're sending a werewolf to do recon on your boyfriend?" He held the phone back to her.

"Nope. Wade sent himself. Must have seen that the Executioners were playing his local team and decided to go." She stopped short. "So *Wade*'s a werewolf?"

"No such thing." Donovan turned back to the papers shutting down the conversation. He hated that word. But this wasn't the angry dead stop he'd done in the past. This time he had a hint of a smirk on his lips.

Yeah, well, she was a mermaid. So who was she to judge? Her brain stuttered again. "Where's Walter today?"

"Don't know." Donovan shrugged, but didn't look up from where he was handwriting some odd code on a paper in front of him. "She said she wanted to go find something."

"What the hell could that be?"

"Seriously?" Now he did look up at her. He set the pen down and ran his hand over his chin—the chin she only just noticed that he hadn't shaved. She wasn't sure if he grew facial hair at the same rate as other men, fully human men, but she'd long ago noticed his grew thicker. Donovan had a fine down of hair on his face—unnoticeable until you inspected him—like on babies and old people. She'd only looked for it once she knew what he was, once she had a reason to check. He sighed into the hand. "With Walter? It could be anything, right? I mean she might have a lead on an awesome fried fish joint or she might be tracking a CIA criminal. I really don't know."

"Good point." Eleri wondered where their new third had gone. But Walter wasn't really their third. Didn't have the clearance or the forensic training to be. "Any ideas on how to tell Westerfield we fucked up and Walter saw you change?"

That was going to have to be dealt with soon, and Eleri wasn't looking forward to it.

"*We* didn't fuck up. *I* did." His look was hard, accepting.

"Nope. *We* did."

"You can't pull seniority and claim my screw-up—"

She interrupted. "If she'd found me when we were together would you do anything different?"

He responded with silence. They both knew he wouldn't let her go down alone for something to do with their partnership. She wouldn't either.

She knew it. "So, shut up. We just need to figure out how to tell Westerfield and that will happen a lot easier if you think in terms of 'we.'"

He nodded and she hoped his agreement was real. He didn't understand partners, not the way she did. Not yet. She nodded back. "Let's be sure to ask Walter where she was today."

"And if she was scouting restaurants?"

"Then we ask her to show us the best one. I'm tired of snow and these damn four walls." She held her hands up. "I ordered a rush on the DNA. Just a few days."

Donovan sighed and Eleri felt it in her muscles. The bones waited, laid out on the tables around them. Three skeletons, almost complete. Eleri looked at them, hoping something new would come to her, but nothing did.

She looked again. The piece out of Number Two's skull probably didn't conceal a death blow. But the fact remained that they couldn't be sure. Number Three and Number One looked good at first glance but the anomalies in their bone growth were extreme.

Eleri knew the patterns; children grew into adulthood at a variety of rates. They also hit different marker points at different times and some of the ranges overlapped, but many just didn't. Having the molars entirely in, but the bones not fused on Number Three just didn't make sense. It was possible that it was an abnormally large child.

Those thoughts tugged at the back of her brain. Though she couldn't put her finger on it, she knew it didn't add up. This was not the skeleton of an abnormally large child.

"Got it!" She almost yelled it at Donovan, startling him with her realization. "I'm calling the lab back. I'm ordering telomere checks."

"For aging?" Donovan knew about telomeres—caps on the end of every chromosome—but he wasn't buying in like she did. "Is there an advance in that science that I'm not aware of? I mean, we know they degrade with age, but there's no direct count or correlation we can point to."

She opened her mouth, but he beat her to it.

"We also know there's something wrong with these skeletons, so degraded or even non-degraded telomeres may not tell us anything."

"I know," she answered, "but it's another nail. These guys are so weird—" she waved her hand at the remains around her "—that I suspect in the end all we'll have is things that point in one direction. Besides, I'm a lot more likely to buy in to the theory that this is a child if the telomeres aren't degraded. The other option: the connection as one of The Disappeared holds up a lot better if I had any evidence this was a thirty-plus-year-old."

"Except, we have to determine time of death." Donovan was looking at her. "If it was decades or so ago, that changes the age necessary to be one of the Disappeared."

"I don't think that body could have laid in that field with no one noticing for a decade." Eleri had never bought into that theory; in fact, she'd dismissed it so easily that it was almost forgotten.

"You're assuming it wasn't moved."

"How would that happen? All the bones intact?" That would be a big endeavor. Sure, it could be done. But the concept was weird enough to almost completely rule it out.

"A few of them were missing," Donovan pointed out.

She turned that over in her brain for a bit. Her stomach grumbled, reminding her that the basic necessities held for the live people in the room. "We also need to find out about that building."

"Yeah, about that." He tipped his head back and forth, equivocating. "Last night I—"

"Did you sleep at all?" She interrupted.

"Not much. But I can't find Axis anywhere. Not really."

"What does that mean?" She felt her brows furrow as her stomach protested again.

"It's everywhere. Everything is called Axis. It's possibly the most common company name, corporate program name, or group name, ever." He was leaning on his elbow on the counter. "But an 'Axis' that might be out *here*? Nothing. The weird thing is that there shouldn't be *anything* there, not in that part of the forest. There's not even a business registered under that name in this part of Michigan."

"Did you check satellite images?" she asked.

"Oh yeah. Again, nothing. According to the sat photos, the building really doesn't exist. Everything is blurred out on every view . . . which means someone is doing it on purpose. Probably the government."

18

Donovan scrubbed his hand down his face. He felt the stubble that sprang up like AstroTurf, just as stiff and just as obnoxious. His sigh brought only a twinge from his ribs; for that he was grateful. The rest of it he could do without.

He and Eleri had spent the entire day before in the lab, though Walter had run out to get them lunch. It was a nice gesture, but the food was cooling before she made it back through security. Donovan would have been more than happy to get out of the windowless lab. For a man who needed free space to run—in either form—this lab was purgatory at best.

"I know," Eleri told him. Her voice was the first thing to break the silence in probably an hour. She was tapping away on the computer, trying to find out something about the building. He'd been examining the skeletons.

Day two on it and despite switching tasks and bringing fresher eyes, neither of them had anything new. He was tired, frustrated, and ready for a break.

The knock at the door was not what he expected. He

jumped at the same time Eleri did, both of them ready to answer the door just for something to do.

"You go." Eleri put her hand out, waving him forward.

Donovan was startled to find both Walter and a deliveryman standing there. Waving Walter inside, he spoke to the man at the door for a moment before signing for the full genomic results on the skeletons. They hoped to have 820's full results, too.

Closing the door, he walked back to where Eleri and Walter now stood over a paper map she must have brought with her. Setting the envelope on the table, he joined the conversation.

"Here." Walter pointed to a spot on the map. "This is where the building is. I marked the four corners. It's basically square, with a square courtyard in the middle. One side is two stories, but the others are all one story. The upper floor is dormitories, and under the dormitories are classrooms."

She was rattling off all kinds of stats about the building, still talking while she pulled out a white paper and pencil schematic.

Donovan interrupted. "Did you draw this? When?"

She was nodding as he talked, and Eleri filled in.

"She went out scouting yesterday. Marked the building on the map—so we don't have to go by our guesstimate anymore. We can check satellite pictures now. And she went inside and mapped it. Look."

He was looking. The map was precise and obviously not the first time Walter had done this. It wasn't even on graph paper. "You did this out in the snow?"

"It's just snow," she answered first, then caught a little more of the question. "Cartography classes in the military. Gotta know what you're up against. I can match to aerial photographs, too."

She was looking at the page again, examining her drawing. But he was looking at *her*. It was hard to believe that when he'd met her, she was homeless in Los Angeles. She'd been living in an abandoned lot downtown with a handful of other disenfranchised veterans. It had become clear very quickly that she was not as damaged as it may appear. She was smart, able, and well-trained. She'd found them here, found him out, and continued to amaze him.

"I went inside, obviously, and it was more interesting than the outside," Walter was saying.

"What about the outside?" Eleri pushed, thumbing through a file of pictures Walter had snapped of the exterior.

"It's blank. No markings."

"We noticed that, too." Donovan rejoined the conversation, pulling his head out of his own thoughts. "Like it wasn't ever labeled at all."

Walter nodded. "I thought that, too. So I checked. Every inch I could see. But I can't find anything. Not on the brick, not on the doors or windows. Not just removed or painted over, either. There are no anchors, no remaining marks where letters were scraped away. Nothing."

"It is out in the middle of nowhere." Eleri said.

"That's what makes me think it was never marked." Walter pulled another page out. This one was full of notes, handwritten in precise script. Walter's. Donovan looked over her shoulder as she dragged her finger to a note and looked up. "I found a few documents, the oldest from 1986. But honestly, the architecture bears hints of the seventies."

"Really?" Donovan asked. "I thought it was horrendously generic."

"It was," Walter agreed, "but it still has the spray foam ceilings, with the big, circular glitter embedded in it. I scraped some to see if it was the original covering, and it was."

Donovan watched as Eleri's eyebrows rose. He agreed and held his tongue, too. Walter kept talking.

"I spent this morning online, looking up a few things.

According to my research, by '86, that ceiling type was well out of use. But it was the preferred ceiling coating in the late seventies. Also, the windows say late seventies." She looked up at them then. "The frames, the type of aluminum. I looked it up."

Donovan was nodding now. He didn't doubt Walter.

"Shit," Eleri was muttering. "Another brick in the wall."

"What?" Donovan asked.

"Los Desaparecidos. That was in the late seventies."

"It fits." Donovan felt some of the empty places in his brain, some of the question marks, start filling in. "Las Abuelas may be onto something." He jumped up. "We have the first set of results."

"Oh?"

He stopped. The word was so un-Eleri-like. Turning, he looked at her and watched as she motioned with a small shrug and a twitch of her eyes in Walter's direction.

Starting to shrug back, Donovan stopped himself, recognizing that the half-shorthand sign language wasn't going to work. He turned to Walter. "Can you excuse us for a minute?"

"Take my maps or no?"

"No."

With a nod, she stepped outside the lab door. Whether she knew that it automatically locked her out or not, she'd heard the click. Only the code or someone inside could get her back in.

Eleri spoke first. "We have to officially hire her."

"Yeah." His agreement on that idea was easy, on the execution, not so much. "Which means we have to bring it up to Westerfield again."

"Or wait until he asks," she offered.

"If you're okay with that." He was willing if she was. Then again, it really was ultimately his furry ass on the line. Donovan decided right there that if he was getting sent up river for it, at least Walter would be acknowledged. "Yes."

"Okay," Eleri was standing even before she said it, making him wonder if she'd decided before he did. But he didn't complain.

"Come on in." She opened the door for Walter, still waiting patiently in the hallway.

Walter came in, military proud. She was maybe used to waiting in hallways while the higher-ups made decisions about her future.

"We're hiring you. Again." Eleri made the announcement.

"That's not necessary, ma'am."

That was Walter, still uber-competent, still on her A-game, but always on duty on some level. Marines didn't get hired, they just did.

Donovan dove in. He was far less indoctrinated into the Bureau than Eleri. She hadn't had another career first, she was Fed all the way. Donovan prided himself on still having a lot of civilian left in him, though he hadn't had that much of it to start with. "It *is* necessary. We can't tell you certain things without clearance. So you have to be hired. Say yes. We need you."

A small smile flirted with her lips, humanizing the Marine that stood before him. She visibly relaxed, "Okay. Then I accept."

Eleri sat back down immediately. "Given the age that you've calculated for the building, we have more evidence for an odd correlation we've found." She was talking quickly, excited to be able to tell someone about what little they'd found. "All of the DNA samples have come back with a letter—"

Donovan was already ripping open the new envelope, ignoring Eleri's update to Walter as he scanned the results. He held a full genome of each of the three samples, not Eight-twenty. He couldn't read the string of Gs, Cs, Ts, and As, but the results started pinging in his head.

Slowly, his face contracted into a solid frown. It couldn't be right. He kept reading. He would have said the results were wrong, but it was computer matched. Wrong once? Coincidence. Sure. But on all three? Whatever it was it was real.

"Donovan?" Eleri's voice broke his thoughts. "Are they Los Desaparecidos? Does the mitochondrial DNA match?"

He hadn't even looked. He held a finger up to hold them off, reading as he moved closer to them. It was almost a full minute of silence before he turned back to them.

"Yes." It was the only thing he said at first, his brain still turning as he flipped the pages back and forth. It was almost another minute before he looked at each of them, landing on Eleri's green gaze. "On two of them."

"Two?" she asked, stunned.

He nodded. "The mitochondrial DNA turned up matches to two specific women in the Abuelas. We have names, so it's definitely not a mistake." The mitochondrial match proved that these kids were a direct lineage through the female line, hence the group of grandmothers—Las Abuelas—using their own DNA as the basis for the search. He looked further along, rattling off the names of the women the DNA matched to. These women not only lost their daughters, but their grandchildren along with them.

"Wow." Eleri was suddenly behind him, managing to look over his shoulder despite the fact that she was almost a full foot shorter than him. "Jesus. One of them is already gone. The other is well into her nineties."

"Well, their grandkids are gone, too." Donovan added. The old medical examiner in him popped out, stating the facts with no concern for the feeling, often grieving, humans on the other ends of those facts. He was almost glad one of the Abuelas was dead. Not only were their grandkids gone, but something had been pretty wrong with them when they were alive. Bones didn't wind up altered like that for no reason.

There were names on some of the pages—Argentinian names that meant nothing to him. Names of the grandmothers the mitochondrial DNA had matched to, and names of the people the skeletons had once been. But that was a hard call, too. The children had disappeared very early in life. Sometimes it was a pregnant mother who was disappeared, the baby taken from her upon birth. These skeletons had likely never really lived a life under these names. It was more than likely they had never known these names. He flipped to a page and handed it to Eleri. It was the story of one of the skeletons.

Donovan headed to the second one. Name of the Abuela whose DNA had matched at the top. Name of the missing child under that, or simply that the child would have been due on a certain date. Many had no idea if the unborn child was male or female. In at least two of these cases, he and Eleri would only be filling in missing gaps in long waiting records. In the third case, there would be no reunion, only more bad news after decades of waiting. His heart didn't turn over the way Eleri's would, but it shifted.

"Wait." He put an arm out to stop Eleri from walking away. Only then did he look up and spot Walter, sitting at the desk on one of the utilitarian lab stools, once again patiently waiting.

"Here." He finally relinquished control on the papers he was holding tightly, laying them out across one last open desk top. In a moment, he and Eleri had the black surface covered with an organized layout of the pages. Rows and columns delineated which skeleton and what kind of information the pages held: information about the Argentinian connection, the full breakdown of the genomic code, additional information about heritage and genetic background.

The background wasn't surprising. All three were South American, some genetics specifically pointing to Argentina, a few smidges to Peru or Brazil in two of the cases, some traces to native tribes, probably from the area. There was a little Western European in the mix on two of them, but nothing that stood out. The genetic coding said that all three of these were South

Americans whose skeletal remains had wound up in Michigan
for some reason. The genetic matches to Las Abuelas said that
at least two of these skeletons specifically belonged to babies
that had been stolen by the dictatorial Argentinian government
at the time.

"This one's not one of the Disappeared." Donovan pointed
to the one that hadn't come back as a match.

"Not necessarily. The government stole children without
knowledge of which women had mothers who would follow
up. So perhaps he is one of them, but didn't have a live family
member or one who was local and could join Las Abuelas. The
fact that it has strong Argentinian genetics is pretty damning."
Eleri shook her head.

Donovan felt his head shaking in unison with hers even as
Walter watched them with detached bemusement.

Eleri was talking under her breath. Whether it was to
herself or to him didn't matter. Donovan understood it. He
listened with one ear as he sat at the computer and used the
info given with the results to log into a secured server that
would open reams of data on each of the subjects.

"So at least two, probably all three, are some of the Argentinian Disappeared, given the genetic markers. And something
was very wrong with them while they were alive." Her hands
migrated to her hips as she finally stopped moving. "Still the
biggest thing we know for certain about all of them is that
they're human."

"Yes, *we* do." Donovan turned his screen toward her. "The
machine doesn't."

"Holy shit." She blinked, then stared at the results. "Wait, it
says human."

"Only ninety-five percent match," Donovan countered,
pointing to the first set of results. He scrolled through the long
list of scrambled, probably meaningless genetic information,

until he got to something interesting he'd spotted at the bottom of the lists.

"That one's ninety-seven." Eleri pointed to the second set of information. Her voice had leveled out. "That's well within possibility. We used fully skeletonized remains. The sample could easily be degraded."

"True." He flipped to another window. "This one's only Ninety one."

"Shit." She leaned forward, as though the data would say something different if she could just get close enough. "No other matches. Just human."

"Not quite. Dig further." Donovan widened one of the windows to include what he was seeing. "So look here." He pointed. "Human is the highest match and nothing even comes close to it. But if you run down to where it tried to match other things, there are three blips."

Eleri read them off. "Gorilla. Black bear. Polar bear?" Her tone twisted almost the same way her expression did.

Though they didn't "match" to the sample, the percent match of the genome was much higher than it should be. And much higher than any other animal. When he looked at cross-matching to birds, fish, even other mammals, the genetic code overlap was in the tiniest of partial percents. These were coming in at two and three percent each. He grinned, "Ready?"

"For what?"

Donovan flipped to the second profile, showed her the percentage human match again, then scrolled down to the blips again. "Gorilla, Polar bear."

He flipped again. "Look at this one. Lynx, canine, orangutan."

"Holy shit." Her words were reverent, but spoke exactly what he'd thought when he first saw it.

Those kinds of matches, even in the low percentages, they weren't errors.

19

Eleri stared at the screen, her head balanced in her hand while her eyes crossed. Her stomach rumbled at her and only the clock on the wall told her all she'd missed.

Donovan and Walter had headed out for dinner some time ago. She'd waved them off, wanting to look again at the slides, wanting to see if she could visually discern the weird levels of animal overlap in the genetic codes. Never mind that she didn't recognize gorilla bones microscopically or even macroscopically. She'd been trained on the standard human/not human scale, and anything else she recognized, she'd learned out of her own curiosity or from seeing it so much. So she could recognize a deer scapula and a variety of woodland creature skulls just from experience, but partial lynx DNA in the cross sections they'd taken of the long bones? No.

Pulling her phone from her pocket she saw she'd missed three texts from Avery. At least that made her smile. Heading for the door, she meandered through the relatively empty hallways toward the bank of vending machines. The windows mocked her with her own reflection, the darkness beyond a reminder that she'd spent her whole day in the lab. Inside the lab the landscape was visually, disturbingly similar to being out in the snow. The white walls—like the snow—simultaneously went on forever while still managing to close her in.

Her brain churned. How did the Disappeared get to Michigan, into the US at all? What was wrong with them?

She wanted to talk to the Abuelas, or someone who could speak for them. She wanted to ask if anything was wrong with the babies. But how would they know? Prenatal testing and imaging were not the norm in those days—most people were still surprised at birth by the gender of their child. So how would they even know if the babies had genetic disorders?

Honestly, there were holes all through that line of thinking.

If she called, she would have to explain that she had these bones and that the genetics had matched. She wasn't ready to do that, the case was nowhere near ready. If she had good news, that would be a different story, but she had only a decedent— dead person—and no information about what had happened to him.

Eleri toyed with the idea that the defects were experiments induced by the Argentinian government. That theory was dismissed almost as soon as it formed. If it were the case, the pregnancies would have been induced after the women disappeared. These women were pregnant enough that their mothers had known about it. While there were workarounds to interfering with the growth of an already developing fetus, most of that technology developed well after these women and their children were taken.

She allowed her internal systems of checks and balances to work through and throw out several other options until she found herself standing in front of the vending machines before she was fully aware she'd made it that far down the hall.

A candy bar and a soft drink weren't what she should be eating, but what she would be eating. When she got back to the lab, she started texting to Avery before giving up and calling him.

He didn't answer, but the sound of his voice on the service was nice. She left a message before finishing a candy bar that had become boring before she hit halfway. Within minutes, she was back where she'd started. Head in hand, looking at photographs of bone slices.

They all looked different, but nothing popped out at her, nothing she hadn't seen before. The densities were odd. The central column that held the marrow was a little too narrow; the thickness of the bone itself was too big or too small. The formation of the bone should resemble a sponge, almost coral-like. These did, but not in the normal ways.

Eleri wanted to bash her head on the desk. Knowing that there were small amounts of genetic code from other animals explained a little of it, but raised even more questions. There wasn't a lot available on bone densities of gorillas, lynx, and bears. So the densities made more logical sense in that light, but she had no real evidence. Just her own "Hey, that makes sense," but she sure as hell wasn't any closer to "why."

She rested her head in her hands then, staring down at the desk while her mind wound around it. The gears slowly churned to a slower pace. Her breathing steadied out.

Retracing her steps, Eleri considered where they found the skeletons. She visualized the layout of the field, the way the bodies were arranged. She tried to think about what effect that would have on the bones. She needed another test. She should write that down . . . but she was thinking about the landscape, about the seasons the bones would have been through to be so clean and untouched under the snow like that.

There wasn't grass over them, so the field would have been cut or low-growing. Wildflowers maybe? They had all been gone by the time the bones were found, so it seemed reasonable. Eleri visualized it, tiny purple and white flowers, with the body in the middle, somehow unnoticed. It began to decompose before her eyes, but something in the trees grabbed her attention.

Walking on, Eleri entered the trees, noticing the warmth of the forest. This time the ground under her feet was covered in the thick green of tiny plants pushing upward. In a few spots, brown, loamy soil showed through, making a trail. It aimed her off in an odd direction, but she followed, anyway.

She headed deeper into the forest, the warmth of summer wrapping her like a blanket. Eleri breathed deep of the wild scents of the trees and dirt. She walked the trail for a while not knowing how long she was in the woods, but feeling safe, protected, while she wound her way through. Eventually she arrived at the little white house.

The door faced her this time, oddly cut into the corner of the small building, the little triangular porch. Again, she walked up the one step onto the porch and turned the knob, pushed the door inward.

This time the woman was in the front room. Slowly, she rocked, stitched, ignored Eleri.

This time the doll she sewed was bright red. The thread she pulled through like blood. The stitches like cuts. They slashed wide across the doll, not neat marching rows like the other doll. Eleri sat at her feet and watch as she sewed on various arms and legs without care.

A strange feeling of peace settled over Eleri despite the disturbing images of the odd doll. Low music played over her, coming from the woman, from the rhythm of the stitching. Slowly, it got louder. Pushing at her, nudging her from her spot at the woman's feet.

Her cell phone. Why was it ringing?

Her eyes fluttered open, the dream falling away to the sight and smells of the lab and the insistent sound of her phone.

Scrambling to answer it, she almost dropped it, but managed to push the button before it quit.

"Hello?"

"El." The smile in Avery's voice woke her fully, bringing her own smile.

"Avery! I think I fell asleep in the lab."

"Did I wake you up?" He almost laughed it.

"Yes, and it was a good thing. This case is making me weird." It was what she could say.

"Oh, I think you were plenty weird before." He laughed aloud this time. "But the weirdness doesn't make this case any different than any of the others you talked about, does it?"

She wanted to say "no" but couldn't bring herself to do it. This case did feel different. She felt watched. All the time.

GJ STOOD in snow up to her knees. She was damned tired of it, but she was more tired of having her research pulled out from under her just when it was getting good.

She sighed into the cold air, her frozen breath a visible reminder of her ire. Absentmindedly, she rubbed her gloves together as though that would warm her hands.

The building stood in front of her, a box holding secrets she needed. There was too much at stake to ignore it. GJ knew her grandfather was holding out on her. All those years she'd learned so much. His mistake had been in feeding her curiosity and then thinking he could keep secrets.

This building wasn't one of his, theirs, not a family holding, but it held secrets. They were part of the weave she'd begun seeing strange patterns in. So GJ stood in the cold even though she hated it.

The building had no markings. But it had doors.

GJ was ready to use a crowbar, a gun even, to open the lock.

But as she readied herself then tugged on the handle, she found it opened almost disappointingly easily. Footsteps around the building indicated that she wasn't the only one who'd been here since the last snowfall, but the area around the doorway was pristine. There was no covering over the door, so the area was open to the wind and precipitation. She trusted the lack of marks, and the drifts would be hard to fake.

As she headed inside, her instinct wanted the interior to be warmer, but it wasn't. In fact, the sun was blocked, somehow leaving her just a little more chilled. None of this stopped her. Her grandfather always said, "When GJ gets something in her head, it's safer for everyone else to just get out of the way."

She found the irony, if not the enjoyment, in that thought now.

Walking the open hallway, she looked into empty offices, opened drawers, peered onto top shelves. As each room subsequently turned up more and more nothing, she got colder and colder, but she didn't stop. GJ had to find something. She hadn't come out here for the big fat nothing she was left with.

The vast emptiness, the utter abandonment of the building, bothered her. She began humming softly to herself.

The bleakness was easier to handle with the human noise in the air. She wandered into classrooms long let go to dust. There were few actual toys. Most were tests disguised as games. GJ recognized dexterity tests, high IQ puzzles, physical challenges. What she didn't recognize were just plain old games.

In some of the rooms, the chairs were small, kindergarten size maybe. Two rooms over, they became regular school-sized, along with the desks. The teacher's organization remained— the desks still haunting the room in a neat circle.

Here at least, there were a few scraps of paper. She devoured what she could find, tossing most aside upon seeing that they were just standard school assignments. Sentence graphs, short essays, the occasional math problem, all taunted her with their normalcy. She wanted—*needed*—the unusual. Something was up, she could feel it.

She climbed the staircase, looking up as she did. Bedrooms, more like dormitory rooms, loomed at the top. Also empty, they too appeared to be sparsely furnished even when they had been occupied. Many of the beds were twins, or even smaller, indicating again that children had lived here.

GJ picked up and turned over books—mostly classics—and more of the puzzle games. Her voice lifted again, the mild humming ringing through the empty walls.

She found only scattered papers, some dated as far back as 1979, the childlike scrawl leading to more questions and fewer answers. A handful of pages said "Axis" at the top. Several things she found said "Axis Project," but mostly she found nothing of value. Nothing that would begin to answer her questions about the skeletons out in the national forest. Only more questions. Only things that could set her imagination running free. But she prided herself on the science her grandfather had instilled in her heart. She had no evidence. All she was looking for was evidence. She found none.

GJ was heading down the stairs the first time she heard it. The creak, the pop of an old building settling or of a footfall, she couldn't be sure. But she stopped dead and waited.

When she didn't hear the noise again, when enough time had passed that she was confident enough to move, when she believed she had sorted out the building noises and not that of a human creeping round, she headed down the stairs again.

She walked down a different set of steps from the one she'd come up, stopping at the window set into the wall. Looking out it at the snow, she smiled at the bitter landscape before her eye snagged on something.

Footsteps. Fresh in the otherwise undisturbed snow.

They led into the building. Through a window? She couldn't be sure. Her face pressed against the glass, she still couldn't see straight onto the window on the story below. If she remembered correctly, the window would lead into one of the chain of offices that ran the side of the building.

Shit.

Someone was coming in and out of the building. Someone besides her. Very recently.

There was no more time for exploring. The building wasn't as empty as it appeared. She listened for a moment, waiting to hear the sounds of others, but she heard nothing. When she was convinced she was alone, she turned the corner on the landing of the steps and ran smack into the biggest man she'd ever seen.

He grabbed her arm in a death grip, lifting her slightly off the ground. "Why are you here? Why have people come to Axis?"

Stunned, she failed to answer, managing only to gape like a fish. She was in over her head and she found she'd be incredibly grateful if only he would let her live.

When she didn't speak, he asked her again, in what she believed was Russian. This time she frowned. Shocked.

He asked again in Spanish. Which she understood, but still failed to answer.

Then he asked in Chinese.

20

It was nine-thirty in the morning when Eleri and Donovan walked down the hallway to the lab. Later than she liked to start. But Walter was with them again and Eleri managed some real sleep after her weird dream and her phone call with Avery.

The strange little white house didn't come back into her sleep again. In fact, nothing she remembered did. She called that a good night, though she was starting to wonder why she wasn't dreaming about the case. Usually being so immersed in something sparked whatever connection she made, but it wasn't happening this time.

Unless the odd little house *was* the connection to the case? But that wasn't making any sense. Not that the house did at all.

"Excuse me?" The voice cut her thoughts just as she reached the door to the lab they'd been assigned. Other agents walked the hallways occasionally, but mostly in this wing it was labs, so the only traffic was those delivering or picking up lab samples. So much was delivered via electronic methods that the foot traffic was low.

Eleri started to answer, but Donovan beat her to it. By the

time her brain fog processed what was happening, Donovan was conversing with the woman and signing for yet another envelope.

Eleri turned back to the lab door, reaching first for the keypad lock and punching in the code she and Donovan had chosen. It was when she grasped the knob that she felt the zing of awareness and stopped dead.

Donovan put a hand out to brace against the door as he almost ran into it. He'd been expecting her to open it. Only Walter had the reflexes to stop on a dime.

Eleri looked at them, seeing two faces identical in confusion if not in physical reaction. She must have frowned at Donovan.

He held up the envelope. "Full genome results from Eight-twenty." His pause was momentary at best. "What's wrong?"

"Don't know." She shook her head, only knowing that something *was* wrong. Expressions flitted across her face, she could feel them but not stop them. The confusion, the dead certainty, the puzzle of not knowing where the feeling fit despite its strength.

Walter saw it all. "What's wrong?"

Though her words echoed Donovan's exactly, the meaning was very different. Donovan understood what Eleri was going through—at least from the outside he did. He knew to stand back, to trust her results even if no one understood the methods. Walter had none of that.

But she wasn't slow.

Eleri was reaching for the doorknob again, no one getting in her way, when understanding dawned on Walter's face. Her features, usually schooled to soldier stiffness, were quite pretty as the thought hit her.

"You . . . ?"

Eleri watched as Walter pointed to the doorknob and then to Eleri.

For a moment, she wished Walter was just a soldier in the

lowest function, just a gun who only did as she was told. But that was so far from what Walter really was that there was no skirting the truth. She nodded, but didn't have time to explain. She grasped the knob again.

This time images came with the feeling. The feeling itself came sharper, clearer. Violation. Theft of her things. Their things.

It must have shown on her face. Walter and Donovan stared at her. She could see their shocked, confused, upset expressions behind the overlay of the images.

The lab was trashed. Here in the FBI building, someone had gotten in.

Eleri was pushing at the door, the whole thing so fast that the code was still active and the door swung wide. Her eyes only confirmed what her brain had seen.

"Shit!" Donovan nearly yelled it.

The tables were clear, cleaned off. The papers she'd carefully sorted all missing.

The three of them shoved into the room, both Walter and Eleri reaching for their sidearms, though only Walter was wearing hers. Eleri had forgone her own, thinking that she didn't need it inside the Bureau building. She'd been wrong.

Walter led with the muzzle, executing perfect corner turns around the steel lab door and into the back alcove. Eleri wanted to lead, but knew enough to stay back, let Walter go first. Instead she let her eyes roam.

The place wasn't tossed, not like she'd expected with the initial zing she'd gotten off the doorknob. But, to her eyes, it had clearly been thoroughly gone-through. The only evidence of theft was a few pieces of work and their records. The lab looked clean.

"The bones." Donovan said the words bleakly.

She'd already seen that. The tables were empty where the skeletons had been laid out.

Her heart pounded. Three nearly full skeletons, gone. Someone came ready to steal them. They knew what they wanted and were prepared. "They must have come prepared with boxes or bags. No one could have carried bones of these sizes without drawing attention. No one could have just put them in a pocket."

Donovan was nodding, but still looking around frantically. "The slides." He'd pulled on gloves and rummaged through the desk. "They're here!"

She looked over as he held up a few loose slides and then the wooden box they'd been filed in. "All of them?"

"All of them." He smiled, but it quickly fell off his face as he asked her. "Papers?"

She shook her head. "All of them."

Someone had both the bones and the results. Both the initial no-match test against the FBI database as well as the results from the NamUs and DoeNetwork websites. They also had the weird results from the full genome matching.

Shit!

"I have the login and codes. We can get the info back online. But damn." She was opening her mouth to suggest they report it, but Walter spoke up.

"What tipped you off?" The gaze was clear, the question direct.

For a moment Eleri entertained the idea of getting away with it. Of telling Walter that she spotted a pry mark or lock pick scrape on the door. But it didn't have a manual lock, and she didn't notice anything. She'd touched the knob before understanding that she shouldn't. Though Donovan was preserving evidence with his gloves on, she'd destroyed it on the doorknob most likely. She wished she'd gotten the heads-up *before* she touched it. Then again, whoever had broken into the FBI lab probably hadn't left prints. Dejected at the idea, Eleri turned back to Walter.

"Just felt it," she confessed. Walter already knew Donovan's secret. What was one more?

"That's why you two are partners." It was a statement more than a question, Walter's finger tracing back and forth between them, as though she was sewing ideas together. The gun still stuck in her grasp, loose but at the ready.

Eleri looked around a little more, pulling on her own gloves before touching anything. It took her five minutes to assess that —aside from the bone slices—everything they'd collected was gone and everything they didn't need was left alone.

She was furious. "We have to report it."

Donovan looked up at her, but it was Walter who spoke.

"What's the probability that you're reporting it directly to the people responsible?"

"High." Eleri spoke it through clenched teeth. Much higher than she wanted it to be. "But what's the alternative?"

Donovan stopped looking through things for any kind of evidence and stared. "We don't report it."

"But we're *in* the Bureau building." Eleri pointed out, then realized that neither of these two fully understood what that meant. Donovan had only been a Feeb under NightShade; he didn't understand how the Bureau worked. She'd been in for close to a decade, what she now referred to as "regular Bureau." She sighed and explained. "It's strict. You'll lose everything for not following protocol."

"Will we?" Donovan asked before taking a breath in, apparently only then realizing that Walter was in the room and he was about to discuss the NightShade protocol in front of her.

Eleri simply shrugged, letting it stand as her answer given the current company. "If we don't report properly to a branch we are not assigned agents of, then yes, we'll be in massive trouble."

She could see the thoughts passing on Donovan's face with the absent nod he offered of agreement. He was thinking that they didn't have a home office at all. She picked up the phone in the office and called in the report.

Inside of three minutes, there were twelve agents swarming the small lab. Six of them were in Tyvek and actively hunting for fingerprints, blood stains, and anything else they might find. Eleri, Donovan and Walter were stuck out in the hallway. Five minutes later, they were split between three separate offices, getting questioned.

Eleri answered everything they asked, three times.

She understood exactly what they were doing. It was just different being on this side of the table. By the time she was released, both Donovan and Walter were out and waiting on her. Without speaking, the three of them turned by mutual agreement and headed down the long hallway and out of the building.

They were all in the rental car and before anyone spoke, Eleri turned the key and drove them to a nearby chain restaurant. Because what better way to talk about classified information than over rolls and butter and burgers?

She was sipping at a tea she'd dumped several packets of sugar into before she spoke. "We have the bone slices. What else do we have?"

"Web access to the DNA data. Though we are no longer in the sole possession of it, if that becomes important," Donovan added.

"We have Walter's drawn blueprints of the building," Eleri added, noticing that Walter Reed wasn't participating. She was quietly eating the bread and watching the exchange. Eleri tried to ignore her. "What do they have?"

"The skeletons, the print versions of the files . . ." He paused, then swore. "They have all the files Walter took from the Axis building. I'm just glad we changed the password on first login for the access to the full DNA profiles. They only have the one originally assigned."

"Anything else?" she was wracking her brain, but couldn't think what else they might still have. They had memories of what they'd seen. They'd documented most of what they'd found, but her heart dropped at that thought. "Did you report that whoever-it-was took the photos of the anomalies on the skeletons?"

Donovan nodded at her, his expression as glum as hers. "I didn't find the camera either."

"Shit," she muttered as her burger arrived, her curse startling the server. "Oh, I'm so sorry. I'm upset about something else."

The food was placed in front of them and Eleri took a bite before she realized Walter was staring at her. She was chewing and left it to Donovan to handle Walter.

He did. "Eleri is a moneyed Southern belle. What you heard is her innate Southern accent. It comes out with alcohol and anger." He took a bite of his burger, considering the topic closed.

Walter just raised an eyebrow, before sinking into her own food. "Did you not back it up?"

It was the first thing she'd asked, her first participation in the conversation since they found they'd been cleaned out.

Eleri finished her bite, wishing she could enjoy the burger more. Mostly she loved food. Rich cheeses, juicy meats, soft breads, and crisp flavors. But today it was all flat. She was angry. Not a good seasoning.

"Sure. The lab is supposed to be so secure that it's safer to *not* send information out via hardware or email. So we can probably pull it from the home computer but we don't know yet." The crime scene techs said they had to check the computer first: look for traces of searches, deleted data. Eleri's team could check the system once the scene was cleared. It was weird again being on the other side of the yellow tape. She spoke to organize her thoughts. "But the hard copies are gone.

I'm as upset about what they have as what we lost. Why would anyone want it?"

They sat in silence for a moment, each contemplating the problem. Who would steal their things? Who knew the case? Who knew which lab they were in? Or at least could find it and get into it without physically picking the lock? That would have at least set off alarms. None had been triggered. Or they'd been quelled as soon as they were triggered. "Everything points to some kind of inside job."

It didn't make her feel any better.

"Well, I made copies. I do a standard backup for myself. And my information is my own. So no rules to not do it," Walter announced around a bite of Philly cheesesteak that looked like a good sandwich but resembled neither cheesesteak nor anything from Philly.

Eleri fought to keep her mouth from opening and hanging there. Only the years of etiquette training stopped her. "All the maps?"

Walter nodded. "All the files. I made photo and print copies for myself. So at the very least we still have all the Axis papers I found."

"I love you, Walter." Donovan spoke it plain, but Eleri's eyes popped open. She didn't think Donovan loved anything. Or at least he didn't love anything out loud.

Walter busted out laughing, the expression transforming her face. And Eleri's lunch got a whole lot less bleak. "Well, then we aren't dead in the water."

They finished their food on a happier note and headed back to the Bureau, hoping the techs were done with the lab and they could begin their work all over again.

Outside the door, another delivery girl walked up to them. "Eleri Eames?"

"Yes." She looked up, then at Donovan and Walter. They weren't expecting anything else. They had the last of the genomic data on Eight-twenty in the delivery Donovan received just before everything went to shit.

He didn't seem to know what was in the envelope. Eleri took it and checked the return address. "Nynette Remi."

"Is that your grandmother?" Donovan asked as he nodded to the tech standing sentry to the lab so the woman would let them in.

"Grandmère." Eleri said absently, then noticed that once again Walter was puzzled. "My great-grandmother. Mother's side."

It didn't appear that Walter had looked at the envelope, but she must have. "That address is from New Orleans. Lower Ninth Ward . . ." She let the words trail off. That area was not what anyone would refer to as the "moneyed South."

"Yup. My grandmère is quite the creature." That was all Eleri was willing to say as she pulled the tab on the envelope.

Her grandmère always managed to find her in odd locations, even when Agent in Charge Westerfield sometimes didn't even know where they were. Grandmère sent her and Donovan and one of the other agents each a gris-gris on the last case. But this envelope was flat. Sticking her hand in, Eleri felt three smaller envelopes. Thick paper was rough under her fingers. She pulled them out, not surprised to see they said "Makinde" —an old pet name for Eleri. "The Dark Wolf"—clearly Donovan.

Eleri expected the third one to say "The Agent in Charge" if it was for Westerfield. Maybe even "The Brown Wolf" if she wanted it delivered to Wade. Nothing Grandmère did ever made full sense to Eleri. So she was surprised to find the third envelope was addressed to "Lucy Fisher."

Well, she nailed that one on the head. Eleri handed the parchment letter over to the surprised woman. And who wouldn't be?

Then she opened her own, curious as to what was inside.

The loopy scrawl was clearly Grandmère's. The words shocked her.

—*EMMALINE WILL BE FOUND SOON.*

GJ WAITED in the high-end hotel room, watching out the large windows as the snow fell. At least this time she could watch it and not live it. At least this time she was warm.

She pushed the sleeves up on her sweater and took a sip of the hot tea she'd ordered from room service. It was a lot of money for a drink, but she couldn't leave the room.

Her thoughts wandered while she waited. She knew it was done. She'd gotten the text. No one would suspect either of them. At least not for a long time. She was banking on that.

For years, she'd prided herself on being good. She was as straight an arrow as they came. Just like her grandfather. Then she'd learned more, and her arrow had bent. Her compass had skewed and hadn't yet found its home point. She was her grandfather's granddaughter after all.

The knock came at the door, startling her when it shouldn't have.

She jumped but then pulled herself together. It wouldn't suit to look nervous. When GJ pulled the door open, she was as she always was. Calm, cool, collected. "You have the bones?"

"And papers, too," he answered.

21

Donovan held the letter in his hands. He didn't usually get letters. Not hand-written ones. Lucy/Walter looked almost as bad as he did. Though Eleri had opened her note, he and Walter were each holding theirs like it smelled bad.

As he watched, Eleri read and turned sheet-white.

"El?" His own letter was forgotten. His arm went around her as though to hold her upright, though in general he knew she didn't need it. At least the feel of her shoulders under his touch was steady as a rock, even if her face told a different story.

She didn't speak. Just turned the letter around to face him.

—*EMMALINE WILL BE FOUND SOON.*

DONOVAN BLINKED, the words and Eleri's expression soaking in.

"Emmaline?" he asked as though Eleri might not understand, but she understood that he was asking about her grandmother's meaning.

"Emmaline?" This time it was Walter asking. She must not have seen the emotion in Eleri's eyes. Normally Walter stayed silent.

Donovan turned to her and explained. "Emmaline was her little sister. She was kidnapped at age ten. You might have heard about it on the news. It was a big case. Emmaline Eames. She was never found."

That was the simplest version he could give of it, but there was so much more. He turned back to Eleri.

"El. Does she not know?"

Eleri shook her head. "She knows. Or at least I think she does. She's always hinted that she knew." Now she looked up at him. "Like she knew the same way I did."

Donovan understood. Eleri had dreamed of Emmaline after she was gone. Then she dreamed—years later—about Emmaline's death. Donovan understood it rationally but he found it hard to empathize with what he had no base of feelings for.

He turned to Walter to find that she was silent. Usually, her silence freaked him out a little. It was preternatural. He'd gone through Quantico, trained for the FBI. He excelled at defensive driving, but let Eleri drive most of the time they were out and around. He'd passed marksmanship, still thinking of his Hippocratic oath each time he pulled the trigger even on a paper target. Though he'd learned in Texas, on their first case, he could pull the trigger and kill someone.

Donovan was turning back to Eleri when Walter opened her note and frowned. She blinked twice and held the note up for him to see.

—Trust the girl.

.   .   .

FROWNING AT THE WORDS, thinking he hadn't been included, Donovan tore open his own note. Pulling the folded paper out, he flipped his open and read it.

—*YOU HAVE NOT YET FOUND the one you seek.*

DONOVAN SUCKED AIR IN. WHEN "GRANDMÈRE" had sent the gris-gris in Los Angeles, his had a wolf on it. With no input whatsoever, the old woman had seemed to know exactly what he was. Even if she just thought the wolf was some kind of spirit animal, Grandmère was on target. So why was this note so lame?

He wanted to find her and say, *No shit, Sherlock.* But he held his tongue. At least on that count. "Your grandmère is sending some weird messages, Eleri. Is this normal?"

She shook her head, still looking a little stunned. "It's not absolutely out of the norm. I mean, when I was a kid she would once in a while send something. But not like this. Not to strange locations or for people I know." She looked up at him at last. "She nailed it last time."

"So you're wondering if she nailed it again this time?"

Eleri nodded, her eyes still wide.

Donovan tried to pull her off track. "Well, none of these things applies right now. Let's get going through what's left in the lab and catalog what we have."

She nodded at him, her eyes clearing as she headed into the ruined space and back into what she knew. What she did best.

DONOVAN SAT at the computer and began going through the recovered files. The folder he'd saved the photos under was still there, but he had to look inside to see if the photos survived. As he clicked, each inspection, each opened photo let his shoulders relax a little bit.

"Donovan?" Walter's voice came over his shoulder.

"Yes?" He didn't look up, hoping he could talk and check at the same time.

"Look." She must have picked up the card from Grandmère, his card. He'd set it on the counter before sitting down. She held it down into his line of sight now. "There's a date on yours."

Donovan frowned. He hadn't seen that. He'd been too busy reading the words. His message was lame. But maybe not. "It's dated a week from today. Weird."

"This *Grandmère* is always this weird?" Walter asked.

"Well, yeah." Eleri's voice joined in and Donovan was glad that she was the one who said it. "Honestly, it always pans out." She shrugged but continued to go through the papers she'd stashed under the table. Given the noises of appreciation she was making, Donovan was thinking she was happy with what she'd found.

The skeletons would be missed, but maybe the case wasn't dead.

Her voice confirmed his suspicions. "I can't tell if everything is here, because this is a file I hadn't gotten to run through yet, but it seems nothing was taken. Looks like stashing it under the table was actually a good idea. Also, look!"

She held up what looked like a felted liquor bottle bag. The drawstrings at the neck were pulled tight and he had no idea what was in it. "The small bones! Remember we had a few ankle and finger bones that we couldn't classify? Well, I put them in here last night, not wanting them on the table, since they weren't identified! So we at least have these."

He grinned at that and reported, "Photos are all here."

"Nothing here that shouldn't be," was Walter's check-in.

Smart to look for other things that might have been left behind —things that might ID the thief. But there was nothing.

Donovan sighed. Though he was grateful something was left, there was so little of it that the entire inventory had taken less than ten minutes. A knock from behind him had his head popping up.

An agent stood in the open doorway—no point in shutting the lab now. Everything was in plain sight, and as Eleri had declared earlier, they would be in charge of security now. *Secure lab, my ass,* Donovan thought.

"Can we help you?" Eleri asked, the steel-but-sugar tone in her voice tipping off Donovan that she didn't like something she saw.

"I'm afraid I'm here to help you, except that I can't do that." The agent grabbed at his tie, straightening it in a nervous gesture.

"Please explain?" Eleri was tense, she'd almost crossed her arms, but then hadn't. Donovan couldn't read her, not anything other than her discomfort. He could practically see the gears turning in her head, but he couldn't tell what she was thinking.

"I'm with the techs who came through the place. I'm a forensic scientist."

Donovan wouldn't have known that from the coat and tie. For a moment he glanced down at his own slacks and long-sleeved T-shirt. He hardly looked like an agent himself, but at least he did look like a field scientist. Donovan stood up then, allowing his height to help bolster whatever Eleri needed. He went and stood beside her, her junior partner. "What do you have for us?"

"That's the problem." The man straightened the tie again. Donovan didn't like it either now. Though if that was because he didn't like the man or because he picked up on Eleri's feelings, he couldn't say for certain.

"We didn't find any prints."

No shit, Sherlock. Donovan thought. "Did you expect any? Whoever got in here broke into a secure FBI lab. Leaving prints is an idiot's game."

"True," the lab man responded, this time rubbing sweaty palms down the nice slacks he wore. "We vacuumed for hair, fibers, tried for DNA traces."

"Nothing?" Eleri asked as though she already knew the answer. Donovan thought she might.

"Nothing," the man confirmed. "I'm sorry. We'll keep looking into it."

"You'll pull the security footage." Eleri told him; she didn't ask. "The hallway has a camera. We should know who came in, right?"

"I don't know." He straightened the tie a third time. Donovan clenched his fists, both wanting and not wanting to deck him. "I'm not part of security—just the forensics lab. But, sadly, what I understand is that the cameras were disabled and there's no footage." He shrugged as though there was nothing he could do.

Something about it rubbed Donovan the wrong way. All agents were trained to be calm in the face of struggle, anger, whatever. But this man was a forensic scientist. He worked in a lab just like this one. The fact that this one had been cleaned out, robbed when it should have been secure should have shaken him more than it did. He should be angered that the FBI security had been so cleanly breached and that his results showed nothing. But he wasn't.

For a moment, Donovan considered that Eleri's instincts were just better than his. That she'd picked up on this before he did. But then again, her "instincts" were superior to any other human's, at least any he'd met.

Eleri did an about-face then. "Well, thank you for your help. I hope you find something."

While Donovan was still working to keep his face impassive

in light of her sudden change, Eleri held her hand out, offering a shake. In her case, she held her fingers out with a touch of a regal bearing. It was inherent in her upbringing. Donovan had seen it since day one. He also saw the moment their hands connected and Eleri's fight to keep her own expression plastered in place.

Then the man was gone, turning and heading out the door. Donovan turned to Eleri, but she was standing stock still.

Only for a moment. Then she turned sharply away from Donovan. She glared at Walter and without explanation whispered harshly, "Follow him!"

Walter was in action and out the door before Donovan could even process any of it. "What did you see?"

"He did it. He robbed the lab. But he doesn't have the bones anymore. He gave them away already." She wasn't focusing on anything, the words pouring out as her eyes darted back and forth as though she could catch them in her sights. "He didn't lie."

She looked up at him; Donovan watched as her eyes swam and darkened as the gears in her head connected. She must be putting pieces together.

Her words suggested he was right.

"He vacuumed the place, collecting fibers and hair and cells, just like he said."

Donovan knew this; all the agents had files so that forensics could rule them out from a scene. Even Walter had been printed. They had to say she'd been in the lab and that her fingerprints shouldn't be counted as criminal. Donovan was starting to tie the parts together as Eleri said it.

"He ruled himself out. Cameras down, so there's no footage of him entering or leaving the lab. He has free rein of the facility." Her voice was getting faster as she talked. "Then he comes in as the tech and the first thing he does in the lab is rule himself out as a possible suspect. They'll never find him."

"But you did." Donovan smiled as he closed the door. They'd propped it open when they inspected it, but now it was better in its intended position. Then he caught what he'd missed. "You stood up to talk to him hoping for a chance to touch him."

She nodded.

Then Donovan turned back to her. "Do you think he'll spot Walter following him?"

Eleri just stared at him.

"Okay," he laughed. "Dumb question." Walter had followed them, too, and they'd never caught her. Even when they thought she was following them. Walter made them look like rank amateurs.

"So now what?" he asked.

Finally, Eleri focused on him. She just shrugged. Usually, she was so together, but he understood. She'd taken a hit with the letter from her Grandmère about her sister. Emmaline had never been found, so while Eleri knew—just *knew*—that her sister was dead, her family didn't. Eleri had grieved her sister's death; she even knew when it happened, about ten years after the girl was kidnapped. But her mother and father still held out hope that Emmaline would be returned. Eleri had no way of telling them it would never happen, not with her sister alive anyway.

With everything Donovan had been through, he still didn't think he'd had anything as rough as that. Eleri had dreamed of Emmaline for a few months, but things had been blissfully silent for a while now. That was probably over for her.

"How about we get the hell out of here? We need to set up a new shop." He was done with this lab. "I'm texting Walter—" she wouldn't let something like a phone interfere with her stealth "—and you decide what we're taking."

An hour and a half later, they left. They hefted two duffel bags, though neither was full. They hauled the wooden boxes with the slides, though they had no microscope to read them with. The cloth bag with bones was tucked inside the same bag. The other held papers and the files from the Axis building.

It had taken longer to clear out than he'd expected. He'd thought to just grab their things and get the hell gone. But they had to print the photos, move them to a mobile file, then erase the computer. They had to use the microscope to grab photos of what they were seeing on the slides, before re-cataloging them and . . . and it was more work than he'd expected.

In the car, he turned to Eleri to admit what he didn't want to. "We have to get back to the Axis building."

"I know." She sighed. "At least it's getting warmer?"

Warmer was relative, but the robbery put things in a different perspective. They pulled out from the covered parking of the Bureau and into cold sunlight.

"Normally, I would never do this in the car. But today, I'm declaring this space our mobile lab." Donovan ripped open the envelope he'd had since just before finding out they'd been robbed. "Let's see what Eight-twenty's DNA can tell us." He scanned the pages.

"Well?" she asked. "Does he match to any of Las Abuelas?"

Donovan grinned. "Yes. She's deceased, but a clear match."

"Son of a bitch." Her voice was soft as she turned the wheel with one hand. Donovan didn't pay any attention to where she was taking them.

"Yeah, and get this: he's almost three percent lynx. Two percent polar bear."

22

G J gripped the steering wheel tightly, her knuckles turning white until she forcibly relaxed them. The state highway patrol car pulled up behind her as her heart beat a little faster.

There was no reason to pull her over. None that she knew of, anyway. Well, there was. She had three human skeletons in the trunk of her nice rental car. Not only was it illegal to trans-port human skeletons, but a little bit of an online check into her background would reveal she good and well knew this.

Her knuckles were turning white again. She flexed her fingers, before dropping one hand and steering with just the other. Hitting the button on the radio, GJ began to sing along to the song that came on, even though she hated it.

She had three, illegal, stolen, human skeletons in the trunk. Stolen from the FBI. And a bank transfer that would show she'd paid for them. She held her speed as steady as she could until the patrol car passed and she sang along about some dude who thought he was hot shit. She did it badly, but enjoyed the slowing of her heart when the officer looked over at her, then back to the road as he passed.

She was so close.

After Bobby dropped the lab stuff off, she'd waited a tense and boring half an hour before grabbing her things. Calling for the bellhop to take her bags down to valet was as nerve-racking as having the state trooper behind her. But in that hotel, carrying her own bags—all four of them—would have raised more eyebrows. Then she'd hit the road.

She stopped on the shoulder as soon as she was out of town and re-packed everything. So she could grab one bag that held all the bones, the papers, the pictures and her one change of clothes and overnight kit. Thirty minutes farther down the road, she stopped at the bed and breakfast she'd made a reservation at. Then GJ hauled in her one bag and played tourist, keeping her new valuables too close.

This morning, she'd suffered through a polite and wonderful breakfast. Her things were farther away. The room unattended. But who would go search her things? It didn't make any sense, so she covered her nerves by lingering over a cup of coffee with the owner.

After that, she said a kind goodbye with what she hoped was an utterly forgettable smile and hit the road again. She had passed Peoria, Illinois a little ways back, then Farmington, past A4 Junior High where some of her summer friends had attended. At last she turned into the long drive to her grandfather's house, though "house" was a loose term.

Her grandfather was a long-tenured professor of anthropology in Chicago. The private college paid well, if the house was anything to go by. Her current prospects weren't as good, maybe due to the university climate.

GJ climbed out of the rental car and grabbed the suitcase she'd repacked. Later she could come back for the spare clothing, her actual things, but she was keeping the stolen goods close. It sucked, because the bag was big and the entry was up a flight of stairs. Sorting through her many keys, she plucked one and opened the door to the side entry on the apartment.

The place was dark, stale. *Good.*

No one had been in here for a while. She'd need to go into the main house and say hello to the staff. She could lay low here for a while. Maybe even cobble together some excuse to go down into her grandfather's own lab, into the back rooms. Into the drawers and cases he'd shut her out of. She was still pissed about it. Pissed enough to take bones. Pissed enough to use one of his former students, now Agent Rander, as a thief for her cause. That had been bad. She almost regretted it.

But no going back now.

She stashed the suitcase in the back of the closet, pushing the few hanging clothes she'd left here in front of it. She would get the other bags later. They now held the clothing from her trip. Her camping gear, the ghillie suit. The gun.

Pushing through the door that connected to the main house, she went on a hunt to find someone she recognized. Eventually she found someone in the kitchen.

"Sally!"

From the jolt and the hand to the heart, Sally was more than surprised to hear her own name shouted from behind.

"I'm so sorry." GJ came around in front of the woman with a smile and was immediately enveloped in a big hug. Big enough to nearly crush her.

It took almost half an hour to catch up. GJ talked about school. About her professors and her dissertation. Sally talked about her grandson, Wilson. She talked about "Dr. Marks," GJ's grandfather, and his recent trip.

GJ was just taking it to heart, happy that it sounded like he'd be gone for a while, when she heard other footsteps. Footsteps that she knew well.

"GJ!" he yelled out in surprise. "You're here."

She loved him. But her heart sank.

ELERI HIGH-STEPPED THROUGH THE SNOW. At least it was shallower than last time. She could tell because she wasn't breathing heavily after just a few miles of walking.

She was the middle of the chain this time, with Walter taking point and Donovan at the rear. Walter had been back here to case the place and was taking them through an alternate route. They'd ridden snowmobiles in as far as they could and then went the rest of the way on foot. It was faster but there was still time for her mind to wander.

She'd dreamed of the house again. Of the woman sewing feathers and ribbons onto the doll. This time she wore a yellow dress. Still the old woman didn't speak. It wasn't her grand-mère. She knew that—she *knew* it, even if the woman had no face. Not that she could see.

Eleri's feet were getting cold. Her fingers had had enough of this damn weather. And she didn't like leaving what little they had back at the hotel room. But hiding in plain sight was really their best option. So they had a mid-level place with cameras and internal entrances to each of the rooms. They made sure the little amount they'd rescued was in the central room of the three they had. That the only attaching room was keyed to them, too. Walter jacked the locks, so if anyone tried to go past the "Do Not Disturb" signs, they would find they couldn't. They were also on the fourth floor. Eleri sighed, sucking the cold air into her lungs. They had done what they could.

She almost ran into Walter's back when the woman stopped abruptly. One finger went into the air, signaling the agents to stop behind her. Walter whispered, "He's here."

Eleri's brain snapped into sharp focus. She scanned the surrounding area, but saw nothing. She breathed in slowly, taking in what she could, despite the fact that Donovan would be much better at it than she.

That thought was answered by her partner almost instantly. Having inhaled, just as she did, he said, "He is."

Tapping him on the sleeve, just hard enough to get his attention through all the layers, she asked, "Is he the only one?" For a few long minutes, Donovan didn't answer. He tested the wind. Turned to face a different direction, did it again. Eventually, he said, "Yes. Just Eight-twenty."

Walter was checking out the area, looking at the front of the building, the side they were facing. Eleri knew what she was looking for, but she didn't quite know Walter's methods. Walter motioned them forward, and Eleri followed.

Cautiously, they made their way to the doorway. The area in front of the building was open, the trees falling away the closer they got. Though she was looking everywhere, she didn't see it coming.

Inside of a breath, she went from being the middle of the chain, to being on her side on the ground. Only a half-moment too late did she register the hit to her side, the bulldozer-like weight of the man who'd taken her down.

His surprise worked in his favor. He grabbed her as she went down, rolling with her even as she fought to be free of the large, strong hands that held her tight.

Her knees smacked the earth, shooting pain up her legs, down to her toes. Though she got her arms underneath herself, to push up against the earth, she was yanked upward.

A thick arm wrapped her neck and upper shoulders, putting pressure just below her windpipe. She was jerked backward against the broad chest, her brain only then registering what she'd seen. The blur had been Eight-twenty, and he'd singled her out of the line.

"She's my shield!" he said it loudly, to Walter and Donovan, now both standing with guns drawn at him. Or more accurately *at her*, because Eight-twenty was behind her, his large arm rested on her shoulder, a semi-automatic handgun big enough to be a .45 aimed at her partner and special ops hire. He said it again in three other languages, as though he hadn't figured out yet what they spoke, or maybe what their native tongue was, what they would need in times of duress. He yanked her back again, her neck jolting.

Eleri pulled her hands up, grasping at the forearm across her throat, realizing that again, it was bare. She tugged against it to no avail. That was when it hit her.

This asshole had pegged her because he picked her as the weakest link. *Fuck him.*

Eleri looked at Donovan and Walter, knowing that they saw, even though neither gave a single eye blink to acknowledge her. She mouthed the words, "I've got this."

She'd already set it up. Rolling with him, grasping at his forearm as if she had no idea how to defend against such a rudimentary hold. He was a good fighter, a big guy, but not that well trained. She was taking a slow breath in to ready herself when he yanked back again and she got pissed.

Reaching her hands around his forearms wasn't easy, but she didn't need to completely encircle them, she just needed a few key spots. *Got it!*

Screw "applying pressure," she dug in the tips of her fingers. They were covered in leather gloves or she would have gone with fingernails. She hit the nerve ganglion just below his elbow and the bones on the back of his hand.

Eight-twenty offered her only a grunt of surprise as his grip on her suddenly failed him.

With his thin shirt, he didn't bulk up like she did. Her clothing would minimize the damage she could do, but his light clothing would help him feel it. Without a windup, she threw her elbow into his lowest rib and heard a crunch. She hoped she broke it. Weakest link? *Fucker.*

She wasn't done either. The loosened grip, the distance she'd put between their torsos—she took advantage of it. Her back was still to him. The hand holding the gun had stayed aimed at her friends while she hit him. So she grabbed it with both hands, pulled forward on his arm while pushing her shoulder back for leverage and tucked the gun downward, throwing him over her own puny shoulder and onto the ground.

It was Eleri on her feet then. Eight-twenty should have been on his back, but he rolled right up, pushing her back.

He stood, gun aimed at her, Eleri standing between his gun and her partners. He was still trying to use her as a shield. But he was close.

Eleri felt the flare of anger as she looked him in the eye. He flinched. She took advantage.

Using the palms of both hands, she clapped his gun hold in a scissor hit, breaking the straight line of his wrist and aiming the gun away from her. But she didn't stop the movement; her hands followed through, leaving his with no option but to drop the gun. In a move she'd practiced a thousand times, she caught it.

With only the motor-memory of practice, the gun was in her grip, aimed at him. "On your knees."

His chest heaved, his eyes flaring at the gravel in her voice. She hadn't expected it, but she felt it, the force behind her anger.

She heard the clicks of heavy plastic and metal as Walter and Donovan came around either side, backing her up. They held their own guns on him now.

Slowly, Eight-twenty lowered himself to his knees.

For a moment, they all stood there, the three of them watching him for any twitch. Eight-twenty breathed heavily, looking wary, angry.

Walter must have decided the two feds had the man under control because she turned to give Eleri the once-over. Barely glancing her way, Eleri experienced her own jolt of shock at the fear/bewilderment that laced the usually unflappable soldier's expression.

Walter opened her mouth. Closed it. Then opened it again. She whispered, "Your eyes."

Eleri blinked. *What?*

Eight-twenty looked up at the sky. He said something in Chinese. Then Russian, then Spanish, which was when Eleri caught it. Her breath hitched. Then he said it in English.

"Do not bury me with them."

23

Donovan took a deep breath as he felt for the first time the way his ribs had changed. He hadn't noticed when he did it.

Eight-twenty kneeled on the frozen ground in just jeans and a long-sleeved T-shirt, his hands laced behind his head. He was under control, his threat diminished. Eleri had been in between Eight-twenty and the two of them the entire time. There had been nothing he could do. Eleri had it under control.

Donovan didn't.

He'd started morphing at the sign of threat. Eleri's eyes had flashed into that black-zone thing they'd started doing. She had something else going on there, something even she wasn't aware of. But whoever was fighting her saw it, and it scared them. Whether the edge she had was fear or more, Donovan didn't know.

What he did know was that he'd seen the fight and started to change. He rocked back on his heels, noticing his legs had partly flexed. The tendons had pulled his ankles up, leaving him standing on his toes. His fingers had flexed in and his jaw pushed out.

Donovan rolled his shoulders now, putting his bones and tendons back into human place. He wondered if Eight-twenty had seen anything. Then he had a second thought.

Back into place, he stepped forward. "Can you change?"

Eight-twenty shrugged. He hardly moved. Donovan blinked.

Something was off. The man set his hands on top of his head, not laced behind his neck as most people did because they saw it on TV. Eleri told him to kneel, but he'd automatically put his hands on his head . . . as though he'd been put in this position before.

"Can you change? Lynx? Polar bear?" Donovan had never heard of that before. He knew of the Lobomau—the gangs of people like him running in the streets of the cities. But he'd never heard of any other animal shapes. This man was part lynx, part polar bear. Small parts, yes, but . . .

Donovan's head pounded and spun. Was he part wolf? Genetically? He'd tested his full genome, looking for odd genes, but he hadn't tested against animal matches.

Eight-twenty shook his head.

"What do you do?" Donovan asked, only then realizing he was still holding his gun, almost gesturing with it. He'd been taught skills to counteract that tendency, but they must have failed him in the moment as his head swam with staggering thoughts. He pushed his focus back to the matter at hand. He could run his own blood tests later.

Eight-twenty's answer surprised them. "I survive."

Eleri stepped back, her own gun never wavering. She was far more trained than he was.

Knowing that El and Walter had the situation contained, Donovan re-holstered his gun. Walking around behind the man, he let his physician's brain take stock.

Eight-twenty was big. He was tall, stocky, slightly hairier than normal. But there was more.

Looking at the hair on the man's arms, Donovan recognized his own attributes. The hair didn't look human. His finer eyesight saw that the shaft of each hair was thicker than normal. Also, the hair was pale, like the small amount on his head. But as Donovan examined it, he saw that it wasn't blond. It was just pale—whiter, silvery, the mid-range color of an animal trying to blend into the landscape here.

Under his skin was a layer of fat, not normal on a man with his musculature. His shape and development would indicate a very low body fat, but Donovan saw it in the curve of the arm, even in his legs under the jeans. Eight-twenty's stockiness wasn't just bone and sinew, it was also fat.

Though he was on his knees, though his muscles were lax, Donovan had seen what he was capable of, the speed and agility he could work with. Almost like a lynx . . . or a polar bear.

Standing in front of him, not truly sure what Eight-twenty was capable of, Donovan leaned down. "Where do you live?"

"Here." His voice was strong. He answered in English, though that was reasonable given that Donovan was asking in English.

"Here, Michigan?" On second thought of the DNA results, Donovan asked again. "Here, the US?"

Eight-twenty looked confused. "Here. Here, Axis."

"You grew up at Axis?" Donovan was walking around the man, surely intimidating him. He was being held at gunpoint. He was being questioned outside, in the snow, on his knees. His answers were untrustworthy at best, but Donovan couldn't stop. "In that building?"

Eight-twenty nodded.

Eleri and Walter stood back, guns aimed, letting him know that the questions were his to ask.

"When did you leave?"

Again he looked confused. "I didn't." He shrugged awkwardly, his hands still flat against his head. "I'm still here."

Donovan was almost as confused as the man was. Though he considered "man" was possibly a term best applied loosely. It took a moment to gather his next question.

"When did they leave?"

There was a pause. A moment where his gaze darted side to side then up to the sky. "Who?"

"The others." Donovan didn't have names for them, but there had clearly been other people here. A while ago.

"Which others?" Eight-twenty's eyes no longer darted but looked now at Donovan in a way that made it clear he thought Donovan had no idea what he was asking about.

Sadly, he was correct.

Donovan didn't know what he didn't know. He glanced to Eleri, Walter. Neither seemed to have a direction for this. Neither offered their own questions.

Eleri's breathing had changed back to normal. Her eyes were their usual unusual shade of green. Her skin tone had reverted back to its normal mixed-African/Pilgrim coloring. There was nothing about her that was normal, except that she was her normal self now. Calm, collected, badass.

Donovan did the only thing he could, he fudged. "Tell us about Axis."

This seemed to confuse Eight-twenty. "It's a building."

Donovan frowned. That didn't match what he'd just been told, what he'd found. This interrogation wasn't working. Eight-twenty either didn't understand or he didn't want to say, or maybe even both. They were all standing out here in the cold. Though there was less snow than before, it was still barely above freezing temperature. It was bothering him a little. The weather was chilly. To Walter and Eleri, it was clearly cold, though Walter was hiding the discomfort better than his

Southern belle partner. Not that Eleri was anything other than professional, but the occasional flexing of her fingers and twitching of her feet gave away that her toes were cold. Eight-twenty seemed to feel none of it.

"Should we head back to the Bureau?" Donovan asked the women. He didn't think that was a good idea, but he wanted to see the reaction.

Again, Eight-twenty looked confused. "Bureau?"

"FBI. Federal Bureau of Investigation," Donovan clarified, though the explanation only seemed to upset the man.

"No. No government. No military." He shook his head, dropped his hands and started to stand up. Apparently an involuntary reaction, because the moment Eleri and Walter jerked to jab their guns at him again, he saw them and sank back to his knees in the snow. "No government!"

Donovan's heart twisted alongside his brain. None of this made sense. The man didn't understand that "the Bureau" meant FBI but he disliked government. He didn't seem to understand that they were feds. Though they hadn't identified themselves that way.

Since NightShade gave them legitimate FBI badges and access to all the Bureau, other agents knew them as FBI agents. But NightShade didn't operate under Bureau directives. They didn't have to identify themselves upon contact. They also had the occasional kill order. Very un-FBI. Donovan was grateful that this case didn't have a standing kill. Still, it was weird as fuck and getting dangerous to boot.

"Inside the Axis building then?" At least they'd be out of the wind. They could sit. Pretend to have a civilized inter-rogation.

They all looked to each other before escorting Eight-twenty through the main door. The way they broke the pristine covering of a new layer of snow, and since it hadn't snowed here in four days, Donovan knew one of two things. Eight-twenty wasn't going inside the building on his own, or he was using some alternate entrance.

Donovan let Eleri get ahead of him, let her push Eight-twenty forward, get him seated. Donovan held back and asked Walter, "Is there an alternate way in here? Is he using it?"

"Old tracks under a window on the ground floor. Could be him. Might have been the woman in the ghillie suit." Walter pitched her voice so it wouldn't carry.

So he'd asked but learned approximately nothing.

Eight-twenty sat, his hands clasped in front of him, his size dwarfing the plastic chair in spite of the fact that it was sturdy and adult-sized. Donovan pulled out his own chair, sliding it directly across from the man, letting Eleri and Walter come up on either side of him. True to form, Eleri sat but didn't put away her sidearm. Walter stood. Eight-twenty had nowhere to go.

Still, he bartered.

"We can ask each other questions?"

Eleri agreed rapidly, too rapidly for Donovan to stop her. He thought to himself, this guy could ask, but they wouldn't necessarily answer. He started.

If the guy lived here now, then what was the story behind that? "Tell us about Axis. When did you first come here?"

There was another pause, yet another look of confusion, before he answered. "I've always lived here."

Donovan frowned, pulled his seat closer, adding to the intimacy of the situation. The quiet of the room, the stillness of his partners, his own nodding head helped. He let his confusion show, purposefully building trust. Interrogation was a skill Eleri had been born with. She swore she'd found out what kind of engagement ring, size, and perfect proposal for a college friend without ever alerting her that she was on recon from the boyfriend-soon-to-be-fiancé. Donovan was certain she'd passed interrogation courses at Quantico without ever showing up for class. He, on the other hand, studied the nuance, the science of connection, and practiced having the questions roll off his tongue.

The man in front of him was an animal. Of sorts. He was literally part lynx and definitely more than a little feral. This was one of the very few times Donovan should be in charge of the questions. He was going to do his best. "Always? You were very small when you moved here? Born here? Or you just lived here a really long time?"

Blinking followed. Eyes darting with thought. The big man was wary, thinking about his answers. Donovan had seen intelligence and calculation with previous answers. This time the confusion was either pure or the man could add "actor" to his resume.

"I don't know. I've never lived anywhere else that I can remember." Seeming to find some peace in that answer, he cut Donovan off before the next question formed. "Why did you take my friends?"

"Your friends?" This time it was Donovan who was confused. "I haven't seen anyone else."

Except the woman in the ghillie suit. But he meant he'd seen no one else like Eight-twenty.

"They aren't alive anymore." The words were calm, almost cold.

Donovan looked at Eleri, sensing her confusion. Then he asked, "The bones?"

Eight-twenty nodded.

"When did they die?" Donovan had lost all control over his questioning. Eleri would have run it better, but he was sure as hell getting some interesting shit.

"Last year."

"You left them out there?" Donovan asked. A nod was his only answer, so he asked another question. "You let them rot?"

"I didn't want to bury them. No more graves."

"There are more graves?" Donovan asked before the words could be stopped or even thought about.

Eight-twenty nodded, but didn't elaborate.

"Where?" Donovan pushed. Luckily, despite the force, Eight-twenty answered. He pointed, toward the northwest corner of the building.

Donovan's eyes flicked to his right, seeing that Eleri was taking mental note. Taking a deep breath, Donovan tried to calm his nerves. The skeletons were this man's friends, though whether that was real or delusion Donovan couldn't tell.

After a moment, he asked a question, "What were their names?"

He wondered. They had family names from Las Abuelas. Had they kept them?

"Victor."

"Last name?" Donovan pressed, though "Victor" didn't strike him as particularly Argentinian.

Eight-twenty shook his head no. "Victor," he repeated, then said, "One-ninety-two. Charlie. Seven-thirty-seven. Five-sixty-three."

Donovan's thoughts stuttered. There were three sets of bones—*three*—but Eight-twenty listed five names. Well, "names" was a very strange determination for what seemed to be more a code. And it matched the military alphabet and numerical coding Eleri had found on the empty folders.

"What's your name?"

"Eight-twenty," He answered. Stone sober. No equivocation.

His name was not a name and it was tattooed on his arm.

This little sit-in inside the Axis building wasn't going to cut it. "We should go into town. Somewhere warm."

"No." Eight-twenty looked spooked.

"Just to our hotel. Not the Bureau," Donovan countered, trying to quell the reaction he saw blooming. So he changed tactics, shifted the conversation to throw Eight-twenty off track. "We checked your DNA."

"NO!"

He stood then, faster than Donovan could follow.

Walter, already on her feet, had her gun out in time to have it knocked out of her hand. The chair Eight-twenty had been sitting on swung in a perfect arc in his grip. It followed through after knocking the gun out of Walter's hand and past Donovan's face. The feet swiped him, missing by mere inches because of his own fast reflexes.

Even as the metal arced by his face, Donovan put the pieces together—the nerves, the twitching, all of it. He was repositioning to stand and defend himself.

That brilliance of hindsight, the flash of certainty, it was the last thing he thought before he saw the chair connect with Eleri's head.

24

E leri groaned. The world blinked into bright blown-
out images then faded away. She sighed, feeling the
movement inside her head. When she blinked again,
the light invaded all her senses and this time she squeezed her
eyes to shut it out.

She reached her hand up to her head, remembering that
she'd taken a hit, but not from what.

Her head was wrong. There was a lump on the side—a big,
leather lump. Eleri blinked again, and this time the darker
image in front of her became Walter. Her eyes closed and
opened on their own and this time she put the pieces together.

"She's waking up," Walter shouted out.

Eleri was alert enough to figure out that she was probably
talking to Donovan. And probably not actually shouting. He'd
escaped the swing of the chair, and she hoped he'd run off after
Eight-twenty—whose name was apparently Eight-twenty.
"Donovan?"

"Hey, El." He leaned into her line of sight, disappointing
her.

"You didn't go after him," she accused.

"Well, El, you were out cold. So I stayed with you." He offered half a grin.

"Walter stayed. You should have gone after him."

"Well, since I'm a physician and we don't have any equipment out here to monitor you for brain injury or anything, it seemed the prudent choice that I stay." His words and his tone were even.

"Whatever." She rolled away, but immediately regretted it. Only then did she realize that Walter was holding packed snow to the side of her head. She tapped on the hand and felt Walter pull away. Some of the snow stayed on her head. She reached up and touched it, knocking the rest of it away.

"Graves." She muttered it. "Graves." Why was she asking about graves? Yes. "We need to go find those graves he said were on the northwest side of the building."

"No. We need to backtrack out of this frozen hell," Donovan countered with a snarky smile on his face.

"No. If we do that we have to come back here again. That's really the last thing I want. We do it now. We're already here. There's plenty of day left." *Right?* She didn't ask that out loud though, just looked out the windows to see that there was enough light and she was probably on track.

"We need to get back." Walter said, though her voice didn't have the conviction that Donovan's did.

"No, we don't." Eleri stood and fought to look normal. "I have my personal physician with me. I'll be fine." She headed toward the doors, thinking it was harder to stay upright and be normal than she felt. But she really did not want to come back out here again. "Let's go find those graves."

This time it was Walter who stopped her. "How will we find them? There's still seven inches of snow on the ground. Not that we would find them now. They may be covered over already with leaves, new growth, who knows?"

"Donovan knows." Eleri smiled at her, feeling the pull of

the facial expression in her temples. It hurt like a bitch, but she didn't want to let it show.

"Donovan?"

"He can smell it." *Ohhhh.* Maybe she shouldn't have said that. If he was mad, she was going to claim traumatic brain injury. "Right, Donovan?"

When Walter looked up at him, he nodded. "I can smell it."

"Like a cadaver dog," Eleri added, thinking again that the best bet was to just keep her mouth shut. *Traumatic Brain Injury*, she repeated to herself inside her clearly damaged brain. That part she wasn't saying out loud. She looked up to Donovan who was shrugging and nodding at Walter.

"Go change. We'll wait here. Then we can find the graves." Eleri instructed him, still feeling as if her neurons weren't working quite that well. But Donovan went.

She was touching the side of her head to check her wound as he rounded the corner away from her. The lump under her fingers was tender. It oozed and when she pulled her hand away, she saw the red of blood on her fingertips. At least they had their kits. Eleri pulled out gauze and held it to her head until he returned. Applying pressure only hurt her, but she did it anyway.

The wolf trotted up to her, looking from her to Walter. Eleri, too, looked to Walter to see how she was reacting.

The Marine leaned back a little, though she didn't actually take a step back. Donovan sat in front of her and lifted one front paw, waiting for her to acknowledge him.

Walter's lips twisted, then she cracked a laugh.

Donovan then turned to Eleri and walked past her. With her hand to her head, she followed, letting him out the door.

The cold hit her cut, but she ignored it.

"The bags?" Walter asked her. There were two. Eleri had planned ahead, knowing there were times when Donovan might need to change, and she would have to carry both the bags.

"Give me one." Eleri turned, her hand to her head. "Also, we should go get his clothes. Don't want to leave things here, just in case."

Walter looked at her, eyes heading up and down, her mouth twisting. "I'll carry both."

"No, it's fine, I—"

"I'll carry both." Walter shouldered each of them easily. "You just get the clothes."

"I was going to put them in the bag," Eleri deadpanned, but Walter's ponytail bobbed in her wake. She left Eleri to dive into the other room and grab the folded pile of clothing. Next she was out the door into the open air, tracking Walter who was tracking Donovan.

An hour later, they had to quit. There was nothing out here.

Eleri had long since let go of her head wound. She wasn't sure what she looked like, probably like she'd emerged from a battle.

A series of sharp barks came from behind a stand of trees. Eleri's head snapped up.

She bolted for the sound. Even with the packs on her back, Walter passed her quickly. Eleri ran, the steady thud of her feet matching the one in her head. It felt like it was going to split, but she didn't stop running.

Another sound, this one deep and growling, came again, closer.

It was Donovan and it sounded like a fight.

Despite the head wound, Eleri's mind raced. Had he encountered Eight-twenty again? Or one of the others he'd named? Victor? Seven-thirty-seven?

And what were they?

She imagined Donovan bitten down on an arm or a leg, but

she knew what Donovan was. Ultimately, she had no clue what Eight-twenty was. Only that he wasn't completely human.

DONOVAN BIT INTO THE ARM, feeling his canines pierce the skin. Warm blood ran in a coppery sluice over his tongue, the metallic tang telling him he'd gone further than he intended. He let out another growl from low in the back of his throat and held on.

He could hear Eleri's footsteps, heavier than normal. For a moment he was distracted, the physician diagnosing the head injury. Walter's steps were lighter, more measured, faster. But he needed Eleri. Walter was new to this. She didn't understand. As new as he was, he and Eleri had a shorthand. He growled again.

As he tugged back on the arm, he inhaled. This man was like Eight-twenty. He didn't smell right. He had feral under-tones. Unlike Eight-twenty, who had meticulous hygiene, this guy had unwashed overtones. Sweat, dirt, anger, fear, all fed into Donovan's senses. Eight-twenty was the alpha. This man was the beta.

He pled, but quit fighting back. "Please, don't hurt me."

Donovan wished he could tell the man that he wouldn't. Eleri would be here soon. She'd tell him. He just had to hang on.

Her footsteps got closer. He could hear her breathing. Smell her. Smell Walter, even as he heard her come to a studied and rapid halt behind him. Walter was reassurance, a backup. Eleri's stumbling steps—despite her injury and his worry—were comfort. Bone deep. Friendship. His side. No matter what.

He didn't have time to contemplate that thought. She was already talking.

"He's mine. He'll let you go. Just answer a few questions."

Donovan stood still. It was exactly the opening he'd been waiting for. But the man tugged again, fear in his eyes. Donovan bit down harder. Just a little bit, he dug in and held his ground. Growled.

Blood ran another trickle and Donovan winced. This man was hairier than Eight-twenty. Not as strong.

"Stop." Eleri's voice cut the air. He heard the *snck* of Walter's gun coming into the equation, then a whisper from Eleri. "Wait."

Donovan felt as much as heard the change in the man. The alteration in his breathing, the change in pressure, the way his eyes darted.

"Call off your dog."

"Answer a few questions and we'll let you go," Eleri countered. Then, without waiting for his consent, she started asking. "What's your name?"

"Victor. Let me go."

"Thank you, Victor. Where do you live?"

"Here. Let me go." He tugged again, but Donovan gave no ground.

"You live here? At the Axis building?" She sounded confused. Eleri had a plan, questions at the ready. The subtle shifts in her tone told him she was getting pulled off track.

"Around here. Let me go." The second sentence was more forceful.

"Were you raised at the Axis building?" Her tone was softer, fishing.

"Yes." He didn't add the command. Victor was resigned, waiting. He'd make a move any moment now. Donovan held, quietly waited.

"Thank you, Victor." Eleri stepped back, reducing her threat to him. From the corner of his eye, Donovan saw her wave Walter back. "Let go."

He felt it as soon as he heard it and let go.

Victor disappeared into the woods in seconds, blending seamlessly with the trees and foliage. Donovan smelled him but lost visual quickly.

"Donovan." Eleri's voice turned his head. He'd heard her coming up to him, but hadn't placed the pieces together.

"Look at me." Donovan raised his head to her, seeing the long wooden cotton swab as she pulled it and waved it at him.

Understanding, he opened his mouth and let her swab it.

"That's got his DNA, too, right?" Walter asked, speaking for the first time.

"Yes," Eleri answered, not breaking eye contact with him. She knew she'd have to wait to find out what he knew. He couldn't talk like this. "But we know his genetic code. We'll rule him out. What's left will be Victor."

Walter nodded, but Donovan was wondering if Eleri's thoughts had taken the same turn as his: should his blood be put through a matching program that might determine just what other genes he had? You wouldn't find them if you didn't specifically look. While he'd looked in the past, there were always advances being made. For a moment, he was afraid what it might turn up.

Had he been in human form, he might have said something about not running the sample. But he couldn't and didn't. Instead she offered water and turned back the way they'd come. "He grew up in that building."

Walter nodded. "It looked that way from my recon earlier. As though a handful of children had boarding rooms there, classrooms, more."

Eleri looked at Donovan, keeping him in the conversation despite the fact that he couldn't participate. He listened with one ear to the words, the other toward the woods. Though he'd heard "Victor" crashing away from them, the sounds were gone now. Either he'd gone to ground or he was too far away for Donovan to pick up.

He smelled the sweet scent of rotting leaves under the layer of snow. He could smell that the snow was old, nothing fresh for almost a week. The trees had the faint whiff of hibernation, and under his feet the soft loam of the earth squished between the pads of his front paws. What had been palm, heel of his hand, and finger prints were now paw and rough pad that both scraped at the soil and felt it.

"We need to get back to the Axis building. We only have so much daylight to burn." She turned back to Donovan. "Are there any graves out here?"

He didn't nod or shake his head, though he could. He didn't smell anything. Decay brought a faint tickle in the back of the nasal cavity, a rough and twisted overtone with a faint sweetness underneath it. The sweetness lingered regardless of the state of decay. He'd smelled it on the bones in the lab, despite the fact they'd sat in the sun for so long. One set was almost fully bleached and still a slight trace clung and tickled at the edge of his senses. He could smell it, sliding up through the loose soil of a grave, but he didn't smell it here.

Donovan turned and headed back toward the Axis building. He could change there, put his clothes back on. Get the hell out of the cold weather that gave up secrets only to take them back.

Behind him, he heard Eleri pick up one of the packs this time, lifting part of the burden from Walter. Donovan couldn't carry any of it, not like this, so he didn't argue about who did. The scent of Eleri's wound had changed; it was clotting, healing, not great yet, but at least getting better.

He trotted through the snow, for a moment imagining how fast he could get back to civilization if he were free to run in this form.

When they came to the northwest corner of the building, Donovan stopped and looked up at the second-story windows. Eleri stopped behind him.

"There's a door on this side," Walter offered up, then led them to another entrance. "There are only two of them. Southeast and northwest."

The snow around the other doorway was untouched, Donovan noticed. Yet someone had been in the building.

This doorway was locked and it took a moment for Walter to pull a pick set and jiggle the tumblers until it opened. It would have been easier to shoot the lock or the hinges, Donovan knew. He'd been taught how, surely so had Walter. The advantage came from being able to put it back as you'd found it, though they could do nothing about the steps they left in the snow.

Inside, he picked up scent and went off on his own. Eleri and Walter could follow as they chose, but as he explored the new portion of the building, he finally had something. A body had been in here. Quite some time ago, but the decay couldn't quite be washed out of linoleum. No one here had even tried, just let the dust settle over the trail left behind.

It ran under the door at the entrance to the courtyard. Donovan sat. Waited.

"Here?" Eleri asked though Walter was already picking the lock.

As soon as the door was just slightly opened, he pushed his way through and into the courtyard where the scent grew. Eleri pushed past him, now seeing with her eyes what he'd seen with his nose.

The lump in the snow was revealed by the melt in a way that hadn't been obvious at all the first time they'd come, when the snow had been deeper. A human form was clearly outlined.

Donovan inhaled the courtyard air, detecting others under the soil. Had he been able, he would have frowned. Were they younger? The smell wasn't quite right, again.

He wished he had the capacity to tell Eleri, but that would take a handful of minutes and a chance to change. He flicked his ears, almost like blinking, but they twitched with the trace of a sound.

Turning his head, he aimed his ears, straining, then he found it.

Footsteps.

Two sets.

He turned toward the doorway they'd come through, letting loose a low growl, alerting the others.

"What is it?" Eleri asked.

But Donovan couldn't answer.

25

G J spent twenty-four hours waiting for her grandfather to leave the house. Luckily, he always had another speaking engagement. Dr. Murray Marks was at the top of his field. It had both helped her and hurt her.

She'd eaten breakfast next to him that morning, earlier than she would have liked to get up. Sally made omelets with toast from homemade sourdough bread. GJ could gain a ton here, but she couldn't refuse Sally or her food.

She'd kissed her grandfather goodbye, at last done with having to pretend she wasn't about to do what she was about to do. With Sally in the kitchen and the gardeners outside, she was surrounded but not watched. GJ headed down the hallway.

The last time she came this way, she'd found something. Something that made her recent skeletons look familiar.

It was an old house with long, dark-paneled hallways. Red Turkish carpet lined the long walk and original art hung on the walls. She was pretty sure her grandfather had bought the whole place lock, stock, and barrel. Though he knew his history, he was hardly an art connoisseur. He would have chosen something different if he'd done it himself.

GJ passed the door to the library. That room, he'd stocked himself. So many forensic texts, histories, anthropological data sets. A good number of them he'd written himself. She passed Sally's office and his. Several other closed, heavy doors held other rooms—storage in a few, a small office that he'd given her, lastly a room where he displayed skeletons and bone bits he'd been allowed to curate over the years.

She was heading to the last door. It opened onto a small closet with a staircase to a cinder block basement. Her grandfather had taken her down there when she was a child. He'd shown it to her, told her that one day he wanted to fill it with the things he collected.

GJ had gone on his archeological digs with him. He collected things for the room. She'd seen the pot sherds, the bone tools, the pieces of writing that he photographed, framed, and deciphered. He photographed ancient graves and drew conclusions about the people and their customs. He was called out to death scenes, and she would tag along on the tamer ones —old skeletons found, bones in the lab used to ID missing people. He'd started her on this road, given her the love of the puzzle, and here she was, trying to figure out the latest puzzle: him.

He'd slowly filled the room with antiquities. He'd showed her a few.

Then a small number of years ago, he'd locked up. It occurred to her that he had a room to display his finds. He had other rooms. He had money to be his own museum these days. So why were these things in the basement?

Three months ago, she'd picked the lock.

She'd seen many of the same things she'd seen as a kid. They were down here still. Why had they not been rotated into the displays? They were fascinating pieces of history.

There were new things there, too. Full human skeletons. Now, as a grad student in human forensics, GJ knew he probably shouldn't have them. Professors were allowed to keep some of the skeletons on loan as teaching tools, but she'd never seen anyone else with a home collection.

Then she'd noticed the skeletons were *wrong*. The rib cages an odd shape. The scapula on the very long side of normal. The femurs thick. Too thick. On the skull, the front of the face was in several pieces, as though the bones had never fused.

He had three like that.

She'd left. She'd searched the literature for more like these. But she'd found nothing. GJ asked subtly leading questions of her professors, but had gotten nowhere. She'd talked to her grandfather's longtime assistant, Shray, and met a brick wall.

Shray Menon stonewalling her was most disturbing. Until then, she'd thought maybe she was crazy. She was a student, after all. Maybe she didn't know what she'd seen, misinterpreted something normal. But the assistant's stuttered answers and his abrupt dismissal, that was what finally convinced her there was something to this.

Now she had bones from other sites. They had similar but decidedly different anomalies, if she was remembering correctly. She just needed to get in and take a look. Compare the pictures in her pocket to the bones down here.

She was reaching for the knob when she happened to tilt her face upward. That was when she saw the camera.

It aimed down the hallway, the red light blinking, telling her it was recording. Probably motion activated.

Her arm was already pulling the door open, just a little. GJ shut it. In a heartbeat, she came up with a dumb plan. Shaking her head, she acted as though she'd opened the wrong door. Then turned and looked at each of the doors in the hallway, as though she'd forgotten which one she meant to enter.

With a sigh and a self-deprecating shake, she headed to her

office where she opened the door easily and ducked inside. As she settled behind her computer, GJ wondered if there was a camera in here, too. Was she acting normal enough? When had the camera been installed?

She hadn't seen it last time she'd been here and she was always in this hallway sooner or later. Her heart pounded, she couldn't control it even though she forcefully slowed her breathing. Her fingers flew over the keyboard, searching for anomalies in bones, as it was what was on her mind, and typing on her computer in here would be normal.

But what if there was something watching her search history here?

GJ erased the search.

She leaned back in her desk chair and thought things through: Shray Menon stonewalling her questions. The locks on the door. The camera after she picked the lock. There was definitely something here.

What GJ didn't like was that her grandfather was at the heart of it.

ELERI TURNED at Donovan's growl, her mind immediately distracted from the "yes" bark Donovan had first issued. She assumed 'yes' meant that yes, there were graves here. But the growl was not about that.

The three of them froze in place, the door to the courtyard still open, Donovan facing it on all fours. He was hunched down, neck extended, fur ruffed along his spine.

Eleri pulled her gun, wondering how many times she would do this today. She didn't even have to chamber a round, it was already there. She felt a trickle along the side of her face and she wondered how she could have started it bleeding again just by pulling her gun. Though she cataloged the feeling, she ignored it.

Walter had her gun out, silently. Eleri took one step forward, as did Walter. Though she didn't hear anything—anything at all—she trusted her partner. His growl, his stare, all told her something was coming.

She waited, standing in the courtyard, unmoving, waiting. Then she heard it. Footsteps, purposefully quiet. Something heavy. Heavier than an average man.

They approached the open doorway, the door swung into the hallway where she couldn't see it. Eleri had the thought with just moments to move.

Gun raised, she bolted. Donovan didn't have the physiology to do it, but she and Walter did. She felt more than heard the other woman beside her, bolting at the same time. She saw the door move and with a burst of speed she reached it.

Just as it clicked shut.

Both Eleri and Walter ran into the closed door, having run so hard they were unable to stop in time. Gun clutched in one hand now, the other pressed hard to the metal of the door, so she could feel the vibrations as the bolt slid home.

Eleri pounded on the door once, but Walter didn't waste the effort.

"Stand back, Eames," She demanded. Eleri's brain, always churning, filed away that though Walter had sometimes called her "Eleri" it was back to "Eames" in times of strife. Always the soldier, she reverted to it easily.

Eleri stepped back. Donovan, too, his paws slowly tracking in the remaining snow in here. The courtyard was eerie with the abandoned playground gathering dirt, dust, and snow rather than children. The rust on the equipment was enough to push bad thoughts into view. Walter and her raised gun only added to it.

She fired rapidly, unconcerned with the noise. First she

took out the main lock at the handle, the bullet melting through the metal there. A second shot in almost the exact same spot attested to Walter's skill and clearly loosened door. With a few quick steps, Walter approached the door and pushed on it. It didn't open. Eleri could have told her that. She was opening her mouth to say so when she realized Walter was testing the door, finding the spot.

One step back and Walter raised her gun. Another step back and she fired at a position just above her head and right into the door frame. Despite the blast to her ears, Eleri smiled.

The door came loose and this time Walter pushed through it, leading the way with special ops precision.

Eleri would have smiled if she wasn't right behind the woman, gun aimed at the ground in front of her. Donovan brought up the rear. Unable to hold a gun, his weapon was his teeth, and Eleri didn't want him having to go there.

They made it into the hallway and followed the direction they heard the footsteps going. Because the building was a square, after the initial direction there were no choices, but they turned the corner and didn't see anything.

Without hesitating, Donovan growled low and took the lead. Though she didn't like it, Eleri let it happen. His nose went to the ground, and a soft *wuff* exited his throat. He wasn't fast, but he was thorough. Eleri trusted him.

Now their order was reversed. Eleri stayed close on Donovan's heels, wanting to read him, knowing how in a way that Walter couldn't. Walter brought up the rear, making Eleri feel safe, at least from that side.

Donovan picked up speed down the hall, his feet loping at a reasonable rate for him. Too fast for Eleri to walk. She sped up her pace and Walter did too. A close pack, they headed down the hall as quietly as possible. Then Donovan turned to a closed door and pointed his nose at it.

Breath paused, Eleri looked at it, one hand on the gun,

one hand signaling Walter to come close. Though Eleri strained her ears, she heard nothing. Still, she knew better. Without speaking, she pointed to her own ear and shook her head.

One slow bob of his head up and then down told her what she needed. Donovan heard someone in there.

Stepping even more softly, if that were possible, and using only hand signals, they lined up to kick in the door. Walter was in front this time, and she slowly, slowly reached out and turned the knob.

She must have hit resistance, because she turned her head to the side without moving her eyes from her target. She shook her head. Eleri nodded in response.

She'd done all of this on autopilot, but hitting this pause made her *feel*. Her heart was pounding. She had no idea what was on the other side of that door. If she'd be met by an animal or a bullet.

Donovan stood still at her side. His breathing stayed shallow, but focused. Walter was unreadable. Eleri forced her own breathing to shallow out, to remain under her conscious control rather than spike like it wanted to.

Walter held up one finger. Two. Eleri braced.

With two movements so rapid they were almost indistinguishable, Walter kicked the door in, leaving her hands free for her gun. Eleri was right on her six.

The man on the floor shocked her. He didn't look right. But as he stood Eleri put it together, she realized the man on the floor was a woman. She wasn't shocked at the door coming in, only at the timing.

The woman knelt in front of the room's storage closet. A trap door was open in the floor and she was pulling papers from the hole. Folders were tightly clutched to her chest. Her expression betrayed both her anger and her fear.

"Hands up," Eleri said, then repeated it in Spanish as it was the only other language she could accurately generate on the fly. The woman didn't move.

Eleri took in her arms, legs, the thickness of them, even as she didn't put up her hands. Eleri barked the command again. "Hands up."

Again, the woman didn't move.

Normally, you didn't shoot an unarmed person who wasn't moving. The woman was frozen, barely breathing, eyes wide, nostrils flaring ever so slightly.

Eleri repeated the Spanish, then waited a beat. If no one moved, nothing would happen. She let the words burst out of her, knowing the sharper, the better with the command. "Hands up. FBI."

Apparently, being told to put her hands up wasn't the issue. FBI was. The woman bolted. Folders still clutched tightly, she didn't push past Eleri as she'd expected. She went for the window.

Only then did Eleri see that it had been opened before they got there. Walter was already heading around her, trying to reach the window first. Donovan leapt straight ahead, but the woman had planned for this.

She cracked the heavy glass as she hit it but slid through the space the rotated pane had created when cranked open. She seemed to hesitate as Eleri trained the muzzle of her gun on the woman. But the hesitation was actually Donovan, managing to snag a pant leg, to hold her back when neither Walter nor Eleri had been able to.

He growled just as the sound of fabric tearing hit the air and then he tumbled backward as the tension holding him in place disappeared. Eleri burst into the fray, her hand touching hair that didn't feel quite right.

Again, the woman pushed forward, dropping the folders. For a fraction of a second, her fear was directed at the papers, manila folders, and envelopes that slipped from her grasp. She looked back at the wolf even as she scrambled forward, now barely clearing the low ledge on all fours. She hit her shin on the way out, making Eleri cringe at the crack of bone on metal.

Donovan went after her, pushing through the metal frame, using the space she'd created. But the woman pushed in on the window, forcing him back. He barely managed to get his feet inside before the sash connected with the frame.

She gathered the folders that fell in the snow on her side of the window. Some were now crushed between the metal parts of the window, some she just gave up on. Holding what she could, she disappeared into the forest and into the fading afternoon.

Walter was already on her knees, picking up the papers. Eleri holstered her weapon and asked, "What are they? What's so important?"

"Records?" Walter inflected it like a question. "Intakes. Shipments. Deliveries."

Eleri knelt down beside her, looking over manifests and listings. There was something in the coding that bothered her.

Donovan nudged her, then did it again until she noticed the single blood drop that spattered on the page she was looking at. She reached up, feeling the cut bleeding again. But she simply pushed at it, as though that would stop it. She frowned, then stopped, thinking it might pull at her cut.

"These invoices—" she waved the papers she was holding. She'd figured out what was wrong. "They're for *people*."

onovan sat on the edge of his finely upholstered but uncomfortable chair. The table in the middle of the suite surely had seen a few meals, and probably many businessmen and women working on laptops or tablets, but it likely hadn't seen this before.

He set the needle down and reached for the forceps.

The suture set was just part of his usual medical kit. He'd fully expected to use them on himself, but right now, he was just grateful he had it. Donovan pushed the needle into the skin at Eleri's temple. It was swollen both from the original injury and with the Xylocaine he'd injected. The edges looked raw even though he'd cleaned them.

"I'm only passably decent at this," He told her again.

"I know. You suture Y-cuts in dead bodies." She managed to dismiss him without moving her head in the slightest. "It's in my hair, so no one will see it."

"Thank goodness," he mumbled. He'd have been mortified if he had to see this on her face or even her arm. Stitching was a skill and one that should be kept up. He hadn't. It was a pretty crap job. He knew it even as he tied off the last stitch. "It will get the job done."

She reached up to touch it, but Donovan pulled her hand away. "Keep it clean."

He added antibiotic ointment from a portable squeeze pack. Eleri had some stretchy headband already around her neck that she pulled up and over the squares of gauze he held in place.

After tossing what was used and putting his kit back together, Donovan looked over to see Eleri talking to Walter. She was just a woman in a headband, not someone who'd recently been chasing random people in the wilderness in Michigan. Certainly not someone who did all of it while actively bleeding from a head wound.

They passed papers back and forth, organizing them into separate piles. Then, they weren't just stacking the papers, they were following by date. Two of the most intelligent and highly trained people he knew, and they were performing ridiculous clerical tasks.

He went to pick one pile up and Eleri quietly pushed his hand away and handed him a different stack. Taking them, he began thumbing through the pages.

They were invoices, just as she'd said. The shipments were all coded. "How did you figure out they were for people?"

"Look at the dates. These are birth dates, and honestly, they correspond a little too well to the dates of the Disappeared. And then look at the listings with the invoices. They don't say 'people' per se, but age, height, weight, gender. That could only be a person."

Donovan was looking. "Children. Not just people but specifically small children." He'd seen enough of them in his work as a medical examiner. Too many of them, actually. He knew what a toddler looked like by the numbers. He then fanned through other pages. "These are infants."

"Yeah." Her voice was solemn. She'd already figured it out. "Check this."

She handed him a page that made him want to vomit. It read, "Stock loss."

His heart took the hit, even though he often thought nothing could truly disturb him after the M.E.'s office. You see enough kids beaten to death or neglected to death by their parents and you had to become immune. Apparently, it had either worn off in his now almost one year with the FBI and NightShade, or it had never really been there. Maybe it was just about the numbers. He murmured, not even realizing he was doing it until he heard the sound of his own voice. "They lost over fifty percent of their *stock*."

With a deep breath to steady herself, Eleri nodded at him.

Even Walter looked a little tight around the eyes and mouth. He didn't expect anything of her, no reaction at all. So he was shocked when he actually looked at her and it seemed to make the fine muscles in her expression even tighter.

Her voice quavered as she announced, "I'm going to the restroom."

She stood quickly, pushed her chair in, and left.

So she'd been hit by it after all. It humanized her, at least. Eleri looked up as Walter walked away, but she stayed with her papers. She'd seen more than anyone knew. She'd *been there* for some of it. Seeing and feeling everything but unable to *do* anything about it.

She could handle a few invoices. Even if they were for children.

"There's a five-year span . . . so far." She pointed to the earliest date then to the latest. "That's by what I've found. It may be wider."

Pulling out the chair beside her, opposite the one Walter vacated, he asked, "Does it match?"

She only nodded. The headband and the pert hairstyle in

her shade of strawberry blond looked out of place in the midst of the horror they were finding.

He asked a follow-up question. "Given the 'stock loss,' what's your estimate on the number of kids?"

"Right now, I'm thinking thirty."

"Thirty total kids delivered there? Or thirty dead?"

She put the papers down and if she had been wearing glasses she would have pulled them off to deliver her numbers. "Given the labels, the invoices, and the percent loss, . . . thirty dead. That's by figuring we met Victor and Charlie—both of whom match the military lettering system we stumbled upon earlier."

"Which means they made it to V." He nodded. That was twenty-two. "Then the numbers."

"The letters came first." She sorted through the invoices. "These seem to match up." She handed one paper to him then another. "It looks like they didn't get assigned a letter or number until they arrived alive. So the named ones are just the ones that made it."

"Do you think the others are buried in the courtyard there?" he asked her.

In response, Eleri stared at him. "You would have a far better answer to that than I. You smelled something, and I haven't had a chance to ask you."

"Yes, graves. And yes, the smells were just a bit off. But old, so it was hard to say exactly how they were 'off.' If that makes sense." He shrugged and heard a noise behind him as Walter emerged from the bathroom.

He looked over to find a sheen on her eyes again, but no other outward signs. She must have known that they knew. She simply said, "I'm good."

"Could you tell if there were a lot of buried bodies or a few?" Eleri looked at him. She'd only been out with him when he'd found single graves before. All dogs could smell cadavers;

with the trained dogs it was just a matter of training them to alert when they smelled something specific. For the two of them, it had been about training Eleri to read what he was signaling when he couldn't talk.

"I don't know. More than one. More than two, actually. Beyond that I can't distinguish it."

Walter's expression had shifted. The sheen was gone in her eyes and she was wary of him again.

He understood. Scientifically, he was cool, interesting. But when a layperson tried to wrap their mind around it, it didn't sit well. Still didn't make it stab any less that she was looking at him that way. The day had been hard enough.

He looked her in the eye. "It's me. It's who I am. Deal or leave."

"I—" she started, but he cut her off, riding some tide he hadn't known was crashing in.

"You have metal parts. And Eleri here can read images and feelings off things she touches. She dreams other people's lives." He paused for the barest of seconds. "We've all got something. You've seen mine. Deal or leave."

Walter barely paused, then nodded. She pulled out her chair from where she'd politely pushed it in when she left and proceeded to sit down. Donovan guessed that meant she was in.

For some reason that eased the tightness in his chest more than he wanted to admit. He told himself it was good to have friends even if it also meant being exposed. That was the hard part.

Leave it to Walter to not ask the usual questions—if there was such a thing—of Eleri. She only said, "You knew the lab was ransacked before we went in."

Eleri nodded. "I saw it in flashes. Not sure how useful it is to see on the other side of a door I would have opened inside two seconds, but yes, that was how it happened."

"You didn't even touch the doorknob much. Had the person touched it, they would have had prints," Walter pointed out. "That's how you knew to have me follow the guy from Forensics."

Eleri nodded, and Donovan wished it led to more than just that he went to the fourteenth floor of one of the local nice chain hotels. Walter lost him then. While they'd gotten the listing of people staying in the hotel, with rooms on that floor, nothing had matched up to anything of interest. Over three-quarters of the rooms were rented and over half of those were just for the day. There was no telling which occupant was the one they wanted.

Donovan held onto the list in hopes that something would pan out in the future. But for now, he had nothing.

"I wonder how the numbers were chosen."

Eleri shrugged. "I'm just hoping they weren't numerical. He's eight-twenty. That's too many."

"That has to be too many," he agreed.

"By tomorrow night we should have two more DNA samples," Eleri said, changing the subject a bit.

"Are we willing to bet on whether or not we get the letter from Las Abuelas?" He stood to get a bottle of very expensive water from the fridge. He held them up in offering as Eleri held out a hand. He threw the bottle to her, and she caught it easily, more easily than a pure-bred Southern belle should have. He reminded himself she wasn't pure-bred at all. He offered another bottle to Walter.

She was turning him down when he said, "It's on the FBI."

"Well then." She held her good hand out too and caught the bottle cleanly, just as he'd expected she would.

For a moment he looked at the two of them. The three of them were a motley crew, but they worked well together. They'd gotten blood from Victor—from when Donovan bit the man—and then also just barely enough from the windowsill as the woman had left.

"And, no, not willing to bet on that," Eleri said. "Too likely. I think we'll get both."

Walter didn't ask. She kept up well on her own.

"So we have to go back tomorrow." Eleri said.

Donovan only groaned. If he never fucking saw snow again, he'd be happy.

Seeming to read his thoughts, Walter put in her two cents. "The temperature has been above freezing for a few days now. It's possible most of the snow will be gone."

"It's the middle of the winter. I'm just grateful it's not under five feet of snow." He sighed.

Suddenly, Eleri's eyes widened and she scrambled back to the papers on the table, nearly knocking over her water in the process. "Not under snow. Arizona. It's not under snow."

She held up a small stack of papers. "They shipped some of the children to Arizona."

"What?" Donovan asked her. "Was it an alternate station? Like this one? Another Axis location?"

He was looking over the pages now too. But it seemed only the pages Eleri had already sequestered mentioned Arizona.

They'd picked up the folders the woman dropped. Trying to put the files back in the correct folder when possible. But there was another stack they hadn't even gotten to. Once they'd collected the blood from the windowsill, they went into the closet and pulled out all the other files she'd been rifling through.

They purposefully hadn't sorted them in with the others. The woman pulled her stack out for some reason, and none of the three of them was willing to mix them back up until they understood what the difference was.

Donovan turned the conversation this time. "She was different. Her face was flattened, her nose broad."

"Kind of like Downs or Fetal Alcohol Syndrome," Eleri added, "but that doesn't make a lot of sense."

"Right. Downs is a possibility. But she didn't really look like she had it. If she did, it was the mildest and oddest case I've ever seen," he told her. "The nose was right, but the tilt of the eyes wasn't, the thickness of her skin didn't look right. Not Downs."

"Probably not Fetal Alcohol either," Eleri added.

Both of them were a bit surprised when Walter chimed in. "The mother was a protester. She might have been a functioning alcoholic, but even if she was, they wouldn't have given her alcohol while they waited for her to give birth. Why keep her around for the baby then give the baby trouble?"

Eleri nodded agreement. "So it *could be* Fetal Alcohol Syndrome, but not likely at all. Do you think it has to do with the hybridization?"

It took Donovan a moment, but he understood what she was talking about. The various small percentages of animal DNA that kept showing up in the full genome sequences. "I don't know that's the case, but it's possible."

Just then Eleri's phone rang.

It was almost eleven at night. Donovan smiled. "Avery?"

The look on Eleri's face stopped him. Then her voice answered him in a cold tone. "No. Westerfield."

She answered. "Hello, sir?" It took a moment. She nodded, even though he couldn't see her, even though she didn't speak. She uttered only one other word. "Yes."

Then she moved her thumb, hung up, and set the phone down.

"He said we need to send Lucy Fisher back to her own hotel room and call him back on speaker phone."

27

Once Walter was out of the room, Eleri took a deep breath and looked to Donovan.

"No time like the present," he said, deadpan.

"What's with the present?" she asked back, knowing she was actively avoiding calling their Agent in Charge. "It's eleven at night. We could have been asleep."

"Seriously? He knew Walter was not only with us but in the room." Donovan put down the water bottle he'd picked back up and set down several times in his own set of fidgeting movements. He was as nervous as she was, clearly.

"True." Eleri looked out the window. They'd left the drapes open onto the city skyline. She liked knowing they were in a populated place, not out in the open with the snow and the cougars and the weird people who didn't want to have anything to do with them but understood more than they were saying about Axis.

Even though the papers and all the problems followed them inside, there was something comforting about being ensconced in the hotel rooms. Westerfield had blown that comfortable feeling wide open. "I don't think that trick of moving small objects just by thinking about it was his only talent. He's in charge because he sees all of us."

"You should be more careful with Avery."

"Ew!" She recoiled at the thought. "That is so disturbing." Her water bottle was empty now and she chucked it at him for giving her that thought. Westerfield better not be watching their private lives. "We have to call in. He knows we're stalling."

She punched a few buttons and waited while the phone rang once. He answered with a smooth, "Good evening, agents."

"Hello." She wasn't up to using his full title. Not at 11 p.m. Not when she was still reeling somewhere inside from the invoices that said they were shipping children around the world.

"Hello." Donovan's greeting mimicked hers nearly perfectly for lack of feeling. Westerfield would run the call. He always did. All they had to do was wait.

"So you still have Lucy Fisher with you," he opened. That was a fun one.

Eleri looked to Donovan as she answered, "Yes," though she didn't really know why she did it. Obviously Westerfield already knew this.

"She followed you?"

This time she broke form. Usually she just answered him, went along on whatever path he dragged them down. "You already know she did. What do you really need to know?"

"You're working with her again." He paused, and Eleri didn't fill in the gap. She held up her hand to Donovan and stopped him from responding, too. As if he was going to just jump in and tell Westerfield everything. Ha.

Westerfield filled in what he had. "You've hired her. I see that on the paperwork. Have her doing recon again. Is she worth it?"

"She's worth twice that much," Donovan answered, making Eleri's eyebrows blink up rapidly. She agreed, but that wasn't what surprised her. It was Donovan's sudden defense. Whether that was because Lucy/Walter knew his secret or because he felt something more or because he was just tired of Westerfield yanking them around, she had no clue. She'd have to look into that. Later.

"Good to know. Give her a raise. A big one."

Well, if Eleri's eyebrows had jumped before, she was pretty sure that they left her head this time. "Did I hear you correctly, sir?"

"Yes, you did." He gave his usual beat, and she could imagine him sitting there with his forearms braced on the edge of the desk in front of him, the quarter walking silently across his knuckles, back and forth. It made Donovan's fidgeting with the water bottle positively inelegant. But she had no idea if she was making it up or if she could really see him through the distance. "You have to pay her more. More than she's worth. You fucked up."

"What?" Jesus, this job was tough. Westerfield jerking them around was only worse. "Why?"

"Because she knows about you. She followed Donovan. She was at his place during his down time, then she followed you both to Michigan *before* you hired her."

"You know all this how?" She was going to make him say it. She wanted him to admit he was spying into their lives.

"Because you hired her. She showed up on my billables. So I checked out how you hired her and paid her in the same day. Meant she was already in Michigan. So I checked her flight records."

Fuck.

That was disturbingly ordinary. And reasonable. He was, after all, a Special Agent in Charge of a full division of the FBI. A division that didn't really exist. And she had no clue who he reported to.

Feeling a little better that he wasn't spying—or maybe just

that he wasn't going to admit it—she decided to be a little more generous and cut him some slack. "Of course."

"So, I concluded that she saw Donovan in his altered state and followed you. Sounds like something she would do." Another beat of silence from Westerfield, and another heartbeat passed in her own chest. "Does she know about you, too, Eleri?"

Shit.

"Yes." She didn't add *because we basically told her.* Because the fact was, Walter was going to put it all together anyway. She was no dumb blonde. She let the one word stand as her answer with Westerfield.

"Then you have to overpay her. You have to buy her silence."

Eleri didn't like where this was going.

"And if she breaks that silence, you have to remove the problem."

Donovan stood in the courtyard of the Axis building. As himself. He didn't need to be in wolf form right now—they had huge heaters aimed at the ground, thawing it layer by layer.

He was grateful to be in his human form. Why he was colder this way was a mystery for another day. Right now, he was glad to be cooler. Right now, he was hired muscle.

He thought about his paycheck, about his job description. All the training, the classes, the practice at Quantico. Never once had he been told, "Be prepared to spend a day shoveling."

But there was no one else to do it. No one was out here except the other strange people they'd run into. And they weren't going to come help.

In fact, Eleri was hoping that the three of them being out here, digging up the graves would draw the others out. So far, they'd seen exactly no one. Not even the cougar and her cubs. Not the strange woman in the ghillie suit.

That one Donovan wanted to happen. Walter had a grudge on for that woman and if they ran into her again, Walter was going to take her down. Walter was quiet, stoic, smart as a whip, and you just didn't fuck with her.

He rammed the shovel into the ground again, glad he was in good shape. The ground was frozen and the going was very slow. Eleri was sweating; she'd taken off her jacket and pushed up her sleeves. The barely above freezing temperature was keeping them all from overheating. As a physician, he was already on the lookout for when it would try to kill them as soon as they quit.

He was working at a faster pace than Eleri. This didn't surprise him. He was a foot taller and male to boot. He should be faster. His only disadvantage was his ribs. She had her head injury—still covered neatly, this time with a knit ear-cover that she wouldn't take off because of the gauze.

It was that Walter was working faster than him, that's what got him. She was out-shoveling both of them.

"Slow down," he told her.

"Why? So you can beat me?"

Jesus, the woman was even missing a hand! She made the prosthetic work for her, that was for sure.

"No, because if you hit a grave or a body at that speed, you'll damage it. And we're collecting evidence." He rested on the handle of the shovel while he talked, feeling the cold seep in around his edges. "We're supposed to be hand digging the whole thing. With trowels at the most. Best tool is brushes and fingers."

Eleri smiled at him. "You were paying attention."

"Yes, ma'am." He'd had a little of it when he was the medical examiner. Every once in a while, he'd be called out to a partially exposed grave and work with the anthropologist or forensic specialist. But most of what he knew, he'd learned from Eleri.

"There's no way fingers and brushes are working in this frozen crap." Walter grinned at him.

It shocked him. He liked her grin. She was getting more comfortable around them and he was getting more comfortable around her. Drinks, he decided, the three of them would go out for drinks when they were back in town and clean. He and Eleri did it. They needed to include Walter this time. Just for a break. They all needed it. He shoveled out another small triangle of packed earth. "Nope. Brushes won't cut it today. Neither will trowels. But these are old, children's bones. At least, that's what we expect. We can't damage them."

With an understanding nod, Walter went back to her work but at a slower pace.

It was Eleri who first hit pay dirt. "Got something." It was quickly followed by, "Shit."

"Shit?" Both he and Walter asked at the same time and gathered round the hole Eleri was digging.

They'd started by attempting to push a pointed T-bar into the ground, searching for softer spots that would indicate a grave. The frozen ground did not give much. They were each digging in a hole suggested by what the T-bar told them. So it wasn't random.

He looked down to where Eleri was scraping at the spot, pulling dirt back off of something blue and soft. His heart clamped, wondering if it was a baby blanket of some kind, but he pushed the feeling away. There wasn't room for that here.

In another moment, he saw there was some kind of scrawl on the blue, that it was cardboard. And in another few minutes, they saw it was a shoebox. The lid was wet, breaking and crushed in on whatever was inside.

Two more minutes and they saw it was an infant. He

clamped down on stray feelings as he dropped to his knees and started the rough job of hand excavating.

Eleri and Walter stood over him. "Go. Work on other spots," he told them. "Unless you want to do this, El?"

"Nope, you can." She moved away and he heard the shovels hit the earth at almost the same time. This time though, he felt it through his knees as it rattled through the ground.

It was rough work, reaching down into the dirt, pulling it back using only small trowels. He'd prefer fingertips, but that wouldn't work in this frozen dirt. They'd brought spare work gloves for exactly this. Waterproof, thin, warm. They had plenty of extras so they could trash them as they ripped or got too wet. The job was demanding. He managed to widen the hole and reveal the set of bones.

Blue and gray shreds of old, wet cardboard clung in places that he didn't have the dexterity to pull off right now. "Come back."

"I've got another one," Walter announced. He hated it, but it was what they'd come for. He knew there were graves here.

Eleri pulled out her camera and photographed it. It was the best they could do. There should be field lines representing north, and measurements. They used a tape measure and got an estimate for depth.

The infant was under less than two feet of dirt. They didn't really care how they'd buried the child. He looked up to Eleri. "What do you know?"

He didn't want to disturb the bones yet.

She was just estimating, he knew that, but he wanted her to see it as it was before they pulled everything up and bagged it.

"About six to nine months depending on size. Nutrition is okay. Maybe some Mongoloid heritage, judging by the shape of the nose. But that's not conclusive in infants."

Mongoloid included five heritages: Pacific islander, Chinese, Indian, Inuit, and Native American. Infants were notoriously hard to get that read on. Teeth helped and this little guy had none. Not any that had emerged yet.

"Boy or girl?" Walter asked.

"Good question." Eleri looked up at the other woman as Donovan started pulling the child out, bone by bone. "You can't tell sex by the skeleton until the person hits puberty."

"Wow." That was all Walter said, but something about watching the bones come up and get laid out on a tray—a baking tray they'd picked up at a restaurant shop that morning —made her turn away.

They pulled up three more infants in the next two hours, none of them getting the attention they deserved. With the snow lower, they'd ridden ATVs all the way up here to the compound. And Walter—their best driver—had a trailer on hers so they could haul back any bodies they found. Even these three wouldn't take up much space.

As Eleri was pulling up the third, reminding them all to eat and drink water, and Donovan was digging, Walter said she'd hit another one.

Knowing what she was doing now, she'd pushed back the dirt, revealing the top of the box. So far, all three had been buried in what appeared to be cardboard. The second two had blankets around them. Though given what they knew, Donovan figured they'd arrived here already dead, and were buried in what they came in. One had a diaper.

"This is different," Walter said. "The box is bigger."

Eleri glanced up sharply from the hole she was shoulder deep in and looked concerned. "Bigger? How much?"

"Adult-sized."

"Shit." Donovan said the word right on top of Eleri. Maybe they were spending too much time together. But he didn't have any other friends. Apparently the one friend he did have, they did things like dig up dead bodies together. Oh joy.

"You get it, D." Eleri spoke into the hole she was in. The

ground around them looked like it had been attacked by land mines. "I want to finish this one correctly. Not interrupted."

He turned to Walter and directed her through the process of scraping clean the box. She was right. It was cardboard, taped up, though the tape was old and peeling, just a strip of silver laid along the decaying pieces.

"Burying them in cardboard was silly. It just rots and caves in," he commented, as though anyone needed that opinion from him. It just meant they had another clingy, wet layer to peel away to see the skeleton underneath.

But as they excavated it, Donovan stilled.

The bones were wrong. Again. These had never really fused. There were places where it appeared the cartilage of infancy had never formed bone, though clearly the size of the person had continued to get bigger. The arthritis at the joints was growing almost out of control and the contorted position of the skeleton may have been his position in life, rather than just how he was shoved in the box.

But around his neck, Donovan found a chain. When he pulled it out it said, "Tango."

28

Eleri hated this lab. It was crowded with black top tables and work that grad students had left over the holidays.

She'd forgotten there were holidays. She needed to call Avery, her mother, her friend Haley Jean, Grandmère—though getting Grandmère on the phone was tough. She was grateful now that she'd written the woman a letter in response to the notes Grandmère sent them all. But a thank-you hardly seemed appropriate. She asked after Emmaline.

Closing the lid on one of the machines, Eleri pushed a button and peeled her gloves, dropping them into the trash can. There was no way to avoid the trash they generated. Someone—most likely the holiday janitorial staff—would know they had been here. The students might see the reagents were low on the machines.

This time Eleri and Donovan were running their own DNA tests. The university had everything they needed. It was why they'd chosen it, why they'd strong-armed the head of the department. He insisted on staying with them until Eleri had flashed her badge at him and told him it was FBI business and thank you very much for his help, now get out of his own lab.

He lingered at the doorway for a while, then down the hall. That was yesterday, but today he wasn't here. Walter had disabled the cameras in the hallway, pulling the wires so she could hook them back up when they left. Tomorrow, Eleri told herself. Tomorrow they would leave.

They'd sent one sample from each new skeleton to a variety of labs. It meant possible inconsistencies, but they couldn't afford to have so many samples at the same private place. There was no guarantee of secrecy, no reason one of the employees might not catch on. But, while she could run her own DNA tests, she wanted a backup for ancestry. She wanted to know if these samples, too, would trigger the letter from Las Abuelas. She would bet good money they did. But she couldn't do that on her own. They didn't know what the marker set was that Las Abuelas were looking for. What they could do was genomic sequencing. But it wasn't easy.

Eleri rubbed her hands through her hair and headed back down the hallway to the other lab where Donovan was laying out the bones. This time, no one was breaking in and stealing their finds.

"Hi Walter. Anything interesting?" Eleri asked cheekily. As though anything might go down in an abandoned school two weeks after finals and four days before Christmas.

"Oh, you know it." Walter was no good in the lab. It seemed they'd finally found a skill Walter Reed didn't possess. So Eleri and Donovan were doing everything by hand.

She pulled the large, green-painted, ugly door open to see her partner working on the small space he'd cleared. He had two trays—one on which they'd laid out each bone at the site, and the second where he was moving the body to, piece by piece, recording everything.

She'd drilled core samples, pulling what she could from the

bone in the younger skeletons and the pulp of a tooth in the older ones. There were three older dead by the end of the day. Four infants. A lot of work.

"I am not up to this grad-student level of lab grunt work," she told him.

"Oh, but you were good with shoveling?" He tossed back.

"Touché." She tilted her head, only then realizing she'd managed to develop a good crick in her neck. Probably from hunching over the desk, measuring and pipetting tiny samples of clear liquids from meticulously labeled bottles. She'd smelled fumes that took her back to her school days. Then she hid her samples in the deep recesses of the cabinets, knowing that was safer than taking it all with them. She still worried about it being found out.

"We are our own lab students. We are our own crew. We are the whole unit, El. I think it was you who told me that." Donovan looked up as he finished dropping yet another stinky, clear liquid into another tiny test tube. He snapped the top and shook it.

"Lunch," she declared, weary to her own bones.

"Absolutely. Tell Walter." It meant another thirty minutes to hide everything and lock back up. But her machine was still running her samples and they should be ready for the next step when they got back.

Lunch was a necessary break, even though they all stayed quiet. Each stared in a different direction, lost in their own thoughts. Eleri chewed her burger and texted Avery, promising to come find him as soon as the case was over. While she waited for each return text to blink silently onto her screen, she wondered if Avery was for real. If he was truly okay with her long absences, her inability to discuss her job. She thought about the women who threw themselves at hockey stars and how he told her he'd had enough of that. But if she didn't trust him, then what did she have?

So many times she simply made the decision that she wanted to trust. She didn't want to be the agent who never had a relationship. But she also didn't want to be the fool. She searched him using her phone, but didn't see any pictures of him with anyone else. She smiled when the next text popped up and tapped a message back as she realized her salad was finished.

Donovan's plate was already empty and he was chatting with Walter. Eleri hadn't even realized when the conversation started and that she wasn't involved in it. Her game was off.

"Let's get back to the lab," she announced cheerfully, only to be looked at like she was crazy. She probably was.

Half an hour later, she'd matched the tag "Tango" to a few of the papers in the file—not that any of them made any sense. She had an intake form for him. Later she had papers on him at various intervals, though she would guess she didn't have a full docket.

She pulled the finished polymerase chain reaction—necessary to sort the DNA—and spent the next several hours alongside Donovan in the lab while Walter stood guard. Eleri was sitting at the computer in the corner when it came up. "Donovan, look. Look."

He leaned over her shoulder. "Is that right?"

"It's incredibly consistent. Not a computer or tech error. The only thing would be if we switched Victor's blood sample," he thought out loud.

"Look." She pointed again, this time to a print-off. "This is where I pulled your blood sample out of this one. See? You're XY and here's your code. Removed from the sample. So this is definitely Victor's sample."

"Son of a bitch." He murmured.

She couldn't help but mutter, "*Daughter* of one. Victor's genetically female."

And Victor was also gone. Eleri found herself sorting her

visual memory for anything she could put into place that would hint at Victor's female genetic coding. She'd been convinced he was a man. The voice was male, the build was male, even the way he carried himself. She couldn't think of anything. Then she did.

"Donovan, you bit him, you fought with him. Did you know? Is there anything—looking back now—that would agree with this?"

Donovan's eyes looked downward, focusing on a random point in front of him as he thought. Then he said, "No. No there wasn't. He smelled like a man. Moved like one. I'm shocked by this result. In fact, I'd check it."

"We already did. We sent it to the other lab, too. Remember? If that comes back XX then we have to believe it. But everything we have here says we didn't screw this up." She leaned back in the seat but to where she could still hit the mouse and keyboard. "Look at the rest of this."

The match list pulled up. He tested at four percent wolverine and three of ermine.

Eleri couldn't wrap her head around it. "Wolverine and ermine? What in God's name was going on in there?"

If only they could find a mission statement, but they hadn't found one. She started talking her way through it, knowing that speaking it out loud would help. Donovan would help.

"They had all these kids. They were shipping them like stock. Now we find the bodies and they all have these hybridizations. What was the point?"

She swiveled the chair around to face him. "We have to call in a crew and clean out the building."

Donovan took a deep breath, thinking. "We also need research. We need to know what the hell Axis really is. It's definitely bigger than us. How do we do that?"

This time it was Eleri who needed a moment to think. "Normally, I'd call my agent in charge and tell them what we need and they would either contact someone to arrange the crew or they would tell me how they wanted it done. That's what we did when we needed agents on the ground in Los Angeles."

"But these aren't agents on the ground. It's definitely a non-standard op and our agent in charge just suggested that we had to keep our source silent or enforce that silence ourselves." Donovan looked as shaken as she was at that.

"Yeah. That directive to take the kill if we found it necessary was just a warning flag. We may have a broader order than we thought." She didn't like the way her chest squeezed at the idea. She didn't like any of it. Never had. "We can't use that order. Ever."

"No shit. But that's going to get tangled. We will eventually have to make a decision to pull a trigger." He was staring at her. He wanted something.

"Never on Walter." She looked him in the eye. Didn't waver. "Regardless of what she tells or doesn't. Never on Walter."

He nodded in return. "So how do we do this?"

"I don't know. But I do know who to call." She picked up her phone and started to sort the buttons, but she didn't use that phone for the call. Instead she picked up the phone on the desk. It took three tries to figure out how to dial out. When she did, she called Wade.

"No answer?" Donovan asked.

She shook her head, but hung up after five rings. She dialed again. Again she got no answer. And she hung up after five rings. Donovan frowned as she called a third time. If this didn't work, she would call his house. But after the first ring she heard the click.

"Eleri?" Wade's voice was a comfort in and of itself and she caught the edge of a smile as she heard it.

"Of course."

"You have trouble?" he asked, getting right to the point. Why else would she be calling from an unknown number?

Using an old code they'd devised to let the other know who it was.

"When don't I?" The smirk in her voice was enough to let him know it wasn't life or death. "Why are you still in your office?"

"Who's office are you in?" he countered. He must have seen a caller ID from the university. Wade was both a former Night-Shade agent and a scientist. He'd mentored her during her early years as what she now called "regular FBI." When she grew up, she wanted to be Wade.

"I've hijacked a university lab and I have seven sets of skeletal remains, pulled from one grave. There are more there. Plus there have to be papers in the building by the grave." She took a breath but kept going. "So we also need research."

"Go through Westerfield." He said it without inflection, as though reciting a line he'd heard too many times.

"Yeah, not sure on that one." She looked up at Donovan as she said that. He was sitting on the lab table, one leg braced on the floor, arms crossed.

It took a few minutes to sort out the workarounds Wade suggested. He'd dealt with Westerfield before. And Wade had left NightShade. While Eleri saw NightShade as an opportunity —a chance to use all her science, to acknowledge the hunches and dreams and not wind up in a mental hospital or be investigated for being too close to the crimes—Wade's leaving should have been a clue to her. She'd stayed in anyway.

When she hung up she turned back to Donovan. "We can do this. But first we need the rest of this data. We go in with as much data as we can."

They hit the machines again, sorting samples until they had everything they could. The sun went down, leaving only darkness in the high horizontal windows that lined the lab.

Eleri stood over the data she'd printed out. Tango had traces of wolverine, moose, snowshoe rabbit, and lynx. All at levels over four percent. "These are huge. That's way too much hybridization."

"Do you think that explains Tango's age? The arthritis?"

"Maybe." Eleri conceded. It was possible. "Infant number one has snowshoe rabbit and seal. Each over five percent. Infant number two has seal, moose, and reindeer. Each over four percent."

She went to the next page and the next. "Infant number three has moose and wolverine, but at under two percent each."

"No two combinations are the same," Donovan said. "So they were simply experimenting?"

"So if this happened at Axis, then these infants all arrived alive. They weren't part of the 'stock loss.'" The term still turned her stomach. "We need to find the lost infants. The ones who arrived dead. It would appear they are buried or interred elsewhere. We need them for comparison."

All Donovan would do in return was nod. It was nasty business.

She turned her attention back to the numbers; they were easier to deal with. "It's not entirely the case, but there's a definite trend here. It doesn't seem to be the number of kinds of animal DNA that correlates, but the overall percentage of it. The higher it is, it seems the faster they died.'"

29

G J's heart pounded. She reached out to touch the bones in front of her.

It had taken far too long to get here. She'd had to call the power company and complain about glitches in their service. She set up an appointment when her grandfather was out and counted on them having to shut the power to fix the glitch she'd fabricated.

That had taken care of the camera. She picked the lock and snuck down here, not knowing how long she had. GJ had to get out before that camera came back online and it had taken too long to find what she was looking for. Her gloved fingers searched for full skeletons and boxes of bone chips.

But as she looked quickly at each specimen, she'd begun to doubt she even remembered it correctly. Had she fabricated the whole thing? Imagined the strange skeletons? She didn't know.

Finally, she'd pulled another drawer and found it.

The scapulae were longer than normal, thicker, the normal growth slightly off. Pulling her camera from her back pocket, GJ turned on the flash and shot pictures in the dark. She rotated the bones and photographed another angle before carefully putting them back as she'd found them. Her heart knocked as she prayed her grandfather didn't notice.

She picked up the femur and noted the heaviness, that it was slightly thicker around as well. That alone didn't account for the weight; the density had to be higher, too. It was more like a four-legged creature, though the skeleton was clearly human. Or mostly human.

She set the jaw aside, though she noticed the back molars were more spiked than most humans' were. Then she rolled the skull to face her and checked the maxillary sutures.

Her mouth fell open, seeing what she remembered. What she'd convinced herself was just a trick of the mind. But here it was. Usually the bones of the face fused early in childhood making the skull one solid piece. Though this was clearly an adult skeleton, the front facial bones were still separate.

Shiiiiit.

The word sounded through her brain but didn't stop her from snapping pictures. Quickly, she lined the bones back up and slid the drawer shut. This was the second drawer with one of these skeletons. If she remembered correctly there was a third.

Footsteps above her head made her freeze, her chest clenching as she waited for the power to come back on. It didn't, but the footsteps traced the hallway overhead. She heard the hinges as each office was checked.

"GJ?" The sound was faint, but clear. Sally. Wandering the house while the power was out, looking for her lost charge. Some days, Sally remembered GJ was a grown woman, almost with a PhD of her own. Other days, the housekeeper seemed to think she was still five and that a little power outage would mean she needed cookies and a hand to hold.

GJ didn't answer. Didn't move. Didn't breathe. She just waited for Sally to try the door to the stairs that led down here, but the woman didn't. Why would she? Her grandfather had probably trained Sally well that there was no point in even trying the door.

GJ listened as the footsteps went the other way down the hall and the voice called out her name a few more times. When at last it got too far away, she let out her breath with a *whoosh,* then just as quickly sucked it back in.

Time. She was running out of time.

She pulled the next drawer open and found the third skeleton. Just a few quick snapshots of the overall layout. She didn't have time anymore to field the individual bones.

GJ pulled another drawer open, finding a fourth skeleton that had the same problems or alterations. Three was more than coincidence. Four was a disease, an issue, a subset. She pulled the next drawer.

Damn. A fifth one!

She took another picture just as the lights flicked on.

Again, her heart stopped. This was going to age her five years. How the hell was she going to get out of here? The camera was lining back up and there was no way she could get up the stairs and relock the door without being seen.

There was no other door in or out, her grandfather had made sure of that.

Slowly pushing the last drawer shut, GJ headed for the stairs. No cameras down here. Her grandfather wouldn't want anything recording what he had. Human skeletons—she'd learned in legal classes—probably shouldn't be a citizen's possession. Anomalies should be studied in a university by students, not sit here untouched.

She climbed the stairs slowly, on a suicide mission. She would have to open the door, the camera would catch her. Her grandfather would know she'd been down here.

Suddenly realizing she was still wearing gloves, she snapped at the blue latex, peeling it and shoving the trash in her back pocket. She pushed them down until they couldn't be seen. If she could get out the door—if there was a way out of this—the gloves in her pocket would be a killer. It would mean she intended to come down here and not leave fingerprints.

GJ reached for the knob, her stomach turning. Coming down here had been bad. She'd breached her grandfather's trust. And it didn't matter that she'd been right, that he was keeping odd skeletons in his home. The anger he would feel would be justified.

Then again, maybe he wouldn't see the footage. If she left no hints she'd been here, he would have no reason to look. With that hope she climbed the last two steps.

She took a deep breath and reached out for the knob. Then she yanked her hand back. No gloves.

She pulled one of the spares she'd shoved in her front pocket and slid her hand in just as the power blinked out again. This time she took advantage.

GJ yanked open the door and stepped boldly into the dark hallway. Turning back, she pulled it shut with her gloved hand and scurried away, peeling the glove as she went. The power blinked back on then, just as she stuffed the latex into her pocket, but she was already halfway down the hall, the camera at her back.

DONOVAN LEANED back into his seat and asked for a ginger ale from the flight attendant. Walter sat next to him on the plane, her prosthetic hand folded into her lap as she accepted the small cup the attendant handed her. It was the first time he'd ever seen her self-conscious about it.

He tried to ignore her odd actions. They were so un-Walter-like.

Eleri was in the seat in front of them. Through the space, he could see she was reading something on the small e-reader she kept tucked into her purse most of the time.

It was Walter who started the conversation. "Is everything in Michigan okay in the hands of the crime scene crew?"

"Who knows?" Donovan shrugged and tore the foil off the tiny peanut packet he'd been handed. "I've never worked with them. I have no idea if they can keep what they find there secret. Or if they know enough to know they aren't digging up anything more than infants and children."

There was no one in the seats behind them, so he was relatively comfortable with the low level conversation. He leaned in closer to Walter. "I have no idea if they can do the job or if they can report on it or hold the information to themselves."

"That's no bueno." Walter tilted her head with a small smile.

Just then he realized she smelled good. Bad time to realize that, he thought. So he talked to cover it. "We have to go to Arizona now. Those papers point us to another facility there."

Walter had gone back to her room the night before. They all had. While Walter had slept in the adjoining room, Donovan and Eleri had rooms off the main suite. At one a.m. Donovan came out of his room to find Eleri still awake and at the table.

She was sipping what looked like hot tea and thumbing through the stacks of pages. She didn't look up, but she spoke knowing he was standing there. "We have to go."

She'd pointed to a spot on the map, out at the edge of what he could read was Pima County. He looked closer: the Cabeza Pieta Wildlife Refuge. A huge swath of unoccupied land.

At last she looked up at him. "See any striking similarities?"

"Sure. National land, a huge patch of it. No nearby cities. But this is a good bit out in the open. It's mostly desert." He shrugged, fully awake by then, his brain chewing on what she'd fed it.

"That's exactly where the other sets of invoices lead." She sipped the tea as though they weren't speaking of infants and toddlers. "And look what I found."

Donovan had turned on the coffee maker and sat down to look.

Now he relayed that same information to Walter, who'd been greeted that morning then shuttled onto the first flight Eleri found.

He still held the open packet of peanuts that seemed hardly bigger than a bite. He tossed them back before leaning into Walter's space again. "She pulled up a satellite map of the area, and it's censored."

"Censored?"

"Blurred out. There's a program in the sat system that won't let people get to the data that's there. There are a small handful of places like that in the US. It turns out, this is one of them."

Walter ate her own pack of pretzels, but she ate them one at a time while he crumpled the foil from his own "snack" in his hand. Donovan noticed she didn't lean away. Then he told himself not to notice.

"So we're headed right into the heart of that?" She turned her head to look at him. She was too close.

Donovan backed up just a little bit. "It's complicated. We'll fly into Yuma, buy ATVs, puddle jump to Ajo, then ride in and check it out."

"Do we have an exact location?" she asked, her brow furrowing.

"Of course not, just the blurred area. So somewhere in there."

"No snow." She gave that wry half-grin again. "But we may be wishing for it out in the desert."

This time when he leaned back, he let his eyes fall shut. Maybe he was paying for those late hours last night. He wondered about it for a few minutes until his ears hurt and Walter was shaking him awake.

"Donovan. Donovan." She whispered to him until his eyes fluttered open. "What were you dreaming?"

"Hmmm?" He looked at her through still fuzzy eyes.

"You were growling."

He had no answer for that.

"Don't worry," she told him. "No one heard you. I coughed to cover it when you got loud."

"Thanks?" It was all he could offer as he shook himself fully awake.

Eleri had made plans for them. They were moving as soon as they hit the tarmac in Yuma. A car took them to a meet point where they were handed the keys to a gassed SUV and all their equipment.

Walter was the one who said what was boggling Donovan's brain. "It's an SUV towing ATVs. That's too many letters."

"Oh no," he replied, "It's an SUV towing ATVs for the FBI."

"But you've missed the good part." Eleri pointed out as she took the keys and let Donovan and Walter throw their luggage in the back. "On the trailer are three ATVs and a *trailer*. We have a trailer hauling a trailer."

"This was your big plan?" Donovan asked, knowing they were all deflecting their concerns about what they were walking into.

"Oh, yes. Now get in the car." She cranked the engine and pulled the door shut.

Donovan motioned Walter into the front seat and they headed out just as his phone pinged. Email.

He opened it, then held the small screen up as though the two women could read it from the front. "It's the lab. *Shockingly,* all three of the samples we sent to this lab triggered the letter from Las Abuelas. This was the lab with two infants and Tango, right?"

When Eleri nodded in response, he continued. "At this point, we don't really need any more confirmation. It will only be interesting if one of the DNA profiles doesn't trigger the match to the Disappeared. We already know the animal hybrid profiles on these guys. This is just confirmation of the work we've already done."

"We get a login for that?" she asked from the front, steering them into the parking lot of a grocery store.

Letting Walter lead the way through the store, they stocked up on lightweight coolers, sports drinks, jerkies, trail mixes, and energy bars. Donovan was as excited about the food as he'd been about the treks into the national forest in Michigan. He tried to add a candy bar to the cart, but Walter expertly plucked it out and put it back onto the shelf.

"That will melt."

He sighed. He didn't like when she was right. He put it back in the cart. "I'll eat it in the car."

Three hours later, he was stripped down to his T-shirt. While his helmet and face plate protected his eyes, his skin took the stings of flying sand where it was exposed, but the heat was too much for him to keep sleeves on.

He was about to fall asleep to the monochrome of the landscape passing by. Eleri had rented them a matte, dun-colored SUV. The ATVs were desert camo. Even their clothing was designed to blend in. When the sand blew, he was afraid he'd lose one or the other of them in the landscape.

"Look." Eleri's voice came digitized through his helmet.

Donovan blinked and looked again.

Chain link, old and degrading, crossed the desert sand. Huge swaths of it were falling down, posts bent as though pushed down by the sky or melting in the mid-day sun. It didn't take long to find a hole big enough to drive though.

Over a short rise, a building came into view.

"Holy shit." Walter said what they were all thinking.

The building was identical to the one they'd left behind in Michigan. If there had been any question about the two being linked, it was no longer an issue.

They were through the door inside of ten minutes. Unlike the other building, this one looked like it had been abandoned rather rapidly, if a long time ago.

Cups were left on the counter and plates in the low sink. Chairs sat behind desks and looked as though they'd simply been pushed back and left behind. In the offices, the file cabinets were full.

Eleri pulled one file then another. "They don't say Axis."

"No," Walter agreed. "They all say Atlas. What is that? Axis, then Atlas?"

Donovan felt his head snap up. "I know."

30

Eleri held the papers in her hand as Donovan said he understood. She did, too, but she didn't speak. She kept rifling through the pages, her brain soaking in the written words as well as Donovan's spoken ones.

"Axis is the second bone in the spinal column. It's in the neck, and it has a spike on it. It's the piece the whole head rotates on."

"And Atlas holds up the world," Walter filled in.

"More than that, it's the top bone in the spinal column. The one that rotates on Axis," he added.

Eleri knew that. As soon as he said he had it, she connected the anatomy, too. What it meant, she didn't know, only that the two were definitely related, but . . . "Which one was first?"

"Axis." Walter answered with conviction, puzzling Eleri and finally getting her to look up.

Walter kept talking. She pointed up. "The ceilings in here have a much smaller kernel spray foam on them, and the windows—while the same size and shape as the other building, have a different mechanism. I told you I dated the other building by some of the features. Well, these features were common about half a decade later."

Well, damn. The ceiling foam. The window handles. Eleri should have paid better attention in shop class. "Good eyes," was all she said.

She looked at Donovan. "She's right, the invoices are for several years later."

Invoices for children again, from Argentina. Children who would trace back to Las Abuelas. Children who would likely have a variety of animal genes in their systems.

She held up the files. "Yes, this place is second. The others were labeled Alpha, Bravo and so on. These are AZ-Alpha, AZ-Echo, AZ-Juliet and so on. They've re-used the names. But this is clearly a secondary list." She thumbed through again.

"So AZ-Juliet—is that Juliet from Michigan moved here? Or is it another child entirely?" She was thinking out loud with that.

"I think this place is separate," Donovan said. "I'm trying to remember the names, but I don't think they line up. Do they have a Charlie? A Victor? A Tango? We know those exist in Michigan."

"Or an Eight-twenty," Walter added to the list.

They dug into the file drawers in earnest, none of them forgetting that the last compound had the occasional person running around it. It took them thirty minutes to find the file they wanted. It was Walter who found it.

"Tango!" She practically slapped the folder into Eleri's hands.

"Look." Eleri pointed. "Male. Our Tango was female. They're definitely separate." She held onto the file, confident there was more here. "So they were shipping kids both places, but there first . . . Next question: Were these kids hybridized with animals, too?"

"Well, that's a little extreme." Donovan corrected her. He

was right, these kids weren't really "hybridized."

"Why is it extreme? Isn't that what they were doing? They were making animal-people," Walter said.

For the first time since she got here, Eleri slowed down. This, at least, she understood. The rest didn't make any sense, but she understood the science. "It's not like an animal-human hybrid. So, a few years ago, scientists made a glow-in-the-dark puppy."

"A what?"

"Yeah, a dog that glows in the dark." Eleri watched Walter's expression change. "They used jellyfish DNA, because the jelly-fish have bioluminescent cells. So they isolated those genes and transplanted them to the dog embryos."

"So the dogs were part jellyfish?" Walter asked.

"Technically, yes. Just a few percent. They weren't like puppies with tentacles or open circulatory systems—" At the look on Walter's face, she added, "You can ignore the last one."

"I got it," Donovan chimed in.

"Of course you did." Walter punched him in the biceps. "You were one of the science nerds." When she turned her attention back to Eleri, Eleri didn't let her eyes move or her face give it away, but she saw Donovan open his mouth in pain and his hand reach up to touch where he'd been hit. He covered it, and she kept talking.

"They were puppies. Almost entirely dogs, just a handful of genes from the jellyfish. This is like that."

"So they can just pick out genes and insert them into the baby?" Walter asked.

"No. Reasonable question, but no." Eleri set the paper down. "We currently think the average mammal has around thirty thousand genes, but while we can find the gene itself, we also have to know what it does and how. And that's more complicated. We don't know so many of those. We can insert them, but it usually doesn't work . . ."

She let the last word trail off as her brain caught on it. "Donovan, it—"

"—usually doesn't work." He was nodding at her. "They also didn't implant in embryos."

Eleri felt her focus change. She felt the desert push in from beyond the windows, the heat in the building contained from the windows and brick. She could smell the fine layer of dust on everything. "Or did they?"

"How?" Donovan asked. No one was pulling files anymore. It was now a brainstorming session in the middle of a building in the middle of the desert. "The women that the Argentinian government took were already pregnant. They could have implanted them into the fetus. Would that be—"

This time she cut him off. "—why they kept the pregnant women in the first place."

Walter watched them as though she was at a tennis match. "You two are having the creepiest, most disturbing conversation I've ever seen. On several levels."

Eleri could only nod. She wanted to acknowledge that, but she wanted to keep on the roll they'd started. Her brain kept turning over and she was connecting things she hadn't seen before. "Some of the kids showed up as toddlers. That would be too late. The trauma lines we saw in the teeth indicated that trauma was much later than in utero."

"Maybe that's why it didn't work." Donovan's expression turned down.

"So they knew it wouldn't work a lot of the time and they did it anyway?" Walter looked as disturbed as Eleri had ever seen her. Thwarting terrorist attacks was easy for her. This wasn't.

"Yeah. It looks like they did exactly that," Eleri acknowledged it. "Clearly, from the number of graves we found, it didn't work."

"Victor's still out there. So is Eight-twenty." Walter pointed out.

"So it worked a few times." Donovan paused. "We need to take these papers and get out. We need internet."

Eleri went on instant alert. "What?"

"I can't tell if someone is here or not."

"Like at Axis?" she asked. At least the people there seemed more scared of being seen than much else.

"It's too dry here." He looked nervous though. "I don't smell as well this way. My nose isn't the right shape. I can't tell."

DONOVAN WOKE up face down in a pile of papers. He was just grateful that he hadn't drooled on them.

He'd dreamed of changing—not just into the wolf but into hyenas, dingoes, javelina, monkeys and more. All animals he'd seen in the files. The dreams scared him. He'd fought against children who changed like he did, feral gleams in their eyes. Fangs and claws struck out and he'd fought back. Viciously.

The images lingered with him when he woke.

Eleri looked up, her own eyes bleary. She, too, had fallen asleep on their work last night. Only she'd managed to clear the pages from under her head before she passed out.

Donovan peeled one from his cheek, assisted by the stubble that had grown from barely noticeable to disreputable while he slept.

"That's a good look for you," Eleri mumbled, managing a soft insult before she was even awake.

He grinned as best he could. "At least I didn't drool."

He enjoyed the look of concern that flashed over her features before she reached up to wipe at her mouth. She recovered quickly and looked at him oddly. "Bad dreams?"

"You, too?" He asked even as she nodded. "Bad night."

"Fed by some really bad info," she added. "I need a shower."

Stalking off, she headed into her room and presumably into the attached bath. Donovan also needed a shower, and even as he washed off he knew it was futile. They were headed back to Atlas today. Even though the heat wasn't oppressive—it was barely seventy-five—it was dead winter.

At least he was clean while he ate room service omelets with his partner and their bodyguard. At least he was clean while he rode in the air-conditioned car out to their last point to park. Then it was all over.

Three minutes into the ride he had grit between his teeth even though his helmet had a full face shield. His arms were taking a beating from both the fine grain dirt and what must be actual rocks.

Yesterday, they'd come in point blank. Guns in hand for protection, they'd needed information more than security. Today, they were playing it a little more careful. After thirty minutes circling the compound and checking coordinates on the GPS, they found the fence was down in a handful of places and several gates just stood open.

There was little evidence of any activity at the compound, animal or human, though the area was more than capable of hiding any number of sins. People often thought of the desert like the Middle Eastern version—an ocean of sand, but this area was a turbulent sea at best. The ground rose and fell in folds and patterns as though a sheet was rumpled on a lumpy mattress. On those folds, tufts of greenish spikes fought for space with brown sticks that were actually plants in full foliage. The occasional cactus harbored geckos, snakes, birds and even scorpions. Donovan steered his way through it all.

When they pulled up next to the door, they made no attempt to conceal the vehicles. They were here for evidence, not to sneak in. Though the building had once been locked, it was now unprotected.

They'd noticed cameras mounted at intervals along the fence posts, but they were so old as to look retro, and most were sporting some kind of damage that would make it impossible for them to record even if someone tried.

They threaded their way in again, with Donovan paying more attention than before. He was no longer heading through a house of horrors, not knowing what would pop up at him. He had a basic layout. He knew what was here. And this time he saw it.

The dust.

It wasn't everywhere. It should be everywhere.

"El." He kept his voice pitched low. "It's too clean. It's not perfect, but it's too good for a decade since they closed their doors. Way too good."

She nodded at him and tapped at the butt of the gun holstered at her side. She wouldn't speak but was ready to draw down on someone if she had to.

They'd already hammered out a plan—case the building first then go after more papers. Another trip and they'd get Donovan out in form to see if he could sniff bodies. He wasn't looking forward to that trip. There was a reason there weren't wolves in the desert.

Quickly passing the offices they'd been in the day before, Walter led the trio. She hung a right around the corner and, with her gun drawn and a quick signal of finger to lips, opened one of the doors.

She was in, gun leading, footsteps rolling softly despite the echo of silence in the place. She swung wide, aiming to one corner then the other before issuing a soft but concise, "Clear."

They stepped into the space, checked file cabinets before Donovan tapped his partner on the shoulder. "El, look."

Outside the window was the courtyard and a play set almost identical to the one in Michigan. He didn't like the way this place made him feel—as if it was both familiar and foreign at the same time.

The section that was two-story again housed classrooms downstairs and dorm rooms up. Only these looked more like home—or they had before they'd been abandoned. There were signs and art, kindergarten style, hung on the doors. "Echo", "November," "Zulu," "India," and "X-ray" mixed in with a variety of three-digit numbers. These kids were three and four to a room. Bunk beds pushed up against walls.

"El, more kids survived here." His eyes darted back and forth, trying to take it all in. There was evidence that many of the kids were older, too.

"Or maybe they just shipped more here," Walter offered.

"No." Eleri shook her head. "Donovan's right. More of the original military alpha code is represented. More of them made it to an older age. They had better success here."

"Whatever that means," Donovan muttered, his brows pulling together and his ears twitching as he said it. He could almost smell the dust unsettling. Was it them? Was it their presence in the building that made that happen?

No.

He turned then, hands out at his side, not wanting a fight, but ready for it.

"El, Walter." He barely spoke the words but heard the two women turn as a single unit behind him. He'd been last in the room, he was first to face whatever was coming around the corner.

The footsteps were clear now. Light, balanced, soft. Whoever was coming wasn't moving blindly toward them.

He saw the shadow then the man round the open doorway from the steps. But he didn't see the gun until it was too late.

Donovan counted three shots. Four. Five. And he felt the hot burn of metal in his flesh.

31

Eleri stumbled backward as bullets went over her head. But it only took two steps for her to regain her self-awareness and control.

She lowered her torso beneath the gunfire and rolled backward. The move was executed through muscle memory, the same way she'd been trained years ago at Quantico. Her shoulder hit the linoleum and she rotated onto her feet, coming up with her gun drawn at the shooter.

Walter was already on a knee, behind the corner, her gun and one eye trained.

Eleri fired twice in rapid succession, hating the clench in her gut as she did it. She was firing at someone she didn't know, for no reason other than he was firing at her. If it was even a "he."

If she killed, she wanted it to be righteous. Defense wasn't fully on that docket, not when she was the invader. She pulled the trigger again.

Walter was shooting at almost three times the rate she was, but not hitting anything. Eleri would have looked, but there wasn't time.

The bullets stopped.

Eleri breathed and looked through her peripheral vision for the first time. Walter was holding, too. Donovan was down.

"Walter, cover me!" She yelled it as she bolted to the side.

She'd seen Donovan move as the bullets started, but assumed he was rolling into position like she did.

She shook him, her body screaming with tension from the gunfight and the fear spiking through her. Blood was pooling around him, running smoothly along the floor, rivulets following the edges where the tiles came together.

No more bullets came, though Eleri was braced for impact. Her back was to the door, a dangerous position, but Donovan was down and Walter held their ground.

She wished for riot gear, bulletproof vests, helmets . . . he had none.

"Donovan." She shook him again, the word bursting out in a hushed tone.

This time he moaned. Pushed back against her hand.

None of them were out of the woods yet.

"Walter," she barked. "Sit rep."

The situation report was delivered in calm words despite the anything-but-calm situation. "Shooter gone. Holding . . . I'm unharmed."

She added the last part before Eleri asked, though Eleri didn't quite believe that "unharmed" meant the same thing to Walter that it did to other people. Still the woman was reporting in solid English, which was better than Donovan.

Who moaned again.

His hand reached up toward his head.

"Don't move." She pulled his hand back and tipped his head toward her. Her fingers probed at his head.

"Jesus, El!" This time he smacked her hand away.

"Hey!" But she laughed in sharp relief. That was Donovan. "Tell me where it hurts?"

"My head."

"Not helpful." She put her fingers back to his scalp and found the source before he smacked her hand away again. "You have a furrow along the side of your head. Given the groan rather than a scream there are two options."

"Yes, Doc?" He was looking at her with a sardonic expression.

"Either it barely grazed and didn't crack your skull," she started, "Or it did crack your skull and you're too brain damaged to know how much it hurts."

"I'll take door number one." His words were dry, but he held his hand up to hers for a lift.

He was a big guy, so it required standing and bracing her feet to give him any kind of real help. Donovan swung upward, the leonine motion cut short by his duck and cringe at what he must be feeling in his head.

"Here." The word came from behind her and Eleri turned to see Walter holding out gauze still in the sterile wrap. She must have rummaged through her pack without putting down her gun.

Eleri took the dressing from her while Walter continued to hold guard position. "Is there anything you aren't competent at?"

"Forensics, ma'am." Walter's eyes didn't waver and Eleri realized her attempt at praise/humor was only interfering with the woman's ability to hear and stay on sharp lookout. Eleri shut up.

∾

GJ WAS DISAPPOINTED.

She couldn't match any of her skeletons to the pictures from her grandfather's collection. She sighed and set her femur down.

This was all wrong.

She was sitting on the carpet in her apartment bedroom, the skeleton laid out in front of her. She'd gathered the wrist bones, ankle bones, hand and feet bones into eight separate labeled Ziploc baggies with Kleenex for buffer and sharpie noting what each bag contained.

Even though it was a very expensive Turkish carpet her grandfather had brought back from his travels, she still had bones laid out on the floor. She should have them on a lab table or a steel-plated gurney.

It was bad lab technique, to say the least. She knew the carpet was clean—Sally would have vacuumed it to within an inch of its life—but there was no way to put that in any report. She'd been taught that despite all the cool and crazy things she would see, all the different ways that death could come, there was always need of respect for the dead. This fell far short.

Then there was the pesky little problem that it was completely illegal.

When she was downstairs in her grandfather's personal storage, she thought repeatedly about how he was depriving the world of the knowledge there. That his collection was wrong.

Here she was doing the same thing. She'd seduced herself into thinking that her cause was in some way noble. That finding the bones was the most important thing. That while her name might be on the paper, it wasn't about her—it was about the sum total of human knowledge.

Her grandfather had drilled that into her. His work had purpose, served something higher than his own prestige. But he'd gotten a title and tenure and eventually money from the work he did, too. He'd loved all of those things, GJ knew.

She didn't know at what point he'd started thinking it was okay to keep full skeletons illegally. More than that, she didn't know at what point she'd started thinking that was okay, too.

She cataloged what she could, not sure if her newfound morals were from somewhere deep inside or if they resulted from the fact that none of the three skeletons was a match for the ones she'd seen at her grandfather's. Now there were five. He was still collecting.

She had to stop now.

GJ finished her write-ups, thinking that the five skeletons downstairs might have something to do with the ones she had. They didn't match each other, but that didn't mean they didn't match others.

She packed up her finds and got them ready to ship, but she didn't close the box. Then she printed out her pictures from downstairs. And she started her write-ups on those skeletons, too.

DONOVAN LOOKED up at his partner. "You can do it, Eleri."

She sighed. "I don't think so. I wasn't trained like you."

"Have you ever stitched a fetal pig?" He knew she had. No one got through the levels of biology degrees she had without stitching something. He'd already injected himself with lidocaine.

Needles didn't bother him, but sticking himself was a bitch. It didn't help that lidocaine stung as it entered, too. The bullet had burned a trail along his head, just behind his temple. The length of the trail meant he had to stick himself repeatedly. He handled it with a mirror, but he didn't have enough hands to stitch himself. "Do it, El. Or I'll make Walter do it."

"I'll puke on you." Walter's response was as fast as it was ridiculous.

"I don't think you'd ever puke on anything." Eleri turned to the other woman, happy for the distraction.

"I don't sew." Walter deadpanned, then she turned to Donovan. "And fuck you for suggesting I sew. I'm a damned Marine."

With a wry look, he held the forceps out to Eleri with the needle clenched between the teeth. He had it all ready for her. She took it, but not happily. "You're going to look like a damn fetal pig."

He felt her sewing him up. It didn't hurt, just the pressure and tugging as she made angry stitches in his head. She tied off each stitch slowly, despite her declaration that she was no good at it. He picked up the mirror and took a look.

"Wow, El, you were very careful, and it still looks like crap."

"Fuck you," she replied and stuck him again. Donovan was grateful he couldn't feel it.

She tied the last one off and set down the tools. "That's my first human suturing."

"You two match now," Walter told them, her arms crossed.

"Oh my God, Donovan. She's right!" Eleri ran into the other room and came back quickly. She held up a stretchy headband in pink. "This one's for you."

He pushed her hand and the offending hairband away. "I'm good, but thanks." Donovan held the gauze to his head, staunching the small flow of blood that remained. Despite his teasing and the fact that she'd never get hired as a plastic surgeon, she'd done a good job.

"Let's get to the paperwork. I've had enough of this." He stood up quickly and only got a little stirred by it.

"Sure. Except maybe we should all eat and shower first. You especially," Eleri pointed out.

It was only then that he noticed his clothing was covered in blood. He sighed.

It was all his own blood from the single head wound. Ultimately, even Walter hadn't tagged the guy who'd shot at them. Then again, she said she'd been aiming around him, not wanting to kill a man for defending his home. Eleri said much the same. So the man at Atlas either had horrible aim himself or he was doing the same thing. When they went back to the building maybe they would find cartoon outlines of each other in bullet holes.

He showered quickly despite working around his latest wound. In less than thirty minutes he was back at the table and still managed to be the last one there.

They even had a snack platter out. Jesus, he was not used to being the slow, dumb one. Eleri held out a plate and stopped flipping pages for a moment. "I got a call from Westerfield."

Donovan expected more bodies and information from the teams sent in to clear the Axis building, but Eleri surprised him.

"One name emerged from the list at the hotel where the agent took the stolen bones. Arabella Janson." She waited a beat.

"Is that supposed to mean something to me?" Donovan shrugged at her, confused.

"I don't know. I wouldn't expect so. But she's a forensic science PhD student out of Illinois. No one else there would have any idea what to do with the stolen bones. Accountants, salespeople, stay-at-home parents, a few engineers." Another pause. "Her grandfather is Dr. Murray Marks."

"Oh, holy shit." He did know that name. Marks was a very well-established name in forensics. Donovan had seen the man speak twice. "She's Marks' granddaughter? Oh. I've met her."

He had. At one of the talks, Marks had brought her along as an assistant. At the end of his presentation, he'd been mobbed and wound up handing off a reasonable number of questions to her. She'd been an undergrad at the time, but more than competent even then.

"Yeah, I'm trying to find her. We'll see what pops."

"But we're now getting pulled in about three different directions." Michigan, here, and off to find the bones. If they could. If that was even right. Maybe it had been purely coincidental that Arabella Janson was at the hotel that night. No, it wasn't. "The agent who cleaned out the lab and took it to her was a forensics tech. Fifty bucks says he studied with Marks at one point."

"I'm not taking that bet," Eleri said. "Arabella hasn't been home to the apartment in her name in just over three weeks. Shocking, huh?"

"She's our girl." Trying to keep his brain on the right track, he pointed to the files in front of her. "Good reading?"

"Just as horrific as Axis." She stacked an apple slice with cheese and fig jam before popping it into her mouth. "Same shit, different animals."

"Better paperwork," Walter started. She ate her cheese on a cracker and Donovan noticed she didn't go near the blue cheese. Like him.

He settled in and started reading.

First, it gave him a stomach ache. Then, it gave him a headache.

There were records of treatments to infants and small children. Painful transfusions of early virus-genetic transplant therapies haunted the pages in the files.

Thinner stacks told stories of children who didn't weather the therapies well. Their deaths were recorded but not their burial. This time he and Eleri didn't have the bodies or even DNA.

Even the man who'd shot at them hadn't taken a bullet, hadn't left any blood. Still, he'd dropped an empty gun and Eleri took it. Tomorrow they would send it out to lift DNA and fingerprints. But there wasn't a university within range that had a bio lab like they would need. So it wasn't anything they would cross reference on their own.

Right now, all they had were the files.

Several hours later, after Walter had offhandedly declared

the fig jam to be "really good," and they'd cleaned the plate, and read a reasonable stack of files, Eleri declared a halt. "What do we have? Let's compile."

"How many people? Children, I mean. How many children did they have here?" Walter asked.

It took a little bit of extrapolation, but they came up with approximately seventy or so that survived the initial trip.

"Which means probably about a hundred and fifty were shipped here initially," Donovan estimated.

They next listed the names of the doctors signing off on the treatments. They wound up with six names. None of which meant anything to him. "They're all geneticists. Well, five of them. One's emergency pediatrics."

"That doesn't bode well for their expectations." Walter commented.

Eventually they wound up putting that list aside, too and compiling a third one. Animals. In short order they had, three types of monkey, jaguar, sloth, tapir, lemur, agouti, javelina, meerkat, hyena, and dingo.

"We still may not have all of them. There may be more in those." She gestured to the boxes of files they'd already extracted from the building. This time, they'd left some behind because of timing, because of inability to carry them all in one trip.

"It already seems like a bigger list than the one in Michigan." Walter added and Donovan agreed.

"Statistically, yes." He took a breath. "More kids, more animals, more survivors."

"It's cold in Michigan," Eleri said as she looked at a spot on the wall.

"Duh," Walter responded quickly, but Donovan held his hand out to stop her.

"It is. And it's really hot here. The animals used here are

warm-weather creatures. Suited to jungles and deserts and high heat."

Eleri turned to look at him, nodding. "And the ones in Michigan were all cold-weather mammals."

It was like he could feel the gears in his brain turning alongside hers. "It's as if they were building them to survive in the climate. But why?"

leri looked at the card Donovan held out to her and shrugged.

"Today's the date," he told her, waving her grand-mère's oddly worded stationery in front of her.

"Right, but today you still haven't found who you seek." She cited back to him.

"So tomorrow we'll find this person?" he asked, his whole body leaning toward her as though he were interrogating her.

"Whoa. You are making some pretty big assumptions here. I don't understand Grandmère any better than you do." She was walking away from him, cradling her first cup of coffee for the day and wishing she could incant a spell over it and make him stop bothering her. Something about that idea sent a brush of sensation along the back of her brain, but she didn't know what it meant.

"Yours made sense." He spoke it as though that should make his card make sense, too.

"Oh joy." She turned to face him, barely avoiding sloshing the hot liquid out of her cup. "Let's say she's right—"

"Is she ever not?"

That gave her pause. She thought back a moment. "No. I guess not. I mean there have been things that are still open to interpretation, but well, no I don't think she's ever been *wrong.*" She was babbling and she knew it. Eleri started over. "So let's assume Grandmère is right. They'll find Emmaline soon and you and I both know well and good she's been dead for years. Then what? I won't grieve because I grieved a while ago, privately. My mother will once again think I'm a freak of nature and I can't tell her that I've seen Emmaline all this time anyway. She's as alive to me now as she ever was since she disappeared."

"Have you seen her recently?" he asked, no longer waving the card at her. Now he looked concerned.

She hated this part. It made her sound crazy. "Last night I dreamed about the house again. Only this time, Emmaline showed up in my room and led me out to the house. She didn't come inside."

Donovan nodded as she told him about the rest of it. About the woman at the chair sewing, and the man behind her waving Eleri into the next room.

"Was it Aida Wedo and Domballah Wedo?"

Eleri jerked around at Walter's voice, startled at her reference to little-known Voodoo gods. "How long have you been there?"

Walter shrugged. "Since Donovan was asking you about the date on his card. Do you think it was the Wedos in your dream?"

Eleri blinked. Walter had just heard her entire dead-sister-crazy-grandmother-creepy-dream story and asked about "the Wedos" as though anyone had ever referred to the high gods that way. But . . .

"Maybe." *Shit*, maybe Walter was right, not that that helped her understand the dream at all.

Walter didn't seem to mind the rest of it though. Eleri sipped her coffee and wondered how her life was so far off the rails that her coworkers were no longer suggesting she was mentally unstable. Now they just accepted her craziness with their coffee.

She wasn't even really dressed yet. "Me and my coffee are going to go get our damn clothes on and contemplate the high gods of the Rada visiting me in my dreams. Why don't you two do something useful?"

Eleri felt better once she was dressed, though her coffee was empty by that point. She emerged with a plan but found Walter and Donovan already neck deep in a brainstorm without her. "What do you have?"

"Not much," Donovan admitted. "We know they were genetically modifying the kids—probably well into toddler-hood—which seems pretty late."

"By today's standards," Eleri commented.

He frowned.

"Well, we know that glow puppy was one of three surviving puppies from the implanted litter of eighteen."

"*Eighteen?*" Walter interjected. "Holy shit. What if they'd all taken?"

"Well, we have low expectations of implantation on modified eggs."

"In English?" Walter looked back and forth between the two of them, noting that Donovan understood just fine. "Sorry."

"They don't expect all eighteen to work. They were right, only three grew into puppies. Only one even showed evidence of the red glow—the gene they'd implanted." Eleri poured herself another cup of coffee as if she wasn't talking about scientists trying this shit on children. "But remember, the glow puppy was in 2009 and these guys were doing this in the late seventies."

"They had no clue what they were doing," Walter murmured.

"I don't know. As many kids as survived?" Donovan shook

his head. "Maybe they did. Their survival rates seem better than the dogs."

"I guess so. They were definitely ahead of their time. But why?" That's what Eleri still couldn't wrap her head around. "They were changing these kids, altering them with animal DNA. The kids in Michigan are altered for cold and the ones here for heat. But *why*?"

Both of them looked at her like they had no idea.

Donovan offered up what he could. "Shall we throw out whatever dumb shit we get until something hits?"

"Do it." She thunked her coffee mug onto the table and noticed she was the only one who was drinking it.

"It was the height of the Cold War. The kids were from South America."

"I was under the impression that the kids were just a ready source. I mean, these were the children of the Disappeared," Eleri added. "And it seems they were for sale."

Some of the wealthy in Argentina were given the children to raise as their own. Eleri thought about it. "Maybe there were more children than places and this experiment needed children."

"It was an experiment?" Walter asked. "Really? At first I thought it was a school or home. Maybe for wayward kids."

"School for animal-hybrid kids?" Eleri grinned.

"One—this dude exists." She jabbed her thumb toward Donovan, who raised his eyebrows and shrugged. "And two—you said this was a safe space to throw out dumb ideas."

"I never said it was a safe space," she deadpanned. "But you're right on both counts. The paperwork does look like lab work and experiments on quantities of DNA."

Donovan started rifling his way through the pages. "I didn't count everything, but it looks like they used higher percentages of animal DNA early on and they had higher death rates then. They lowered the percentages and got better success. Though . .

." He looked for a moment or two more while Walter remained silent and Eleri sipped at her coffee. "They had better survival rates here than in Michigan."

"Do you think it was the cold?" Eleri asked.

"I have no fucking clue." He leaned back in the chair as though giving up. "Why would they create human-animal hybrids? Design them to survive in cold and hot temperatures? Who knows if there are only *two* facilities?" He laced his hands behind his head and Eleri noticed Walter was tapping away on her tablet.

"There are only two facilities."

Two heads snapped her direction.

Walter looked up. "Well, if the naming convention works, you're out of spinal bones to name them after. Atlas is the top one, right?"

"She's right," Donovan added.

Walter turned her tablet around. She'd blown up a picture of a *TIME* magazine cover. Two reactor silos shadowed the cover with the yellow headline "Nuclear Nightmare."

"Three Mile Island?" Eleri asked.

"They were afraid of nuclear war," Walter said. "Is this maybe a factor? They were trying to create super humans."

"Supersoldiers," Donovan added, almost reverently. "They've always been after the super soldier."

Walter held up her prosthetic hand. "But they have me."

Eleri laughed out loud at that one. "Back then, they didn't know you were coming." Her brain turned back to the last argument. "They were trying to make supersoldiers. Jesus."

There was silence around the table for a moment as they each contemplated what had happened at both the compounds. Then Eleri did what she had to and took the reins. "Can we follow up on our list of scientists?"

She split the names up evenly for research. She managed another cup of coffee while she looked. The first doctor she checked out was Dr. Robert Adesso—a geneticist with a specialty in mammalian genes.

Prior to 1976, he had a home address, a wife, two children. He was a respected professor at Arizona State University in the physiological sciences division. Eleri found old phone records, newspaper articles, and school documentation on him. Using the Bureau access to scientific research, she pulled a variety of papers he'd published.

She was still reading when she tipped her cup up and discovered that she'd hit bottom yet again. She had to lay off the coffee today. Or start laying off it.

Adesso was deep into research regarding genetic sequences and the physical traits they produced. He'd done a handful of tests inserting genes into live animals. Much of it failed. And this was just what he published.

"I don't get it." Walter looked up from her own research, her frustration showing. "The first genetic sequencing was in 1995. So how did they sequence this stuff in the seventies? I'm sure I'm missing something because of the science."

"Two things," Eleri started. "First, you're referencing the full genomic sequencing of a bacteria. Individual genes were sequenced long before that. Also, you're talking about what's available to the public. There were probably a bunch of steps before that became widely known. So the science was there long before they let it go public."

"These guys appear to be working ahead of the public know-how and with only individual genes. Their success is surprising, really," Donovan said.

Eleri hated calling it "success." She returned to digging up anything she could find on Adesso. Eventually, she gave up on finding anything more recent. She'd checked him against a variety of databases. His wife received public assistance in relatively high amounts to this day and he'd never been declared dead. Turning her search to the other name on her short list, she hit pay dirt.

Before she could say anything, Walter spoke up. "Both of mine are dead."

Eleri looked up. "You have actual notices? Because Adesso disappeared off the grid in '76, but was never declared dead."

"Nope. Dead," Walter said. "Dr. Dena Fillin was a viral geneticist. She went off grid in '77. Paperwork on her resumes in 1987. She went back to work with a pharmaceutical company. Retired in '98 and died in 2002. Dead."

Eleri agreed. That was a good trail. "The other?"

"Dr. Albert Watoto." Walter told a similar story with him. He disappeared from all documentation for about ten years and then came back to the real world. She had death information on him, too. "Heart attack in 1999."

Donovan gave his rundown of Dr. Jun Wen. She had a PhD in bacterial, moneran, and plant genetics as well as an MD. A research scientist by trade, her story was nearly identical to Fillin's. Wen held on until 2010, when she died of complications of cancer.

"Dr. Benjamin Schwartzgartner is still alive."

"*What*?" That was the best thing Eleri had heard yet. Her head popped up. Maybe they could interview him.

Donovan shook his head. "He's in a home. Severe Alzheimer's."

"I still want to interview him. Maybe something is in there." She could hope that his mad ravings might just be about the work he did in the middle of the central west zone of Arizona. It was dumb, but she clung to it.

"My first guy is missing—Dr. Adesso went off grid about the same time as the others. But never came back on." She showed them a headshot she'd found of him. Full seventies hair, collar, and all.

"Maybe we'll dig him up," Donovan volunteered. "Do you think maybe he's buried on site?"

"Possibly." She shrugged. "Now do you want to hear about what I did get?" Eleri didn't give them time to answer. "Dr. Len Morozov? MD with PhD in human genetics. He's in prison, right here in Arizona. He was jailed for violating his medical license. In 1985."

"What?" Donovan's frown managed to be at odds with his open mouth. "Did he not disappear from public record the same as the others?"

"He did. He just reappeared as a prison inmate. So the trial, the accusations, any of his victims? I can't find anything. Only that he's convicted of some kind of pharmaceutical fraud that terminated his medical license."

"Let's go interview him. He's better than the dementia guy." Donovan was already standing.

"We can't go yet. We have to go back into Atlas for more of the paperwork." Eleri shook her head. She didn't want to do it either, but they didn't have a team to excavate the building either. She hadn't called Westerfield yet, and there was no telling if he'd want a second team—assuring that no one tech person knew enough to put the case together. Or if he would want to use the same team—thus minimizing the number of agents who knew anything about this case at all. Either way, Eleri and her small team would be holding the fort here for a while.

The reports from Axis said the building had been cleared of papers. The bed sheets were collected for any lingering DNA. The windows and shiny surfaces dusted for prints. Three spots of blood they'd found were being tested. They were still digging bodies out of the courtyard and had found another site that had a small mass grave with infants and toddlers only. Eleri was convinced that would prove to be the "stock loss" they'd read about. She also had people tailing Agent Bobby Rander who'd ransacked their lab—not that they'd turned up anything. Each morning Eleri got an update on Arabella Janson, too. She still hadn't touched a credit card or returned to her apartment. Eleri was beginning to wonder if the grad student had gone back out into the forest and gotten herself eaten by the cougar. And why hadn't anyone claimed her missing yet? So far, Eleri had a glut of evidence and exactly dick-all for conclusions.

"We can't go interview Adesso today. He's been there for over thirty years. He should still be there tomorrow. But those papers at Atlas? We're the only ones who can go get them and yesterday someone was defending the building with a gun. That's our first priority, before that evidence disappears, too. Suit up."

She was in her last set of riding-in-the-desert gear that was clean. Two minutes after she started her ATV she was filthy, sweaty, and irritable. The only thing worse than the ride was the physical labor of hauling paper—possibly the densest material on the planet—and the tension of knowing she could be shot at in any given moment. She was a water lover, a swimmer extraordinaire, a damn mermaid. She couldn't think of any place less suited to her.

Still she did the work and tried not to bitch. Not even when her energy bar was gritty with sand that rubbed at her molars. She was grateful when she got back into the SUV and let Walter drive. If Eleri hadn't been sitting in the back seat, if her gaze hadn't been wandering, she might not have seen the woman sitting in the gold sedan outside the back entrance to the hotel.

Eleri popped out of the car before Walter even brought it to a stop. Her gun was unholstered and she jerked the car door open, shocking the young woman inside. Yanking her out by the arm, Eleri slammed her against the side of the car and stepped immediately back, her gun aimed center mass. "You're under arrest by the Federal Bureau of Investigation."

33

onovan heard the car door slam before he realized what had happened. By the time he was out his own door, Eleri had her gun trained on the woman by the car. But because she was directly in his way, Donovan couldn't see who she was talking to.

He pushed his own door open as Walter pulled into the spot, jacking the car into park. His feet were on the ground, closing in on Eleri as she stayed close to the woman.

Her voice carried to him. "You had no right. It's a federal crime and I should take you in."

"El," he said it as softly as he could. His hand reached out, going for a gentle touch on her shoulder. The woman didn't look dangerous. Her jeans looked worn but expensive. Her shirt hung off one shoulder in a studied way. Her hair, however, looked as if it had been cut by an angry child.

She jerked her head to one side and Donovan saw her face. Arabella Janson. He couldn't help the words that came out of his mouth. "Where are the bones?"

She'd stolen, commissioned, or at least was involved in the

theft of three full skeletal bodies from a secure FBI lab, as well as possibly being the one who took the finds from the site.

Seeing her face, he understood Eleri's anger. Quickly, he ducked a look at his partner to see if her eyes had changed color. Donovan breathed a sigh of relief that they hadn't. He stepped back then, letting Eleri take the lead.

"I have them. I have the skeletons." The woman was putting her hands up, or at least trying to. "They're in the trunk."

Donovan, for all his callousness over dead bodies, still cringed at the idea of this woman driving around with these skeletons in the trunk. "Keys?" He held out his hand.

"Don't move your hands!" Eleri's voice and hands worked synchronously to stop the woman from reaching into her coat. The grad student cringed. She looked to Donovan, her eyes showing deep-seated fear. Donovan didn't have much sympathy.

"My keys are in my pocket. Left front side." She pushed her hip toward Donovan.

Tentatively reaching inside a woman's front pants' pocket wasn't high on Donovan's to-do list, but getting those skeletons back was. He used one finger to slip the ring out. Only one key graced the ring along with the plastic tag from the rental car company. He clicked the button, popping the trunk.

A row of plain black duffel bags marched neatly in the space. He unzipped the first one, finding neatly nestled long bones protected by foam pieces. They looked hand cut for just that purpose. The square cardboard box looked like it was from a craft store. Donovan guessed it held the skull. A series of plastic baggies stuffed with tissue and small bones held the remainder of the skeleton.

He checked the other duffels and concluded that there were three relatively complete skeletons. "It looks good," he told Eleri. "I think it's all here."

"Is it tagged?" she asked him, never taking her eyes off Janson.

It took Donovan a moment to understand—she wasn't asking about labels on the bones, she was asking about radio tags. Eleri appeared at his side as he realized Walter had come to the scene—quietly as always—and taken over restraint of the suspect. That was probably for the best all the way around. Eleri had personal feelings about what Janson had done. So did Walter, but Walter was one to keep those feelings out of her split-second decisions.

Eleri rifled through the bags with a little less care than Donovan would have liked. "I don't see any tags."

"Did you put trackers on these?" she hollered toward the driver's side where Walter still held the woman back.

The look on Janson's face was so confused that Donovan believed her when she shook her head and said, "No."

"Walter, handcuff her," Eleri ordered as she picked up one of the bags and casually motioned Donovan to get the other two.

"El, you just pulled a gun in a parking lot." He tucked himself in right behind her.

"I— I— I don't usually carry cuffs, Ma'am." Walter said, though her gun never wavered. "I'm not military police."

"Shit." Eleri murmured it under her breath. Then she sighed. "You're right." Turning her attention to Walter, she ordered, "Bring her in. Unobtrusively."

Then Eleri stopped in front of Janson and issued another warning. "We're going inside, and you won't make any kind of noise or draw attention. If you do, we'll smack you to the floor and arrest you without concern for the scene. We'll tell the world what you did and why you're arrested. We'll see how well that goes over with your grandfather."

The surprise on the girl's face showed that she had no idea they knew about her. This time, Donovan tucked himself in beside Janson and told her, "She means that. We know who you are, and we suspected you of the theft for a while now. So any surprise you thought you had here, you don't."

Janson offered a curt nod and let Walter lead her around while Eleri simmered as she booked another room and took them all to it. She wasn't going to take Janson into the room with the papers on Atlas and Axis, or the slides and small bones her theft had missed the first time. Though none of those things were left out where they could be found, she wouldn't risk Janson getting near them.

When they arrived at the room, she sat the woman at the table. Eleri opened her mouth, then closed it. She looked at Walter, covered in dust and grime, then at Donovan, who probably looked the same. Eleri looked it, too.

He opened his mouth, "Do you want a shower first? I do."

"Yes." It was the first reaction she'd had about anything other than her anger. "Walter?"

Walter stayed with Janson while the two of them took the skeletons up to the other suite, risking being found if they'd missed a tracker of any kind, but Eleri thought it was safer than leaving Walter with Janson and all the evidence.

Fifteen minutes later, they headed back down two floors.

"Your eyes didn't change." When Eleri only nodded, he continued, "I smelled only fear on her. She didn't seem to be hiding anything."

Another nod from his senior partner as she slid the key in and opened the door to a hyperalert Walter. Despite all the training he'd had, Donovan still couldn't squelch the shock of adrenaline when he faced the barrel of a gun, even if it was held by a friendly as friendly as Walter.

She immediately tipped the gun away.

"Your turn to shower." Eleri told her, though it was clearly both an offer and an order.

Walter nodded and holstered her weapon as she left the

room. Donovan followed Eleri's lead. Though they hadn't discussed it, Eleri established herself as bad cop immediately, which made him good cop, or at least less-bad cop. He didn't unholster his own weapon; neither did Eleri, though she stayed standing. Donovan pulled up a chair, facing Arabella Janson.

"Who are you?"

"You know who I am." She looked confused. "You know my name."

"I want you to tell us. I want you to fill in anything we don't know." He rested his elbows on spread knees and laced his fingers. It wasn't his usual position, but it pushed his torso forward, more into her space. The clasped hands told of comfort, of his trust of her—he didn't need a hand near his weapon.

She nodded and started in a measured tone. "My name is Arabella Jade Janson, but most people know me as GJ."

"GJ?" He offered a small half-smile with the question. His acting skills were subpar at best and he hoped he pulled it off.

Her easy response said it did. She no longer smelled of fear, or not as much. "It's for 'Grandpa's Joy.' My grandfather is a horseman and he swears a horse by the name of Grandpa's Joy ran for the Triple Crown the year I was born. He's always called me that. It stuck with all my family and most of my friends. You didn't know that already?"

"No. Tell us about your grandfather." Also part of his interrogation classes. Dance around more comfortable sources first. Get the subject relaxed and talking.

"Grandpa is Dr. Murray Marks. He's a world-famous forensic archeologist. He took me out on digs when I was little. As he crossed over into anthropology, he tried to instill that love into me. It worked, mostly, though I disappointed him by going into contemporary forensics." She offered a small shrug. "He's mostly forgiven me, but I couldn't follow directly in his footsteps. I had to make a name for myself. Though I don't have his last name, everyone still knows whose granddaughter I am. Everyone still questions anything I do as my own."

For a flash of a moment, Donovan wondered if that wasn't part of the appeal of the Bureau for Eleri. It was so far out of the realm of her family history that she would never have to battle her last name for her own place. And her family name was bigger than most. He turned his attention back to the young woman in front of him and used the title she'd assigned herself. "GJ, do you want a drink?"

"Yes." She nodded to back up the statement, at least she didn't babble this time. Of course she was nervous, she was being held by the FBI under threat of arrest on federal felony charges.

It was Eleri who asked what she wanted and went down the hall to fetch a drink from the soda machine. She missed part of the conversation, but Donovan kept going.

"Why did you come here?"

This time she shifted before answering. Her eyes darted away and her sigh deflated her a bit. "I was trying to undo what I did."

"You have a ghillie suit? You were in Michigan?"

She nodded, caramel-colored curls bouncing in her ponytail. She was twenty-six but looked a bit younger. Probably part of being a perpetual student. "I was after skeletons."

"You got them."

"I'm sorry." She looked at him before she looked down, indicating the words were truth. "They weren't the ones I was looking for. I'm returning them."

"I don't understand." He shook his head, leaned one elbow on the table, and didn't look away when he heard the door open. He recognized both Eleri's footsteps and her scent. It was just the faintest trace from the hallway, but enough to keep his eyes on GJ Janson as the door behind him opened.

Eleri interrupted them with the crack and fizz of three cans of pop, the crackle of bags of chips and Cheetos. He could smell the orange cheese powder they used. Suddenly he was hungry, even if the food being offered was chemically flavored chips. He took a few, motioned to GJ and prompted her to continue her story.

"I was looking for a certain kind of skeleton. So when I found the first bone, I wanted to keep it, match it. But I had to turn it in."

The first skeleton, the one that triggered all of this.

"I was on a legitimate dig when we found that one." She became more animated in the story, now that it wasn't part of a felony. "I was called in on a search and recovery. We found that bone as well as the ones we'd gotten the tip for. My bone was given to me—well, to the university—to process and then it was taken away."

He nodded. He knew about the first bone. "But you went back into the area after it was closed?"

"I was there for a while before you showed up. The ghillie suit was only added when the boundaries were closed for a weather warning that didn't seem to exist, so close after the FBI took my find. I just wanted to see what was found."

"Well, you did. And you stole the other finds back."

"They were odd, too. I thought they might be what I was looking for."

"But they aren't?" He wondered how these odd and crazy skeletons with their variety of issues somehow didn't meet her requirements.

"No. I'm looking for specific mutations. I've seen them before, considered working on it for my dissertation. But I haven't been able to find enough instances of this particular mutation to support any theories." She shrugged again as if it were no big deal that she'd stolen federal property and then returned it because it didn't suit her needs. Donovan didn't call her on that.

GJ seemed to catch on. "I shouldn't have done it. I was angry—I'm an adult, that's no excuse, I know. I'm returning them now."

"How did you get Special Agent Robert Rander to steal them for you?"

Her head jerked back. Another surprise bit of info she hadn't anticipated they had. "Please don't prosecute him."

Too late for that, babe. He was a federal agent who stole from FBI labs for money. They'd only left him out there hoping he would lead them to her. Donovan shook his head as though, no, of course we won't process that criminal. He prompted her, "He was one of your grandfather's students . . ."

She nodded quickly. "He's older than me. I was a high school kid when he was one of my grandpa's grad students. I tagged along all the time and Bobby was one of the few who was nice to me. So when the area closed and when I saw you all out there, with your soldier to protect you, I called Bobby and asked if the FBI was out in the forest."

So she must have spotted Walter following them before they knew their old friend was out there tailing them. *Sonofabitch.* Had they been so damn blind the whole time?

GJ didn't stop talking. She was a near perfect witness, didn't know when to shut up. "So I got all my camping gear and the suit and went out looking for more. Anyway, the skeletons got stranger, and I had to compare them to the originals with the mutation I was looking for, to be sure if there wasn't a link."

Donovan nodded again as the girl's smell changed. She was actually excited. She was probably going to be arrested and in prison for a long time, but she was excited about the science of it. Jesus, she was almost as nerdy as Eleri and him. What did that say about them? Only that they had federal permission to steal shit, that's what.

"So Bobby Rander told you where we were? And then you hired him to break into the lab?" Donovan pushed again, taking a slow inhale of the air as she talked. They didn't teach that in Quantico. They couldn't, not when it was actors or other students they were pushing to lie to each other. But the smell of a person was almost as good as anything else. The signals coming off GJ made him appreciate his partner. Partners, actually. Walter didn't lie. She just kept her mouth shut, military style if she couldn't speak the truth, and Eleri told white lies with no compunction. She'd told one family how beautiful their chicken-themed decor was, as sincere as could be. And the only other times she'd lied to him, she'd been lying to herself as well—so no signals of fear or deceit.

GJ nodded. "He even told me you were coming here."

Donovan nodded, but that was when he picked up the change in Eleri even as he tried to hide his own. How the hell had anyone known they were coming here?

34

G J pushed herself back into the seat, the tone of the room changing as the door opened yet again and the soldier came in. She was the one who'd hunted GJ down in the snow and held a gun on her. The soldier was the one who'd put her in the position to drop the bag of stolen bones and leave. That was the reason Bobby Rander was involved in any of this. GJ did not like the soldier. Her attention was pulled back to the man in front of her.

She was trying to answer questions honestly. She'd figured the FBI would catch up with her sooner or later. She didn't need the bones, hadn't found what she wanted, and she honestly felt bad about it. Mostly. The science was so important —bigger than her. It was important for human knowledge. And if it gave her a thesis that no one could claim was built on her grandfather's name? So what if the two overlapped a little bit?

"Tell me what you know about us," the man said.

That was a lot. She started with the simple info Bobby had gotten for her. "You're Agent Heath—Donovan Heath and you have an MD." He seemed to be waiting for more, but she didn't have anything else on him. She looked up at the strangely beautiful strawberry blonde and added, "You're Agent Eleri Eames. The way Bobby talked about you, you're kind of a big deal."

That made the reddish-brown eyebrows go up, but it didn't stop the chips from going into her mouth. GJ continued, but this time she didn't look at the person she was talking about. "And that's your soldier, protection or something. You call her Walter, but I don't know her name."

"Rander told you we were coming here?" This from Eames. Eames had held back in some kind of good cop/bad cop game but GJ had been grateful for that. Just speaking with this woman made her nervous. You'd think she'd be more afraid of the tall man, but the women here seemed far more dangerous than him.

"Yes, it didn't seem like any big secret." But looking at their faces now, it clearly was supposed to have been. *Well, shit.* What had she stumbled into? "I came here to return the bones. Whatever you're studying, it must have to do with that weird, deserted building and all the kid stuff in it."

"That's right," Heath again. Her gaze swung back to him and she reminded herself that her grandfather would get her the best lawyers and that her cooperation here was a good offense for any criminal charges they might bring. She squelched the thought that Bobby Rander wouldn't be able to afford the same lawyers. Heath's voice pulled her attention. "You were in the building there. What do you know about it?"

"That it had kids' stuff in it. There were a few people living on national land. They were weird, too. They had strange gaits and odd development that made me think of the skeletons I'd found—you'd found . . . whatever. But they lived there around the building, maybe in it."

"What else?" He pushed.

What else could there be? She shrugged and waited while they watched her. "I don't know."

"Do you know the name of the program they were running there?" he asked.

"I think Axis. Just because I saw it on a few file folders." She shrugged again and was met with another question.

"Why are we here?"

"Existentially?" She was getting tired of them asking things she didn't know. Then again, she was the felon. Heath merely raised his eyebrows at her. She answered as expected. "No, I have no idea."

Her stomach growled then. Heath's did, too; they all heard it. The day was getting late and she was getting low blood sugar and it was making her cheeky. "Is dinner included in this interrogation?"

It was Eames who offered her a deadened expression.

Could they keep her here without food? "Don't I get a phone call?"

"That's if you're in jail. Under police arrest." Eames answered this question, too, but then turned to Heath and the Walter woman and started asking them what they wanted.

It was decided that there was a vending machine and a questionable Tex-Mex place within any reasonable distance. Thus they decided to hedge their bets on the Tex-Mex. GJ wanted to ask if she was going to be fed, too. But worst-case scenario, she had a handful of ones in her pocket, so she could eat out of the vending machines. She didn't say anything.

They sent Agent Heath and the soldier to fetch it, leaving her here with Agent Eames. As the other two left the room, something about Heath's shirt bothered her, but she couldn't put her finger on it.

"Hey, what's so cool over there?" Eames' voice cut her attention.

"Nothing."

Eames continued with technical questions. Had she taken bone slices? No, but clearly they had. She'd seen that some of the long bones were now in two pieces. Had she done DNA testing? No, it hadn't occurred to her. Her stomach growled again. Eames ignored it. GJ decided she would, too, but if they came back without anything for her, she was going to lodge a protest.

"Where have you been since you were in Michigan?" Eames didn't bother with pleasantries or with pretending this was anything other than what it was.

"At home."

"No. You haven't. We've been watching your apartment."

That shocked her. They were watching her? She had nothing to say to that. She'd thought they would want the bones back. So she'd brought them. She didn't want to be a felon.

Eames managed to shock her again. "You haven't been home and you haven't used your credit cards since before you went into the national forest two weeks ago."

Shit. They were very dedicated to finding her. "What do I have?" No, that wasn't right, they'd taken her stuff. "What *did* I have?"

"You had full skeletons pertinent to an ongoing Bureau investigation. And you knew that."

Thanks. Eames was no help at all.

GJ was at a complete disadvantage here. She should never have come. Sighing to herself, she muttered, "I should have mailed them to you."

"Using the post office for human remains is a felony," Eames quipped.

"What's another one at this point?" Okay, her blood sugar was way too low. Being rude to an FBI agent who'd started the conversation by declaring she was being arrested was a bad idea. "At least I wouldn't be here."

"We would have had you as soon as you went home or used any of your own accounts." Eames just stared. Damn, the woman had that you're-of-no-importance-to-me stare down pat.

How was she supposed to respond?

"What did you conclude from the skeletons?"

Oh God, another question? "Not much, other than they're honked up and my blood sugar is low."

Eames only nodded, pushed the bag of chips at her. There were about three left, but she didn't offer any to the agent. The salt made her thirsty, but her soda was empty. She wasn't about to bitch again about food.

Agent Eames stood up and walked away, leaving her sitting there, not knowing what was happening. Was she really arrested? Would she get a lawyer? Food?

GJ believed she was doing the right thing. She'd done the wrong thing for the wrong reasons, but now she was doing the right thing. At first, when she'd pulled up and sat in her car, she'd felt better about herself, but now? Not so much.

Checking the other bags, she found a small Cheeto and ate it quickly, licking the orange salt and chemicals from her fingertips. Then she sat quietly for some time while Eames puttered in the tiny kitchenette. It wasn't classy in any way. This was likely the only hotel in the area. She'd wondered why they were here. They probably weren't going to tell her.

Her maudlin thoughts and hunger were interrupted by the return of Agent Heath and the soldier, "Walter." That couldn't be her real name. But the smell of food steered her thoughts. Her mouth watered.

There was a small table with two more chairs around it. They must have pulled these two out to have their little chat with her. There was no way they would all fit.

She was thinking these thoughts as Eames brought her a glass of ice water and the other two pulled out four Styrofoam boxes. Four could possibly mean there was one for her. Her stomach clenched and she watched the two slowly set out plastic utensils and hack the tops off the Styrofoam with a pocketknife, probably trying to make it all fit at the tiny table.

As Heath leaned over, his shirt pulled tight against his back. He was lean and strong. GJ saw what she'd seen before, but this time why it bothered her became clear.

She couldn't stop her mouth. "Your scapulae are unusually long."

They all stopped what they were doing and stared at her.

His ribs didn't seem to have quite the usual rounding for humans. She couldn't see anything else, but her mouth ran anyway. "Is your maxilla maybe not fused to your zygomatic and frontal bones?"

"HOW IN HELL DID SHE . . . ?" Donovan was stunned.

He'd been starving when he came into the room, but his appetite fled the moment GJ Janson asked her questions.

He and Eleri had left the room, putting Walter in charge. Eleri at least had the foresight to gather up two containers of food and two sets of plasticware. She'd forgotten drinks though, so they were sipping tap water out of plastic cups. Not that Donovan ate much.

"I don't know." Eleri sat back. She'd at least eaten something. "Whatever it is, she's spot on."

In spite of the fact that she'd managed to eat something, her eyes darted everywhere. Eleri was thinking, trying to put things together, but she wasn't landing on any one thing.

"How?" His thoughts were pinging off the inside of his skull. GJ knew about his physiology just by looking. Or did she? "We have to re-question her. Find out how much she knows."

This time, Eleri's eyes landed on him. "She said she stole our skeletons because they were odd. GJ was looking for a particular anomaly in the skeletons."

"She has skeletons that look like me. Like *me*." It hit him then. Did she have his father? Past relatives? "I want to ask her where she's seen them before."

He stood up to go, but Eleri grabbed his hand, tugged him back down. "You can't go flying in there to ask questions. Honestly, we already gave too much away by running out of there like our asses were on fire."

Crap. He'd given it all away with that surprise. Hadn't he been trained not to react like that? Apparently, it hadn't stuck.

"Let's do something else for a little while. Then let's get our shit and our questions together before we face her again." She was together, even if he wasn't. "Walter is feeding her, holding onto her. We can stay here for a while."

Donovan popped up onto his feet and stalked the small room. His emotions were running away with him, emotions he usually didn't like to admit he had. He practically ran into a wall before he turned and headed the other way, not that it did anything.

"Let's do something else." She stood up and grabbed his hand, dragged him back to the edge of the bed where she opened up her laptop. "I just got an email. Results. Turn your brain to this."

She pulled up her account and used the link to create a login to the genetic testing facility. They were spreading their testing out across a variety of testing centers, not wanting to trip alarms on any one facility.

"There's no letter from Las Abuelas," she mused.

"Does that mean the DNA didn't trip the code or does it mean this facility isn't distributing their message?" He found he did feel better with his thoughts aimed a different direction.

"I don't know." She pulled a copy of the genetic code from her results, loaded it into a public-access program and set it to running.

Donovan watched as the small icon whirred. There was

something soothing about watching it spin. But it didn't take long.

"One hundred percent human." He was stunned. "But we have records. They were doing the same things here."

"Was he a control subject? Kids they didn't do anything to?" Eleri wondered out loud.

"Doesn't make sense. Normal kids are everywhere. There are no records on controls."

She shrugged. "We don't have all the records. We haven't even gone through the records we do have. The fingerprint on the gun was lifted. Let's match."

She pulled up a secure Bureau program, and pulled out the small hot-spot they carried. "Do we load it?"

It would triangulate them to the Bureau. "It's fine, but we need to get Bobby Rander into custody. He's the only one who's following us. If he doesn't know Janson already found us, he may still be tracking us."

"He already found us here. He sent Janson already. So using this only tells them what they already know." She held it up. "I say we plug it in."

He nodded at her, wondering what it would turn up.

In a few moments, they had a perfectly scrambled signal. The lab used some alternate light sources and captured a good picture of the print before they collected the cells for DNA testing. The scan was part of the report. Eleri uploaded it and started checking points on it. Then she set the system to match it.

They had twenty plausible matches for them to reference against. She'd set the matches to "blind"—listing them only by the case number. That way they couldn't see a name and be influenced about the match.

"No, not this one," Donovan told her. There were three points he saw that made it a quick rule-out.

The next one Eleri ruled out just as fast.

The third one was a match. They looked at it for as long as they could. A single error could make it a non-match. But when they had twenty points of correlation, she looked over her shoulder at him. Donovan nodded.

They waited for a name to pop up.

Dr. Robert Adesso. Government employee. Classified Science Division.

35

Eleri sat with Walter over breakfast. She'd sent Donovan down to relieve their friend from GJ Watch. They'd left the two of them on the other floor after dinner the night before. She called Walter, told her what they were planning. Even fetched the bag GJ had in her car with her overnight stuff and took it to them. But Eleri kept GJ and Donovan separate until this morning.

They'd decided he wouldn't talk to her about her observations. GJ could ask him questions and he would catalog what she knew, but he wouldn't answer anything until they knew what they were working with.

"Did she say anything else about Donovan last night?" Eleri asked between bites of eggs.

"Not that I understood. She asked about his scapu— lah? Lay? Again. And I'm pretty sure that's his shoulder bones, but I don't know. So I told her I didn't know and that he looked pretty normal to me." Walter also spoke between bites of her breakfast burrito, braving the Tex-Mex again.

Eleri was glad they could have a conversation with Walter actually at ease rather than at the military version of it. Eleri braved the next question. "Did she ask about him . . . changing? Anything like that?"

Walter shook her head. "Nothing even close."

But the question was did GJ have no idea what Donovan's skeleton meant? Or did she know exactly what it meant and she just wasn't asking?

"So her name is Arabella Jade, right? Arabella Janson?" Walter asked, a frown on her face.

"But she goes by GJ? Does she not understand how initials work?"

Eleri barked out a laugh and almost spit her eggs. "It's something her grandfather called her. She said he always called her 'Grandpa's Joy.' GJ."

"Oh, good. She seemed bright." Walter finished up her breakfast and then cleared her plate almost the moment the last bite was finished. "I hated thinking she didn't know how letters worked."

Another thought hit Eleri. "Do you like her?"

Walter turned, the paper trash from her breakfast still in her hands. "As in, am I interested in her? No. I don't swing that way."

"No, not what I meant." Eleri laughed again. She hadn't been trying to suss out Walter's sexual orientation. Truth be told, she hadn't given that any thought at all, not for a girl named Walter who almost always wore fatigues and gear. Eleri suffered a brief moment of wanting to doll Walter up; she was really beautiful. Then she realized that put her dangerously close to becoming her mother and she squelched the thought. "I meant, is she easy to be friendly with?"

Walter shrugged, her fine-boned face very expressive when she wasn't stonewalling. "She's friendly. Smart. Talks about a lot of things I don't have any background in, so she winds up doing a lot of explaining. But she doesn't seem like your typical bone thief. Not that I'd know what that profile is."

"I'm not sure I know what it is either. But Donovan and I need to get to the prison." She stood up and leaned on the back of the chair. "We need to get to Dr. Morozov and now we have a forensics grad student to babysit. You up for it?"

Totally deadpan, Walter asked, "Do we have play plans?"

Another laugh, then the thought came back that Westerfield had told them to terminate Walter if she broke the secret. "No play plans. You can take her with you to get lunch. *Shit*. No car."

"Tex-Mex is within walking distance."

"You're brave." Eleri commented.

"It's warm but not hot. It's winter." Walter shrugged.

"No, I meant Tex-Mex three meals in a row." Eleri grinned. She liked Walter far too much to enact Westerfield's order. And she suddenly realized she trusted the woman in front of her far more than she trusted her boss. "Walter—has anyone contacted you about Donovan? About me?"

Walter shook her head. Her expression mirrored her thoughts about the sudden change of subject.

She didn't know why she said it, but she did. "Agent Westerfield, my agent in charge, told us we had to watch you now that you know about Donovan."

"And you. At least some of it," Walter added, though her tone wasn't menacing at all. "I'm pretty sure there's a lot more to you than I've seen."

"Probably," Eleri agreed. Donovan was convincing her that there was more to her than they'd seen, too. "I'm not at the top of my food chain. I am here, but it's limited. My Agent in Charge has . . . some ideas I don't agree with."

Walter just nodded. "Am I safe, or should I be worried?"

"You're safe as long as you don't say anything." Eleri felt better with Walter knowing where she stood. "Honestly, it's the same order Donovan and I are under. My boss's name is Derek Westerfield and he has some abilities of his own."

"Not just you two . . ." She mulled that for a minute.

"No."

As she watched, something dawned on Walter's face. "That woman in L.A. The gray-haired one. She's like Donovan, right? You know her?"

Too many questions at once. "Yes, she's like Donovan, except she's a cold bitch—literally—and probably a killer. And no, she was a surprise to us, too."

"They don't all know each other? There's not like a were-wolf network?" Walter seemed to realize how that sounded even as she asked it. "Sorry."

"No they don't. And Donovan and I have to call Westerfield and get to the prison. If you want to take the car, pack up Janson and take her now."

Walter shook her head and went downstairs to relieve Donovan.

When he came upstairs, his stance spoke of his discomfort at talking to GJ—talking to someone who knew—but it was important. It was going to be a morning of discomfort. So Eleri just dove in. "Did she ask about you?"

"About what I can do? No." He seemed somewhat confused. "She asked about my bones. The weight of my femurs, the fusion points at my maxilla and nasal bones. She asked if my zygomatic arches were particularly thick or had a crest. She kept looking at me oddly."

"So she knows your bones, but she doesn't know . . . you."

"It's as good a guess as any," he offered. But he looked worried. He should be. Arabella Jade Janson was a threat, even if you called her "GJ."

"We have to call Westerfield." She held out the short end of a thorny stick.

"Of course we do." He sat down hard and in a few minutes was talking to his boss.

"She found you?" Westerfield asked, not disturbed at all by the news. "Good."

"Good?" Eleri echoed. This man never gave her the response she expected.

"Yes," he replied calmly. "You wanted to find her. I fed your location to Agent Rander, thinking if they were in touch, he would tell her."

"You led her to us?"

"Yes, and now I have an easy but solid charge to level against Rander. All without exposing anything about your case." He said it as though it was as simple as that. "We'll bring him in now."

At least that was something positive. If Agent Rander knew what they were studying and where, he was now out of the picture.

"Thank you." She tried to keep the question out of her voice. In an effort to end the call, she nodded to Donovan. "We're off to interview Dr. Morozov. He's in a prison complex in San Luis."

"He is?"

Oh, that he didn't know?

Donovan raised his hands, palm up, silently asking her the same thing. She answered the voice on the phone. "Yes. We'll upload notes from our interview when we're done. In the meantime, Walter Reed/Lucy Fisher is watching Arabella Janson."

They hung up and headed out. Two hours later they still were in the middle of nowhere and she was glad she'd started with a full tank. The scenery was delineated only by mild differences in color. The greens were gray, the browns were pale, the stillness of desert winter was everywhere. The wildlife—which she knew must be out here—was entirely hidden from view. It was as though the landscape was going by on an endless loop.

Donovan stared out the window and she could almost see him itching to run. To change and go for a wild lope off into the sea of sand and prickly plants. He couldn't. Not just because they didn't have time. He also was likely too injured. He'd taken damage to the ribs, his head; he'd spent most of this case battered. She wasn't much better.

At least both of them had started to heal; they wouldn't look like war victims when they went into the prison flashing their badges. They hadn't given warning they were coming—didn't want any time for Morozov to prepare.

It was nearly a three-hour trip, door to door. Though the prison was listed in San Luis, it was still about ten miles from the edge of town. At a population of thirty thousand it was about ten times the size of Ajo, but still small.

When they pulled into the parking lot and passed the high chain link and the rolls of razor wire at the top, they tripped something. Whether it was a digital alert system or just some guy on watch who saw a strange car coming in, Eleri didn't know. It didn't matter, the result was the same. As they approached the front entrance, the door opened, held by a portly man in uniform.

"What can I do for you nice people today?"

When Eleri showed him they were nice people with FBI badges they were quickly led into an interrogation room and Len Morozov was escorted in a moment later. They were catered to with sodas and offers of chips. Morozov was offered handcuffs attached to the table.

"Why am I here? Who are you?" He seemed so belligerent, his white hair standing up like he hadn't brushed it in almost thirty years. His orange jumpsuit hung on his frame as though he'd gotten smaller since he put it on that morning.

Eleri placed her hand on Donovan's forearm and took a deep breath, hoping he'd catch the hint to do the same. He could detect so much that she was completely blind to that way. "When was your last visitor, Dr. Morozov?"

"Ten years ago. My wife came once a year. Then she died."

Eleri had seen that he was married, no children. He was rotting here in this prison, alive for no reason other than that he hadn't died. For that at least, Eleri was grateful. "I'm so sorry."

They all sat that way for a moment, Eleri waiting to see if Morozov would open up the conversation. He did, but didn't give anything away.

"Why is the FBI at my door?" He looked back and forth between them, rheumy blue eyes questioning.

Eleri turned to look at Donovan, who offered only a small shrug. He didn't have anything to add to her ideas. Maybe that was good, that he didn't pick up anything special. So she dove in. "We found your name on some old scientific paperwork and wanted to come ask you about it."

"Ask away." He spread his hands palm out until the chains yanked, stopping him. Eleri found the gesture disingenuous. She didn't let it show.

"You were initially doing work on transgenic creatures. How were you delivering the novel genes?"

He lit up, just like she'd hoped, launching into a lengthy explanation of early bacterial gene delivery systems. He talked about viral mechanisms—things she thought were developed long after he'd been in prison. Maybe that was just the timeline the public was aware of. Or maybe he was lying. He discussed rats he'd encoded to have long human hair on their head. Monkeys with more developed vocal chords. He bragged how he'd given the pair to a linguist and a psychologist, told them to teach the monkeys to talk and learn if language was what they'd thought it was.

Eleri let him go on.

When he seemed to run down, she asked him, "What did you implant into humans?"

"We made humans with thicker skin and with higher metabolism and . . ." He stopped then, his internal monitor taking over and realizing what she'd asked specifically. That kind of genomic work had always been illegal in the US. If he'd done what the public papers said he did, he should have been protected by immunity.

"Why are you in here?"

There was a painful silence, during which the door to the hallway opened and a uniformed officer stepped one foot inside. "Is everything okay here?"

He was looking at Donovan, who responded easily, "Of course."

If that struck Eleri as odd, the feeling passed quickly. As soon as the door closed, she asked again, "Why are you in here?"

"Because I realized I was playing God. I'd been given a toy chest to play in and I was playing." He looked contrite for the first time. "One of the interns turned on me. I said it was just homesickness. Told him he needed to get himself together. He left. At least now . . . I *think* he left. When the second one turned on me, she told me what she really thought of what we were doing. And it got through."

He paused as though editing his story. "I packed up. Left the facility. Laid low. I called the news stations and planned a press conference." He took a deep breath. "I was arrested in my cheap motel room just outside of Tucson. I was charged with treason, which doesn't even fit with anything I was doing, and I was in prison with no chance of parole before I said word one." He looked at them now, as though they could absolve him.

They couldn't. Eleri knew that. She had a few more things she needed to confirm. "Your conscience was because of the number of deaths?"

He nodded. Less chatty now.

"And Axis and Atlas were about designing humans to withstand nuclear radiation aftermath?" She was leaning forward, even as he started to shake his head.

No?

She stared at him. *They'd been wrong?*

"It was about the climate. Do you remember when we were first making climate change public?"

Oh, shit. She did. Involuntarily, she looked to Donovan, who was nodding, putting it all together.

Eleri remembered an old *TIME* magazine cover, probably only months off from the one Walter pulled. It featured a penguin and presented the "coming ice age" as the result of carbon dioxide in the air. "That's why Axis was first? You thought we were plunging into an ice age."

He nodded. "We held that belief just long enough to make it public before we realized we'd interpreted the data wrong. It was the biggest mistake we as scientists made. People believed we screwed up and didn't know what we were talking about. We were right, we just were only right for the early numbers. We did get colder first, but it was part of extreme weather. Then we saw the bigger trend: warming."

"That's when you moved to the Atlas project." It wasn't a question. It all lined up: the two facilities, Axis's earlier start date. "You kept working both of them in case the data swung back."

Her brain was churning, registering his nod.

"And also because we saw the extreme weather changes coming. Some places would be colder. But most of it didn't pan out." This time, he leaned forward. "Yes, I was upset about the deaths of the children, but they were dead anyway. You have to understand that."

She did. She didn't like it. But she understood that to a man working on it from the inside, that would be the piece that would let him destroy their lives. She nodded as though she agreed.

"I was concerned because they planned to release them into the public."

Her eyes widened. She felt Donovan tense beside her. Under the table his hand clenched her knee and from the corner of her eye she saw him give a subtle nod. Presumedly, that meant Morozov was telling the truth. She wasn't in a place to ask.

"So I killed them all." That, he looked remorseful about.

"But—" She was interrupted by the door opening again. She'd learned long ago to stop mid-sentence, not to give anything away.

"Interview time is up," The man in the door said.

"No. We're FBI." Eleri stood, planting her hands on the tabletop. "We're almost done."

"I'm sorry. I'm under strict orders." He was in the room, locking a second set of cuffs onto Morozov before keying the ones attached to the table open.

"No." Eleri put her hand on his. "FBI." She flipped open her badge again.

"Not a problem. Just tell my boss, I'll bring this one back. But it's my job, ma'am."

She hated *ma'am*. "Just stay here while we call your boss in."

But he didn't. The guard whisked Morozov out of the room while she was on the phone, climbing the ranks of officers. "Go." She mouthed the word to Donovan, who ducked out after Morozov.

Her partner was back in just a moment. "They blocked me at the gate. Locked it behind them. Nothing I could do."

On the phone, she was told that they would have to come back next week. The prisoner had limited time per week for interviews—they'd exceeded it. Some kind of federal regulation.

Her brain hurt. That was seven kinds of stupid. She was the fucking FBI. She and Donovan should have authority over the prison even at the state level. They weren't taking the prisoner out. Just interviewing.

Her brain was also trying to get around the fact that they'd been wrong about the point of the two projects. She was in the car just getting ready to say so to Donovan as she started the engine and called the prison to complain.

When she hung up she turned to Donovan, stunned.

"He's dead. Another inmate shanked him and he bled out within moments of being led back to his cell."

36

D onovan was uptight each time he was around the grad student. He didn't know how much she knew, only that it was too much. Eleri managed to stay much calmer.

It also didn't escape his notice that Westerfield had made no mention during their call of GJ Janson being their new sidekick or of what she'd known. Donovan tried skirting around things the day before, the few times he'd talked to her, but he was done skirting. The drive to the prison had taken almost all day. It was time.

Eleri was in the other room with GJ now, leaving Donovan and Walter here. He stood up and stretched. "I have to go. I can't handle the stress of not knowing."

Walter jumped up as though to stop him, but rushed past him. "Wait."

She returned, jabbing a piece of paper at him. "What's the date?"

He was confused for a moment, but then realized that the paper was the note Eleri's grandmère had sent. *Trust the girl.* She asked again, "What's the date?"

"It was two days ago."

"When she showed up." Walter nodded. "It's her. She's what you're looking for and we're supposed to trust her . . . Eleri said her grandmère isn't wrong. Just go ask. Shake off the stress. We have a lot to do."

They would need him full-tilt, that was for sure. He nodded at her and headed for the door. The elevator made him tense. The carpeting in the hallway made him tense. He had to calm down. He'd been found out before and he was still here. He'd survive whatever GJ Janson knew, too.

She and Eleri were talking when he walked in, but GJ's eyes stayed on him. "It's amazing," she murmured.

"What?" Eleri was looking at him, and he could see she was trying to hide what she knew. Trying to let Janson spill what she knew or didn't.

"There's no external evidence of the disease." She looked at him the way a scientist did. The way the doctor did when he broke his ankle and ribs and the ER wanted to do a full-body panel to see what was going on with Donovan. "Or mutation," She added hastily. It wasn't polite to call people diseased.

No, no external evidence.

She kept talking. Maybe unaware of the way her mouth was rambling. "So that means the issue could be a lot more prevalent. I could be walking by people on the street who have this and never know it!"

Donovan looked to his senior partner. That conclusion, at least, was true.

GJ was off in her own head. She was a bona fide scientist—the talking to herself, mentally putting her pieces together. And Donovan didn't like that what she said was right.

She twisted her head up to him. "Can I X-ray you?"

"No." The reaction was knee-jerk. "No. You can't."

GJ turned away, inadvertently pacing the small room. "But I can get other X-rays. I can search hospital records. I can—"

"No." Eleri's voice was firm. "No, you can't."

"Because I'm under arrest? It just didn't seem like I was really being arrested." The insecurity was back. For good reason.

Eleri stood up. "Here's the deal. You leave now. You give us everything you have on the skeletons as well as all the evidence itself, and we won't arrest you."

They'd discussed this. Arresting a citizen—a forensic scientist—would open a can of worms. GJ, by way of her grandfather, had enough money to get a lawyer big enough to make a public stink. Right now, the only crimes they had her on would open their case to the courtroom or worse, the media. None of them wanted that. What they wanted was for GJ Janson to disappear. That wasn't going to happen either; the girl talked way too much.

Eleri continued, her stare sharp and meaningful, just shy of the black-eyed anger she could project these days. "If you breathe a word of this to anyone, write any papers on it, anything, we *will* arrest you."

The stare stopped the pacing. The last words seem to stop the girl's very breath. Donovan expected her to pack up and flee. It's what any sane person would do.

She didn't. Instead she breathed out the words, "Oh God, what did I stumble on?"

Eleri gave her another glare. "You don't know. You haven't seen the worst of it."

The way Janson reacted, she was warned but she didn't see the black eyes. Her look didn't convince Donovan he was safe. Though she did pack up and leave, he didn't believe it.

With his hands laced on top of his head, Donovan turned around. "I don't trust her, despite what your grandmère says."

"I don't know either," Eleri admitted. "But I don't want to deal with what Westerfield considers cleanup. *Our* cleanup."

The very thought turned Donovan's stomach. "So that leaves trusting her as the only option."

"It would seem so. My best hope is that Grandmère believes she's trustworthy." Eleri turned away. Then she turned back. "We need to see if we can find Adesso. He's out there."

"He's also shooting at us now."

"So we wear protective gear," she said. "Which will be oh-so-exciting and fun on a high seventies day. Gear up."

They met up with Walter, and donned helmets, non-Newtonian liquid vests, boots, and sweat apparently. He'd nearly soaked through his T-shirt by the time he was shoving a gun into his holster and ammo into his belt. This was not his usual MO. Though there was a level of comfort in the motor memory from training for this, this was still not easy for him.

"I wish we could put this on later." But he knew they couldn't. They had to ride in wearing full gear, because they had no idea where Adesso might be. When he might come out of the woodwork.

They rode in on the ATVs, the trailer slowing them down, though Donovan had no idea what Eleri expected to bring back on it. Any paperwork they might have left behind? Dr. Adesso?

He didn't want to ask. Instead he kept his eyes scanning the far too-open terrain around him. Donovan didn't trust the low scrub to not be hiding things. Hiding people.

He had trouble swallowing and wanted to believe it was the sand and not fear that closed his throat. Despite his need to steer, one hand strayed to the gun at his hip. It was more reassuring to look to his side and see Walter there. She had a long gun slung over her shoulder, sitting patiently, as though it belonged there. He'd seen her use it, nearly flowing into her hands when she needed it, a kind of deadly magic. It was just a matter of practice, he knew, but it looked damn cool when she did it.

He breathed easier then, inhaling sand inadvertently.

He coughed. Then coughed again. He'd breathe easier as—

"Eleri! Eleri." He spat sand as he said it into the comm system. The two other ATVs began to slow and he turned with them, a very small circling of the wagons.

"What?" Eleri asked, peeling her helmet away to reveal concern at his change of plans.

He looked back and forth between the two of them. Eleri would handle this fine. But Walter? No time like the present. "I go in better as the wolf."

Eleri's head jerked back. "I don't know if you noticed, but they don't have wolves out here."

"Yeah, I noticed," he added wryly. "But Adesso is clearly willing to shoot at people. I don't think he would have a reason to shoot at an animal."

He could get in, check around, sniff the place out, maybe even find Adesso. He could do it as a wolf in a way he never could as a person.

Eleri shook her head. "As the wolf you have no weapons."

"I'll have my teeth and my strength and I'll have no reason to defend myself, because who's going to shoot at a dog?"

"You're not a dog. You're a wolf. And you're out of place," she argued, clearly not liking the idea as much as he did. "He might shoot you just for that. He has to be suspicious after we went in and took all the paperwork we could find and surprised him on his own turf. No."

"Yes." His feet were on the ground, boot tracks wedged into the sand and scrub. She was wrong.

"No. I won't risk you that way." She was starting to put her helmet back on. She was the senior partner. She had final say.

"No." Except she didn't really. "It's my risk. You and Walter will have my back." He was climbing off his ATV and unbuckling his helmet.

"Donovan," Eleri protested.

"Eleri." He responded in just the same tone, brooking no

argument. "We were shot at once. We're heading in wearing full gear and looking for a fight. If we get this guy at all, it'll be no good because he'll most likely be dead."

"But we won't be." The set of her lips betrayed her anger.

"Last I checked, the job requirement was much more extensive than 'not dead.'" He peeled his jacket and began working the clasps on his vest.

"Stop removing your gear," she barked, but he didn't.

"You can turn around or get an eyeful." He peeled his shirt. The desert air felt much better against his skin, though he was wary of a bullet flying at him from out of nowhere. It didn't happen and he went for the buckle at his pants.

"Jesus, Donovan." She turned away, but he saw she was still watching the horizon, keeping an eye out.

"I need the tarp." But as he said it, he saw that Walter—who'd stayed silent during the argument—was already on it. "Thanks."

He ducked under the plastic sheet, growing hotter as he rolled his shoulders and popped his jaw. He opened and closed his mouth, pushing the front of his face out in a manner that GJ Janson hadn't yet deduced.

The fur trapped his body heat, just as it was intended to do. He hated it, feeling like he couldn't breathe. But then he shook his head in the rolling manner of all canines and nosed his way out from under the tarp. With one look back at them, he headed off for the closest hill. Once he cleared the crest, he would be able to see the Atlas building.

"Donovan, I want to stay in right behind you," Eleri said as he loped off.

He shook his head softly side to side, hoping they would see the "no," and understand. Then he took off.

Over the hill, the hot sand slid between his toes with each step. It slipped away, refusing resistance as he tried to run. He was already breathing heavily, panting in the heat. The building was growing in his sights as he got closer, the brick both beckoning and repelling him.

But he was at the door before he could think about it more. He heard the ATVs stop beyond the hills, out of sight. He appreciated it, though he could almost hear them sneaking up beyond the wind break.

Donovan stopped at the door, but didn't attempt to open it. First he put his nose to the seam between the double doors and inhaled. The same man had been here, recently, though Donovan couldn't quite tell the time frame. Since the last time they'd seen him? He didn't know.

Up on his hind legs, Donovan reached for the door handle. It took three tries, but he maneuvered, shoved, and pushed his way inside.

Aside from the heat, it reminded him of Axis. It was eerie, the same tables and chairs, same arrangement. Different smells. Donovan paused, listened. No sounds came from inside the building.

He sniffed his way along, nose down, following the faint scent around the corner. He smelled the man; he was here. It became more obvious when he turned the corner and saw the boots planted square at the end of the hallway. Following a line of sight up from the feet, he saw legs, torso, and that damned gun, pointed right at him.

Donovan stood stock still for a moment, not even breathing. Adesso stared at him as though he knew what Donovan was, and Donovan didn't twitch.

Not for five whole seconds before the heat got to him and he had to suck in a breath. Under the sound of his own lungs sucking air was the click of the safety sliding on.

His shoulders relaxed and he walked forward, only then thinking he may have cued Dr. Adesso that he understood the gun. He loped up and stuck his head under the man's hand. It was a gesture he hated, but it worked. He'd done it to Walter once upon a time. Then she'd figured him out.

He sat through the old man scratching his head. Having his head rubbed felt good, but being coddled like a dog didn't.

"You lost?" The voice wasn't as strong as the boots and gun would have indicated. The words came at the same time as a hand felt around his neck. "Wolf half-breed?"

So he recognized that Donovan wasn't just a lost dog. That made sense. He was a mammalian geneticist; he would know his wolf from his dog. Donovan was in trouble if he recognized that Donovan wasn't any kind of wolf. It hadn't taken Eleri long, and she didn't have a veterinary background. He'd have to play along, hope the man didn't notice.

"No collar. Well fed. Friendly." The analysis boded well for Donovan. "But probably half-wild. You shouldn't exist." He said it with a smile in his voice to cut the poor quality of his assessment of Donovan.

He walked off, favoring his left leg a little. Donovan wondered if they'd done that to him the week before. Then again, the healing bullet burn on his own head was from a gun fired by this man. The fact that he had another gun today meant he hadn't lost his only firearm. He'd managed to find another.

Following Adesso down the hallway, Donovan padded along, trying to appear casual, wishing the man would speak more. Eventually he did.

"Thought I heard people. May have just been you, but I'm not taking any chances this time." He used two different keys to open a bolted closet. Inside was an arsenal. Adesso started picking out guns.

E leri stopped outside the doors to the Atlas building, Walter snugged up alongside her, ready to enter and clear the place if necessary.

Wait.

Eleri signaled it, glad she'd gotten some military training, that she could signal without speaking and Walter would understand. Groups all had their own signs, but Walter had picked theirs up very fast.

Though she was practically covered from head to toe, Eleri peeled her gloves. Walter frowned, probably most concerned about leaving fingerprints. Though Eleri understood that wasn't her best move, she needed something more.

Grandmère said Emmaline would be found soon. Something told Eleri she would need to be at the top of her game for that. Her family would implode. She was going to need her skills at peak performance. So she put her hand flat on the door frame and closed her eyes. Walter could see the world around them; it wasn't unsafe.

But she got nothing.

She tried again, worried that Walter would think her

stranger than she already did. That she was holding them up. Donovan was inside. At the very thought, her stomach turned with fear. But was it her own, or his?

She couldn't tell.

Trying to calm herself down and feel something—*anything* —Eleri signaled for Walter to open the door. This time they stepped inside and she tried again. Inside the building, if Adesso was here, if anyone was here, they were much more vulnerable.

After a moment she gave up.

"Get anything?" Walter asked sotto voce.

Eleri shook her head. What good was her skill if she couldn't use it? The random impressions were a bitch— sending her on chases to hunt down evidence and find suspects the moment she woke up sometimes. It filled her with shit she didn't need and left her high and dry when she did need it.

Walter started for the other end of the big room. She slid soundlessly between the chairs, her rifle aimed and ready for the nothing that seemed to be coming.

Eleri was stepping away from the door, closing the distance between her and Walter when the cold hit her.

It clenched her chest, icy fear reaching fingers into her, snaking around her heart. It hit her like a memory she didn't possess: an image from behind, of a man striding down the hallway. A handgun rested easily in the grip of his left hand. His right hand held a rifle as though he was ready to spray bullets through a room.

"Walter!" She didn't shout it, her training too ingrained to be overcome by something as simple as bone-deep fear. "Get *down!*"

Eleri was diving for the floor as the door opened. There wasn't enough time for her to see where Walter went as she flipped a table and tucked herself behind it. The table was a cheap, industrial model and she was confident it wasn't going to protect her from much, but she was better off if he couldn't see her.

The sound of bullets hitting the walls around her and the wood-chip-and-glue construction of the table in front of her kept her in a tight ball, her own gun clutched in her grip as she waited for the right moment.

Her eyes tightly shut against the sound, Eleri saw instead the man at the end of the room. She felt his grip on his weapon and the anger that permeated him at their presence.

Her fingers still gripped her gun as she considered staying low or popping up to fight. Trying to slow her heart rate wasn't working. Staying small was a gamble. She'd been shot at before, but she was better at chasing, searching, and even hand-to-hand. Odd thoughts to pop into her head now, when she might be about to die. Her mother would be so pissed.

The decision was taken out of her hands. She didn't know how she heard it, but she did. Walter must have popped up from whatever she was behind and opened fire. But Eleri couldn't let her be the only one defending. She let go of her firm grip on the fetal position and got on her knees.

Leading with the muzzle of her gun, she looked over the edge of the table and was grateful for the full gear as something pinged off her helmet. She flinched inside, but squeezed off two shots before she ducked back.

He'd seen her.

Bullets were now flying her direction rather than randomly. She hit fetal position again for a moment before taking a short, deep breath and popping back up. She fired three shots this time before she even focused on the man, but she winged him.

At that moment, Eleri was more than grateful for her training. But she was maybe more thankful for Walter's. From the sounds, she hadn't let up fire for more than a second.

Shit.

"Don't kill him!" She didn't want to yell it. Didn't want him to know he had an advantage. But more than that she didn't want to lose the only witness she had to whatever shit was still going on down here.

"Seriously?" Walter bit the sound back.

There was no good answer. Walter should protect herself first, but Eleri wanted to talk to him.

Taking advantage of a momentary break in the fire, she popped up and fired again. Missed again. *Fuck.*

"You want him alive?" Walter asked, just as the sound of gunfire started up again.

Eleri didn't get to answer.

She heard the steady pop of a nine mil interlaced with the heavy steps of a not-too-heavy woman. Shocked, but not thinking, Eleri popped up over the top of the table and her mouth opened at the sight.

Walter was walking straight toward the man, two hands on her firearm, squeezing off shots. In short order, Eleri watched Walter switch to one hand, then drop the gun as she ran out of bullets.

Her other hand came up then, her backup weapon in it. She never missed a beat.

Eleri fought through her awe to provide backup.

Adesso ran out of bullets and panicked for a moment before holding his hands up.

"I hit you," he said to Walter as though saying it should be enough to topple the woman coming at him.

Walter held fire, but continued forward until her gun was in the man's face. "I'm metal." She held up her prosthetic hand. "And you're done."

Eleri had a moment of confusion. Walter only had one good hand. She must have wedged the gun into the prosthetic and worked the limited mobility of the fingers on that hand. *Holy shit.*

"Eames?" Walter prodded her.

Yeah, all she had to do was talk.

"Dr. Adesso?" Eleri kept her peripheral vision on the empty fully automatic gun at his side. She had no idea what other weapons he might be hiding. He'd come out shooting rather than asking questions. She didn't trust him. He'd also manipulated kids. Stolen children.

He stared at her, dead behind the eyes.

She'd seen this look before. Hostile witness. "Adesso?"

All she needed was a yes or no. Not to identify him; she recognized him. Definitely older than the picture she'd seen. Definitely harder worn. He still didn't answer.

Though her eyes didn't flicker, she saw Donovan coming up behind him. He'd been directly behind the doctor. For a moment, her brain scrambled, trying to figure out how to get him out of this. She could use him in his regular form. But she didn't know how, she had Adesso to keep an eye on.

"Come in. Sit down. Please notice that we didn't kill you and we only returned fire." She gestured sarcastically to one of the chairs that was still standing. Then she pulled up a table. "Oh, look, this one doesn't have as many bullet holes as the others. Sit."

He stared blankly at her for another moment before she got too exasperated and lost her shit. "Oh, please! You are eighty-two years old. You're Dr. Robert Adesso. You're an animal geneticist. And you worked on children. You hybridized *children*. Want to explain?"

"No."

"Oh, goody. An answer." She pulled up a chair across from him as Walter stepped up behind him, motioning to check him. Eleri nodded.

"Walter is going to pat you down, take your weapons."

"Her name is Walter?"

"I'm the fucking FBI. You did genetic work on stolen children and you're questioning the name of the best damn soldier I've ever met?"

Walter's lips turned up slightly at that, but her good hand didn't stop the pat-down. "By the way," she whispered to the surly older man, "I can still pull the trigger with my metal hand. Don't test me. You aren't that fast."

Walter found three handguns on Adesso. Each time she pulled another one, he stiffened more—if that were possible. Eleri never broke eye contact.

She did reach into her back pocket and pull her ID, setting it on the table between them, badge and info up. His eyes flicked only enough to see that the badge was real. Eleri wasn't sure if she outranked him. Though she was part of a government division not publicly acknowledged, so was he.

Walter stood behind him, her arms in the standard "at ease." Eleri let the silence sit for a moment before she spoke again. This time she turned away from Adesso and offered a smile to Walter, trying to think how to phrase this. "Can you . . . tell Donovan where we are? Take his things."

A slow nod showed comprehension and Eleri pre-empted the next question. She stared at Adesso as she said it. "I'm good here."

She didn't say anything else as Walter carefully gathered Donovan's clothes. Before she left the room, Walter patted Adesso on the shoulder. "Don't make her mad."

Eleri hid her reaction to that. She wanted to both laugh and cry. She couldn't control it. Had never seen it. But she didn't let Adesso see anything other than a blank stare that matched his own. "You can talk to me or not. But I didn't kill you. I don't really want to."

He blinked. He breathed. Though there was nothing she could put her finger on, she felt the shift starting in him. Trying to use that feeling to her advantage, she looked for the right way in. She needed information, not another dead body.

She couldn't afford another incident like Morozov.

That was the ticket.

She leaned back and started talking. "We went to see Dr. Morozov in prison."

Adesso inhaled sharply and stiffened again, but still didn't speak.

"We don't know enough to help, but we know enough to cause a lot of problems. And we know enough to know that whatever you've held onto here for so long is about to crumble."

He blinked again. Eleri kept chipping at his wall. "We saw Morozov. He said he killed them all. But he didn't, did he? Some of them are still here."

She saw Donovan and Walter then, coming around the corner. Some tiny portion of her brain spiked jealousy that Walter might have been allowed to see him change, but she pushed it away. What was at hand was far more important. Donovan nodded in response to her last statement, lifted his head and inhaled—not to smell, but to gesture what he'd done.

There were others. They were still here. Just like at Axis.

Eleri sharpened her focus on Adesso, felt the surge and the anger for what had been done to these children. Were they living feral in the desert the way others were in Michigan? Probably. They were adults now. The ones that survived. Adults with whatever problems the scientists had inserted into their cells.

She fought the surge. She didn't want her eyes to turn black —whatever that actually was—she wanted Adesso to trust her. She threw out an accusation, hoping he would defend himself.

"Are you still experimenting on them?" She bit the words like bullets.

He shook his head, then he cracked. "They are mine. I protect them!" His fist pounded the table. "You cannot have them."

"I don't want them." She shook her head and gave him a sad but genuine look. "I don't. I just need to know what's going on."

"No. You don't. You need to leave." He was leaning across the table. "They have been through enough."

She leaned in, too. "At your hands."

That took a little righteousness out of his ire. He still managed a response. "Whatever Morozov said that sent you here, it was a lie."

"Maybe it was." Eleri leaned back. This wasn't going to be pretty. "But maybe it triggered someone else to come here, too."

His eyes flared, his nostrils twitched, his shoulders slumped a little. Reaction. She could read it. It was Donovan, standing slightly behind the man who shook his head "no." Whoever they were, they hadn't been here yet.

Eleri ignored the flash of a frown that crossed Walter's face at Donovan's pronouncement. Damn, Walter was getting in very deep with them. Westerfield's comments about what to do about the soldier flitted through Eleri's mind, leaving a trace of bitter flavor behind as they went. There was no way she was enacting option one. She trained her focus back to Adesso.

"It doesn't matter if they've been here yet or not. Someone is onto this. Not just us." Eleri pushed. Her silences were timed to get him to speak.

He frowned at her. So she played her card.

"Morozov died in a 'random' prison shanking just moments after being dragged from our interview."

She watched as Adesso's eyes widened further in fear at each word she uttered. He should be afraid. She whispered, "Now, tell me, how many are out here?"

38

S he shouldn't be here. GJ knew that. She also knew she could no more fight her inherent personality than she could turn the ocean. Instead, she turned the wheel.

There were tire tracks off the road here. Bigger ones, not a truck but not a little compact car either. About the right size for, say, a good sized SUV. She was no expert, but it looked like a set of trailer tires followed. They'd had a trailer when she'd seen them go by.

She'd been eating her breakfast, ready to drive out of town —though "town" was a strong term for the place—and she'd seen the oddly matte-colored SUV out the window. ATVs stacked on the trailer suggested they were heading out into the desert.

GJ knew her curiosity wasn't right. But Agent Heath, he was one of *them*. He was a living, breathing specimen of the skeletons her grandfather collected. As far as she knew—and she admitted she didn't know much—her grandfather had never seen a live one. If she brought him one, maybe he would talk to her about them, rather than shut her out.

Not that she was going to kidnap an FBI agent, but she

could learn about him and use that info as leverage into her grandfather's research. That's why she followed.

The question was did she use what she knew about her grandfather's research or just information to get Agent Heath to talk to her? If she already knew he had some mutation and that it was maybe more common than he thought, he might see that she meant well.

Okay, GJ didn't really believe that, but she held out hope. And she turned off the road into the sand.

The road was bumpy at best and she crawled along feeling like a felon. Why shouldn't she? She'd been arrested for the first time and let go with strict warnings. The arrest had been deserved. She'd trailed FBI agents in a closed national forest. She'd stolen directly from them and she'd arranged a felony committed by another FBI agent.

GJ hit the brakes.

What had she become?

The dust embedded in the sand around her billowed up, leaving her in a cloud of her own sudden realization. It wasn't pretty.

She sat there for probably five minutes. Thinking. Should she do this? Her brain went back and forth.

She'd been committing felonies to move her thesis forward. Then to follow up on her grandfather's research . . . if it could be called that. *Shit.*

Still, Agent Heath was a living person with whatever that mutation was. He surely couldn't have those bones and not have some physiological results of that. What were they? Had her grandfather met any people living with it? Was it an already identified disease? She hadn't asked her grandfather, and she hadn't been able to find anything. She was a grad student; she should be able to find it if it existed. But she'd feel stupid beyond measure if she went back and her grandfather simply said, "Of course, it's such-and-such disease."

GJ sighed into the car. If she found them, what would she do?

She'd stay back and watch. That was all. Maybe Agent Heath moved differently, maybe if she watched him long enough she could record some other symptom besides the elongated shoulder blades, the odd shape of the rib cage. Maybe she'd see evidence of the slightly thicker long bones—not that she had any idea how to see that on a living man without an X-ray, but she had hope.

Observing people on public property wasn't illegal.

She put the car back into drive. The cloud of her own dust had cleared a bit and she could see better. The symbolism didn't escape her. But she slowly followed the tire tracks until she came to the abandoned SUV and the now empty trailer.

They'd pulled the ATVs and ridden in from here. Too far to walk then. She crept forward until she found the ATV tracks and figured she'd go until she had to turn around. At least she still had a mostly full tank of gas.

When the ground got too rough, she opened her bag and rummaged for socks and her best sneakers. She grabbed a bottle of water and pulled her phone off the charger. She'd go until she had to turn around or she found something. Not her best plan, but . . .

GJ walked until she cleared a small hill and came up on an old, old fence. She was huffing from the exertion—her exercise seemed to always come in bursts—and she told herself from the heat. But she sucked in her breath for another reason entirely.

A brick building stared at her. Here in the almost literal middle of nowhere. And she recognized it. It looked just like that Axis building in the middle of the snow in Michigan.

GJ walked through a hole in the fence.

∾

DONOVAN SMELLED her before he saw her.

Immediately he looked to Eleri, sitting calm in her chair while he and Walter stood nearby—Walter to keep Adesso in that seat, and Donovan to read him.

There was no way to signal Eleri without telling all of them.

It was gone a moment after he detected it. A shift in the wind, something stirring through the building, he didn't know. But GJ Janson was at the Atlas building.

He must have breathed some level of his frustration out, because Eleri looked up to him, questioning. Should he tell her? Or just leave?

Janson was no threat, but maybe he could use her. With one finger he signaled to Eleri that he was headed out the door, then he turned away even as he caught the cloud that passed across her features. She would have to read Adesso now without him, but she could.

Walter started to follow him, but he motioned her to stay behind, still unable to say with certainty there was a grad student who should have been nothing more than a pest but was causing real problems.

Donovan opened his mouth and squeezed the muscles on the side of his face. He wouldn't look right, half-changed like this, but he needed to smell. He needed to know if he was getting close to her, to track her, but more than that, he needed to be sure he didn't run into any surprises.

There were traces of other people here. Inside the building. Stronger in the common areas. They weren't using it much, but they were still using it. Checking out the window—his eyes were great in the dark, but not much for the desert—he scanned the area in the direction back to the road. Sure enough, walking toward them, sweaty and giving off an all-too-human scent he could easily detect now was GJ pain-in-his-ass-Janson.

Eleri told her to leave town and not get charged with federal crimes. Apparently that offer wasn't sweet enough. He sighed to himself. The best thing to do would be to wait. Otherwise, she'd see him when he opened the door and he'd have to run her down—if she was smart enough to run.

For a moment he entertained the thought that she would see the place, take a glance around without entering, and leave. But as she got closer he could see her thoughts in her eyes, in the pull of her forehead, the twitch in her jaw. She recognized the building.

She wasn't going to turn around.

He stepped to the side of the door and waited. Despite the soft sand and her sneakers, she didn't approach silently. He heard Eleri still running her soft/hard interrogation on Adesso in the other room. He heard Walter only minimally, breathing, never moving. Her control was amazing. As a man who sometimes just needed to crawl into a different skin and run wild, he was in awe of her discipline. In fact, it was that very factor in each of them that allowed her to find out about him in the first place.

He listened as GJ stopped on the other side of the door and took a drink from her water bottle. She seemed to be contemplating coming inside. If she did, it would make things a lot easier for him.

His brain skittered away with a new thought. Why had Walter come to his house when he'd been recuperating from his ankle break? They'd emailed a few times, but she'd been in contact with Eleri, too. She hadn't gone to Eleri's house. Had he missed a flag? *Shit.*

He heard GJ wipe her hand on her jeans, a soft, raspy sound. The jeans were probably the reason she was sweating like she was. This was winter around here. She wasn't dumb enough to be this unprepared. She'd stolen from them, successfully. She'd worn a ghillie suit in Michigan. No, GJ Janson, who didn't seem to understand how initials worked, had not planned on being here today. But how did one just make an impromptu jaunt to the Atlas building? Atlas, by its very nature, was hidden away.

She'd somehow followed them.

Her hand on the handle startled him from his thoughts. The click as she pressed the latch and pushed her way inside made him tense.

One. Two. He waited until she crept inside, turned, and saw him before he sprang at her.

He'd thought she didn't have a weapon—the flimsy plastic bottle of water notwithstanding—but her hand came up, baton extended and ready for a solid blow. His training kicked in; it worked better when he was angry, rather than scared. And he was angry.

They'd let her go. They hadn't written a warrant for her. They'd decided to trust her with what little she did seem to know about him. They'd dropped federal felony charges, for God's sakes, and yet, here she was, pushing her way into a situation that was barely contained.

He rushed into her attack, rather than turning away. Though he brought his arms up together and defended, he was well inside the zone where she could successfully strike him with the extended baton.

GJ's arm came down in the arc she'd started and couldn't help but finish, crashing into the back of his fists as he brought them up, disrupting her movement.

"Ah!" She cried out with the pain of the too-abrupt stop.

His teeth clenched. Even as he felt the push of anger, wanting him to change, he fought it back, his teeth clenched against the sound. Making a sound, acknowledging a hit was a point for your opponent. GJ gave that to him. She wasn't a trained fighter at all.

She stepped back, tripping away from him and crashing into the door. She probably couldn't make more noise if she tried. There was no way that Eleri and Walter and even Adesso didn't know she was here now. And Donovan was pissed. If he was Eleri, his eyes would have shot black. As himself, he felt his lips peel back and the low growl of anger escape through those clenched teeth.

Dammit, he'd handed her something. Not again.

Swinging his right arm up—she was holding the baton in her left and he let himself think, let himself catalog the ways in which she was a bad fighter—he blocked her movement even before she calibrated another swing.

With his left hand he knocked loose the water bottle she still clenched in her other hand and wondered if she'd really thought it was a weapon. It hit the linoleum, making a crunch and a thud at the same time, but now the noise didn't matter as much. They would all be hearing this fight. Donovan intended it to be a very short one.

Still holding GJ's arm as she twisted, he shoved her face-first into the door. It wasn't very nice, but she'd left nice far behind when she didn't get out of town. She grunted with the contact and managed a distressed, "Hey!"

He shoved her again. Stripping the baton from her grip, he yanked on her other arm. It kept her from fighting back while he pocketed her weapon. Then he pulled her hands together, turned her palms out, putting pressure on her shoulders and at the last moment realizing he didn't carry cuffs. *Dammit.* Maybe he should have rethought that.

He did have zip ties and inside a minute had each wrist encircled and the two effectively tied together. Only then did he turn her back to face him.

Her mouth shot off again. "Hey! You have no right to arrest—"

"Bullshit. I have you on federal charges. Several of them." He fought another growl that threatened to escape his throat. It wouldn't do to enlighten her further about the anomalies she'd already noted in him. It was best if she thought she'd just discovered a bone disorder.

"You dropped those charges." She somehow found the justification for her own anger.

Donovan didn't see it. In low tones, he explained. "We simply didn't file the charges. They're still out there, waiting, and you didn't leave town. So don't go thinking you met the requirements to have them dropped. And I'll thank you to shut the fuck up."

"I—"

"Shut up." He pushed her against the door. Not enough to hurt her, but enough to rattle the sound loose from her mouth. Then he grabbed her by her zip-tied wrists and shoved her in front of him as he made his way into the room where Eleri still sat at the table, still stared at Adesso as though he would just tell her everything and Adesso stared back at her as though she would never know. Walter stood behind the man, not touching him, but just as effectively keeping him in his seat as if he sat on a land mine. She'd shot him with a prosthetic hand and Adesso understood that kind of skill. Donovan did, too. He just couldn't figure out why it was hot.

"Look what dragged herself in." He pushed GJ toward the questioning, small crowd.

He saw GJ start to open her mouth and he yanked on the zip tie that held her wrists together, stopping her before she started.

Adesso looked back and forth between the three of them, his eyes widening with every glance. Donovan absorbed some of the naked fear in the man's eyes. Did he know GJ? Was she deeper into this thing than any of them knew?

Donovan was looking to Eleri for answers when Adesso burst out, "You were followed? *What have you done?*"

Under the words and far in the distance, Donovan thought he heard a noise.

39

Eleri suppressed a groan when Donovan appeared in the doorway with GJ Janson cuffed and protesting. How in hell had the girl made it here?

Normally Eleri fought against calling—even thinking about —grown women as girls, but it was a damn default when they were being idiots. GJ had no idea what she was getting into, but despite an easy out, a sweetened pot of no-federal-charges and more, the fool just couldn't seem to do what was best for anyone, let alone herself.

With each dumb step she waded deeper into the murky waters of what they were doing.

"You were followed!" Adesso said once, but when he said it the second time, looking at Eleri—accusing her personally this time—he jumped up. "They followed you!"

Eleri didn't know who "they" were, but she highly doubted GJ Janson was part of the group. She wanted to ask, but she needed more information first. Looking to Walter, she frowned, ready to speak the words, but Walter didn't need them.

With her own answering frown, Walter shook her head. GJ

336
A.J. SCUDIERE

had not followed them. When they'd driven in, Eleri had specifically asked if they were being tailed. Walter had specifically paid attention. If GJ had managed to elude Walter, then she was only playing at being a fool and something far worse was going on. Eleri didn't think that was it. She did see Walter's face as it came together.

"She didn't follow us, ma'am," Walter reported, her hand on Adesso's shoulder, her explanation coming easily even as she guided him back into this chair. His outburst didn't faze her; her calm was the kind of thing only the best soldiers ever fully mastered. "She tracked us."

Eleri understood the difference. They'd left marks. GJ wasn't behind them on the road, but she'd figured out where they'd been headed. The roads out here went one way for a long way, so if she'd seen them turn this direction back when they were close to town, they may have been easy to find.

Shit.

They hadn't covered their tracks. She hadn't thought anything of it. *Fuckfuckfuck.*

Morozov was shanked in prison, he'd been pulled away from their interview before they finished. Clearly, someone wanted him there, and recently someone wanted him dead. Someone was watching him. Several of the doctors who'd worked here on the kids had been scattered. Some had been sent home, maybe the loyal ones. Some had disappeared and some had been disappeared—Eleri saw the irony. But she hadn't connected "them" watching Morozov in prison to "them" watching over Atlas. Over the building here.

So Eleri could convince Adesso that they were safe. That GJ was not "them" and he was okay. But if she told him that, then she also told him that she was too dumb to cover her tracks.

Donovan twitched and she looked up at him, but he only frowned. They needed Morse code, or something similar but less commonly understood. She needed to know what he knew, not just that he knew something.

Turning back to Adesso, she gave up. Whatever high ground she thought she held, she didn't. She'd been hacked and now tracked by a grad student—one with good connections mind you, but a grad student nonetheless. "You don't have to worry about her." She hoped to hell she was right about that. "She's tracking us, not you."

Adesso's expression remained stony. He didn't speak. Just looked at her with that cold glare.

Between GJ butting in and Adesso offering nothing, Eleri had enough. Leaving Walter standing behind the doctor and Donovan in control of GJ, Eleri glared back. She smacked her hands on the table top, not feeling the pain of the wood-chip-and-glue splinters she'd pressed into her palms. She let her anger show on her face, not worried about whether she was doing that black-eye thing Donovan told her about or not.

"*You* experimented on these kids. *You* knew they were kidnapped. *You* treated them as lab rats, as less than human. You *killed* them." She towered over him in his seat. She could see him pulling back and she could feel the heat of her own anger rolling toward him. "You don't have any right to act like their protector now."

His breathing sped up, his chest heaving. His face aged as she yelled at him. "You're right. We all did it." He looked away. "But they were already dead."

The words were a strange echo of Morozov's words in the prison interview. "Is that how you justified it?"

He only nodded. Adesso didn't look at her, at any of them. The defiance was gone, fled in the face of his own former sins.

"So you protect them now to make up for that?"

He didn't answer. Still protecting them. She wondered if these "kids"—fully grown adults now—loved or at least respected him for that protection. Or did they hate him for what he'd done before? She didn't have time for speculations on that. She needed to find what was left of the Atlas and Axis kids and figure out what to do with them.

"Where are they?"

This time he looked at her again. "I won't tell you. They deserve their privacy after all we did."

She thought of something then. Eleri had been shocked by Morozov's death. "Morozov said he killed them all. What did he do? Why didn't it work?"

From the corner of her eye, Eleri watched as GJ absorbed the revelatory information being let out before her. GJ Janson was in serious trouble. Whether or not they brought the Atlas and Axis kids in to Westerfield, they were now bringing GJ in front of him. He'd be the one making the decision. Given his remarks on Walter, Eleri wasn't sure what he'd say about a grad student. Would GJ just disappear?

Again she reminded herself that GJ had ample warnings and she'd dug her own hole. With trust in her colleagues to keep things running around her, Eleri turned her laser focus onto Adesso again, in hopes she could squeeze something more from him. She repeated herself, "So what did Morozov do? And why didn't it work?"

There was a silence while he stared at her. She stared back. They were in the middle of nowhere, but if he wanted to play stubborn, he was playing against the wrong girl. Plus, she had backup. If he did, she hadn't seen it yet. She leaned back, crossed her arms and waited as if she had all the time in the world.

Except she didn't.

"El." Donovan's voice broke the cold war between her and the doctor. She flicked him a look. But even in that fast moment she saw him frown. His eyes glanced upward, as though he listened into the distance.

She looked at him more closely then and he mouthed the words to her, "I thought I heard something."

She was pretty sure Donovan almost never *thought* he heard anything. He could place footsteps at distances she couldn't fathom. With that acuity, he also had developed the memory to identify people by their footfalls, places by the smell they left on clothing, animals by something in the way the light fell on them. His senses were so much more fine-tuned than theirs. Eleri had joined the FBI straight out of college. She'd known that's what she would do with her life since she was ten. But Westerfield had figured out what Donovan was. Something in his medical examiner files? His success rate at finding poisons and cause of death? She didn't know. But Donovan had been recruited specifically to Night-Shade for exactly this reason.

"Is he saying you've been followed?" Adesso once again looked at her with accusation.

She wanted to smack him. "Shut up. Let him listen."

But Donovan only shrugged. When she gave up, she turned back to Adesso. "What did Morozov do? He said he killed them all."

"Obviously he didn't." The wall was back. All emotion gone.

"But he tried."

Still nothing. For a moment, she fantasized about just shooting him, Indiana Jones style. If he wasn't going to speak to her he was useless. But that wasn't actually true.

She sat down. "We already know that you took these kids and subjected them to painful and illegal genetic therapies. You basically hybridized them with a variety of animals and you tortured them."

"We didn't torture them. The treatment itself was gentle."

"But not what happened to them after that." She'd accused him of worse than he'd done, getting him to defend himself and leak information.

He seemed to realize that he'd done it, but he made some kind of decision. Adesso shook his head "no."

"A lot of them died from it," Eleri posited.

He didn't answer. He didn't get a chance.

"El. Someone's here." Donovan had managed to stay silent until now.

Adesso turned on GJ. "Who are they? Why did you bring them here?"

"I didn't do anything!" she protested. It was a relatively weak gesture given that she was handcuffed.

Eleri asked a better question. "How many?"

"At least two cars. Big ones. Lots of feet on the ground. Relatively silent. Hard to hear."

Shit. That meant professionals.

With a sudden burst of thought, she blinked and turned to Donovan. "Westerfield? Our people?"

He shook his head and at her answering frown—he could tell that? But she'd asked, hadn't she?—he said, "Not trained the way we were. Walk is different. Not feds."

Double shit.

She grabbed Adesso by the arm. "Who would come here?"

The fear in his eyes made her wary. He looked to Donovan. "What are they wearing? Do they have full face masks with gas?"

Donovan looked flustered for a minute. "How . . .?"

Eleri explained even as she jerked him to his feet. "He can't see them, he's listening. Who are they?"

"I don't know. But they've come twice before. Both times they killed some of the remaining kids. Left them out to rot." He looked truly remorseful, not seeming to connect that he'd helped put these people in this situation in the first place. "I have to sound the alarm."

"What?" *There was an alarm for this?*

"So they'll know to get safe. They've lost too much already." For a moment he looked desperate, frantic, frightened. Then a calm settled over him. "Follow me."

He ran down the hallway with no concern for any of them shooting him in the back. Eleri ran after him.

Donovan yanked on GJ's arms, wondering how much he should protect her. She'd been nothing but trouble and she'd turned into something worse since arriving at the Atlas building. He didn't know what to do with her, but he couldn't leave her behind, so he pulled her along, keeping her upright when her feet stumbled, ignoring her protestations.

Adesso's pace picked up, his old frame sprinting in a burst that looked like it belonged to a younger man. "Here!" he shouted and pointed into one of the offices. It looked random, but Donovan was certain it wasn't.

It took less than ten seconds to prove him right.

Adesso dove into the closet and turned to Walter. "Help."

They dug their fingers into the corners for a moment then pulled up a door leading to stairs. Adesso propped it open with his shoulder, motioning Walter down the steps. She ducked but made short work of it.

Donovan pushed GJ in after her, knowing Walter could handle the girl whether that involved catching her from a stumble or fighting her off. He and Eleri stood at the top of the steps and looked to each other before he turned to Adesso. "You next."

He might have sent Walter into something terrible, down some awful rabbit hole, but there didn't seem to be much choice.

Adesso paused.

"They're at the door," Donovan told them all. He heard them spreading out. With what Adesso had asked earlier, he now imagined them decked out but not showing any logos. Something from the same shadow agency that had made Axis and Atlas in the first place? He didn't know.

"I'm not coming," Adesso said.

Donovan knew better than to let anyone—friend or enemy —put them in a hole and close the door on them.

"Stay here and wait. I have to go." Adesso bolted down the hallway, leaving Donovan to catch the door.

He and Eleri stood silently, not letting the heavy latch fall shut on Walter and GJ, but also not putting themselves into what might very well be a trap either.

Adesso's footsteps rang through the empty hall and Donovan easily heard the metallic rub of the stairwell door opening. The old man's feet pounded up the steps and faded into softer and softer sounds. He was overhead. His steps became erratic, as though he were dancing quickly through the room. Donovan didn't have much time to wonder what was happening.

A siren, probably mounted on the top of the building blasted a short, heavy sound. Then again. Then again. The rhythm kept up for five short blasts before it was interrupted by a spurt of gunfire and fell silent.

Donovan looked to Eleri, who appeared to be thinking the same thing he was: Adesso had gotten the warning out, but whoever the intruders were, they'd shot him down.

Sure enough, no more sounds came from above him. Not the siren, not the shuffle of feet, nothing.

In the distance, he heard the doors down the hall, and they didn't open softly. They were kicked in despite being unlocked. This was a hostile invasion with no options for negotiations.

"After you." He motioned to Eleri but she was already partway down the steps, gesturing for him to follow.

He let the door fall softly closed over his head, pitching them into near total darkness.

"I'm right here." For a brief moment of total blackness a hand curled into his. Donovan was startled by both the bursts of gunfire coming from overhead and the shot of calm that counteracted the natural fear that bullets carried with them. He squeezed the hand as his eyes adjusted, his lips curling into a small smile.

"It's not Eames. It's Walter." She spoke ever-so-softly into the graying light around him. He could see her eyes, bright in the bits of reflection he could detect. Saw how she looked toward him without focus in what was pitch black to her purely human eyes. He picked up the acrid, sweet scent of spent gunpowder and gases and over that the hit of pheromones he hadn't expected.

His chest tightened, but he tried to play it normal. "I know. I can smell you."

Footsteps tread the floor above them. "Shhhh," he warned them all, but leaned closer to Walter. It was up to him to organize. They were blind, relying only on the gross sounds they could hear. Feet. Bullets.

He could distinguish numbers, trained movements vs. untrained. Maybe count how many were there. He could smell and see who was down with him. It was just the three women. No surprises. Not a booby trap set by Adesso.

Donovan knew he could rely on Walter's skills and Eleri's

gut. He had his senses. It was GJ Janson who seemed the most useless, and he didn't trust her despite Grandmère's card.

He turned to her, getting into her face so she could feel him. He knew she couldn't see him. Her unfocused eyes contracted in fear as she sensed his heat or maybe his breath. "Janson, if you make so much as a peep, I swear I will gut you myself and leave you here to rot. Do you understand?"

Her mouth opened, then closed when she thought better of it. Though he'd asked her a question, he'd also threatened even a peep. Realizing he could see her even if she couldn't see anything, she offered a slow, controlled nod and didn't relax until he said, "Good," and slid away from her.

He needed to pay attention to what was going on overhead. Donovan closed his eyes, focusing his brain on the sounds and smells. The bursts of gunfire spoke of fully automatic weapons. He wracked his brain, trying to think of any agency that used full auto and he couldn't come up with anything. He didn't like it.

Whoever they were, they were well-trained. They moved as a unit. More than once, he heard gunfire from two separate parts of the building at the same time. He listened again, searching for and finding the rhythm of their work.

"El, they're shooting the place up."

Though it was dark, she knew full well he could see every-thing. Her expression clearly read, "No shit, Sherlock," and he almost burst out laughing then and there.

"No, I mean they aren't shooting anyone. They got Adesso, and they're searching, but none of the sounds indicate they actually found anyone. They're just shooting into walls and making a show of it. It's an exercise as much as anything. They don't know we're here."

She shook her head. "They don't know exactly where, but they do know we're here. GJ tracked us. They'll have seen the signs of more than just her being here. They won't stop until they find us, or they bomb the place. We have to get out."

"They'll cover the doors. Someone will be left there." GJ's voice was soft, terrified, but Donovan had zero sympathy. Had she followed any one of the instructions she'd been given, she wouldn't be in this mess.

"She's right," Walter added, her hand snaking to rest on Donovan's forearm, as though to reassure him she knew it left a bad taste in his mouth to follow anything GJ said. "They'll have left a post, in case we evade them. They have full autos. I can overpower one man, maybe two. If we go out past them, we might not lose everyone, but with those guns, we'll lose someone."

Donovan was quiet just long enough for GJ to softly gasp. He shrugged into the blackness, knowing she couldn't see him. Maybe that was better.

"Did Adesso close the door to this office when he brought us in?" Eleri asked.

"No," Walter answered before Donovan could say he didn't know. "But then he went back out it as the two of you came down, did he shut it then?"

Donovan closed his eyes, trying to remember if he'd seen it, heard the click, something.

"Yes. He closed it," Eleri offered. He didn't know if she'd seen it with her eyes or felt it as she often did. He didn't really care. He believed her. So he made a small contingency plan, in case she was wrong, but Plan A was that the door was closed.

"They'll open it as they come by," he figured out. "They're sweeping all the rooms. They'll open this door and fire into the room, into the closet." He'd never been so happy to be hiding below the floor. "We'll have to wait for after that."

So they'd get out with the door open. At least they wouldn't have to open it themselves and maybe draw attention. He looked for a positive and didn't really find one. He also didn't think his group could be quiet enough to not alert someone they were sneaking down the hall. GJ worried him the most. He'd heard her coming from a mile away; they would, too.

"The window?" Her voice was soft, the peep he'd warned her against making. But she seemed to know she was the biggest risk. The suggestion was for herself as much as for any of them.

The others probably still couldn't see in the near-complete darkness. But Donovan saw Walter, her eyes darting up and left as she thought. "The windows here are different."

It was how she'd known this building was constructed after the first. He glanced at her mouth as it pursed in thought, looking almost girlie, as though she let go of the outer shell in the black. As though she was Lucy.

"They open sideways, with the crank. So we'll have to climb and slide through to get out." She was still tipping her head back and forth as she thought, no longer the soldier but the brain. For the first time in a long time, Donovan felt a shot of something needy and raw. And he was supremely grateful that they were in the utter darkness and that he was the only one who could smell pheromones.

The only ones coming off Lucy were the kind he expected: controlled fear, stress, the ones that came from a lifetime of awful situations and surviving them. Eleri was much the same. GJ was all over the place, not trained, and about to piss her pants. *Good.*

"What do you hear, Donovan?" Eleri's voice pulled his gaze her way, her eyes reflecting to him like the paranormal creature he was now convinced she was. "Are they close? Is it a good time?"

As if to punctuate her words, a burst of gunfire ripped the air in a distant part of the compound.

"It's upstairs," he said back. He could smell death—probably Adesso, but he couldn't be sure. Not stuck down here, not with the scent of bullets and ripped building materials floating through the air. "They've checked this room and left it. Now is as good as I can tell."

He inhaled again but got nothing more than he'd had the minute before. They were pinned. Despite being ready to come into the compound—vests, eye protection, and more—they were not prepared to go up against whoever was coming in. They were SWAT or better. *Shit*. He should have stayed at the medical examiner's office.

"I'll go up first," Eleri said, and he could both see and feel her moving toward the stairs. Or just to the right of them. To save her from crashing a shin, he grabbed her arm and tugged her in the right direction, at the same time holding her back.

"I'll go." Donovan used his hold on her to maneuver himself in front of her.

"I've got it." Walter was back, having erased Lucy from her face. She headed toward the stairs. She was aimed correctly, even though she couldn't see. Of course she was.

But she had force of conviction, and he stepped out of the way, pulling Eleri with him. Walter's words overrode them the same as her steps.

"I'm up first. I've got the best shooting skills." No one argued. "I'll cover us. This space is the equivalent of the trap in the office at Axis, the secret stash of files. So I know where we are in the building. It'll take a bit to get the window open and get through. Send Bait out first."

"*Bait?*" GJ squeaked, maybe recognizing what she'd really gotten herself into.

"You have no other skills to offer." He countered.

"I'm a forensic scientist!"

"Shut up." He barked it in the lowest tone he had, brooking no more from her. "You should have thought of that before you trailed FBI agents off the road and broke into a government facility."

"How was I supposed to know—?"

He cut her off. "You saw our badges. And this place is marked and has a fence, with razor wire. So if you'd like to spend your final minutes convincing me that you're a complete idiot who didn't see all those signs, then all I'll do is be even more convinced that you're the first one out the window. Shut up and take the damned opportunity to stay alive."

She nodded finally. Reluctantly. Donovan fought the urge to tell her what a bitch she was being. Walter was still talking.

"Once Bait gets out, Donovan next. We need you to take a . . . look around and determine if we can get out that way." She was staring straight at him. Blue eyes caught broken shards of light and sent it back to him.

"Ready?" he asked her.

"Go."

She was the only one who seemed able to make it happen. She was three stairs up and cautiously pushing up on the flooring above them before he'd grabbed GJ and then Eleri and lined them up.

Eleri was stuffing something under her vest, poorly. Donovan frowned. "What are you doing?"

"There are files down here. I have to take at least one."

More files? This place was all files. "No, Eleri."

"We have to know if we need to come back. Adesso is dead." She paused as the door above them cautiously opened, blinding them all for a moment.

"Donovan." She grasped his arm. "These are the files Adesso hid from the world."

It hit him then. They had to come back. But first they had to get out.

As the light formed into soft shapes around him, he saw Walter's fist in front of him, signaling. She snapped the gesture to two fingers pointed forward. He tensed.

Go.

E leri blinked in the harsh light, her brain flitting to
Donovan's eyes. He'd grabbed her arm, tugged her
where she wanted to go. Were his sensitive eyes even
more blown out than hers right now?

Whether he could see or not, he was up the steps, tucked in
tight behind Walter.

Eleri pushed GJ in front of her, urging the girl's feet up the
steps despite her obvious fear and lack of vision. Walter was
right—GJ had to go out first. The rest of them were trained. She
was the civilian, and the danger was likely from within. Still
Eleri had a mean knot in her heart that decided if GJ Janson
did get shot, it was her own damn fault. Using her knife, she cut
one zip-tie, unbinding the girl's wrists. "Go GJ. You're safest in
the front."

She couldn't hear over the sound of her own feet. Or maybe
it was GJ's. That girl was like a herd of horses and slow as
sloths. Eleri fought the urge to turn back and grab more files.
They were gold. They had to be. But she couldn't carry any
more.

She climbed the steps on the faith of Donovan's ears. Walter's aim. Her own purpose. Her heart thudded. Not from fear. Adrenaline, definitely. More from the sudden realization that she could die here, now, and she would die as part of a team.

She'd been a teammate in name before. Part of the profilers unit. She'd been a junior partner—J. Binkley Raymer had showed her the ropes in the FBI and was an excellent teacher. But she'd never been his full-fledged teammate.

It was here, shoved in a secret underground room, with a werewolf who wouldn't admit what he was, a soldier who was part metal, and a pain-in-the-butt grad student that Eleri fully belonged. This was her team.

She put her hand on GJ's shoulder, "It will be okay. We've got you."

Dragging the girl toward the window and the even brighter light that hurt her eyes, she fought not to flinch at the sound of gunfire coming from yet another section of the building. They seemed to be doing the spray-and-pray method without the prayer. She kept her head low and thought of her teammates' safety.

It came automatically, the prayer her grandmère had always used, incanting it each time the girls left her house. Eleri whispered it repeatedly, under her breath. "Bon Dieu, keep us safe. Bind us from trouble. Aida-Wedo protect us from this forest we walk." She inhaled and stepped up onto the ground floor, and started again. "Bon Dieu, keep us safe."

GJ turned to look at her, maybe wondering if she was issuing orders or giving tips. Eleri shook her head and pulled her toward the window. Their silence might mean their lives at this point, and silence wasn't GJ's strong point. She put her finger to her lips and put her other hand onto the window. The pane felt a little cool in the heat.

She glanced back at Walter and Donovan, finding them ready at the door, standing guard against bullets they couldn't possibly stop without blood. Eleri hit the old-style crank, cringing at the sound she couldn't help. Her soul for some WD-40. But it didn't exist.

Gunfire hit down the hallway as the crank resisted her efforts. She pushed harder, knowing Donovan was inhaling, listening, that Walter had her finger on the trigger, ready to at least give as good as she got. Eleri pushed harder.

It still didn't give.

"El." The single syllable on Donovan's tongue was a warning. They were getting closer.

More gunfire punctuated her thoughts, ripping them apart. It was louder than before. And it didn't make any sense. Why did they come in stealthy and then open loud? Why did they keep shooting? Though the building was large, there seemed to be a good number of them. They should have put holes in every wall by now, so why were they still shooting?

Unless they were trying to actually put as many holes in the wall as possible. Though why they would do that . . .

They knew someone was here. They didn't care if they killed the people inside—obviously. A concerted and quiet search could have ferreted out whoever was hiding. Even FBI agents. But they were still shooting.

No point unless the holes in the wall were getting put there for some purpose, or if the noise was a cover.

"Donovan!" she turned to him, trying to keep her voice low though her new panic threatened to boil up.

He saw it as he turned to look at her, maybe he smelled it on her, that she *knew*.

With a deep breath that didn't give her half the information Donovan got when he inhaled she reset her heart rate and focus. She stared at her partner, getting his attention by the expression on her face. "They're going to blow the building."

Then she turned back to the window and inhaled. Whether her eyes changed or not, she would never know, but she felt the energy in the room rush into her, push out through her hands, and she grabbed the crank and forced it open. The window pushed outward. But only a few inches.

It hadn't been opened in years. She was fighting time.

She did it again. Breath. Energy. Push.

Another few inches.

Again.

GJ put both hands against the glass and pushed with her, making the job just a little more effective. It would have been horribly stupid, pushing on glass like that, but it was reinforced, industrial. Or at least Eleri believed it was.

They pushed again.

It still wasn't wide enough. Gunfire came again. Near the end of the hall.

She could place it now. They were concentrating on the corners of the building. It wasn't so much that she'd figured it out but that she'd *understood*.

Once more.

With GJ's frantic help, the window cracked almost a foot. There was a panel that went to the floor, but didn't open. The glass portion began almost three feet up and the lever arms blocked the bottom part of the opening.

It didn't matter. It would have to do. Eleri stuck her head into the space the window had created and hoped it was protected. She looked both left and right before feeling dumb and looking up. No one was out there; they were all too busy destroying the building.

"Go." Eleri pushed at her. The girl was relatively thin. Any extra space she needed, she could get as she shoved her way through. "When you get out, *run*."

GJ nodded even as she hooked one leg out and grabbed

onto the metal edge to pull herself through. She didn't look back.

Eleri left her there; she wasn't the girl's keeper. She ducked back into the closet and pulled up the door they'd let fall shut.

"You can't—" Donovan reached out to pull her back, but Eleri deftly slipped through his grasp.

"I have to. It will all be gone in a bit." She was holding the heavy door over her head as she descended the stairs into the dark. "Hold the door?"

He started to, then followed her down a few steps—as far as he could and still keep the door propped, allowing them some light.

Walter didn't ask what they were doing, and she didn't follow GJ out the window. Ever stoic, she held her post. Jesus, Eleri wished she had half that woman's courage or conviction. And she hoped none of the invading troops—whoever they were—found themselves facing Walter. They would regret it.

Scooping up fat manila folders with loose pages was harder than it seemed. Which ones did she save?

Eleri picked the biggest, hoping they would have the most information, and she wondered about the lives they were leaving behind. Lives gone. Lives kept on paper records and stored in a shelter in a defunct building, all but erased. She couldn't let that change her thinking, she knew.

"Faster," Donovan urged, even as he used his free hand to take files from her and try to find a way to carry them himself.

"As long as they're shooting, they aren't blowing it up. They'll exit before it goes."

He nodded once, acknowledging that she made sense. Then he whispered, "You were right."

She wanted to say, "Of course I was," but she bit her tongue. It wasn't the time. That was the adrenaline speaking.

"Now that I'm looking for it, I can pick up explosives. I think it's a plastic, hard to smell. Not volatile, no real fumes. They are going to blow the place, El. And I haven't heard any gunfire for a full minute."

Shit.

Eleri froze.

G J fell awkwardly to the ground below the window. Her ankle twisted in the loose hot soil, but she ignored the stabbing pain as she stood up and looked around.

She fully expected to be shot and die on the spot despite the fact that Agent Eames stuck her head out and looked around before telling her it was safe and shoving her out the window.

GJ had needed a moment to prepare. She hadn't gotten it.

Keeping pressed to the edge of the building, not wanting to draw attention to herself, she shimmied down to the corner and plastered herself to the brick. She peeked one half of one eye beyond the worn edge and looked.

The ground was trampled to the doorway where she'd come in. The gates hung open, the lock freshly broken despite the gaps in the fencing, the hinges pulled at odd angles. But she didn't see any soldiers.

Instead she rolled until her back was flat against the wall again. She tried to slow the heavy pounding of her heart, to stop the thick slushing in her ears as the blood rushed by with each adrenaline-fueled beat. She would not die today. She would not die here.

GJ took a cue from Agent Heath and listened to her surroundings.

She heard them.

Muffled voices, the occasional low burst of communication through their radios. She heard feet shuffling as though these soldiers waiting outside had grown bored as their friends tried to kill her. She needed to get away.

Staying tucked up alongside the building, and scraping her back in the process, GJ headed back toward the window. She knew time would feel like it dragged as she was all hopped up on fear and anger. But no one else had yet tumbled out the window. Shouldn't at least one of them have followed her out?

Perhaps they were all dead.

That thought launched her forward, straight away from the building. Staying low, she tried to crouch behind scrub and tall grasses that surely weren't big enough to hide her. She must have looked ridiculous had any of the people out front turned this way. But they were still around the corner from where she was. They couldn't see her.

Was she better off standing and flat out running? And where were the agents? Why weren't they behind her?

She considered turning, looking for them. But she didn't have it in her. Too late, she heard gunfire and hit the ground. Her breath soughed in and out, making her suck in fine grains of dirt and searing her lungs as she refused to cough.

It took a moment fighting her own attempt at air before she realized it was coming from behind her and not at her. Only as she carefully looked over her shoulder did she even remember the upper story, that there were likely soldiers up there, watching her crawl away.

Quickly, she checked herself for red laser dots. Finding none, she looked at the ground around her as though these clearly highly trained soldiers might aim next to her instead of at her...

She squeezed her eyes, opened them, and bolted. Holding her breath, GJ ran for everything she was worth. She didn't stop, didn't look back, and didn't think about the people she left behind until she was over the ridge. At that point, she couldn't see them anyway.

She pushed farther, and farther, then hooked a right, figuring the ninety-degree turn would send her back toward her car. It might be sending her right back into the soldiers, but she'd see them first wouldn't she?

GJ didn't know. She just knew she was hot, hungry, thirsty and scared. She patted her pants for the keys she'd stashed in her pocket earlier. It had been only a handful of hours, but it felt like she'd aged years.

The agents told her to stay out of it.

God, what would her parents do if she disappeared? Her grandfather? They would look for her, but she would be gone. Eventually they would figure out that she'd rented a car and come here. They would find the car way off the road in the middle of the desert . . . And that would be the end of the trail. No one knew what she was following. No one even knew she was in this town. Her parents still thought she was at her grandfather's and would think so until they called in and found out she'd left a handful of days ago.

She had to get home.

She felt bad about the agents and the soldier. But going back would probably put them in more danger—she'd pretty much proved she wasn't any help. And they would be glad to see the last of her.

So, tired, dejected, and with all her big ideas shot down, GJ trudged on. She cringed at each noise, waiting to feel the sting of a bullet.

~

ELERI HELD the files against her chest, clutching them like precious dolls.

"We have to go," Donovan uttered.

She was holding out for more gunfire, more noise to indicate the invaders were still in the building. Still setting their charges. Whatever Donovan heard—or didn't hear—he was pulling her out from the shelter. He could have done it by his strength alone, but she didn't fight him. He would have dropped the files, and they were likely going to be all they had from this place.

Planting her foot on the top step, Eleri hoisted herself up into the room. The first thing she saw was Walter's back. The soldier was still standing, still ready, still aimed at the closed door, ready to fight anyone who burst through, or take a bullet if that's what came first. "Walter."

The woman didn't turn, but offered a blink-and-you-miss-it nod to indicate she'd heard and was ready for whatever order Eleri issued.

"Let's go."

"You first, ma'am," Walter told her without turning. She would hold her post until the last moment. For that, Eleri loved her.

There was no thought as she crossed the small distance to the window and struggled to push herself through the odd V left by the crank-open window casing. The hinges tried to catch her clothing and hold her there. The lock wanted to grab at her and pull her shirt, but she didn't let it. Rips be damned, she was getting out. Because Donovan had to come out next.

Eleri's booted feet hit the ground without the benefit of

sight. Her eyes darted from one side to another and she saw nothing of GJ Janson. Nothing of soldiers. She turned and whispered back, "Donovan."

Through the window she saw him grab Walter by the back of her vest and drag her toward the window. Maintaining her feet, Walter still didn't turn away. Donovan didn't let go of the woman the whole time he was climbing out. One hand stayed firmly wrapped in whatever he managed to hold onto on Walter's gear and the other held the files tightly to his chest.

"Here." He thrust his files at Eleri, leaving her no option other than grab them or let them fall. They were her gold, but Donovan was reaching through the window and bodily lifting Walter out.

In that moment, Eleri saw Walter at her real size. Barely five-eight, slim, athletic, she fit through the window as easily as GJ had. She was on her own feet before Donovan set her down, but not before Eleri saw something she'd not seen before. Some understanding in the way Donovan and Walter interacted, something she would have investigated on a normal day, something communicated without words.

"She checked the corner." Walter pointed to tracks in the soft dirt leading away and then back. "Then she headed straight out."

"Do we trust her assessment?" Eleri asked.

"I think we have to." Walter looked around and up, then stepped out into the open space. She tracked GJ's footsteps with confidence, and Donovan kept pace. Eleri fell in behind them.

They'd made it maybe fifteen to twenty steps when Donovan grabbed Walter, halting her forward movement. Stepping steadily, Eleri almost ran into the back of them.

"I hear something. Shh." He stood stock still for just a moment, then his nose went wide a split second before his eyes did. "Get down."

He brooked no argument, tugging at them both.

The jerk to her arm let some of the files slide and one hit the ground, exploding in a flurry of white paper.

Eleri's heart stopped. It was a beacon right to them. If anyone were on the upper floor looking out, they would all be dead the two-point-five seconds it would take a well-trained sniper to take out all three of them.

She started chanting, wanting that energy back that she'd had at the window. That rush that came with her anger and need didn't seem to be as easily called with her fear. "Bon Dieu, keep us safe—"

A gloved hand smacked over her mouth and she was yanked backward, her fingers still reaching for the floating pages. She hit the earth with a hard thud, her legs reaching out as though she could somehow sit on enough of the escaped signals to stop the visual noise.

"Shut up, El." Donovan let her mouth go. "Look."

She felt that Donovan and Walter had already seen what she was slow to spot.

"Be still," he admonished harshly, suddenly the senior agent. In a flash of insight she saw him as a child, huddled in the corner of his trailer, trying to be invisible during one of his father's rages. He understood this. She needed to follow. "We can't stop the pages from catching their attention, but we can be invisible when they look this way."

His arm was a vice. Though she'd figured out what to do, it didn't matter. Donovan wouldn't let her go anywhere.

They were rabbits. Sit still. Don't blink. Pray.

Only, praying was what she'd been trying to do.

It didn't matter because the soldiers were filing out of the facility. They came out in steady formation with a speed and cohesiveness that resembled liquid pouring out. They filtered through the doors and directly into the vehicles in one contin-uous motion. As each of the three armored trucks filled, it started and turned away.

As the first one pulled out, she thought she recognized the combination of tires, digital desert camo, and formation. They were Army.

What in the hell was the Army doing here? The Army didn't get orders to go in shooting, not like this. Was she wrong?

It was the last thought she had before the world exploded.

43

onovan felt his head roll as though it wasn't attached to his body. His ears pounded with a roaring noise he couldn't place. Somewhere in his thoughts he knew the sound should bother him, but he just couldn't muster the worry.

He breathed deeply and felt the leaden weight of his limbs and his thoughts and he drifted away.

It was a while later that he heard it again. This time it had a cadence and an urgency to it, but he was bone tired and wanted to go back to sleep. The breath was seeping out of his lungs and the blackness crept in at the edges. He felt like a drowning man who'd given up the fight and accepted his fate. He could gaze about at the underwater world with appreciation for just a few moments.

Instead the cadence of the droning noise changed. It became a three-part beat that the back of his brain recognized as his name. Once he pulled the rhythm out, the sounds, too, became clear.

"Donovan."

"Donovan."

The third time, it sounded odd.

"Agent Eames."

Walter's voice came through the haze at the same time a crack opened in the dark and a blinding light forced him to squeeze his eyes shut. It was the only thing that alerted him they'd been open at all. So why hadn't he seen anything?

At the same time he tried to open his eyes just a crack his chest tightened at the realization that he was "Donovan" while Eleri remained "Agent Eames."

Still, he could hear nothing beyond the pounding in his ears. See nothing beyond the brightness of the light. But he did feel. He felt the loose, coarse dirt sifting through his fingers as he tried to push himself upright. Small sticks caught in his grasp and his brain started the slow shuffle back to reality.

The overwhelming scent of dirt and desert filled his nose, but mixed in was the fresh sting of recently broken brick, the fumes of exploded C4. He'd been right, it was a plastic. It was easier to identify in the aftermath—after it had been exploded into the air.

His brain jolted. *Aftermath.*

They'd blown the building.

"Walter?" He reached out, his fingers brushing the softened-by-wear fabric of her sleeve. More than that, he could smell her. He couldn't identify it exactly, but there was an overwhelming scent of competence, some pheromone people gave off when they knew what they were doing, something the opposite of sweat. No one believed him when he tried to explain he could smell it, but everyone understood that dogs "just knew."

"Walter?"

"Donovan, I've got you. We need to get going." She was pulling him to his feet. Steadying him, turning away.

He heard her then, talking to Eleri. He blinked into the clouds of debris that hung in the air. On the upside, the dust obscured the trio from any remaining troops that might be watching for them. He couldn't even see the building through the mess.

As he watched, Walter started walking. She pulled the two of them along with her.

"Are we going the right way?" Eleri asked as she pulled out safety glasses and then discarded them. The dust was mixed into the air, nothing she could do about it. "I can't see GJ's footsteps anymore."

"I've got it. We're going on compass readings right now." She held up the military-grade piece.

Of course she had a compass, and of course she'd known what direction they'd come from. Donovan didn't even question it, just put his feet into her boot prints and followed along.

Lifting the front of his T-shirt from under all his gear, he used the knit as a filter. It was a piss-poor filter, but none of them had time to get in their packs and . . .

His pack.

The files.

"Eleri. The files." It was the first time he'd looked directly at her. They'd both been communicating only dully, only with Walter, the only one who was alert and on her feet.

Eleri's startled gasp caused her to choke on the air, but it didn't stop her from turning around, patting herself down. She sighed with relief. "I stuffed as many as I could inside my vest. They're still there. We should get the others, though."

With a sigh of resignation, Walter turned around. Donovan couldn't tell if she'd remembered the files and simply decided to ignore them in favor of escape or if Walter had actually forgotten the effort they'd expended to save them. Either way, she dutifully turned and headed back toward the point they'd started from.

White pages began fluttering at the edges of his vision as soon as he started looking for them. Stepping out of formation to grab one, Donovan folded it, stuffed it into a pocket and turned to rejoin the little line only to be startled that the line was gone.

He was alone in the brown-gray cloud of the explosion. Through the haze, he could see small plants at his feet. One had a few branches all broken toward his left, letting him know just how close they had been to the blast and how lucky they were to have survived. But now?

He had no compass. He didn't have Walter's skills. He didn't have Walter.

He took two steps back in the direction he thought he'd moved from before his brain finally kicked all the way on. He wondered then if he'd hit his head and then decided that, given the explosion and the proximity, the answer almost had to be yes. Donovan wised up and checked the ground, grateful to find his own footprints.

Managing to track himself back to where he'd left the group, he was again startled to find that Eleri and Walter weren't there. Obviously, they'd moved forward. Or backward as it were. Donovan was looking now for two sets of prints—the women, without him—to follow, when Walter appeared out of the grime.

With easy efficiency, she reached out and latched onto the shoulder strap of his vest. Tugging him easily forward, she reached for his pants. His eyes went wide at the gesture then immediately squeezed shut as the grit in the air assaulted them. Her hands tracked his waist and he fought the urge to suck in air as his brain scrambled again. He'd spotted Eleri over Walter's shoulder just before his eyes involuntarily snapped shut in pain.

With no idea what the woman was doing to him and apparently lacking the brain cells to figure it out, Donovan stood still and wondered if he was being assaulted. Then he examined how much he wished that were the case and how very wrong it would be.

He was reaching out to grab Walter—the cognitive dissonance of having her hands on him and knowing she would never do that finally getting to be too much—when she said, "There!" and tugged on the waist of his pants.

He opened his eyes, managed not to manacle her wrist, and looked down at her declaration.

She'd snapped a carabiner onto him, tugged at it and smiled. He followed the thin wire back to her own waist as she demonstrated the retractable line she'd tied onto him. Turning away, she clipped it onto the back of her own pants. Eleri, it appeared, was ziplined to Walter's front. So apparently while he'd been getting a little bit turned on, she was lacing them up like toddlers out for a walk. *Good to know.*

As he saw the next page—this one yellow—flutter at the edge of his vision, he was comforted by knowing he could find his way back. Sure enough, he felt the reassuring tug, tighter and tighter as he walked away. As he grabbed the paper from the ground he also wrapped his other hand around the line and began a walk back toward where Walter was, not just where she'd been.

"I'm giving us one small circle to grab what we can. Then we're out of here." Walter seemed to have dismissed Eleri as the leader of their little group.

Eleri didn't seem to care. "I've found five pages." She held up what was probably the last one she picked up.

"I got a stack!" He was like a kid in a candy shop. A war-torn candy shop where the candy was notes on kids having been tortured years ago. But he'd been excited when he'd reached for the yellow page only to find that a clump had stuck together.

Eleri managed to find a manila folder with pages still inside. Whether it was the whole folder remained to be seen.

Donovan grabbed a few more of the pieces that fluttered at the edge of his vision. Several pages looked freshly torn, their missing pieces nowhere to be seen. It was another grim reminder of how close they had been to the blast.

He listened for the trucks. Assumed they'd left. Maybe that had been the rumble he'd detected as he'd come around. The sound of the tires would have been amplified through the ground beneath his ear. Meanwhile, he didn't hear anything. Then again, the grit and debris in the air was only just beginning to clear; it would muffle a lot of sins well within the normal borders of his hearing. He could only hope he'd detect any danger before it arrived. He couldn't count on Walter for everything.

Too soon they were back at the beginning of their loop. Even he could see that they'd hooked back up to their original tracks. Without comment, Walter began again leading them out the way GJ had come, but after scaling two small rises, she turned to Donovan. "Can we go back to the car? Do you hear anything in the way?"

"I don't, but we won't see them with any warning if I'm wrong." He shrugged, not sure either of them could see him now, despite the fact that the grit in the air was finally starting to clear just a little. He wasn't sure if a high wind would be a blessing or not.

"If we can't see them, they can't see us," Walter countered.

"Unless they have thermal imaging. Which they will." Eleri finally jumped into something besides finding the missing pages.

For a heartbeat Donovan waited for Walter to pull a thermal imager from one of the cargo pockets on her pants and say, "But I have one, too." Instead she only nodded.

Here he'd expected her to produce whatever they needed. He half suspected she had some Harry Potter wand hidden away and she just conjured equipment as necessary. Without magic of her own, she made Eagle Scouts look like they just weren't trying hard enough.

"I don't hear anything. I'll keep my ears open and tell you if I do." And he didn't. No trucks, no cars on the road. More telling, he couldn't make out a single pair of sneaker-clad feet scrambling through the dirt and the twigs. She must have run far and fast. Though the more he thought about it, that was actually good. GJ Janson had maybe escaped the explosion.

They didn't encounter anyone on the way back. Somehow, the car stood exactly where they'd parked it.

"Guess they figure they buried us?" Donovan asked the others.

"Probably they don't care. The building and supposedly all the records are gone. It doesn't matter if we are, too." Eleri looked at both of them. "Then again, if it does matter, they would wire the car."

They spent fifteen minutes, hot, exhausted, and running on fumes, checking the wheel wells, undercarriage, and engine before deciding it wasn't wired, rigged, or set to explode in some other way. They couldn't find any radio trackers or GPS locators either and Eleri turned off the one in the car. They slid into the seats, dirty and ready for showers. Still, they all paused, preternaturally still, while Eleri started the car. When it didn't blow up, they let out a breath collectively. Donovan felt his head loll back in the seat and he didn't remember the drive much beyond the trailer bouncing around without the weight of the ATVs.

When they finally pulled into the hotel, Eleri parked the car around back. "We'll try to draw as little attention as possible. Go straight to our rooms. Avoid any people."

He was getting ready to ask her why when he looked at her —really looked at her. They were covered in dust. Where they weren't dusty, they bore streaks of some black grease that may have been from the explosion. Eleri had another cut on the side of her head and he wondered how he was only just now noticing that.

"Once you're cleaned up, let me take a look at that, El." He was turning to check Walter when he realized none of them had realized Eleri was hurt. "Walter? Are you in one piece?"

It only occurred to him when Walter responded with a nod that he didn't really know if he was in one piece himself. So he did a quick check, found both his legs intact, wondered what Walter would think about that, and then pulled himself out of the car. He walked a beat behind Eleri, surreptitiously checking her gait, looking for swaying or anything else that might divulge a more serious head injury than it appeared.

"I'm fine, Donovan," she said without looking back. Okay, maybe not so surreptitious after all. In the same breath, as she pushed through the door she'd opened with her room key, she said, "Oh, no, you don't."

Though GJ Janson managed to push past Eleri, she didn't get past Donovan. His hand shot out and he grabbed her arm, smelled the shampoo she'd used within the last ten or so minutes and was suddenly jealous that she'd beaten them back by a margin. She probably hadn't checked her car for explosives. "You're not going anywhere."

"You can't arrest me!"

"Yes, I can. I can also detain you and put you in federal prison." He yanked her back, realizing then that her bag was bouncing along behind her.

GJ Janson had been ready to fly the coop.

44

Donovan lay on his sofa, bone weary, with a rum and Coke. He wasn't sure he liked it, but he didn't dislike it either. He did thoroughly dislike beer. But whether that was because he associated it with his father or because it actually tasted like horse piss, he didn't quite know.

He'd showered, gone to take care of Eleri's cut, and found GJ Janson handcuffed to an anchor ring embedded in the back of the room safe. Actually, she was cuffed to a cuff linked to another set of handcuffs. Eleri wasn't a sadist; she was just an agent without a lot of options or trust. He'd then called Walter who said she was fine and lying down to rest.

Donovan wasn't sure he believed Walter ever rested. Lucy Fisher was a super-soldier. Now if she'd said she needed to change her batteries, he would have bought that hook, line, and sinker, but he'd let her be. He'd ordered room service—a fat burger, rare, which he'd immediately picked the lettuce, tomato, and onion off of—and ate everything on the plate. The fries were passable on any other day. Today, they were ambrosia.

Then he'd thought it through, pulled out one measured

bottle of rum from the mini-fridge and made himself this rum and Coke while he sat back on the mostly comfortable couch in his room and contemplated life. He didn't think about whether Eleri had let GJ go—convincing her there was nowhere to run—or had simply made a bed within reach of her safe. He didn't think about the butterfly bandages he'd put at the edge of Eleri's hairline or his concern that it might scar after being rubbed full of who-knew-what had been in the air or what she'd rubbed her head into upon being thrown by the blast.

It had been a few hours. Walter was probably starting to feel the aches. She'd be clean—she'd been clean when he called her. Each of them had retreated into a shower almost immediately. But she might have discovered a cut or bruise. He told himself she had field training and that she would be as competent in this as in everything else. He also told himself that field dressing something was no substitute for having an actual doctor look at it.

He was studiously ignoring the fact that he was a doctor for dead people as he pulled on a shirt and opened his door barefoot. One door over, he knocked, then knocked again.

It was too dark inside the room to see if she checked the peephole. He stood in front of it, clearly friend, not foe, and he should have been more careful. He heard the chain pull back as he contemplated that he'd been too few feet away from an explosion that could have killed him today. If he listened carefully, he could still sort out the high-pitched ring that was a few of his ear neurons still firing from the blast. All those thoughts stopped dead when the door swung open.

"Donovan." The word was as sleepy as she looked.

He'd woken her.

He'd woken something else.

He'd woken Lucy. Lucy had blond curls that tumbled, shiny, to her shoulders. Lucy smelled of synthetic wildflowers and clean sheets and a hint of whatever she'd washed her pajamas in. Lucy smelled of vulnerability. And sex.

She stepped back awkwardly to let him in and he stepped into the room pushing the door closed behind him. Only then did he see her reach down across her body toward her leg. She clutched at it as she took another awkward step back.

She hadn't settled her prosthetic fully on. Her loose pajama pants covered it, but the tank top didn't hide that her left arm simply stopped about two-thirds of the way to her hand. His eyes roved in the dim light from the bedside lamp and he watched as she ducked the missing hand behind her back.

"I just wanted to check you out." *Okay, that sounded wrong.* "I mean, make sure you didn't have any cuts or anything that needed a doctor."

"I told you, I'm fine." Her eyes darted away.

Shit.

Walter Reed, with her metal prosthetics in place, could run and jump and shoot a man. She was the Terminator. Lucy Fisher, on the other hand, was clearly insecure. He'd never seen it before. Any of it. Not Lucy with her hair down. Her nose looked regal instead of stern. Her eyes wide, not just all-seeing. The tank top said "woman," not "Marine."

When neither of them spoke for a moment, Donovan realized the silence had gone awkward. He banked on awkward meaning something and powered through. "You're right. You told me you were fine. But I wanted to come up here."

Again, the arm moved farther behind her back.

"It's okay."

"I know. You're a doctor." She sighed and stepped back. But she missed.

The unsecured leg gave way and she teetered backward. Her reflexes were lightning fast. He shouldn't have been surprised by that, but Donovan dove for her anyway. Before she could protest, he'd lifted her, holding her off the ground.

"Put me down. I'm going to lose my leg."

She meant the prosthetic, but he grinned and raised an eyebrow. "Shake it off. I've got you."

She pushed back on him and he put her down, watching while she hopped and pushed her leg back into the setting. She didn't look at him. Lucy was shy.

Donovan opted for honesty. "You know, I believed that you were fine. I just wanted to come up. Tell me to go or stay. Your call."

She didn't say either of those words. "I'm a master on the battlefield. I know what I'm doing out there. But the rest of it . . . I don't know."

"Like I know either. Clearly, I don't know what to say to get you to say yes." He stepped back, reaching for the door. He finally admitted that he'd hoped they'd come together in some mutually recognized blaze of passion. That had not happened.

His hand was on the knob, he was opening his mouth to say "Goodnight" when she spoke again.

"I'm a freak."

He strode into the room and stood directly in front of her. He used his height advantage to tower over her, angry. "Did you seriously just call yourself a freak? To *me*?"

She opened her mouth like a fish, stepped back, hit the edge of the bed and flopped backward all in one move. Any level of competency he'd seen before was gone. He would have laughed, would have felt the hole it poked in his heart to be able to see Lucy Fisher like this. But he was still mad.

"You've seen me. You've seen me change. You know what I am. How can you possibly call yourself a freak? How can you possibly think I'd judge you? I'm not even sure I'm fully human."

She offered a sweet grin and a shrug in response to his anger. "Maybe you don't need birth control?"

"Not that lucky." His anger sizzled. "Tell me to—"

She cut him off. "Stay."

ELERI SMILED INTO THE CAMERA. "I miss you."

Behind her, she heard the low, snotty tones of GJ. "I missss yoooo."

Eleri ignored it. Instead she paid attention to the hiss on the screen. "What happened to you?"

Avery managed to make it sound only as if he cared that she was beaten up, not that she looked like shit. She knew she looked like shit.

She grinned and tilted her head. "Building exploded."

"Were you *in* it?"

She laughed. Finally. After this crap day, she needed it. "No, only very nearby."

He knew enough by now that he couldn't press and he didn't. "You okay?"

"My partner is a doctor."

"He practiced—past tense—on dead people. None of this is comforting me." Avery offered a sad smile at her freshly washed hair combed back off her forehead.

Eleri had the hotel bathrobe on and pulled up around her neck. She'd thought through getting dressed before she called, but she didn't have it in her. "I just needed to hear your voice."

"I just need to *pee!*" GJ yelled at the top of her lungs.

"You have a guest?" Avery asked.

At least GJ's voice was obviously female. "Actually, I have a prisoner."

"For real?" His eyes blinked, he got closer to his camera—probably on his computer—and he blinked again. "I didn't know the FBI was in the prisoner business."

"Oh, absolutely. It's all very hush-hush."

"I. Have. To. Peeeeee."

"Okay, not so hush-hush. She's a huge pain in the ass. And she's tried to disappear on us . . ." Eleri didn't know. Looking back over her shoulder she asked, "How many times have you tried to sneak off?"

A glare.

Eleri followed it with, "How badly do you want to pee in the bathroom rather than on the floor?" Turning back to the phone, she whispered, "I'm sure that violates about fifty clauses in the Geneva Convention, but she's a pain in the ass."

This time he laughed.

"Four! Please." GJ's voice came from the background.

"Email me your schedule. I need to see you as soon as I'm done with this case." She'd held him off before and wished she hadn't. At the time, she'd wanted to be sure they'd last through his crazy, long game season and her never-ending round of cases. But now she knew, and instead of having Avery, she had a case hanging over her head, an obnoxious grad student wailing in her hotel room, and a pile of files on the small corner table. "I have a prisoner to escort to the ladies."

"I can't wait 'til you get here." He offered a sad smile.

"Me either."

In less than a minute, she was back to being Eleri, FBI Bitch, according to GJ. Even as she uncuffed the girl, she watched. Eleri would not put it past her to try to take a swing, knock her out and get away.

"Thanks." It was sullen, and GJ rubbed at her wrist with her other hand.

"You know, it wouldn't be sore if you hadn't kept tugging on it. And you wouldn't even be cuffed in the first place if you hadn't shoved me outside the hotel in a blatant attempt to get away."

Another glare.

Eleri ignored it. "So I'd better hear you peeing in there. If you want to get any ideas like using the top of the toilet tank or the hair dryer as a weapon, then you'd better figure out how to make them shoot bullets through this metal door. Anything less, and I will take your ass down and add assaulting an officer to your lovely, ever-growing list." She waved an open hand into the bathroom as though welcoming the queen. Then she smiled as GJ slammed the door.

She stood in the entryway exhausted but unable to sleep. And not just because of GJ. Eleri had a plan for that. If the girl kept up her diatribe all night, Eleri was going to leave her there and rent another room to sleep in. She would just take all her things and go. But as it was, it was her own brain keeping her up.

When GJ emerged from the bathroom she held up her hands. "Washed them."

Eleri didn't really care. She held out the cuffs.

GJ broke. "I'm sorry. Please don't cuff me." Tears rolled down her face, but Eleri wasn't sure she bought it.

"I can't let you free. You've proven you can't be trusted." Eleri crossed her arms, "Your fault."

"I know. But there has to be a better way. Shock collar?"

"Seriously?"

GJ shrugged. "I won't set it off, so sure."

Good God. Eleri wished Grandmère would send her a voodoo doll or at least a protection. "Wait." She knew how to hobble a prisoner.

It took her about four minutes and GJ's cooperation to both cuff the girl's ankles together and then lock the door from the inside, so the girl couldn't get out slowly while everyone slept. Once she was confident she had GJ well and truly stuck, she ignored her.

Sitting down at the small table, she began to look through the papers for the first time. Inside of three seconds, she knew she had a serious mess. Part of the work required just cleaning them. They'd been in an underground shelter for probably several decades. Though the dust in the room was low, the dust in the area was high. Then there was the fact that they'd been through an explosion.

Eleri dampened one of the bathroom hand towels knowing full well she was destroying it. It would see white and fluffy for the last time. She wiped down the first file, getting the folder first, then trying to get the edges. She needed a second wet towel for her hands, she quickly found. It took longer to read the first page than she'd anticipated.

The folder itself revealed that she was holding Bravo's file. Probably one of the first—though Atlas came later than the Axis project. It was likely Atlas's Bravo survived longer than the early children at Axis. Eleri didn't know if that was a good thing or not.

The file was relatively slim, just twenty or so pages. She looked through the admission work—Bravo was female. Initial testing, and first gene therapy—gibbon and rhesus genes. There were follow-up tests. Bravo made it about four months before she began deteriorating. She was dead another six weeks after that.

"Whatcha reading?" GJ was standing over her shoulder.

Not that she should say, but Eleri wasn't thinking clearly. "Documents of stolen infants tortured by some secret US division. Most of them died. Happy?"

"What?" GJ put her hand to her head and sank into the opposite chair. "Really?"

"Yes, really." Eleri closed the file and stared at her. "What did you think was in that building?"

She shrugged in response.

Eleri dug in. "You were out there looking for weird skeletons. You found them. What did you think they were? Skeletons are *people*, you know. At least they were."

"I know. But the ones I found were adults." As though that made it all okay.

To a certain extent, Eleri understood. She, too, could get caught up in the science and forget that there were humans on the other end of the line. But right now she had a handful of letters from Las Abuelas that she had to get back to. She had to tell them their grandchildren had been found and it wasn't good.

"Can I help?" GJ offered, her voice smaller than Eleri had ever heard it. "I can clean them for you, if you want."

"Sure." She didn't know why she said it. But she handed the towel over and watched as the other woman carefully cleaned the next file. After a minute of watching, Eleri turned back to reading.

She plowed through file after file, growing more and more frustrated. Some of the pages were in code. Just a scramble of letters that made no sense. Obviously they did, but not to her.

Her brain hurt. But, finally, she was tired. It felt as though all her energy drained out through her feet suddenly, and Eleri put her head down on her hands for a minute.

Before she knew it, GJ was shaking her awake. "Agent Eames. Agent Eames."

She hadn't been deep enough asleep to think anything other than that she needed to get up and go to bed. She had to tap out. She was standing before she realized that wasn't it.

"This doctor, I think his name is Marojon or something—"

"Morozov," Eleri corrected automatically.

GJ nodded. "I think he was killing them. In his notes, in the coded ones, it looks like he was killing them all."

"You can read the coded ones?" Eleri was leaning forward, one hand on the table, the other grasping the robe.

GJ nodded.

45

S uddenly fully awake, Eleri stared at GJ. "What's the code?"

"It's mostly amino acids." She shrugged. "There are a few other notations in there . . ."

"I checked that. It didn't work." Eleri frowned. She had a bio background, she'd thought of amino acid coding when she first saw it.

"They aren't all human. These are specific to gibbons," GJ added. "I once had to categorize proteins found on potsherds. The non-human ones indicated food storage. The meats were interesting."

"Gibbon? Gibbon was a meat you found?" Eleri frowned.

"No, but just like there's a limited number for humans, there's not that wide a spread—for the most part—of amino acids found in mammals. So I recognized some of them."

Eleri wanted to hit herself in the head. She'd dismissed it since some of the codes were unrecognizable. Of course they were animal codes. She went back and looked at the pages.

"It's not like I can just read them," GJ qualified, "but I

copied them into a program and the gene or the protein can sometimes be identified."

Eleri struggled to the other end of GJ's proclamation. She didn't want to, and couldn't, release classified information, but she needed to know what GJ had found. "So why do you think he was killing them?"

The change that came over her was amazing. GJ was no longer on the defensive. No longer a child at the mercy of being punished by the FBI agents. She was a scientist having crossed the threshold of discovery. Shuffling through the folders with a dizzying combination of urgency and respect, she dug until she found two or three of the ones she wanted.

"These," she pointed. "Early on, they were testing combinations of gene therapies on these kids. They seemed kind of random."

Eleri nodded. Though GJ didn't know it, Eleri had found all those same things. "Go on."

"But the kids who got over five percent of the genome of a particular camel," she flipped to a different stack, "they *all* died. All within a matter of days."

GJ was starting to understand what was going on. They knew some of this from Axis, but GJ might not know that. Eleri listened.

"The higher doses in general were fatal. But that one was particularly fatal. I mean, the other high doses killed, too, but a lot of them took longer. This one was fast. But look here—" GJ carefully opened a folder to one of the last pages. "And here." She moved another, and another. "See? Within a matter of days, Marojon—I mean Morozov—administered that dosage to all the kids. When they showed up for their check-up, he administered what they had to know by then was a fatal dose to each kid."

Eleri agreed. But she had to push. "Why do you say they 'had to know' that it was fatal?"

"Well, here." GJ pointed. "This patient, Oscar, was the last one who got that high of a dose. The last note in his account says statistically it was the over five percent of the camel DNA. Also, there's no administration of that dose again until Morozov gave it to all the kids." She looked up. "It was a seven-year span. They didn't give it to *anyone* for that time, and then he gives it to *all* of them? He knew."

Eleri nodded. She'd underestimated GJ and she didn't like it.

This time it was GJ who looked up and asked the question. She almost had tears in her eyes. "Why would he try to kill them?"

Eleri answered as Morozov did. "They were already dead anyway."

"What? Were they terminally ill? I didn't see anything about any other diagnoses. They had physicals all the time." GJ was shaking her head. "Who would put their kid into this program anyway?"

There was nothing Eleri could say. GJ didn't know about Las Abuelas. She didn't know about Victor at Axis. About 820. Eleri sighed. She was searching for the words when GJ caught on.

"Were they kidnapped?"

"Yes," Eleri answered quickly, hoping to stem further questions along this line.

"We have to find their parents." GJ was on her feet. "We have to tell their families."

Again, Eleri worked to stem the questions without breaking classifications or giving the student any cause to go off on her own seeking justice. "That's our job. It's why the FBI is involved in this case."

At least that seemed to calm her.

Eleri was just sitting back down, just thinking about maybe trying to get some sleep. Maybe trying to put this much aside for a few hours. Though she doubted she could sleep. She was thinking about what to tell GJ when the other woman spoke again.

"They didn't all die, you know."

"They didn't?" Eleri knew that, but how did GJ?

"No." She shook her head. "Or at least I have to assume they didn't. He recorded the deaths. Most of these folders have dates in them. Notes about the plot the bodies were buried in. But a lot don't. They just go on with information. Morozov was also jailed about fifteen days after this attempt on all the kids. So a lot of them at least survived until the place went defunct. Or some of them."

"Why 'some' or 'a lot'?" *Crap.* GJ was spot on. And she'd even found the amino acid code.

"We have what appears to be the entirety of seven folders and pieces of thirty others." GJ gestured around the room where, for the first time, Eleri saw that all the folders were cleaned. Each of the lone pages set out by itself or stacked in small clusters. The bed was covered. The side tables, too. The TV had been pushed back on its stand making room for five small stacks that sat in front of it.

"Holy shit." Eleri scanned the room again. "You got them all sorted by patient?"

"They have a code in the upper right-hand corner. Plus the naming system, 'Alpha, Bravo, Charlie,' then numbers." She pointed to the nightstand at the largest pile of loose pages. "Those are torn. The file number is missing. Otherwise, yes." She paused for a moment. "From the system and the numbers, I'm guessing there were between a hundred and a hundred and twenty-five kids at the facility total. I don't think it was big enough to keep that many there at once, but it looks like a lot of them died young."

A solemn nod was all Eleri could muster. "They had a lot of . . . turnover."

"Yeah. That's one way to put it."

Eleri looked around the room as exhaustion crept back in. "Let's stack these pages and get some sleep. We'll get back to it in the morning. Let Walter and Donovan sleep."

GJ nodded and hopped around, her feet still cuffed together. But this time she didn't complain. Eleri fought the urge to uncuff her. Having underestimated GJ Janson's intelligence and usefulness, she didn't want to get caught in the middle of the night having underestimated her cunning.

DONOVAN ROLLED OVER, the strange bed not strange in and of itself. The woman next to him did give him pause.

He blinked in the light that wasn't as dim as it should have been. Frowning, he turned away from Lucy and checked his phone. "Shit."

"Running late?" Even her voice was different. Softer, sweeter, more than he'd expected from the Terminator.

"Yeah." The question was did he use the late hour as an excuse to run? Or stay and talk about what had happened?

Donovan didn't know. He was in uncharted territory. By his age, a lot of men were married, had kids. He'd never woken up with a woman before.

He did not want to stay and talk. It wasn't his strong suit. Probably wasn't Walter's either. Then again, he was pretty sure he'd slept with Lucy Fisher—Walter was the Marine. So, talking wasn't going to go down well.

It seemed he had a lot of firsts this morning. He didn't want to run. He'd never slept with the same woman twice unless she initiated it, but he'd never slept with a woman who knew what he was either. He didn't have a clue what he was doing or what he wanted, but he wasn't ready to be done. He opened his mouth.

And was shocked when Lucy's voice filled the air.

"If you're late, you should probably get dressed and go."

He blinked. She was done? His mouth flopped like a fish for a moment before he asked, "You're pushing me out the door?"

There was a silence of disturbing length, but he let it sit. He didn't get up or make any move to get out of bed. If she was kicking him out she was going to have to do it loud and clear.

Lucy held out as long as she could. "No." Another beat. "I just wanted you to have a clean opportunity to get away if you wanted to."

"I don't want to." It tumbled out of him before he even thought about putting it out there first or asking what she wanted.

"Me either."

His breath let out. "I have to admit that I don't know what I'm doing."

"Me either." She'd rolled his way, she was looking at him now and Donovan returned the favor with a smile.

"But I don't want to stop doing it."

She grinned. Huge. He didn't think he'd ever seen it before, this big, bright smile that made her more than just the one who had his back.

Yet, somehow, she still had his back. She pushed at him. "Get up. Get going. Sneak back to your own room and shower and check in."

"Yes, ma'am." Before she could react, he kissed her. Perfunctory and a bit sweet, it surprised him as much as her. But he pulled on his clothes and left the room without saying much else. In his own mind, that had gone about as well as it possibly could.

Not fifteen minutes later he knocked on Eleri's door and was let in. She was more than awake, dressed, and at the table with room service discarded outside the door.

He frowned. "There are two plates, but no GJ. Did you feed her and let her go?"

"Oh, hell, no." Eleri smiled. "She's in the shower. I made her go second. Besides, she's turned out to be useful."

When he listened, he could hear the pounding of water in the other room. It was obvious, he must have tuned it out. "So, how did she wind up useful?"

Eleri was just pulling out folders when a knock came at the door.

This time the woman on the other side was not Lucy Fisher. Not laughing, not at ease once he'd seen her with the prostheses off. This was Walter, the one who never commanded but always earned the respect of everyone around her.

"Just checking in." She nodded at him, no other gestures giving away anything. "Curious if we are going back out there."

"I think we have to. We have to recover any documents we can, though I'm guessing that's hopeless." Eleri reached out and touched Walter on the arm. "More importantly, I think we have a moral duty to go back out and try to find the survivors."

"The kids?"

"If we want to still call them that." Eleri shrugged. "They're adults now. They've been surviving out there all along, but—"

"But they've been using the building as a central point. It's gone." Walter finished the sentence.

"Exactly." The two were clearly speaking the same language and on a topic that had not occurred to him at all.

"Should we bring tents and gear?" Walter asked. "Something to replace what they lost?"

Another nod from Eleri as she absorbed that. "We should. They lost it because we investigated. We don't know if they want to leave or if they even can. We should at least offer." She nodded more vigorously as the idea settled in. Then she looked up, "So you two slept together?"

Donovan almost swallowed his tongue. He thought about

her hand on Walter's arm. "You shouldn't have looked. What did you see?"

She shrugged, but it wasn't an apology. "Only confirmation of what I already heavily suspected."

That gave him pause.

"Come on, Donovan. Granted, you two have been doing a good job, but you've been throwing sparks for a little while now." She turned back to the work. "Plus, you're both late—the same amount late!—both freshly showered, and both looking a little too *normal* to not have done something."

The shower clicked off then, and they all looked to each other. Unwilling to abandon the conversation, Donovan lowered his voice.

"You shouldn't have looked." He wasn't comfortable with what she might have seen. Was it some porno of him and Walter together? Could he handle that? He didn't think so. That kind of ability had been fine when she'd ferreted out his secrets before. He'd been left with nothing to hide. But the Walter thing... It was too new.

"Don't worry. I didn't watch! I just got a message of 'yes,' no pictures or anything." Her mouth quirked.

He was starting to nod, trying to decide if that was okay. If she could just see into his life whenever she chose, could he deal with that—

"Besides, given that I'm pretty sure you can smell when I have my period or I'm ovulating, I just don't think you get to judge," she snapped.

His head jerked back at the bite in her words. He'd never said anything. "You knew?"

"You have a sense of smell rivaling a wolf's—not surprising-ly." She sighed and threw her hands up as though he was being stupid. "I looked up what dogs can smell. It's a pretty disturbing list. You probably know if I've slept with Avery in the past three days. So I don't want to hear it."

She was right. It was an odd relationship, theirs. And he had been getting all kinds of information about her on a daily basis. He could smell mood a lot of the time. Scientifically, he was confident it was low combinations of hormones, pheromones, sweat and adrenaline, but to his nose and brain, it was mood. So he said the only thing he could say. "You ovulated yesterday."

"I hate you." She said it without vehemence.

He looked at Walter and shrugged.

It was Walter who broke the stalemate. "I feel left out."

"You're the Terminator." They said it simultaneously and laughed at each other.

"You have nothing to feel left out about," Donovan reassured her.

Just then, the bathroom door opened and the mood in the room swung away from laughter. They had a task that was classified and they had a non-clearance civilian on board.

GJ walked into the room and waited with a foul look on her face while Eleri re-hobbled her. Donovan bit back a good laugh at her feet cuffed together. It was brilliant, really. Movement, but not enough to get away.

With a raised eyebrow at him noticing her predicament, GJ looked to all of them. "What are we doing today?"

Just then, Eleri's phone rang.

"Dammit." She said as she looked at the screen. Then she held the phone up to him. "Westerfield." Then, with the press of a button and a clear change of tone, she said his name again. "Agent Westerfield."

Though she didn't put the phone on speaker, the conversation was clear to Donovan. Eleri knew it.

Their Agent in Charge's voice was clear. "So, I understand you have a civilian in custody."

46

I t was close to 3 p.m. by the time Donovan loped through the desert. He could smell the soil and C4 still in the air. From where he stood atop a rise, he could see Eleri and Walter, waiting on one side of him, and see the pile of rubble that had been the Atlas building.

He considered throwing his head back and howling, but he didn't like it. It was too showy, definitely not part of his personality and he hated when he needed to do it. He didn't need to now. So he just offered a short nod and took off.

The women were left there waiting with all they'd hauled out on the trailer. No ATVs this time, they drove as far in as they could, taking a new route and using every ounce of four-wheel drive.

Westerfield had sent agents to claim GJ, but meeting up with them had taken time. She'd bitched about being held, asked if she was being arrested and on what charges. Eleri had let fly and Donovan enjoyed the show.

"You have two choices, Janson." Eleri had hung over the middle of the seat, looking into the back where Walter was supervising the now completely cuffed woman. "You can agree to be held without charges. When I can, I'll make a plea to my supervisor and tell him how useful you've been. *Or* you can get arraigned now. Since I don't have time to make a case for you, every federal charge that can be applied, will be. Your call."

GJ Janson had shut her mouth with an audible click. Only a moment later she stated clearly, "I agree to be held without charges. Please feed me."

"You'll be fed." Eleri was exasperated again. Earlier in the morning, she'd been friendly with their prisoner, pointing out the work she'd done and what she'd found. But apparently GJ Janson had her finger on Eleri's last nerve and either enjoyed pissing off his partner or had no idea how not to do it.

Janson's voice was softer when she asked, "May I also have the files since you won't be using them today? Or at least have access to copies of the files?"

"Seriously?" Eleri was almost over the seat that time.

Though Donovan was driving he could see GJ cringing in her seat. He put out a hand to hold Eleri back.

"I just want to be useful!" the girl protested. "I found the amino acid code. I can find more. I can help. Even if you want to charge me, I want to help. Those kids died."

Donovan felt his own eyes roll despite the fact that he thought the woman was sincere. Eleri slid back into the front seat and he could see she was fighting to make a reasonable decision and not just a snap one. GJ had found a lot of information in those files. He heard the soft sound of his partner counting under her breath.

It wasn't until they arrived at the meet point that Eleri handed over the file box with explicit instructions about how GJ was to be given access only to copies and be monitored. Donovan didn't think he'd ever seen someone led away in handcuffs look so damn happy. For her own sake, he hoped she proved useful. Though GJ didn't know it, it wasn't Eleri who would be the big swing vote in her case, but Westerfield. GJ had no clue what she was up against.

They'd then loaded up with tents, water filtration systems, lamps . . . anything they could find in the camping department. Then they headed out here.

The day was dry, hot, and only in winter temperatures. Summer would be brutal. Without the building, he didn't know how the "kids" would survive. As the wolf, he had the best chances of finding them. They wouldn't come out for people. These men and women had lived out here for maybe three decades, undetected.

He loped on, circling the building, an eye out for Army troops.

Westerfield was on top of that. Why had the Army come to destroy it? What had they triggered? But the building was rubble now and there was nothing they could do about it.

After three circles, he'd seen no one. He'd have to go farther out.

He climbed the crest and found Eleri and Walter, alert, but looking bored. With a nod on a pre-arranged signal, he told them the building was clear. They would try to uncover anything they could in the ruins while he searched.

They were covering the supplies with a camo tarp as he headed away. This time he went out with his nose to the ground.

He could smell the soldiers easily. It wasn't that there was anything about them as a person, but the gear was made of synthetics, they sweated more. The C4 they carried, the guns they shot, made for a clear and unique scent trail. Which was a good thing. He had no trouble leaving their trails alone to ferret out the others that might be around.

The desert was the worst. Without a fresh path, with the recent explosion, there was no scent to follow for any of the "kids." There were only bursts of smell that didn't feel right on his nose. They were human, but *wrong*. Humans had a range of smells; he could tell when they'd been cooking, bleeding, fucking, exercising and more. But these were just off-color. He figured it was the genetics spliced into their systems, probably animal scents, but it made them easier to ID.

He found and followed bursts of scent as he came across them, but they always disappeared. The scents clung better to plants, the bushier, the bigger, the better—which was automatically problematic here. Additionally, the plant scent often was overpowering and it took him a minute to sniff around and find the human that had passed by. A leg dragged along through brush, a cuff snagged on a passing spike, a flower picked—all could capture and hold a scent. For a while.

He kept going.

The sun was setting and Donovan realized he'd been following the trails and not paying attention. He had to be at least ten miles from the building, and he had no means of communicating with Eleri and Walter.

Another scent burst caught his attention, this one stronger than the rest. He followed it. Five hundred yards later, it mingled with another one.

A third passed through and disappeared. He couldn't turn back now.

The night was passing into full dark when he saw them.

He smelled the fire first. Small and expertly contained, it lit them and hid him among the shadows. Their light-adapted eyes would have an even harder time seeing him.

He paced the edge, realizing quickly that it was a camp.

Three creosote trees grew in close to each other. Actually overgrown bushes, these had been pruned back. Branches were cut out from the underside and then placed along the spaces between the canopy. More of a lean-to than a true dwelling, it nonetheless provided some shelter. Leaves were woven through the twisted branches, perhaps making the place waterproof.

Over the fire, a spit held what appeared to be a jackrabbit, skinned and roasting. Periodically, fat would drip from the spit, sizzle, and remind one of the people to turn it. They pegged it in place, not needing to constantly rotate it.

As their dinner cooked, Donovan took stock. He also salivated. The rabbit smelled rich to his hungry nose. While they waited, the two chewed on some kind of plant, one he didn't recognize. He was hungry enough to consider asking them for some. He'd packed nothing, as wild wolves didn't carry backpacks with them. He'd yet to find water, but had managed to break and lick a cactus without spiking himself. That had been a while ago.

Thinking back to the people living near the old Axis building, Donovan got closer. The man was hairier than normal, his scent rougher, gamier. The woman was somehow both thin and heavy. Her bones looked solid, her face wide, her cheekbones prominent. Her elbows and knees looked knobby yet dangerous at the same time.

He would not want to tangle with either of them.

These two were definitely Atlas kids. It was entirely the wrong term, but he'd yet to bring himself to call them "patients" or the even more apt "experiments." Both dehumanized them, and it seemed that had been done to them enough already.

While he was thinking, he noticed the man lifting his head, inhaling as though he was scenting the air.

Had he been in human form, Donovan would have felt his eyes go wide. He knew that look. It was the same look he'd seen on his father's face. One he himself made.

Before he could process it, the man stood. "Amanda, there's a dog out there. Stay put."

"Coyote?" she asked, but she didn't copy his movements of inhaling. Whatever she'd been given, it wasn't the same as the man.

"No, wolf maybe? A dog?"

No wonder he was confused. Donovan didn't smell like wolves. He didn't fully smell like a human, either. He smelled like what he was. Obviously this man had never come in contact with his kind before.

It was then that the man picked up a stick. Only the way he lifted it—hefted the weight and settled it easily, ready to throw or stab—had Donovan on alert.

"Cory," she said. Her hand reached out, resting on his arm, momentarily stopping him.

"I don't like it." Cory didn't peel his eyes from the dark in front of him.

He'd pegged Donovan's location a little too well.

"I'm going to go check it out." Cory started outside the circle of light, and Amanda stood up.

"I'm coming, too."

They started to argue about it, but the roar in Donovan's brain didn't let the words through. Two things had come through at the same time. Both were mind-boggling.

Cory's eyes lit up. They reflected the dim light, gathering it for superior vision. Just like Donovan's own. One more step and Cory would see him.

Also, Amanda was pregnant.

Donovan stepped back a few feet. Then a few more as the two advanced on him. Though Amanda couldn't see him and didn't carry a weapon, Cory could and did.

Donovan turned and ran.

Not far, just out of danger. Then he ducked behind a small rise, crouched down and made a decision that might get him killed.

He changed.

With one ear out for Cory sneaking up on him, and both ears plagued by the sound of his own bones popping and slipping into place, he became human. His fingers curled in and uncurled longer. He twisted each leg, pushing the shapes to change. Slowly, he rolled his shoulders, settling them into his new place. The hair on his arms laid down. It receded, he knew. He'd biopsied himself and found that a good portion of the hair shaft was buried just under the surface of his skin when in human form. Now, he was just a man.

Naked.

In the middle of the dessert.

And Cory could see him and smell him.

Donovan was counting on that.

His heart pounded a rhythm in his ears. Cory could probably smell his fear, too. Donovan could. He walked toward the camp with his hands up. Watching them carefully, he saw that they'd returned to their seats, but Cory's nose went up and he sprung to full alert.

"You." The man was surprised and probably more on guard because of it. "You're the dog that was out here."

Donovan nodded. Jesus, he was just giving his secret out for free these days, it seemed. His fear was stronger than the wry thought and he kept walking until Cory stepped forward.

"Don't come any closer."

Donovan stopped. Nodded in the darkness outside the ring of light afforded by their fire. He could feel the heat on one side and cold on the other. In a moment it blinked out as Amanda killed it faster than he could figure out what she'd done.

Then Donovan said something that he was pretty sure wasn't true. It wasn't untrue either, though.

"I'm like you."

47

Eleri picked her way over the rubble of the building. Often on all fours, she would move, freeze, then breathe out when the broken slabs of concrete and shards of brick didn't shift beneath her.

Several times they had.

Jumping to another pile in the debris only started you over on the stable/unstable game. Eleri wasn't sure about the stressors in her life these days. Previously, she'd been great at the job itself. She'd been the top of the board in the profiling unit, but the others had hated her. They turned on her, investigated her. Now, she was happy with her peers, but damn if the job itself didn't periodically try to kill her.

Slowly she stood up, surveying the area around her. Beside her Walter did the same.

They'd imploded the building. Which explained why the trio had survived the blast. It hadn't blown out, only the dust and tiny particles had. Most of it had fallen in on itself.

Eleri understood two things. One—had they stayed in the shelter, even if the room had survived, they would have been dead. They would have been buried under literally tons of rubble and would have starved or suffocated to death before anyone could reach them. And two—the courtyard was relatively intact. But the explosion had sent a shock wave through the air and through the ground. The dirt would be loose. If this place was anything like Axis, they'd buried the bodies in the middle.

She turned to Walter and took a step forward. The ground held.

It was Walter who slipped.

In a heartbeat, Walter was on her hands, the ground moving under her. The slab she was standing on groaned, shifted, and started to slide.

Eleri was too far away, having just made a series of stable steps. She couldn't reach out and grab her friend. There was no prayer, just a run across the most unstable ground she'd ever walked.

Reaching out, praying she could cover the distance, Eleri shouted, "Walter!" as though the other woman wasn't already reaching for her.

Their fingers touched.

Slid.

Caught.

Curling them together, Eleri pulled until she could grab Walter's wrist with her other hand. She didn't know how she'd gotten there, but she was splayed out across more chunks of broken building than was wise. The old adage of spreading your weight was not applicable here. Somehow, she'd automatically done it. She just hoped she hadn't fucked them both.

There wasn't time for the thought. The sound of the massive pieces shifting made her pull harder on Walter.

As she watched what Walter couldn't see behind her, the piece Walter had stood on snapped in two, falling into the middle. Though it made a noise and coughed up dust, it didn't go far. It was only a few feet lower by the time it seemed to settle into its new position.

Eleri tugged on Walter. "Let's get out of here."

"I can't. My foot's stuck." Walter was shaking her head. "Let me undo it."

Of course, it was her prosthetic foot, not her still human and one remaining permanently attached human foot. Eleri hoped the misunderstanding didn't show on her face. "Let me strap you to me first."

"No." They hadn't strapped together in the first place. Though one might use it to save the other, it might just as likely take them both down.

"Let me at least get it out and we can hold it." She hoped that if anything happened they'd be able to maintain that grip. But it was all they had. Slowly, she reached into her pocket with one hand, the other still clinging to Walter.

It took almost thirty minutes for Walter to unhook the prosthetic leg, work the foot loose of the new crevasse that had tried to take it, and then to get it back on. Though it felt like hours, Eleri reasoned that was actually very fast given what was involved.

They held hands on the way down into the middle.

As her foot stepped onto dirt instead of chunks of metal and brick and drywall her heart changed speed. It dropped again when Walter got both her feet onto the ground.

Eleri looked up at the sky. "It's getting dark."

"We'll be stuck here all night," Walter commented. But they had planned for that possibility.

"Let's use the light." She tried to comment as though the last hour hadn't happened. As though she might not have come close to having to recover Walter's body.

She ignored the problem of getting out of the courtyard. The building was a donut. Though they wouldn't go back the unstable way they came, they would have to climb back over to get out.

Turning toward the middle, she started by looking at the jungle gym.

Standard late seventies/early eighties fare, it was metal rod construction, sunk into the ground several feet and concreted in. She knew this because she could see it all. The blast had uprooted most of it. Some of the frame pieces had bent and several were rusted enough to have simply given way and broken.

It wasn't her concern, not in any way other than to point out that this was the play area. The graveyard would be in the opposite corner. Just like in Michigan, Eleri fought to ignore that the children were asked to take recess in the same place as their compatriots were buried. At least for them, it had been normal. Then again, maybe that was worse.

"Come on." She tracked to the opposite corner. The dirt here was looser than in Michigan anyway. The blast had only helped it.

Though the light was getting lower and lower, she had only to look and she saw it. "Holy shit. They did our work for us."

In Michigan, it appeared the children had been buried in cardboard boxes. As though the intent had been to return them to the earth and erase all traces of them as quickly as possible. Here, wooden boxes seemed to be the norm. Though they didn't appear full-sized, that disturbing answer became clear quickly. They'd simply folded the bodies up. Perhaps to save space.

Eleri had learned a long time ago what atrocities humans were capable of. Once the other person wasn't seen as human, everything was easy. They were socks, shirts, pants—just fold them and put them away.

"Wow." Walter had not been trained the same way.

While Eleri's distance was scientific, Walter's was solemn.

In war, the fallen were either brothers or enemies. The Marine was on her hands and knees, examining a wooden box that had been pushed up through the dirt and cracked, revealing the dark and dirty bones of the child inside.

Eleri didn't comment, but she looked down. Her trained eyes picked out a few teeth and small hand or foot bones. She picked them up, pocketing them and not thinking of the irreverence of it all. She simply collected as many as she could. She'd begun thinking of GJ's numbers. Adding them to Axis. Thinking about what she might say to Las Abuelas. Though these two programs would nowhere near account for the number of infants and very young children lost to the Disappeared, it was a good number.

Others had been found already in other places. So this was by no means the only place the children went. But it was one. And, despite the pain and horror, Las Abuelas deserved to know.

She found half a femur, too long to go into her pocket, and she pulled out a mesh bag. By then, Walter was setting up lightweight tripods with small LED lights. They kept them low to the ground and low in brightness, too. They needed the light, but the last thing Eleri wanted to do was draw attention to themselves. They couldn't get out, and the need to work warred with the need to not be discovered.

The act of slipping bones into a bag or her pocket pained her. She desperately wanted to grid and catalog. But the fact was this place was blown up barely twenty-four hours earlier. If slipping bones into bags of what she was convinced were mixed samples hurt in her heart, it didn't matter. She did it anyway.

She used a foldable spade from her pack to hack at the ground—another generally unforgivable sin in excavation—and watched as Walter did the same. The other woman walked with a small hitch in her stride as apparently getting the prosthetic stuck in the fall had damaged it a bit. This concerned Eleri for the climb out, but she couldn't worry about it now.

She couldn't worry about where Donovan was either. He was a trained agent. He could take care of himself—even with no weapons or clothes.

Eleri looked back at the sound of Walter's shovel hitting wood again. The splintering crack was soft, the wood old. Eleri prayed the bone didn't break. She prayed each piece contained enough usable DNA for a sample. She knew most of the prayers would be futile. Even if the children of the Disappeared were here, many might never be identified.

Walter, no longer making faces at holding dirty human bones, held up another one for her. A rib. From an infant. Several more pieces came, tiny, curved. Skull. Also infant. Probably the same one, but given the numbers around here, Eleri wouldn't put much money on it.

It was almost daylight when she heard the sound of rubble shifting. Looking up, she scanned the directions as Walter came to a mannequin-like stop beside her. She heard it, too. Slowly setting down their shovels and bags without a sound, they simultaneously reached for their weapons.

The noise helped pinpoint where it was coming from. With a wave of her hand, Eleri motioned to Walter and Walter cut the light.

The darkness would have been absolute if not for the stars and sliver of a moon. Still it took far too long for Eleri's eyes to adjust. By the time she made out the shape, the creature was already coming over the pile on four legs.

It wasn't Donovan.

∼

DONOVAN SAT by the fire with Cory and Amanda. They offered him rabbit though they still looked at him with suspicion. It might have been the shorts he had to borrow from Cory or the fact that he appeared out of the night the day after their building exploded.

Amanda did the bulk of the talking. "You aren't from Atlas. We know everyone from Atlas."

"No, I'm not," he agreed. Then he lied. "I'm from Axis."

"I don't know Axis." Amanda still looked suspicious, but Donovan saw something dawning in Cory's eyes.

"You know it?"

The other man shook his head. "Only that it was mentioned a few times back when I was little." He motioned to Amanda with the rabbit leg he was eating. "She's younger than me. She probably doesn't remember. They dismantled it."

Donovan nodded. "They did the same thing at Axis. But up in Michigan. In the cold."

"No one here changes like that," Amanda stated, the words a wall she threw up between them.

Donovan understood. No one at Axis changed like that either, but these two didn't know that. Cory could smell him though. Knew he was the wolf he'd seen. No need to argue that fact or prove himself. Donovan skipped ahead. "How long have you been out here?"

"Thirty years next June."

Donovan tried not to blink. That was far more specific than he'd expected. In fact, when he'd gotten closer, the little lean-to was engineered with superior techniques. Containers were buried in the ground offering cool if not cold storage. He'd waited long enough. "Do you have water?"

They'd offered him food but not water.

They shook their heads at him. Looked at him like he was nuts. He tried again. "I've been out all day. Can you show me somewhere I can drink?"

They shook their heads again, but something in their expressions said they didn't really understand. He let it drop.

But Cory didn't. "You weren't engineered for the desert. You need water."

Amanda nodded and got up.

"Maybe I can find another cactus."

Amanda started. "When did you do that?"

"About five hours ago." He shrugged.

"Don't do it again. There are only a few varieties that won't cause nausea and vomiting." She offered a stern look then walked away. "I'll get you some."

"Thank you." He said to her retreating back, unsure if she'd heard him. His brain was still processing that they didn't need water. He turned to Cory. "You don't drink at all?"

"When we find it." He waved with the rabbit bone again. This time, Donovan saw through the dirt on his arm. The tattoo. K. This was Kilo.

He'd seen Amanda's. "You don't use your names?" He pointed to the ink on Cory's arms.

"Not since we left. I was Kilo while I was there. Once they shut down, none of us used them again. We named ourselves."

He saw as Cory's eyes darted to his own arms. Comparatively clean, it was easy to see he didn't have a tattoo. "I was Victor." The lie felt fuzzy on his tongue but he told it anyway.

"We had a Victor."

"They re-used the names," Donovan explained. "What happened to him?" Then he switched tacks. "How many of you made it out?"

"Nineteen." The number came quickly.

"How many are still out there?"

"Seven." This answer came just as fast though Cory didn't offer any other names. "We're all in touch. But we stay separated, too."

"You've been out here the whole time?"

Cory's nod was the only answer as he went back to biting into the rabbit meat.

"Tell me what it was like?" Donovan leaned forward. "I want to know if it was like Axis. The buildings are the same, the notes are the same."

Cory breathed in, probably looking for truth. At least that part was entirely true.

"I was here as long as I can remember," he started. Once he'd made the decision, he seemed anxious to tell it. "Other kids were brought in. They seemed to think we didn't know some were dead when they came. But a lot of them died quickly."

He looked away. "Each week we got lessons and activities and injections. Sometimes they did biopsies."

It occurred to Donovan then that Cory and Amanda's manners were odd, but their vocabulary and grammar were excellent. They were educated. Then left to die in the desert.

"When I was fifteen, Dr. Morozov did something. He showed up at everyone's weekly check and gave us all a vaccine. Then most of the kids died."

"That didn't happen to us. Was that hard?" Donovan leaned forward.

"You know, kids died and were buried or simply disappeared all the time. They said some of the kids graduated, and they didn't get graves, but I'm not that dumb." Cory finished the rabbit leg and gathered the bones. Standing up, he went to the edge of the camp and threw them far in different directions.

When he returned, Donovan asked him the most pertinent question. "Do you want to live in the city? Or in a house? We can do that now. The government will help."

Cory barked a laugh. "Nothing more from the government, thank you." He paused. "They blew the building yesterday. Don't know why they waited thirty years to do it, but now they're offering you cities and houses?"

"Also tents and water collection and purification systems," Donovan said, thinking that he'd headed the wrong direction.

Another laugh. "That just shows they have no idea what they're doing. We don't need tents or water. We could use some books though. Read each of ours about twenty times. Maybe some tools. But not tents."

Donovan shifted the topic away from his gaffe. "Do you know where we came from?" He asked as though he had no idea; that made the lie bold. Donovan felt it in his chest and hoped that Cory couldn't see it.

"No." Cory sat down again. "I read some of the manifests. We all did. Once the building was defunct, we read our charts and each other's. We read the manuals, stole the books from the library, took some of the supplies. It was a storage facility, nothing more. But it didn't contain any information on where we came from."

Cory raised his hands uncertainly. "We know where babies come from. We came in at different ages, so we weren't made in a lab. They have invoices for us, so we were received from somewhere, but we don't know where. We thought we might have been kidnapped, but there are so many of us. All from the same shipping source." He shrugged.

"Do you want to find your birth families?"

"Now? After what they did to us? No." It was an answer for him. For Amanda. For all of them.

It was an hour later that Amanda returned with water for him. The source must have been very far away. Donovan drank greedily, thanked them and asked if he could find some of the others.

"We don't give that information out." Cory looked him in the eye. Despite the rabbit and the borrowed shorts, he still didn't trust Donovan.

Donovan understood. "I have to get back to my friends." He didn't say "partners." Didn't mention that Walter was military or that he had an FBI badge.

They'd been playing this all wrong.

48

E leri's hands had a small tremor. She'd wanted it to be Donovan coming over the remnants of the building. She'd known it wasn't, right from the start, but she'd still wanted it to be.

She might not have his ears, but she could tell his footfalls from other animals. Walter's alert stance said she understood the same thing. Her hands didn't falter.

Eleri's eyes adjusted from turning off the light, but maybe a little too late. By the time the shapes around her were forming, the creature was already on the top of the pile.

It had four limbs, bent up in the middle like a spider. It walked through jerky movements, still lithely climbing over the rubble. It didn't falter when the pieces moved beneath it. It just kept coming.

Eleri watched all of this over the sight of her gun. She didn't shoot. She didn't know what it was, but she didn't lower her gun either.

Why it came at them, she didn't know. They shouldn't look like easy prey. This would mean the creature was either starving or sick or both. Or else, it simply wanted to meet them.

None of that seemed like a good option.

As the pile became steeper, the creature turned to back down toward them. Eleri gasped.

It was a person. Either severely deformed or simply climbing very oddly, she couldn't tell, but it wasn't coming over the pile on two legs like she and even Walter had done.

Starting to lower the gun, Eleri motioned back to Walter to do the same. She didn't put it away, didn't even alter her grip in one hand, but she decided not to be a threat herself anymore.

"The light, dim, aim it that way," she whispered and Walter moved to change the settings and get it in place, turn it on low.

When it came up, Eleri blinked as did the . . . man.

As she watched, he hit the bottom of the pile. Less than fifty feet from where they held their ground, he paused, twisted and stood up fully.

He stepped forward haltingly. This bipedal movement wasn't as easy for him as the awkward spider-climb over the pile.

Maybe it was a mistake, but Eleri lowered her gun further. Though she was hyper alert for a threat, he appeared no more able to harm her than the dead bones at her feet.

As he walked into the circle of light, she caught sight of his face. Though his arms and legs were twisted and difficult for him to stand on, his face was long, his jaw set to one side as though it had been badly broken and not reset. His fingers curled as if with severe arthritis. Nothing on him appeared properly formed.

The only thing that worked as intended was his voice. It was deep and melodious, if angry.

"You blow up our building and now you dig up my brothers and sisters?"

Eleri stepped back as if she'd been slapped.

Perhaps his disability was all a ruse, but her disrespect of the dead was very real. She felt the weight of the bones in her pockets; there was no hiding the ones in the bag she carried. "I'm sorry."

It was Walter who came forward. "We didn't blow up the building."

He tipped his oddly shaped head and narrowed his eyes. "You wear their uniform and tell me that you aren't them. I'm not faint of mind."

Walter looked down at herself. "No, this is a generic digital desert camo. Theirs was specifically Army. Did you see the trucks?"

Eleri watched as Walter stayed calm, describing the insignia on the back of the trucks and on the vests they wore.

"That's all correct," he replied. "But it only proves you know what was on the truck. Not that you aren't them."

"I'm a consultant, but I was never Army. Marines, Special Forces." She looked to Eleri for a miniscule nod before continuing. "This is Special Agent Eleri Eames of the FBI. I'm her associate now. We didn't blow up the building."

He looked back and forth between them until Eleri pulled out her badge wallet and nudged Walter to pull out the papers she had listing her as an authorized associate working on behalf of the FBI.

He stumbled closer, checked the documents carefully and then stepped back out of reach.

Eleri spoke into the sounds of the night. "We didn't blow it up. We were inside right before it went. But we may be responsible for it. I'm sorry."

He shifted his focus. He looked at her bag. "I knew them."

They were bones now. It had been a while. "The Army came in and blew the building. If we're going to collect these and get them returned to their families, we have to do it now."

"In the middle of the night? That's not suspicious at all." He stared at her.

She stared back. "This whole program was suspicious. I

only know bits and pieces of what they did to you. I'm trying to set it right."

He looked up and down at his own mangled body. "None of it can be set right."

Eleri had to acknowledge that he was correct. "There are people waiting for you." He had to be one of the Atlas kids.

"I'm not waiting for them. This isn't the usual reunion." He raised his eyebrows, his misshapen face surprisingly expressive. The droll line of his mouth telling her that he knew that she knew what had been done.

Eleri played another card. "Morozov is dead."

There was a beat where he froze. "He's in prison."

"We went to see him. We interviewed him. He was pulled out of the interview and sent back to his room. He was shanked and killed before we left the building."

"You did it?"

She shook her head. "We had nothing to do with it, but I think our visit triggered it." Eleri swept her hand at the destruction. "I think our investigation triggered all of this. I'm so sorry about your home."

"This isn't my home. This isn't anyone's home." He looked at her like she was stupid.

"But it's running water and shelter and . . ." At least they were collecting those things. Right?

No, not according to him. He didn't answer. He stood there at the very edge of the light, wearing only his old, thin tank top and shorts that had seen better days. His skin was dark. His hair sparse on his head. His limbs twisted.

She looked now at his arm. 221. She'd read his file. It was one of the partials they'd saved. But the combinations of treatments the kids had been given varied so wildly that she couldn't remember what had been done to him. So she just asked. "You're 221. What did they give you, do you know?"

"I know. I'm not 221. Not anymore." He hardly moved, the answer clearly having hit a nerve with him.

"What do you go by now?" Because who else would run around with those disabilities or that number tattooed in exactly that spot on his right arm?

"Tonio."

"I'm Eleri. This is Walter."

"I'm not that dumb. That's Lucy."

Eleri smiled. "Yes, her legal name is Lucy, but she's gone by Walter Reed for the last several years."

"That's a military hospital on the East Coast." He spoke well. Educated.

Walter pulled back her sleeve and showed off her metal arm. Tonio nodded.

"How did you get the name Tonio?"

"We picked them ourselves when they let the place go. Once we realized no one was coming back, we headed out and named ourselves." His mouth quirked again. "We'd been watching soap operas."

Eleri smiled. It was so simple in the midst of all the mess. They named themselves after what they saw on TV. "You didn't use the building?"

"We stole the books and divided them up. A few of us took our pillows or blankets. Mostly we just went out and didn't come back much." He took another uneven step toward them. "If you know what they did then you know why we didn't need to come back for water or supplies."

Her breath hitched. "They succeeded."

"If this is success." He held his arms out toward her, the joints clearly not formed correctly. "Morozov tried to fail."

"I do know that," she said. "But you lived. How many of you lived through it?"

"Almost half of us. For a while. Enough that the others took too long to figure out what Morozov was doing. Once they figured it out, they put him in prison, but it was the beginning of the end of it."

"How?"

"I don't know. I don't know if the other doctors grew a conscience like Adesso. Or if they fled. Or if Morozov talked and what was going on here was finally exposed to someone who did something about it. But one by one, they abandoned the facility." He waited. Looked at the sky. Looked back at Eleri. He'd been holding off on asking and she figured it out before he said it. "Dr. Adesso was the only one who used the building. Was he in the building when it went?"

"Yes." She didn't pull her punch. He didn't deserve that. Besides, it seemed he already knew the answer. "But the explosion didn't kill him. They did. He was up and sounding the alarm. For you?"

"There are seven of us."

"I thought almost half survived."

"For a few weeks, more than just days." Tonio's eyes said that he would miss Adesso. His mouth answered her question. "Nineteen of us made it out when the place shut down."

"But only seven now."

"It's been a long time." He wasn't looking at her again.

There were only seven now.

"Tonio." She waited until he looked at her again. "I don't know if or when these guys are coming back. I want DNA to identify these kids. If I don't collect it now, I don't know if we'll ever be able to."

"Are you asking me for permission?"

"Yes." She waited. She would stop if he said so. She couldn't right this crime. These children had endured torture for years only to be abandoned at the end. They'd been turned out to live in the desert, one of the harshest landscapes on Earth. Morozov's defect gene already injected, the damage already done, the kids who survived were set for success. Seven of them still lived.

Tonio turned away. He walked to the edge of the rubble and in the shadows squatted down. He turned his legs out at the hips and pushed his shoulders back. His voice carried.

"I can't give you that permission. But I won't deny it either."

Then he proceeded to climb up and over the rubble again.

Eleri and Walter watched him go. It was going on 2 a.m. They had to get out of here soon and get some sleep. She had to find Donovan. Eleri had no clue where he was. And there were too many bones in the ground to get them all.

BY THE TIME Donovan saw what was left of the building in the distance, the moon had moved almost overhead. Probably after 2 a.m. Cory and Amanda had told the time by the sky. They clearly hunted and cooked for themselves. They'd made the shelter and survived with few clothes.

Donovan didn't stop for his own. He didn't change to human; he'd needed to be the wolf to go unnoticed in the night. He'd needed to be the wolf to cover the distance.

His brain scrambled. They'd done everything wrong. The seven survivors didn't need tents and water. They didn't drink often, they survived the heat and the sun just fine without much in the way of shelter or tools. Probably that was the mission of Atlas in the first place. He was shocked.

They'd parked the trailer near the building. Thus his clothes were near there too. He'd been heading that way originally, but then he'd heard it.

Donovan picked up the pace. He was close. Closer than the trucks. Luckily, in this form, he was faster than the trucks. There was no road out here. They were picking their way through.

But it was the middle of the night. Nothing good could be coming. Not from the same engine frequency patterns that matched the trucks that came out here before. These same guys were back.

Donovan breathed deeply and stretched. He ran full-out for the building. When he reached the rubble, he started to climb, but then stopped.

He couldn't go in. It was unstable. He shouldn't climb unless he knew they were in there.

Circling the edge of the wreckage, he found their entry point. The scent was there. It led up and over the broken pieces of the Atlas building. But it was hours old. He hadn't smelled anything suggesting they'd come back out.

Donovan barked. And waited.

He barked again. Three times in short order.

"Donovan!" Eleri's voice was faint. She was on the other side.

There was no way to say he was coming. But there was a way to tell them to stay. He let out five quick barks, and ran.

49

Donovan searched for the safest point to climb over the destruction. He'd circled until he was closer to where he thought they were on the other side. By then, he'd looped almost the entire building.

With uncertain paws, he stepped up onto the unstable pile. At least his weight was better distributed this way. He used speed to his advantage, scrambling up and over, never touching any one spot long enough to still be standing on it if it shifted out from under him.

He was at the top, looking down to see them when he hit a sharp edge and felt the hot sting as his foot sliced. He didn't stop.

They met him at the bottom edge, where the now churned-up courtyard met the pile of building materials. Walter held the light, pulled down from the pole, which she'd abandoned, not wanting to carry it back out. Eleri held a bag in addition to the pack she'd brought in. Her pockets looked to be near bursting and she smelled of loose dirt, C4, and bone.

Though both women scrambled toward him, she was the one who saw the trail of blood he'd left as he came down.

"You're cut." She pulled at his paw to inspect it and started for her pack.

Not enough time.

The trucks were coming closer. The trio's only saving grace was that they were on the opposite side from where the soldiers would pull up. But it wouldn't mean much if they didn't hurry.

He pulled his limb back out of Eleri's grip and started up the rubble with a low short bark, hoping they understood his urgency. He wanted to tell Walter to douse the light, but there wasn't enough time for a change and their communication was Morse code at best. It was safer to keep the light and get out fast.

Luckily, Walter was smart. She set it at dim and aimed it low, illuminating the path for their feet.

Donovan tried to lead them the way he'd come in, knowing it was at least somewhat stable. But the going was slow.

"Help Walter," Eleri said, taking the light. "She twisted her foot, the prosthetic, on the way in."

He skipped back, pushing his shoulders under Walter's hand. He did it twice. Then three times before she conceded and leaned a little of her weight on him.

Eleri led the way, scrambling on all fours, a feat Walter could not duplicate. She took the light and kept it on their path, sweeping it back and forth between her own feet and theirs.

Then the light jerked and Eleri froze as the large piece she was crouched on shifted under her. She waited a single heartbeat then jumped to another spot. Though it, too, shifted, it was only a small fall of rubble as she paused and got her breath.

Donovan stilled, too. His light was gone. He could adjust quickly and keep climbing, but Walter couldn't. Just when he wasn't sure it wasn't coming, the light glowed again at their feet.

Then it traced an arc out in front of them, leading them around the shifting spot. When they hit a stable point, the light swept back toward Eleri and she began to move again, keeping it trained on her own feet. Until, once again, she froze.

What was she doing? Did she feel the ground moving beneath her feet? Donovan didn't. When she looked up, her face was stark.

"Files," she whispered harshly. "I can see them." She peered down into the gap beneath her feet. "I'm going down."

She moved slowly, using time they didn't have. Easing one foot down into the space, searching for purchase.

"Is it worth it?" Walter asked and Donovan was grateful she'd voiced his very concern.

"Yes." Eleri didn't look up. "There are only seven of them left. We don't know that DNA will show who they really are. This is their only history. The only record that they even existed."

Donovan didn't know how Eleri knew there were only seven, but he could ask later. Or so he hoped. He watched her slide farther into the gap.

Donovan acted. Leaving Walter to fend for herself, he closed ten yards between him and his partner and nudged her out of the way. He was built for this. Or at least, right now he was.

It took a second, harder nudge with his head for her to understand what he wanted and even longer for her to pull herself up out of the hole she'd lowered herself into. But as soon as she was out, Donovan ducked down in.

The collapse had busted a file cabinet or something. This spot was in between explosion points. Here the building didn't blow so much as just collapse. There were loose papers every-where. He would never be able to get them all. But he grabbed the biggest one in his teeth and headed back up the rubble. Sticking his head out of the hole, he waited until Eleri took it and ducked back down.

She was right. This was the only evidence these people

existed. Many of the women kidnapped during the Argentinian regime had been assumed pregnant. This was the proof that those babies had been born and lived—or not. He pulled up a second file, a third, each requiring a trip up and down. He grabbed up a section of loose paper in his teeth, twisting them and probably mangling some of the information in the process. He went back down again. A thin file. Again, another grab of loose pages. He felt the rumble of the trucks through the stacked pieces of building he was playing between. Now he was gambling all their lives. Taking the papers back up, he stuck his head out, handing them to Eleri. Once she had them, he started to haul himself up and fully through the gap.

His bloody paw slipped. The chunk of drywall he'd been standing on cracked under his weight and he fell a into hole.

ELERI WATCHED as Donovan appeared in the gap, finally coming out. Even she could hear the trucks approaching now. It must have been why he was in such a hurry.

Then, with a yelp, he disappeared, sliding backward into the hole.

No!

She fought the urge to leap forward, not sure if she jerked and caused the shift or if it started to move before she did. But the slab of intact brick and mortar she sat on shook and broke into several pieces, sending rocks raining down on Donovan.

"Donovan!" She hissed it. She couldn't shine the light down until she knew it wouldn't blind him. He was dark adapted, and those eyes would be hurt rather than helped.

"Donovan!" she called again, trying to keep it low. Sound could carry out here, and if he was okay she wasn't going to condemn them all by calling attention to them any more than the light already did. At least they were on the far side from the trucks.

This time a moan came up from inside the space. It was Donovan, but sounded human. Had he changed?

"Donovan." She spoke again, not sure what she could possibly hear that would tell her he was okay.

This time a short, soft bark came back. Though if that was because he was fine and he was trying to not make sound, or because that was all he was capable of, she had no clue. She was reaching for the straps she'd used between her and Walter when Donovan's head appeared in the gap.

Only this time, after the rubble had moved, he didn't fit.

Fuck.

He wedged his head into the space and pushed. No time for anything else. She could only watch as he struggled. Any movement wouldn't help him, so it wasn't worth risking another shift of their ground. She breathed heavily as he worked his head then left space for one paw.

Then she moved. Scrambling the two feet to put her hands out, Eleri grabbed his bloody foot and didn't let go. She felt him put pressure on her grip, using her strength to hold him up to get the other paw through. She was debating how to grab that foot, too, with his blood on her hands when she saw another hand reaching into the fray.

Walter had his other foot. Bracing themselves, they tugged and tugged until he was through. More than just his foot was cut now, but there was no time for any of it.

Eleri shoved the files and crumpled pages into the front of her jacket and zipped it shut as the three of them scrambled down the other side and out onto even desert ground.

They bolted, Donovan leading the way. Despite all his injuries, he was still the best suited for a flat-out run. He directed them over a small rise and to a set of creosote trees.

They ducked down behind and watched as the first of the soldiers came around the side of building.

She felt the movement behind her but did her partner the courtesy of not watching. Besides, she had to keep an eye—and a gun—out in case the troops spotted them and decided to come after them. But Donovan had to change. If he was taken in as a wolf, there would be almost no way to get him back without trouble. They might even shoot him on sight if they thought he was sick in any way. So Eleri didn't look at him, all her desperation to watch the biological wonder that was the change gone in this moment. She just wanted to survive.

She just hoped Tonio was far enough away that he wasn't caught up in whatever was now going on at Atlas.

The troops were efficient this time and quiet, too. They were setting charges again, though Eleri had no idea why. Behind her, the air stopped moving and she heard Donovan's voice.

"Anyone carrying spare pants in there?"

When it was determined that they weren't—a stunning oversight given Donovan's proclivities, Eleri thought—she volunteered her own.

"Then you won't have pants."

"Eh, I have boyshorts on. Better that than you being naked." She was out of them and handing them over before he could protest. She simply hoped the hip width in her pants covered him. The length sure wouldn't.

She wanted to clean him up, tend to the many cuts and scrapes he'd gotten. An old bruise along his ribs showed up far too clearly in the moonlight. While she was debating the movement, Donovan was showing Walter how to clip out the branches from one side of the tree and stick them through the twisted growth on the other side for cover. As long as the troops weren't in sight, they worked. When one patrolled this region, they sat stock still and waited.

Eventually, they had enough camouflage from that direction, so Eleri washed and tended to each cut of his she could see. His hand was the worst, the gash translating to across the heel of his palm. At least that wasn't a nerve issue. That one got a full bandage.

She was tucking the last of the wrap in tight when Walter hissed, "Cover your ears!"

Eleri barely got her hands to the sides of her head before she felt more than heard the blast.

50

E leri sat at a desk, words blaring past her that she should be paying attention to, but wasn't. Not really.

She wasn't sure the day could have gotten any worse. She'd woken in the desert with one bottle of water between three of them and a four-mile walk to the car. With no pants.

Exhausted, hungry, and thirsty, Eleri and Walter had sloppily shoved all the gear off the trailer, while Donovan went to fetch his own clothes. At least she hadn't had to drive back pantless.

They left all the well-meaning but pointless things they'd brought.

The kids were the creation of the program. Dr. Ben Schwartzgartner had been the impetus behind it all—trying to create a new breed of human that would survive desert conditions in the face of the catastrophic climate shift predicted with global warming. Despite Morozov's attempts to kill them all off, or maybe because of it, they'd succeeded.

The trio had made it back to the hotel. They showered.

Ordered room service, and despite her hunger, Eleri hadn't even heard the knock on the door. She'd been out cold.

What she did hear was her phone going off for who-knew-how-many rings in a row. When she looked, it was Westerfield. When she answered it, she learned that he was in town. And that he was pissed.

Apparently, he'd been standing right here waiting the whole time she got dressed and shoved food in her face and rounded up Donovan. Though Walter appeared at the hotel door with him, Eleri told her to stay behind. It wasn't going to be pretty.

It wasn't.

Westerfield had dragged them in here, where a two-way mirror allowed them to watch GJ Janson flip through files, restack them, and make copious notes on the legal pad she'd been given.

As Eleri's brain cleared, she got the gist of Westerfield's anger.

"You can't just bring in civilians all the time. Last time it was Lucy Fisher and I had to put her on the payroll. Then I had to put her on the payroll again because you—" he pointed at Donovan, "can't keep your damn tail in your own backyard."

Eleri suppressed an elementary-level giggle at that. She also wanted to point out that Lucy/Walter had apparently crept into Donovan's own backyard and it really wasn't his fault she was that good of a P.I., but now was probably not the time.

"Not only that," Westerfield said, ignoring her thoughts on the issue, and Eleri stared straight ahead into the wind of his words. "I had to hire her again for this case. And she knows exactly what you are. You're supposed to solve cases and keep your damn secrets." He pointed over his shoulder where GJ worked behind the tinted glass, oblivious to their yelling on this side. "If you tell me that she knows what you can do, I'll fire you on the spot."

"No, sir," Eleri answered, speaking for the first time in a while. "She does know that Donovan has long scapulae and a bone structure that she's seen in skeletons before."

That stopped Westerfield in his tracks. The small circle he was pacing came to an abrupt stop and he pivoted to face them. "She's seen this before?"

"That's what she said. Said she was studying it," Donovan filled in, even though it was Eleri's job as senior partner to cover him.

"Where has she seen them before?" He was now leaning on his hands on the edge of the desk, towering over them.

"She said her grandfather is Dr. Murray Marks. I'm familiar with the name from my studies and keeping up with the current science. He's seen it, or has a skeleton with it, or something like that. I pushed a bit but didn't want to seem like I was that interested in the topic." Eleri tried to remember to breathe. It was hard to do when Westerfield was on a tear.

"Dr. Murray Marks knows about this?" He seemed incredulous.

"It didn't sound like she knew what it was at all." Eleri leaned forward now. Her best defense that GJ was still in the dark. "She asked Donovan what physiological traits went with the alterations. She didn't seem to know. I think she's only seen the fully decomposed versions, so she hasn't figured it out. I have no idea about her grandfather."

It was clear from the way he stood back up and rubbed at his chin that Westerfield knew the name Murray Marks. And that none of this was sitting well with him. "Son of a bitch."

Eleri didn't respond.

A few blinks, a few thoughts he didn't let them in on, and Westerfield returned to her full force. "You gave her all the files?"

"She's been useful, sir. She figured out the coding of the amino acids and even placed some of the animals used for hybridization." Eleri went on the defensive again. "We can charge her. Throw the book at her and lock her up. But she has been useful, and you can set her free by bargaining with her. She's petrified of jail time." Eleri snorted. "Probably more so of losing her academic status. She's supposed to be moving on her thesis and this ain't it. She'll stay quiet. Just scare her. You're good at that."

Crap. The last part had just slipped out. She hadn't slept enough. Advantage Westerfield. Though he didn't need it, she could apparently do the damage herself.

Westerfield stared at her. Proving her point.

Eleri stared back. It was the only hand she could play.

He stared longer. Longer. Until Eleri was pretty certain he'd simply run out of things to yell at them about. When he finally spoke it was with a different tone. "Go in there and squeeze every useful bit of information out of her that you can."

They were leaving when a knock came at the door and a messenger arrived with a page for him. He looked at it quickly, then up at them. "Walter Reed was right. The Army came back to level the building. They're erasing all trace of it."

Eleri nodded, grateful for the intel. Grateful that it showed that bringing Walter into the fold had been a good idea, not a bad one. Once outside the small room she was able to breathe a little better, then, with Donovan close behind, she turned the knob and walked into the room where GJ Janson jerked up at the sight of her.

~

GJ'S HEART jolted at the sight of Agents Eames and Heath. She'd been in here almost a full day and had begun to think they weren't going to come get her out. By the minute she'd been growing more and more convinced that she was going to rot away in jail on trumped-up charges that were just true enough that even her grandfather's best lawyers wouldn't be able to get her out.

Agent Eames had said her ticket was to be "useful." So GJ worked the files, barely sleeping, eating only snacks from the vending machine and always under the watchful eye of her jailers. She did it for love of the work and fear for her future.

She'd asked for an internet link so often that the wardens had grown tired of bringing in a tablet and watching over her shoulder. They'd said she had to have ten searches before she could request it again.

Her head had been lolling as she nodded off in the metal chair when the door opened and it wasn't an escorted restroom break. She stood upright so fast she would have knocked the chair over had it not been so damn heavy. "Agent Eames. Agent Heath."

In a coordinated effort, the agents pulled out the chairs opposite hers and sat at the table. It was covered in files and notes, too many to move to make room for them. Not like they were here for tea anyway. Some of the files were on the floor now and she almost kicked one as she sat back down abruptly. She needed a bed and about twenty hours sleep. More than that she needed to not spend her life in jail.

"What have you got?"

Her breath caught. They weren't going to interrogate her, at least not yet. It seemed they'd been serious about her being useful. She nodded and dug out her notepad and the crappy mechanical pencil she'd been given. She flipped through her notes looking for where to start. There were so many threads.

Her mouth opened and words fell out. "The building in Michigan is called Axis."

Eames nodded. *Damn it*, they already knew.

"And this one is Atlas. So Michigan was first, as axis is a lower bone in the neck. It's the bone that allows the head to turn and see as far as we do. So Atlas is the bone that sits on that, the sister bone allowing for head-turning." She was rambling and she couldn't stop. She was word-vomiting biology to a forensic biologist and a physician. *Dumb.* "Atlas came after. It's supposed to be the superior program."

They already knew this.

"They were trying to fight global warming. Well, first, at Axis they were trying to fight a coming ice age but that was a mistake climatologists made when they first realized our pollution was screwing with global weather patterns."

The agents nodded, trying to look as though they didn't already know this, but they clearly did.

"I don't know where they were getting the kids, but they had a steady source of infants. These weren't random kidnapping or foster cases gone wrong," she threw out.

"Why do you say that?"

Finally! Something they didn't already know fully. Or they were just messing with her. She had to tell them anyway. "They list the genetics of all the kids. Except the ones that I call 'dead loss.' I'm sorry!" She backtracked. "That's way too harsh a term, but the ones that arrived already deceased—they didn't do a full genome sequence on them."

"It's okay. We understand," Agent Heath assured her. He wasn't very good at it.

Taking a deep breath, she tried to go on like a normal person, or at least a relatively normal one. "The genetic sequences are too similar. They look like they came from a single genetic pool. Not the US—too diverse. But from a singular region of the world. I think it was South America somewhere." She'd tested the sequences as best she could with her school login to the sequencing sites. The wardens had let her, despite the fact that her grandfather's people would be able to trace the school link and the IP address to here. Maybe someone would find her if the agents didn't let her go.

They were looking at each other.

Holy shit. She was right. The kids had come from somewhere in Latin America. In the eighties. So what did the agents know that she didn't?

"Los Desaparecidos! The babies." She stunned herself. It had to be. The Disappeared were taught as part of the anthropological education framework. It was one of the world's great mysteries where all the bodies and evidence had gone.

GJ looked up and realized she'd dug her own hole. She'd needed to be good. She hadn't considered the option of being too good. Of stumbling upon something that they had to shut up. Was now a good time to profess how well she could keep a secret? Request witness protection?

"Keep going," Eames prompted her.

This time, she was more cautious. "They hybridized the kids. They injected them with viral vectors of various genes from a variety of animals. The animals seem to represent the best adaptations of hot climate. So they were trying to build a heat-resistant human." This time she looked at them before she went on. Their expressions were neutral.

"There's a letterhead note copied in one of the charts. They used an outside physician, took several of the kids to him for some kind of treatment. They thought about four of them might have whooping cough. The letter is requesting permission of some oversight agency—it looks military—to take them 'off-base.' Again, a military term."

The pages were riddled with them. These were not military doctors. Not enough lingo, but the area was referred to as a 'base' and the kids rooms were "barracks" and there were enough other small flags to make GJ think the military was funding it or guarding it or something.

Eames' eyes shot off to the side to process that. *New information.* Heath just stared and nodded at her.

"Is that why they blew it up?" GJ asked a question for the first time. She'd seen the trucks. Army.

"I would guess so," Eames replied in measured tones.

It was probably all classified anyway. GJ figured that was the best answer she was going to get. It beat getting slammed to the floor and arrested.

She kept pushing ahead. She wanted out of here and this was possibly her ticket. She hoped.

"Dr. Morozov had some existential crisis partway through the program. He has a few loose pages in here." She shuffled through and pulled them out of the pile set off to her left. Handing them over, she continued. "He was Nixon-level arrogant, but he *was* making gene-spliced therapies in the seventies. He decided they'd gone too far. Too many of the kids were too badly mutated. He designed a kill gene from the earlier tests.

"In his own notes, he calls it 'The Atlas Defect.' Anyway, he added it to the weekly injections and administered it himself. Again, arrogant. It's probably why he was caught and thrown in jail." GJ was on her feet, pacing carefully through the piles on the floor.

The two agents were looking at the paper, then Eames looked up. "It didn't kill them all. Why do you think that was?"

"It did kill all the young kids it came into contact with. It was universally lethal in those initial doses. He wasn't an idiot. I think what he didn't count on was that when he administered it across the board, the older kids could handle it. Either because they were older with stronger immune systems or because they'd had so many gene therapies that this one just didn't shock the system enough."

They'd arrested Morozov. A few of the other doctors had started having tweaks of conscience. The place had crumbled.

"I think the doctors just left. All the notes simply trail off one summer. The last note in every chart is by Adesso. Some are just 'deceased' with a date. Others say 'missing' or 'missing, presumed dead.' He charted other notes in the nineties, too."

No one said anything. So GJ played her last card.

"I get a weird impression off all these notes. Because—aside from the scientific knowledge—why would they do all this? They actually built a human that could survive in extreme desert terrain." She took a breath. "Also, they educated them and kept them healthy. If you disregard the fact that they tortured them repeatedly, they actually took pretty good care of the kids. There are notes about efforts to keep up with pop culture and current events. At one point they upgraded the play yard equipment because theirs was out of date. Not bad, but they wanted the kids to know what 'modern' playgrounds looked like."

GJ knew she was missing something. Something vital.

Agents Eames and Heath looked at each other as though they knew, but they weren't sharing it with her.

"Thank you." Eames reached out and shook her hand, then left.

They were leaving her in here?

51

Donovan settled down at his desk in his home, the familiar feeling oddly unsettling. He'd been home for a week.

After three days to himself, Lucy Fisher had shown up at his door. The fact that he'd invited her was even more surprising. She'd walked out the door less than forty-eight hours ago, taking her own rental car to the airport.

She said she had a case in L.A. that needed her. Donovan suspected she was more watching their space and making sure she didn't step on any toes than needing to get back for work. Though whether she was doing that for him or for herself he couldn't tell.

They hadn't committed to anything, but he'd found himself waffling between the comforts of the familiar—being alone—and the surprising feeling of enjoying her company. Donovan sipped at his ice water and parked those thoughts for another day.

He'd seen Lucy off—he was thinking of her as "Lucy" rather than "Walter" more and more—gone for a run, taken a shower, and worked. This morning he'd settled into his regular routine without kissing her goodbye. He wasn't sure which felt more odd, having her here or not. He paced his usual plan and once he'd checked his email, he returned to his kitchen table.

Even with Lucy here he still hadn't eaten on the glossy antique. It was huge. Perfect for a family dinner or for spreading out papers. Before NightShade it had been autopsy reports. This time, it was his copies of the Axis and Atlas files.

GJ Janson had been discharged on her own recognizance. They'd let Westerfield do that. The man could put the fear of God in anyone. The final agreement was that the charges would be left as "pending" and not filed. No warrants, no need for jail time, *if* GJ Janson kept her mouth shut and stopped trailing FBI agents and stealing from them.

Donovan and Eleri were already in the air before that deal was cut. They'd received an email even before they landed. Apparently Janson had agreed to all the terms and "run out of here like her butt was on fire." Donovan was pretty sure that wasn't what his Agent in Charge would put in the file, but it rung true.

He'd taken a few days off while Lucy was here, but he was back at it now. Combing the files put him officially back on the clock. He called his senior partner.

"Donovan!"

"Where are you this week?"

"We were in Colorado, then L.A., and now Anaheim. All this week."

Eleri was tagging along with Avery, working while he had practice and attending every game. Donovan had never imagined her as a hockey fan, but he'd seen it in the picture she'd sent. There was Eleri Eames of the Virginia Eameses and the Massachusetts Hales up on the jumbotron. Wearing a jersey for what was essentially a blood sport. The jersey, of course, sported her boyfriend's name and number.

Donovan wondered if El's mother had caught wind of this

yet and had a heart attack. But Eleri didn't say anything about that.

"So," he asked, "are you officially a puck bunny yet?"

"Ew." Her disgust rang clear. "That's such an awful and yet appropriate term. Not for me! I hope to God not for me! Hey, you had to look that up, didn't you?"

"Obviously." It had been three days since he checked in. He'd spent yesterday bent over the files, wanting something to add to this first conversation. "You ready?"

"Throw it at me."

He listed the files he'd read for the first time, happy to report that he'd now made it through every word they'd rightfully stolen from both facilities. Eleri had passed that point a few days ago and he tried to remind himself that Lucy was here. That he was on a vacation of sorts.

Then he listed everything he'd seen while reading that grabbed him as odd or extreme. They'd been bantering back and forth when his phone buzzed.

"El, it's Wester—" He didn't finish. She was saying the same thing to him.

"Shit." He rubbed his face. "Group call. A hundred bucks says it's a new case."

"I'm not taking that bet," she said and hung up on him.

They hadn't even finished this one. Sure, they were home, but it wasn't done. He had no choice but to click in to the call.

Westerfield didn't bother with any pleasantries. "How soon can you get airborne?"

Donovan didn't want to answer and was grateful when Eleri said, "Five hours."

Neither of them probably needed that long, but jumping up right now was probably more than he could handle.

"You have to be in the air in four." That was Westerfield's version of bargaining. If the tickets were already in motion, why had he asked?

"Yes sir." It was all Donovan could say. Every job had its perks and its downsides. Though this one had some damn doozies, he'd been challenged every step of the way. His heart rate picked up.

Westerfield barked at them again. "In your email—" Donovan was already clicking it open "—you'll find reports on two other agents, they'll be working with you."

Eleri was asking if they were NightShade, but Donovan had already opened copies of their badges and spotted the diamonds at the end of the lines around the badge. For anyone who knew, that meant a NightShade agent.

There was a dossier on the case, too. "Holy shit."

He hadn't meant to let it slip, but the pictures of the murders were both gruesome and strange.

"Exactly. That's why you're on it. It's a new case to the other agents, too. I just got this handed up to me an hour ago. It's across three states and all we know is that it's definitely a serial."

With that, he hung up and Donovan's phone went dead.

It rang in his hand before he could even set it down.

"Okay, before we start on this clusterfuck, tell me something you figured out about the Atlas Defect. I need something to pretend we closed this case." Eleri didn't even say hello. She didn't have to.

She was still angry that Westerfield wouldn't let them notify Las Abuelas about the matches. If they did, they admitted that the US Army used purchased children in experiments. Eleri still wanted to tell. Donovan did, too, but his eyes weren't turning black over it. He wondered if Avery had seen that trick yet. Her voice pulled him back.

"I need to know we found something of use."

The diversion was welcome, though he wasn't sure he'd be able to shake the murder scene pictures he'd just seen. "Well, they gave the kids injections intending to mutate them. But that doesn't really work. Not at the level they wanted. They should have been working with embryos, not actual infants."

"Good point."

"But they didn't know that then," Donovan pointed out. "So they gave the kids the gene therapies every week. And it looks like they did manage to affect some of the change they wanted."

"I'll say."

"Here's the thing, El. They biopsied the kids. Repeatedly. Even their ovaries and testes."

"They were testing for germ tissue changes?" Eleri asked.

"Yes. And they *found* them." He still was impressed that the gene treatments had managed that. "I told you Amanda was pregnant. If it was Cory's . . ." He didn't know what that meant, other than that the kid carried some of the work of the Atlas program, as well as the defect probably. "I'm not sure why they would want to . . ." But it hit him as she said the words.

"They wanted to make a new race. A new race needs to breed the new traits. Donovan. I found a page that matches a few of the notes. Remember we found some of the files that ended with 'graduated' and a date? I found a list. There are at least twenty 'graduates' on it."

She paused. "Donovan. *They did it*. They sent at least twenty of their experiments out into the population to live their lives and marry and have their own kids."

Even after he'd hung up and packed and was on his way to the airport yet again, Donovan pondered that. The Atlas Defect was in the general population. And it already had been for years.

ABOUT THE AUTHOR

A.J.'s world is strange place where patterns jump out and catch the eye, little is missed, and most of it can be recalled with a deep breath. In this world, the smell of Florida takes three weeks to fully leave the senses and the air in Dallas is so thick that the planes "sink" to the runways rather than actually landing.

For A.J., reality is always a little bit off from the norm and something usually lurks right under the surface. As a story-teller, A.J. loves irony, the unexpected, and a puzzle where all the pieces fit and make sense. Originally a scientist and a teacher, the writer says research is always a key player in the stories. AJ's motto is "It could happen. It wouldn't. But it could."

A.J. has lived in Florida and Los Angeles among a handful of other places. Recent whims have brought the dark writer to Tennessee, where home is a deceptively normal-looking neighborhood just outside Nashville.

For more information:
www.ReadAJS.com
AJ@ReadAJS.com

Made in United States
North Haven, CT
16 July 2023